D0282826

The Sand Café

PUBLICAFFAIRS

New York

The Sand Café

A NOVEL

Neil MacFarquhar

No part of this book may be reproduced in any manner
whatsoever without written permission except in the case of brief
quotations embodied in critical articles and reviews. For information,
address PublicAffairs, 250 West 57th Street, Suite 1321, New York, NY 10107.
PublicAffairs books are available at special discounts for bulk purchases
in the U.S. by corporations, institutions, and other organizations.
For more information, please contact the Special Markets Department
at the Perseus Books Group, 11 Cambridge Center, Cambridge, MA 02142,
call (617) 252-5298, or email special.markets@perseusbooks.com.

Book design by Mark McGarry
Set in Dante

Library of Congress Cataloging-in-Publication data
MacFarquhar, Neil.
The sand café / by Neil MacFarquhar.
p. cm.
ISBN-13: 978-1-58648-368-5
ISBN-10: 1-58648-368-4
1. Persian Gulf War, 1991—Fiction.
2. Americans—Saudi Arabia—Fiction.
3. Dhahran (Saudi Arabia)—Fiction. 4. War correspondents—Fiction.
I. Title.
PS3613.A2724S26 2006
813'.6—dc22
2005053511

FIRST EDITION
10 9 8 7 6 5 4 3 2 1

For all those—starting with my sister, Gail, my mother,
and Claudia—who worked so hard to make sure that
I not only lived past October 2, 1997, but thrived.

No man can live this life and emerge unchanged.
He will carry, however faint, the imprint of the desert,
the brand which marks the nomad; and he will have within
him the yearning to return, weak or insistent, according to his nature.
For this cruel land can cast a spell which no temperate climate can match.

—WILFRED THESIGER, *Arabian Sands*

Twenty years from now somebody
will ask me to go to the beach and
I'll be thinking Sun. Sand. Saudi Arabia.
And I'll turn around and I'll slap 'em.

— A U.S. MARINE
INTERVIEWED THE DURING THE FIRST GULF WAR

Chapter One

ANGUS AWOKE to a foul smell. He rolled onto his stomach and burrowed his head in the pillow, trying to convince himself that whatever reeked could not be in his room. The stench had to be oozing under the door or filtering through the supposedly sealed window.

From the day he checked in, Angus had noticed a funky odor haunting the Dhahran Palace Hotel. After years of excessive air-conditioning and few guests, mildew permeated the wall-to-wall carpeting in the dimly lit corridors—little gray diamonds on a midnight blue background. Stepping into a corridor was like opening a refrigerator kept shut for too long.

Three of the hotel's four wings had been completely shuttered when the press suddenly descended to cover the war from Saudi Arabia. The reporters changed the place nearly overnight, of course, transforming the Dhahran Palace into their own peculiar ant colony.

Still in bed, Angus flipped onto his back. He was wearing a dun-colored army issue T-shirt and olive boxer shorts, unwashed since the abrupt, hundred-hour land war had ended earlier that week. He had been assigned to cover the U.S. Army sweep across southern Iraq through those last days of February. He raised his arms over his head and smelled both armpits. Strong but not foul. He stretched and then brought his arms down, running his hands over his chest and stomach.

At thirty-five, he was no longer the sinewy soccer player he had been in high school, but months of living on coffee and mostly inedible army rations had almost returned his five-foot, eleven-inch frame to its youthful leanness. Muscles ridged his stomach again.

Angus listened for some noise, but the hotel was oddly still now that the press corps had decamped north to newly liberated Kuwait. The caravan has moved so far away that not even the dogs are barking anymore, he thought.

Any war hotel needed one of two essential attributes—it either had to be near the action or had to offer an unusual level of service, like a general manager who didn't blink at billing a hand-woven silk carpet from the lobby store as telephone charges. War hotels tended to be dumps that enjoyed a fleeting glamour while the press corps was in residence, like a faded dancer asked to perform one final, breathtaking leap.

The Dhahran Palace, built smack in the middle of a dismal airport parking lot, enjoyed a rare location. Across a six-lane highway sat King Abdel Aziz Air Base, the main staging area for the hundreds of thousands of American troops who poured into the country ahead of the battle to liberate Kuwait.

The U.S. military's Public Affairs Office, which controlled all press access to the troops, set up shop in the hotel. That's all it took for reporters to besiege the place like land-hungry homesteaders. The three-story Dhahran Palace was far too small to contain the throng—more than 1,000 journalists jockeying for 190 rooms—and skirmishing for space started early. World Press, Angus's employer, had been quick to set up its bureau in the hotel's Royal Suite. A few weeks after Iraq invaded Kuwait, as he sat on a butterscotch leather sectional couch, Angus watched a phalanx of senior news producers from one of television's big three U.S. networks, WBC, march in and start unpacking their computers and other gear.

"ABC already has a suite, so I guess we'll use this one," said the oldest, a swarthy man wearing a crisp white shirt under his khaki safari jacket, looking pointedly at Angus. That had been his introduction to Aaron Black, damn the guy.

"I think perhaps you need an empty suite," Angus answered mildly, but Black and the others pretended not to hear, assuming that even the world's largest news agency would, without question, do the network's bidding.

When Angus told them point-blank that World Press would not move, the chagrined network men summoned the general manager and tried explaining that a famous American television anchor expected the kind of suite designed for the king of Saudi Arabia, if not better. Without it, they hinted, the entire allied war effort might suffer.

Wolfgang Brandt, the hotel manager, was a thickset German with thinning blond hair who always wore dark wool suits, even in August. He was sympathetic but unmoved. In the interest of keeping the peace, Herr Brandt doled out rooms on a first come, first served basis, politely declining thousands of dollars in bribes. Once everyone was firmly ensconced, he quadrupled the rates.

In bed Angus yawned, remembering how the story had erupted with about as much warning as a flash flood when Saddam Hussein jolted the world awake on August 2, just seven months ago, by rolling Iraqi tanks into downtown Kuwait City. Angus felt resentment when he was not included in the first wave of reporters, fearful of missing the action.

A Middle East correspondent stationed in Cairo, he was not among the small band of Pentagon-approved reporters whom Washington jammed down the throat of the Saudi government ten days after the invasion.

With Saddam's tanks pawing Kuwait's southern border and menacing Arabia's oilfields, the aging Saudi royals suddenly faced the nightmare of losing the main source of their bottomless wealth. Despite the religious fundamentalists who became apoplectic at the very idea of infidel soldiers defiling Islam's birthplace, the doddering princes bowed to the need for American troops. As part of the package, the Pentagon dispatched seventeen journalists called the Department of Defense National Media Pool, one of those expansive government titles which sounded like the group would be all the press ever needed to cover the war.

Its members certainly felt that way. They treated Angus and the other foreign correspondents who started showing up soon afterward like a side dish they hadn't ordered.

The smell in his hotel room suddenly became more rank than the memory of the Pentagon press pool. "What the hell is it?" Angus muttered, scrambling to his feet. He jerked open the heavy blue velvet curtains and peered out between the strips of duct tape that one of his jittery WP colleagues had stretched across the glass in case it shattered during a Scud attack. The swimming pool and rear terrace edged by tall palm trees were diced into little squares between the horizontal and vertical bands. It was as if someone had snapped dozens of Polaroids and then stuck them up in rows; the view reborn as collage.

His third-floor room looked out over the six sapphire domes of various sizes that the networks used as their backdrop for most live broadcasts. The domes seemed so exotic, so perfectly Middle Eastern that the television producers hadn't reverted to their usual practice of paying someone with a headdress and a flock of sheep to amble into the background, providing the visual cue that the reporter was in the Arab world. The domes suggested a mosque or the opulent lair of a desert prince. They actually formed the roof of the hotel gym and changing rooms.

Two tennis courts lay just beyond the domes, and beyond that the flat desert sands stretched away. When Angus was a boy, his father, a small-town New England doctor with unfulfilled wanderlust, fired his only son's imagination by reading him to sleep every night from the exotic tales of Rudyard Kipling, Antoine de Saint Exupéry and a host of other adventurers. Even now, surveying the sand sea, Angus remembered a line from Saint Exupéry about the nomads defending their great store of sand as if it were gold dust.

After checking into the hotel for the first time, Angus had stared out at the desert with a similar spirit, seeing in it a Klondike of untapped scoops, of major battles and bold front-page headlines. There had been some, but certainly not the endless string he first envisioned. He had spent far more time inside the walls of the Dhahran Palace than out there. My hotel room, my combat zone, he thought to himself with a wry grin.

THINKING about his room reminded him of the terrible smell sluicing through his nostrils. He couldn't see anything outside that would account for the odor, so he turned from the window. It's got to be coming from someplace in the room.

Dingy veneered furniture crowded every room in the hotel, all of them numbingly alike. The standard issue included twin beds covered with shiny padded bedspreads in a sky blue and mustard paisley pattern. Angus slept in the bed closest to the window. The second one had nearly disappeared under his debris. The chunky table between the beds held a telephone and a lamp with a white, square shade. The front of the table was faced with brushed aluminum sporting a row of defunct black buttons that should have controlled a built-in radio, an alarm clock and assorted other functions.

Clothes—some dirty, some clean and folded neatly in their cardboard boxes from the hotel laundry—were piled high on a squat armchair. Splotched yellow fabric, sagging and slightly threadbare on the armrests, covered its scant padding. The small, six-sided wooden table next to it held a basket of fruit, a weekly gift from the hotel, inevitably sweating inside its cellophane wrapping.

Sheets of papers filled with Angus's scrawl—mostly notes from telephone interviews—were stacked in vague piles across the top of the desk, which also had a television set on one end, a telephone, a reading light and a faux maroon leather blotter holding hotel stationery. An inverted Iraqi helmet sat on the desk, filled with oranges. Beyond the desk, a built-in closet holding the minibar took up one side of the short hallway leading to the door, opposite the entrance to the bathroom.

The room could have been in any U.S. budget hotel were it not for a few Oriental touches. Each headboard curved up in an ogee arch, a favorite motif in Islamic architecture, twin S shapes that met at a point. The arches were made of pale wood and the area underneath them upholstered in the same padded fabric as the bedspreads. A similar arch topped the full-length mirror next to the bathroom door. Finally, a small print above the beds depicted an idealized Arab village, dense black palm trees surrounding little yellow huts. A yellow crescent moon hung suspended in the white sky.

Looking around, Angus paused at the oranges stacked inside the helmet. Maybe they had gone bad. He picked through them, but none were moldy. He lifted the hotel fruit basket. It smelled waxy.

His military clothing and the various contents of his backpack lay strewn across the unused bed and the floor, where he had dumped them when he returned from the Iraqi–Saudi border late the previous night.

The jumble on the carpet included a wrinkled pair of lacy, peach-colored women's underpants. He picked them up and sat on the second bed, staring at them. Soldiers considered lingerie a prized possession and tucked their girlfriend's panties into the webbing of their Kevlar helmets as a good luck charm.

Angus discovered the tradition months earlier, before the war began, when he had been out on desert maneuvers for a few nights with four women journalists who tried to minimize undue attention from the soldiers by waiting until dark to use the crude plywood cubicles that served as desert showers. The showers sat on the edge of the camp not far from a low ridge, which allowed anybody atop the ridge to peek over the doorway. That was one reason the women waited for nightfall. But they failed to anticipate night vision equipment.

About twenty Marines and a couple of male reporters filed noiselessly to the top of the ridge with night goggles strapped to their helmets. The women stood soaping themselves under a sporadic trickle of chilly water in their individual cubicles, not suspecting that directly above them in the black night a line of men stared down. With their skinny night vision tubes swiveled in front of their eyes, Angus thought the men resembled some strange insect species.

He discovered that the goggles turned everything green, with human forms a shadowy blur, like opening his eyes underwater at night in a half-lit swimming pool. He couldn't distinguish the shape of the women's breasts exactly, but the dark circles of their nipples stood out against their white flesh. Clean lingerie lay on top of one towel slung over a door.

"Damn, I wouldn't mind having that pair rubbing my head all day," moaned one soldier looking through his goggles. Angus misunderstood what he meant until another grunt doffed his helmet covered in desert camouflage cloth and pulled out a pair of skimpy black lace panties trimmed with pink satin ribbon. "I got me a pair. My girlfriend was kind of embarrassed, but after a couple months of me begging in every letter she sent some," he said, sniffing deeply as he crumpled them against his nose. "One whiff and you are sure to have great dreams." A few of the other soldiers groaned and attempted to sack the guy to grab the panties, but he quickly tucked them back inside his helmet and strapped it on, laughing.

In his hotel room, Angus scrunched the peach confection to his nose in the vain hope of squeezing out a vague whiff of flowery Chanel No. 5 perfume, just enough to conjure up a woman's presence. But it had long since evaporated. "Oh Thea," he sighed.

Again the stench in his room interrupted his reverie. The second bed sat nearer the bathroom. Angus could see its turquoise tile floor through the open door, the tiles such a vivid hue that they stung his eyes when he snapped the light on each morning. The odor seemed stronger there. He thought maybe he forgot to flush, although the smell seemed too putrid for that. Angus found the toilet bowl clear.

Instead he spotted his construction boots under the sink, the tan leather encrusted with a thin white layer of dirt from months of tramping through sand. It was the boots that stank. He reached down to pick them up and when he flipped them over his throat squeezed shut in a spasm of disgust. Lodged in the Vibram sole was a human finger.

It was a dusky finger, slightly swollen, with strands of flesh and a little splinter of bone hanging off where it separated from the hand. On a quick trip with the military the day before, Angus had visited a now quiet battlefield inside Iraq where the U.S. Army was burying dozens of soldiers killed by its helicopter gunships. As he had watched bulldozers covering the neatly stacked bodies with sand, he had accidentally walked across a mass grave. Angus realized he must have stepped on a hand buried beneath the thin covering.

He picked up his Swiss Army knife from the sink, opened the blade and gingerly pried out the finger, grimacing when it splashed into the toilet. He went to flush but hesitated. One infamous World Press bureau chief in Saigon kept North Vietnamese ears in a bag nailed to the wall. The shriveled ears, which resembled dried apricots, served as a reminder to everyone that despite the decadent living in Saigon, despite the bars and the whores and the endless poker games, a gruesome war loomed just over the horizon.

The Gulf War wasn't anything like that. There had been few whores and little debauchery, at least among the press corps.

Angus knew that hotel affairs usually didn't last long enough to foster the kind of intimacy that might change his life. Story assignments were too short and an automatic "God be with you" was built into any romance before it started. Still, he wondered whether this time might be different, whether his liaison sparked in the Dhahran Palace might resume elsewhere despite its wrenching twists. As usual when he relaxed his intense focus on a story, he was forced to confront just how unsettled his life really was.

On his bedside table sat a hastily scrawled message from the Dhahran bureau chief of one of the most storied newspapers in the United States, confirming what the guy had suggested to Angus in passing. It was the direct telephone number of his foreign editor, the man with the passkey to one of the few newspapers where Angus had always wanted to work. He had found the note shoved under his door when he came back from the border, and had lain in bed staring at it before going to sleep. The note included a brief, glowing reference to Angus's work as a war correspondent. He wasn't convinced he had earned that title.

What war? The overture had lasted nearly three times as long as the war itself. What had the British reporters called it? Oh yes. The Phony War. They were comparing it to World War II, which commenced with a strange lull as well. Not that there was any real similarity.

His initial excitement felt absurd now. War was always the big story, the mainline adrenaline rush that most reporters needed to experience at least once to make a career, to prompt the editors back in the States to sit up and take notice. Angus knew that for the soldiers' sake it would be wrong to wish that the war had been worse or had lasted longer. It had been bad enough for some people.

Angus slumped against the wall next to the toilet and closed his eyes. He didn't want to think about Black, to go over it all again, beating himself up over something that could have happened to any aggressive reporter.

For Angus, the battle of Khafji had been a perfect reporting moment, *his* moment, at least until Black appeared. Trust some TV parasite to always show up at the crucial juncture, like a cowbird planting its eggs in another bird's nest, outsourcing the hard work until the fledglings could fly. Given how it ended, he knew he would live with it forever, condemned eternally to wonder whether he would change anything if given the chance to do it all over. The answer was probably no, but Angus skittered away from that conclusion.

Still leaning against the bathroom wall and slowly opening his eyes, Angus reflected on how grim it was to be the only man left in a war hotel after the vital dateline shifted elsewhere. He could not staunch his sense of loss, his sense that the whole experience was already irrevocably fading.

Looking down again at the detached finger in the water, Angus knew he had no need for grisly souvenirs. He flushed.

Chapter Two

ANGUS first spotted her in the hotel coffee shop. He was sitting alone at a small table and reading a local English-language newspaper, the *Saudi Chronicle,* which specialized in stories about princes presiding over ribbon cuttings. Bland newspapers were a trademark of repressive Arab regimes like the Saudi monarchy.

The paper's daily religion page proved riveting, however, particularly the fervent letters from imported Asian laborers seeking advice on matters of Islamic practice. In the coffee shop that late August morning, Angus was reading a letter from "Reza of Karachi" questioning whether it was acceptable to participate in the dawn prayer without fully bathing after a wet dream.

Angus glanced up from the column annoyed because a group of TV people were bantering loudly as they crossed between their booth and the breakfast buffet, acting like they owned the coffee shop. A couple cameramen were needling one of the women with dumb military jokes.

"Hey Thea, what's the ugliest thing on a woman?" bellowed one bearlike guy weighing a good 250 pounds.

"There's absolutely nothing ugly on a woman; how could you possibly expect me to even entertain such a question?" she answered in mock horror, ladling plain yogurt into a bowl with one hand while nibbling a date with the other.

"A fighter pilot," came the shouted response.

Thea groaned and then laughed, encouraging an endless stream of jokes in a similar vein.

At first glance she did not strike Angus as beautiful. Her complexion was olive, somewhat Mediterranean but not distinctly exotic. Her full, sensual lips framed small white teeth, and her nose, bending slightly over a little bump, was one that a less confident woman might have had reshaped. She was about five-nine with unruly, light brown hair cropped off at the neck.

It was the way she moved that held his attention. Her body was lithe, like a dancer's. Her baggy, long-sleeved white shirt with the collar turned up seemed to respect Islamic sensibilities. But whenever she leaned over the buffet, Angus couldn't help noticing that she had left one button too many undone.

The coffee shop, decorated in Day-Glo shades of lime green and radiating all the charm of a Denny's restaurant, was the clubhouse for the gathering press corps—barely fifty people at that point given the Saudi reluctance to issue visas. It was a beacon in the hotel's otherwise gloomy interior because light poured from its floor-to-ceiling arched windows, which ran across the lobby's entire back wall. The rest of the lobby resembled a tomb, so dark that its brown marble floors and walls looked black. But every correspondent entering the hotel could see colleagues huddled together near the mountainous buffet. The draw of gossip and food was irresistible; they had to know what was being discussed. Officially named the Sand Dunes Coffee Shop, everyone called it the Dunes.

"Hey Thea, why did they make Marines slightly smarter than horses?"

"Are you sure they did?" she answered in an accent Angus could not quite place—it was a little too musical to be completely American.

"So they wouldn't shit during parades!" two men yelled in unison.

Again she laughed. Angus wondered if she really found the jokes funny or was merely humoring her colleagues. Leaving the buffet table, she sat cross-legged in the booth and alternated between eating and playing with errant strands of hair. There was something private about a woman playing with her hair that Angus found intensely arousing.

He was pondering how to say hello when Thea abruptly stood and glided toward the doors. He vaulted from his seat, spilling the last of his coffee, but was too late. Angus hurried after her, figuring she was headed toward the U.S. military press office upstairs.

THE Dhahran Palace was built like an H, with the entrance at one end of the crossbar and all the rooms lining the wings off to the sides. An open central well soared up all three stories in the middle of the crossbar, with sickly ivy plants hanging over the narrow balcony that ringed the second floor. Four chandeliers, each a cluster of long strands of tiny lights designed to resemble falling raindrops, cascaded from the third floor ceiling down to the lobby. They never seemed to throw off any light, though.

The reception desk was off to the right of the hotel entrance. A wide staircase just beyond it along one side of the central well led to the two flights above. The staircase, like the corridors, was carpeted in dark blue, and the walls were clad with the same weird shiny brown marble as the lobby.

The marble slabs were also used to create a short, square fountain that sat right inside the main rotating glass doors. The timid jets of water on all four sides reminded Angus of a urinal. The lobby wasn't an inviting place, and its armless couches in baby blue Naugahyde were usually deserted.

Rushing out of the Dunes, Angus slowed momentarily until his eyes adjusted to the dimness. He headed past the twin elevators tucked behind the stairs. No reporters used the elevators, which were for people with time to spare, for Saudi minders or bellhops transferring countless heaps of equipment and suitcases. Later, long after the realization struck that they were doomed to spend week after week in the hotel, waiting, reporters still launched themselves up and down the stairs with synthetic urgency.

The military press office was housed in the Mecca Banquet Hall, one of several dining rooms on the second floor. All the banqueting halls faced the central well—small ones on the second floor, large ones on the third. Parked outside the Mecca room was a large, rolling cork board painted entirely white. It was the war's main crossroads after the coffee shop.

Reporters commuted all day long between the Dunes and the bulletin board hoping that a sign-up sheet would materialize for rare opportunities like an overnight excursion to troops bivouacked in the desert; what they invariably found were offers to visit a military laundry facility with an impressive washing machine count or an army bakery introducing a new line of raisin bread.

Angus climbed the stairs two at a time to find Thea scanning the board, laughing over a notice headlined "Apology" that a reporter had pinned there: "To His Holiness the late Ayatollah Khomeini of Iran: Over the past years, in common with all other newspapers, we may inadvertently have given the impression that the late Ayatollah Khomeini was the most evil man in the world, a vile tyrant and the gravest threat to world peace since Adolf Hitler.

"We may also have given the impression that President Saddam Hussein of Iraq had in some way been worthy of our wholehearted admiration and support in his gallant 10-year struggle to rid the world of the menace of the Ayatollah. We further may from time to time have indicated that we might in some way have approved of the sale of Western arms and technology to President Saddam Hussein, on the grounds that these were being used to further the entirely laudable purpose of eradicating the wicked old lunatic with the beard and thus make the world a safer place.

"We now realize that the late Ayatollah was in fact a saintly and scholarly cleric whose main concern was to save the world from the evil clutches of the Hitler of Baghdad, the wickedest man in the history of the world, Mr. Saddam Hussein.

"We would therefore like to apologize to the late Ayatollah and family for any distress that these articles may have caused."

Angus started laughing too, and when he finished reading, Thea thrust out her hand.

"Thea Makdisi, CBN," she said.

"Angus Dalziel, WP," he answered. "You a correspondent or a producer?"

"Don't tell me you haven't been watching?" she answered in mock alarm. "Surely the mighty World Press of all people should be watching television to know what the entire planet is really talking about? It's going to be CBN's war."

"That will be the day," he shot back, hastily adding, "However, I'll start watching immediately now that I have such an obvious reason."

She grinned briefly, then asked him if he was a good enough reporter to have a pen.

"You know there is one twisted up in your hair, right?" Angus asked, proffering a slightly chewed blue Bic from the pocket of his khakis.

"I love you observant writer types," she said, taking his pen and poking him playfully in the chest with it.

On the bulletin board that day the military announced a series of chemical weapons lectures, required of all reporters who wanted to spend time with the troops. Every reporter in Dhahran would do practically anything if it meant spending time with soldiers. Thea opted for a lecture that afternoon and Angus wrote his name under hers.

They stood by the board for a while, engaged in the sort of initial conversation that is inevitable between reporters: about the stories they were working on and where they were based and how they snagged this particular assignment.

Angus let Thea do most of the talking. She told him that she took a gamble that spring by moving back to Beirut—where the shaky agreement between the major sects to end the civil war seemed to be holding—to help cover the region for the Cable Broadcast Network. "My boss said, 'You're foreign, you should go work for the Foreign Desk,' and that was that," was how she explained it. "Some senior producers doubt that I will ever overcome my slightly foreign looks and accent, but I am determined to prove them wrong."

Angus wondered if she was fishing for him to agree, but she went on before he could say anything. "Of course now that headquarters in Miami has decided we are the world's network, we can't call it the Foreign Desk anymore; we're supposed to say International Desk," she said, beginning to walk away. "So I risk having $10 deducted from my paycheck every time I tell that story."

"I promise not to denounce you if you will have dinner with me," Angus said.

"Blackmail?" she asked, dropping her mouth open as if shocked.

"Whatever works," he answered, smiling.

"Sure," she laughed. "Let's talk about it after the lecture."

LECTURES convened near the swimming pool behind the hotel, under a yellow-and-white striped canopy shaped like a pyramid that shaded the permanent barbecue and imparted a lemony glow on everyone sitting underneath it. The lectures started in the late afternoon after the broiling heat finally eased down to around 100. When Angus walked up, about half the thirty chairs facing a lectern were already taken by reporters trading grim jokes about the horrible death brought on by chemical weapons.

"I hear the end comes with the victim twitching and foaming at the mouth."

"Then how will we be able to tell if a correspondent just took a hit or just finished talking to an editor back in the States?"

He saw Thea already seated under the canopy and took one of the empty chairs next to her, picking up the handout placed on it. She was fanning herself slowly with hers.

"Is it me or is there something chemical between us?" he said.

She shrugged and gave him a cursory smile as she said hello but did not laugh. Angus told himself to stop trying so hard.

A thin blond doctor, a captain from a reserve unit, walked up to the lectern and started arranging gas masks and other paraphernalia. The prospect of chemical weapons was the one thing that made the reporters covering the war from Dhahran queasy. Saddam had lobbed them at his own Kurdish minority and at the Iranian army in the late 1980s, so everyone expected the worst.

Angus read the handout, which listed frequently asked questions about what to do during a chemical warfare attack.

Q: When do you know that it is time to put on your suit?

A: If you see everyone else walking around in them you probably should too.

Q: What might be one clue that there is something odd happening in the area around you?

A: A big death of animals.

Angus groaned. "These must be questions asked by television reporters," he said, but Thea didn't react.

The officer started his lecture.

"First let's talk about the term 'germ warfare.' I think it is emotional and ridiculous," he said. "It is really biological warfare. Anthrax. Cholera. Typhoid. That is what we are really talking about. Some are more lethal than others. Anthrax, for example, is considered 100 percent lethal. Now the first thing that you should know, and that you should find encouraging, is that in high temperatures biological agents have a very limited life. They don't like ultraviolet light and they don't like heat at all."

"Who does?" moaned a female voice from somewhere in the audience, provoking scattered laughter that choked off when the officer frowned.

He switched to chemical warfare agents. "Three kinds of defense exist. The first and the very best is detection and avoidance. The second is physical protection, meaning the mask, this charcoal-lined suit, the rubber gloves and boots you see here on the table. The third is medical," he said, holding up six syringes and a twenty-one-day supply of pills that came in a little olive green kit.

As the doctor lectured, Angus tried not to think about the sepia-tinged photographs he once saw in a European museum, showing a World War I battlefield at Ypres where gassed soldiers lay with their mouths gaping open, their death masks frozen in the horror of their final moments. Dwelling on the gruesome would serve no purpose.

"For every casualty unlucky enough to absorb a fatal dosage," the officer was saying, drawing rings on a white board with a red marker to illustrate where the impact area would be, "there will be twenty others who will have pinpoint pupils with difficult vision, uncontrollable sweating and testicular disturbances, muscular coordination difficulties and so forth."

Angus wondered if he could risk making a joke to Thea about how a beautiful woman is like a chemical warfare attack—they both cause testicular disturbances. But he figured it was a little early for jokes involving his balls and berated himself for not concentrating on the lecture.

The officer moved on to mustard gas. "It emits a faint odor of garlic and if you smell that, it means your eyes are already injured, if not worse."

"I think Saddam might have pulled off a mustard attack on this hotel already," said a male baritone from the back, "I've been smelling something weird ever since I set foot in the place."

There was more scattered laughter. Angus recognized the voice of Aaron Black, the network bureau chief who had tried to appropriate the WP suite. Middle-aged, he was burly and handsome in a kind of dark way, with close-cropped, slightly kinky hair dusted with gray and a nose that might have been broken once. He grew thick stubble so fast that he could have shaved twice a day.

Angus had heard him joking to someone in the Dunes earlier in the week that he had been born too dark and too smart to be a correspondent. Producers are the brains of any television operation and Black was considered a master. At the Dunes, everyone gossiped endlessly, and Angus had found out that Black started his career in Vietnam, where he did some controversial reporting about U.S. soldiers burning villages and using their rifle barrels to smoke dope. In the military, rumors that Black used his own Zippo lighter on a few village huts to get better pictures had never quite died down. More recently, Black had become infamous among his colleagues for serial philandering with novices and rebuffing all home office enticements to work in the States.

Once the laughter subsided, the military doctor resumed.

"A chemical attack could come any time, so at a minimum everyone must keep a mask nearby and should probably lug around the heavy charcoal lined suit also, at least in the field," the doctor warned. "The mask is the essential piece of equipment to get on first, like the oxygen mask in a depressurized airplane cabin. If your air supply is not protected, then nothing else will do you any good. Remember that."

Everyone shifted uneasily in their seats. The doctor had reached the last line of defense, the one that made them all cringe. Inside the carrying case for the mask was a small canvas bag about the size of a crayon box that held three twinned sets of syringes.

The two green ones the size of a magic marker were filled with atropine, an alkaloid compound developed by the British in 1945 and not tinkered with since. The second set, black and about the size of a large felt-tip marking pen, was filled with a chemical compound called pralidoxime chloride. The third and smallest set contained valium.

The first two were designed to be self-injected, but the valium was supposed to be administered by a medical corpsman who would magically materialize at the right time. It allegedly prevented brain damage from the antinerve serum. There was confusion and grumbling in the audience.

"Wouldn't it be better to inject the valium first, to be calm enough to whap yourself with the other needles?" Angus suggested.

The reporters laughed, but the military guy responded by asking for a volunteer to demonstrate the injection technique.

"Who is feeling brave this afternoon?" he said, drawing nervous chuckles.

"I'll do it," said Thea, jumping up and grinning with evident pleasure that she had been first to volunteer. Angus watched her relish the chance to upstage the men around her.

The officer positioned Thea sideways, her right foot up on a chair with her knee bent, her inner thigh facing the audience, the muscle pressing against the black cloth of her pants. The lecturer started smacking his right fist into his left palm, saying that a decent momentum was required for the needle in the auto injector to break the skin.

"You have to inject yourself right through the anterior lateral thigh," the military guy said, running his hand right behind Thea's knee. Angus felt a twinge of jealousy.

"Do not place your finger anywhere near the bright green end of the auto injector; that will cause the needle to emerge," the officer said, prompting audience members to half rise out of their seats and crane their necks to see. The idea was to grab the auto injector like a knife and stab it down fast but smoothly into the fleshy inside of your lower thigh.

The officer continued. "When you are gassed, you have one minute to inject yourself with the antidote, so there is very little time. Do it without hesitating."

"I might prefer taking a few deep breaths and ending it all rather than even thinking about jabbing myself with that thing," Thea shot back.

There was a burst of laughter, breaking the tension. Thea struck Angus as a natural performer; he guessed she did pretty well in front of a camera. She certainly had her audience of fellow correspondents riveted.

Then the officer handed Thea chunky boots and an unwieldy protective suit lined with charcoal. She was supposed to get into that regalia in a minute or less. The trousers looked like they would fit a baby elephant and the waist kept slipping down around her knees. She hoisted the pants every time they dropped, while the other reporters threw out scattered comments like, "What the hell happens when your suit falls off?"

Thea had flushed slightly, a reddish hue coloring the upper part of her cheeks, and she was sweating. Her bangs stuck to her forehead and sweat dripped down her neck into her shirt.

"To get a sense of what this will entail, imagine running around the desert with an extra plastic bag over your head," the doctor was saying. "Also remember that once you get the mask and chemical suit on, you won't be able to touch your body, especially your face. You better get used to the idea now that you will always have an itch that you can't get to."

"Jesus, I already have an itch I can't scratch and I haven't even tried on my suit," Black yelled out.

Faint laughter again rippled through the gathering, but the doctor cut it off quickly.

"Remember, you have to master this because when the gas comes, the soldiers with you will don their masks before they can get to you and hopefully you won't be twitching by then," he said. "Chemical weapons are intended to create as much mayhem as possible. The main thing is survival."

The lecture left the reporters gloomy. Most had long since gotten over the idea that their jobs were glamorous, but they clung to the notion that what they did was more exotic and exciting than sitting at a desk. The prospect of facing a chemical weapons attack made them wonder what the hell they were doing in Saudi Arabia.

Subdued, they stood and slowly wandered back toward the hotel building. Thea was still trussed up in the chemical gear, and Angus watched from his seat as Black and a few others headed up toward the lectern. Ignoring the fact that Thea was struggling with the unwieldy garment, Black enveloped her with a huge bear hug.

"I'm so happy to see you!" he exclaimed as he wrapped his arms tightly around her and tried to massage her buttocks, grasping a cheek in each hairy hand. Angus was glad that the thick chemical pants were in the way.

Black eventually relaxed his hug and then chatted with Thea, telling her she made them all look bad when she started signing off her reports "Thea Makdisi in eastern Saudi Arabia" while the rest of them were stuck outside the country and signed off "in the Gulf," hoping no viewers would notice.

Angus guessed they'd met while marooned with other network reporters in a neighboring emirate waiting for Saudi visas. He listened for any hint of intimacy beyond the hug, having seen Black envelop several women in that way.

Black asked Thea if she had figured out how to get multiple entry permits so they could drive over the causeway to Bahrain, a country where the bars served alcohol.

"Our visa problems have evaporated now that we are King Fahd's favorite network," Thea bragged. "You saw our interview where he said he would defeat Saddam because he is richer? How great was that! Anyway, after the interview aired he told us we could have all the visas we needed, although I doubt he had the Bahrain bars in mind when he said it."

"Well then the king and I agree on at least one thing, or at least one reporter," Black said, "Let me know if I can help with your stories or with any advice at all, really. Also you remember what the chemical weapons guy said about how you'll get an itch when you get your suit on..." He leaned over and whispered something in her ear. Thea laughed uncertainly and shoved him away.

When she started striding toward the hotel, Angus caught up to ask about dinner. "I'm running over to the flight line with a camera crew," she said. "Why don't you come along? Surely the World Press needs reaction to Saddam?" The Iraqi dictator had announced from Baghdad a couple hours earlier that foreigners living in Iraq would be used as human shields, dispatched to all possible military targets to deter allied bombing. The U.S. military made it clear that it would not be deterred, laying on a special trip to the air base for reporters to garner reaction from the fighter pilots.

"Someone else in the bureau already opted for that," Angus said.

"Well, I'll probably end up cutting my piece later," she told him, smiling brightly. "But let's have a meal soon."

"Definitely," Angus answered, smiling back to hide his disappointment.

Chapter Three

A FEW WEEKS later, well into September, Angus laughed when he walked by the CBN bureau, housed in the Gulf Banquet Hall at the back of the third floor, and spotted a long computer printout pinned to the wall: "Elvis Sightings on the Flight Line: 5." The sign, its letters a foot high and printed in bold black type, reflected the growing frustration with endless trips to the air base, daily excursions offered as a placebo for any real action. There was an almost complete embargo on taking reporters out into desert, where the U.S. Army was gradually deploying in a long defensive line paralleling the kingdom's northern border.

Instead, trips to the flight line unrolled like a second grade outing. A truncated yellow school bus drove up the curved, palm-lined driveway of the Dhahran Palace and jerked to a halt under the hotel's boxy front canopy, two stories high and faced with slabs of while marble. A ten-minute bus ride delivered the reporters to the flight line, the long row of airplanes parked on the tarmac, where incoming troops were briefly available for supervised interviews as they staggered off the chartered jumbo jets transporting them from the States or elsewhere around the world.

No U.S. television network managed to start the day without interviewing a few soldiers for their reaction to the diplomatic news of the hour, or if there wasn't any, the weather. Naturally the WP editors back at wire service headquarters in New York saw so much flight line babble on television that they demanded similar from their staff.

Angus did not regard traipsing to the flight line as war coverage. Actually he started going on the trips to hide. Being on the base with the American military got him away from the baleful eyes of the Saudi minders, the much reviled officials from the Ministry of Information assigned to the Dhahran Palace as press chaperones.

Angus had run afoul of the minders quickly, starting with a shopping excursion downtown.

In the years since Arabia's vast oil reserves were first discovered in 1938, the series of fly-blown hamlets that once dotted the sandy, muggy coastline of the Persian Gulf had developed into an extended urban sprawl that mirrored its American model. Wide freeways linked an anonymous series of strip malls and shopping centers featuring stores like Abdel-Latif Furniture or Al-Ghanim Ceramic Tiles. The malls were interspersed periodically with expatriate residential compounds surrounded by high walls.

Al-Shoula Mall was the biggest of its kind with at least sixty stores spread over three levels, all linked by escalators and anchored on the ground floor with a food court. Angus had popped into the video store there one day to ask what movies were popular and was surprised to discover a Saudi man furtively paying the equivalent of $10 for a bootleg video of the speech Saddam made after the invasion, the dictator growling that the Kuwaiti people themselves begged him to depose the stupid, fat, corrupt royal family.

"That seems like an awful lot of money to pay for one speech. How did you miss it?" Angus asked.

"Surely you don't think they let us see this?" answered the man, who was wearing a long white robe and heavy brown leather sandals but no headscarf. "They didn't even tell us Saddam had invaded Kuwait until three days after it happened."

"Three days? You're joking!"

"C'mon, you must realize that the Saudi press is a government monopoly that makes sure nothing remotely resembling real news actually gets reported," said the guy, who turned out to be an affable chemical engineer educated at the University of Oklahoma and working for Aramco, the giant Saudi oil company. "They didn't report on the invasion, I'm sure, because the head guys for TV and radio were crapping their pants at the thought of making such an important decision. So they no doubt passed it over their heads until finally it reached the king, who said okay. But it took three days to get through all the bureaucrats. God help us if they invade Saudi Arabia. We'll probably find out when an Iraqi tank passes down the street."

"You mean nobody really knew for three days?" Angus asked.

"Some didn't, but of course we listen to BBC radio from London and there are tons of illegal satellite TV dishes," the guy said, waving a little plastic bag with his contraband tape. "I moved recently and I don't have my new dish up yet. If you would like to come over to watch the speech with me, you are welcome."

"Thanks," Angus answered, knowing he was onto a story. "I'd love that, but some other time."

After interviewing a few more people about how they tracked war news, he went back to the hotel to get the official version from the Saudi press office.

Ibrahim al-Misri, the senior minder whose flowing white robe barely concealed a considerable paunch, had studied Romantic poetry at an obscure British university and tried befriending the reporters. He suffered from the naive belief that in return they would file nothing but glowing reports about the kingdom. So he considered it an affront when Angus asked a question implying that the government bungled press coverage.

"The invasion was weeks ago. Why do you care about that now?" he said, glowering from behind a table littered with half drunk cups of tea and coffee in the ministry's suite. Each of the four largest suites in the

Dhahran Palace was decorated in a different motif, and the ministry was housed in the Swiss chalet suite, complete with wooden walls, fake antlers dusty with cobwebs and a real cuckoo clock.

"I was wondering why people have to resort to buying a video of Saddam's speech, why the government wouldn't broadcast it?" Angus said. "There is probably some reason I am not considering."

"At what store did you see this video?" the Saudi official asked, taking a heavy gold pen out of the breast pocket of his robe and uncapping it.

"I don't know, somewhere downtown," Angus answered. After a few similar exchanges he knew he was treading in circles, so he asked point-blank whether Misri wanted to comment for a story or not.

"Off the record?" the senior minder asked.

Angus squelched a smile. Perhaps Misri and the rest were getting press savvy after all. One just had to keep asking.

"Sure."

"No comment," the Saudi official barked.

AFTER that, Misri started whispering to other reporters that Angus was a spy. Some humored him and agreed, but most vigorously denied the accusation to no avail. Angus decided it was best to ignore Misri and hope somebody else attracted his official ire.

The first major event managed by the Saudi minders came when the Iraqis decided that the easiest way to control Kuwait was to let everyone leave, prompting a human flood. On September 16, the Information Ministry hastily organized a bus trip to the Saudi border town of Khafji to interview refugees.

Angus and the other reporters found thousands and thousands of Kuwaitis—their Jaguars, Mercedes and GM Suburbans groaning with personal goods—backed up across six lanes for ten miles into Kuwait. Scared that the Iraqis would change their minds and swoop down on them, they were all honking, wailing and sometimes fainting in the scorching heat. It was like watching blood back up behind a clogged artery and waiting to see where it would erupt.

Television reporters typically wanted to stay at the border for at most two hours—just long enough to film the endless lines and grab a few cursory interviews before rushing back to Dhahran. If they returned by early afternoon, the time difference with New York meant they could satellite the images to their networks for breakfast news shows like *Today.*

Angus wanted to linger. This was his first chance to interview people about life under the harsh occupation; there had been virtually no eyewitness accounts because the few Western reporters in Kuwait when Iraq invaded soon fled. One man told him about a car dealership owner who refused to hang a picture of Saddam Hussein and was taken out of his showroom and summarily executed; another man arrived weeping, saying his twenty-year-old son was one of dozens of young men Iraqi soldiers had just dragged from their cars as they sat in the traffic jam.

Khafji, a quiet town of about 30,000 people, boasted a decent beach motel overflowing with refugees. Others were camping in the sand next to their fancy cars, waiting for relatives to cross. Angus decided to spend the night to interview as many of them as possible.

He had to come out of this war with a fistful of clips that would make newspaper editors sit up and take notice. He had been overseas for five years with little to show for it. A vivid description of the occupation would definitely be a keeper.

Back at the border post, Angus found Misri in the frigidly air-conditioned office of the chief of operations. The minder, smoking and drinking tea, sat slumped on a padded black leather chair behind a desk overflowing with stacks of passports and visa forms. Naturally he hated the idea of Angus staying.

"There will be no change of plans!" Misri said, shaking his head vehemently, the fringes of his red-and-white checkered headscarf dancing around his shoulders.

"Come on, Mr. Misri, there is lots of news here," Angus argued, knowing already that it was pointless—the guy would fear making any such decision. "This is the most news we've covered since we've been in the kingdom and it's a black eye for Saddam. What difference does it make if I stay a few more hours?"

"If I let you I will have to let everyone and that is impossible!" he screeched, furious not just about the request to alter the agenda but about a foreign reporter having the nerve to answer back to a Saudi government official.

"They're television, Mr. Misri; they have no interest in staying," Angus said, still hoping logic would prevail. But Misri was insulted, figuring Angus was talking down to him about his own job and again suspecting that he wanted to hang around for nefarious purposes.

"You can't satisfy an American reporter; you give him the tip of your finger and he would like to eat your whole arm!" Misri screamed. "You will go back to Dhahran on the bus and that is final!"

Angus decided to ignore Misri, slinking away after asking the television correspondent who had been sitting next to him on the bus to answer for him when they took attendance. But the guy was combing his hair or something and forgot. After taking a head count, Misri quickly determined Angus was missing and vowed not to leave Khafji without him. No amount of chanting "Leave him!" from the others would change his mind.

They spent a couple hours roaming Khafji, looking for Angus. He was walking down a side street when the wildly honking school bus skidded to a halt next to him and Misri, spitting with rage, ordered him back to Dhahran. Most of the press corps reacted like a lynch mob.

Aaron Black, dressed in one of his sharply pressed safari jackets with epaulets, threw the butt of his fat Cuban cigar at Angus and spat out the window. "We did this trip just for fucking practice, because we damn well won't get back in time to satellite the stuff to New York," he barked. "And why? To wait for a goddamn wire service reporter. I have a good mind to call the owner of the network and have him get you fired."

Angus stared silently through Black and stalked past him down the aisle of the bus. He found refuge with a veteran *New York Times* reporter who made room on the seat next to him. "Good effort," the guy whispered, which made Angus feel better.

"Why should TV always set the fucking program anyway?" he thought.

As soon as the bus reached Dhahran, Angus turned around and drove the two hundred miles back up to Khafji to report the piece he wanted in the first place. The Saudis were outraged. A few days later Misri and a flock of junior minders came sailing into the WP bureau.

"If you ever go to Khafji again without my express written permission, we will expel you!" he screamed, waving a copy of the offending story at Angus. "How dare you defy the Ministry of Information?"

"What do you mean defy? I came back with you on the bus, Mr. Misri," Angus answered, trying to sound befuddled. "Besides, read the story; it's a pretty grim portrait of Saddam's soldiers doing stuff like shooting people dead at checkpoints inside Kuwait."

Misri couldn't care less. "If you continue, you will never get another visa, nor would I expect any more visas for the World Press!" he yelled, wheeling out of the office.

At least New York loved the Khafji stuff. The foreign editor sent a herogram pressing for more. "Your vivid Khafji piece widely played on front pages across the States," he messaged. "Kudos. Story really gave readers the feeling of being inside Kuwait. Please repeat border interviews soonest."

Angus put him off for a few days but finally had to call. "There's no place I would rather go than Khafji, believe me, but frankly the Saudis are still steaming that I bent the rules a bit," Angus told his editor. "I think maybe I should do refugee stories around Dhahran or perhaps spend a little time with the U.S. troops. I hate to say it, but it is probably a good idea to let the minders cool off, lest they punish us for being uppity."

The editor, spooked at the idea of having visa problems, agreed.

After that Angus passed his mornings shuttling to the military flight line and his afternoons interviewing refugees in hotels around Dhahran.

On one air base visit a kid from Alabama told him, "My daddy says we should roll on up there to Baghdad and stomp a mud hole through Saddam Hussein and walk it dry." Angus had enough material for a mood-of-the-soldiers story that day and figured he would not do better than the mud quote, even if he wasn't quite sure what it meant. So he climbed back aboard the bus to sketch a story outline.

He flipped his notebook open and was puzzling over the quote when someone came up next to him and laid a hand on his shoulder, raising the hairs on the back of his neck. Without even lifting his head, he knew it was Thea. He felt tongue-tied by her sudden arrival, his usual reaction to a woman he liked, so he read her the mud hole quote.

"I swear sometimes it seems easier to translate from Arabic," he said, winning a laugh.

"Maybe you should have asked an officer for simultaneous English translation," she joked, plopping down on the seat across the aisle from him. "So what have you been up to for the past few weeks, besides alienating the entire television contingent of the press corps?"

"So you heard?" he asked.

"What, you thought it was a secret?" she answered. "I'm probably risking my own bright future merely being seen talking to you. But as you are no doubt aware, I love danger."

With the school bus jerking slowly across the airfield and Thea sitting next to him, Angus realized he should forget about his next story for a minute and concentrate on her. He would try to charm her with believe-it-or-not tales from the lives of the Kuwaiti refugees—not exactly standard pickup palaver but all he had to work with right then.

"You know how in most wars, the refugees scurry over the border and drop within sight of their old homeland, convinced they will return in a matter of days?" he asked.

Thea nodded and he went on: "Of course the Kuwaitis weren't terribly interested in living in any kind of temporary tent city. Maybe their nomadic ancestors were happy to squat out in the sand and milk goats, but they have achieved a level of civilization where even the tents they erect in their backyards for nostalgia come with air-conditioning."

She chuckled.

Angus had discovered that Saudi Arabia possessed tens of thousands of unused luxury hotel rooms—visitors being scarce even in peacetime. The Kuwaitis fleeing their country happily occupied them all. Actually not quite happily. Angus witnessed screaming marathons at front desks with everyone demanding suites.

Thea, across the bus aisle, was smiling. Angus struggled to focus on his thoughts and not on her lips.

"The local governor has agreed to pick up the tab," he went on. "But rather than being grateful, mostly they are calling his office to see if he can get them upgraded. Plus they put absolutely everything on their hotel bills. I mean they have been charging things like visits to the hotel hair stylist and the masseuse and..."

Thea interrupted him. "You mean the Saudi government is paying for women to get their hair done?" she wanted to know. "You mean we might be able to get unveiled women on camera looking great and report that the Saudi government is underwriting the moment?"

He nodded and she let out a whoop, "Wouldn't that be a fantastic way to stick it to those warped religious types who fought to ban even veiled women from working on Saudi television!"

"I guess hairdos might be the money shot, but there's all kinds of stuff," Angus said. "The Kuwaitis have charged clothes from the hotel boutiques and birthday cakes for their children from the hotel bakeries and they probably would have charged cars to replace the ones abandoned in Kuwait if only the hotels sold them."

He told Thea that he attended a sort of town hall meeting convened weekly by Prince Khalid, the Saudi king's nephew and the governor of the Eastern Province. A young, good-looking, amiable man, the governor started off by telling the gathering of local notables and refugees, "The Kuwaitis are like brothers; any number are welcome in this country."

"Is that really true?" Thea asked, curling a lock of her hair with her index finger. She had that solemn but wide-eyed look that television reporters so often adopted around their print brethren, not wanting to admit to ignorance but repeating little phrases from the conversation they thought they could use on the air later.

"I think he was just spouting one of those rote Bedouin lines, because the local governorate is bleeding cash. His top aides were muttering that it's time for the Kuwaiti royals to start paying the bills," Angus told her. "The governor's press secretary told me that his boss finally drew the line at paying for deluxe hotel rooms for the small army of Asian maids, nannies, cooks and other servants the Kuwaitis brought with them. The prince ordered all domestic servants returned to their home countries on special flights."

"Speaking of flights, I heard the prince imports high-priced call girls from Europe in his Gulfstream," Thea said. "They are whisked directly to his palace for a fuck and then right back out again without sashaying anywhere near passport control. Is that true?"

"Gee, he didn't bring that up at his public meeting. How odd," Angus said, uncapping and recapping his pen, one of his nervous tics. "And I forgot to ask, being concerned with the silly problem of housing hundreds of thousands of war refugees and their often abused servants."

"You clearly have no future in television," she ribbed him.

"I'll take that as a compliment."

"Dinosaur!"

"Speaking of dinosaurs, have you heard what the Kuwaiti emir and the rest of the ruling family are up to in exile?" Angus asked, swinging his legs out into the aisle and facing Thea directly.

"God, you are just a wealth of information! Where have you been all my life?" Thea said, leaning out of her seat toward him.

"Watch it, you risk catching the print virus that compels one to ask meaningful questions," Angus said and she laughed. "But on the Kuwaiti royals, I really was asking if you had heard anything specific."

"No, just that they were all in Taif and stuff," Thea answered, a crease wrinkling her forehead indicating that she was suddenly worried that she had missed something important.

Kuwait's rulers were housed in the Sheraton near Taif, a green, pleasant town in the low mountains not far from Mecca. Located about 650 miles from the Kuwaiti border, where all the troops were massing, it was about as far as they could get from their country and remain in Saudi Arabia. Angus had been toying with the idea of a road trip to Taif, and he wondered if Thea might be interested. He usually found working amid television cameras worse than maddening, but one camera seemed an acceptable price for her company.

The school bus was slowing to a halt in front of the Dhahran Palace. "What about that dinner we were supposed to have after the chemical weapons lecture?" he asked abruptly. "Maybe we could do that tonight and talk about a trip."

Angus watched her hesitate for a minute, upbraiding himself for paying too much attention to his work and not enough time thinking about his life. If he waited too long she would surely be off with someone else.

"Dinner? In the hotel?" she asked. "What if someone sees us?" She said it lightly, trying to make a joke, but the underlying startled reaction made Angus realize that the television crowd was not going to forgive him for Khafji.

"You can just tell them it was for industrial espionage," he said, smiling because he sensed she was going to agree.

"I am so thoroughly sick of this flight line," she said, standing up out of her seat and helping her crew by hefting their camera tripod. "Let's have dinner tonight by all means, but at al-Hambra or even outside the hotel if there's time, not at the Dunes. I don't want everyone else sitting around eavesdropping and stealing the idea."

Elated, Angus mentally uncorked a bottle of champagne, then laughed at himself for conjuring up such an unlikely image in dry Saudi Arabia.

Chapter Four

REPORTERS rarely ate in al-Hambra for the same reason they avoided the elevators: service in the dark, isolated room unrolled with taxing slowness.

The restaurant, on the hotel's second floor right above the Dunes, was named after the famous fourteenth-century Moorish palace in Spain. Straining to reflect its namesake's sumptuous decor, the restaurant's pink stucco walls were engraved with Arabesques intertwined with lush plants. The tables, lining the walls, were separated from the rest of the room with carved wooden arches. Angus found that the restaurant, oddly for Saudi Arabia, almost achieved the romantic aura of a New York or Paris supper club—the tables were high booths upholstered in red velvet and the only light came from little brass lamps shaped like candlesticks with pink shades. One lamp stood at the center of each table. Even the grating Muzak that played in the rest of the hotel was banished, replaced by the quiet strains of an oud, the Arab lute.

Saudi law required all restaurants to either offer separate sections for men and families or isolate the tables where women sat. Al-Hambra opted for the latter, the waiters placing a carved wooden screen around the front of the booth after Thea and Angus were seated.

"That ought to prevent any spy from denouncing you to the television police for cavorting with a known print reporter," Angus joked and Thea gave him a rueful smile.

"This country," she said, shaking her head. "No wonder so many of my Lebanese compatriots claim they are not descended from the Arabs."

Angus ordered a pepper steak while Thea asked for a Caesar salad with grilled chicken. They agreed to share a pitcher of Saudi champagne, a blend of apple juice and Perrier water with fresh mint. The restaurant attempted to foster the illusion by serving it in tulip-shaped glasses.

"Wish it were wine, Thea," Angus said, raising his glass. "But it feels almost as heady with us finally pulling off this dinner. To the success of any and all future collaborations."

She smiled and clinked her glass against his but did not hold his eyes when he kept looking at her as he sipped. Her green eyes seemed a little lighter than usual, set off by a sea green long-sleeve T-shirt. A fine woolen scarf with stripes in various aquamarine shades was flung around her throat to ward off the inevitable chill from the air-conditioning, still pumping strong in late September.

"So what is a nice Lebanese girl like you doing in a place like this anyway?" he asked. "Plus you said earlier that you had just moved back to Beirut. When did you leave?"

Thea looked somewhere past him as she began explaining that she was half Lebanese and half Swedish. She spent her childhood at various American schools in Lebanon, where her father was a banker and her mother ran one of the city's tasteful handicraft shops. She probably would have ended up following in her mother's footsteps as a pampered, comfortable member of Lebanon's bourgeoisie, if fate had not intervened with the civil war.

"Sometimes I think it odd how the war completed rerouted my life, like a local train shunted by accident onto the express tracks," she said, cocking her head sideways and finally looking directly at Angus. "For the better, I mean. Lebanon is such a small place, reduced even further by the fighting, that I suddenly knew I had to find an escape route. You know when the shelling in Beirut got particularly awful we would flee to my grandfather's village up on Mount Lebanon. One of his brothers, my great uncle, had immigrated to America from Lebanon around 1920, coming back forty years later with a gold ring and a monthly pension from the Ford Motor Company in Detroit. He lorded it over the village, and awestruck relatives never tired of telling me how he had made it in America.

"I always wanted to scream, 'If he made it, why the hell is he back here with the rest of us, trapped like rats in these clammy bomb shelters by the goddamn warlords?' The war made me want to get out so badly that it sharpened my ambition; I knew I needed some form of insurance so that I could escape. I needed to play on a larger stage."

Thea explained that she spent her freshman year at the American University of Beirut but transferred to the University of Southern California because of the war. She was a little vague about her degree, not specifying what she had studied. At some point she began working for the newly launched CBN in its L.A. office.

"I started adult life as the bureau chief's secretary, would you believe?" she said. She worked her way up from there, apparently through sheer scrappiness. News organizations were always short of bodies, so she volunteered to be on call every weekend. Whenever a crisis erupted on a Saturday night—a mudslide in Malibu or a movie star overdosing—she would hustle up the camera crew and get the interviews. Thea told him that she first went on air dolled up in her secretary outfits—big hair and clothes like a flouncy white shirt with yellow polka dots that came with an oversize bow tie. She thought she looked great. But when she overheard two producers mocking her, she realized she had committed a professional sin by distracting the viewers.

"It was one of those immigrant experiences that makes you feel terribly alone, out of place, but at the same time redoubled my determination to do everything necessary to make it," Thea said, her features set in a fierce cast that Angus had not seen before. "I think this sand trap might be just the ticket."

Despite the sudden flash of raw ambition, Angus found himself charmed as he listened, completely captivated by her combination of grit and humor—her laughter often at her own expense—and the way her eyes sparkled even in the subdued light.

"Growing up in Beirut made me something of a war junkie—you know the excitement of all those dashes down to the bomb shelters," she said, adding with a wry smile, "plus I was almost eighteen when the civil war started, so I spent a lot of those first years making out down in the dark."

"You suppose history might repeat itself here?" Angus asked, raising his left eyebrow and allowing himself an abbreviated grin.

"I really don't see myself spending a lot of time here in any shelter," she answered, her face serious, unsmiling, looking him straight in the eye. "This time I am going to be a protagonist, or at least not a potential victim. Besides, artillery barrages don't scare me anymore. I doubt I need the same reassurance, although I suppose time will tell.

"But enough about me, Angus; you haven't revealed a single secret. How did you get into this tawdry business?" Thea asked, taking a small bite of her salad with one hand while pushing an errant coil of hair out of her eyes with the other. "I always pictured foreign correspondents as romantic figures in Burberry trench coats. But so far the ones I've encountered in this hotel seem like nerds with laptops, toting up their front-page stories like accountants and constantly referring to cabinet secretaries back in Washington by their nicknames, as if they were friends. It puts a decided damper on the romance."

"Yeah, I know what you mean about the romance of it all," Angus started. "I wanted to be a foreign correspondent almost as long as I can remember. My father planted the seed early by reading me too much Kipling, I think."

He described how he and his father read *Kim* together so often that by the time he was five they used the traditional Pathan tribal greetings from the book. When Dr. Dalziel came home from his clinic at night Angus would say to him, "May you never be tired," to which his father would respond, "May you never grow poor."

"It is still our first exchange in many far-flung telephone conversations," Angus said, looking up and blushing slightly, realizing it might make him seem like a little kid. He wondered if she could tell he was blushing in the dim light.

"That's so sweet!" Thea exclaimed, running one hand up his forearm, which sent little electric shocks zapping down his neck into his spine.

The sensation stopped just in time for Angus to catch himself before confessing what usually happened next. Whenever his mother was on the line, she would sigh and inevitably scold his father for turning their only son into an incurable wanderer who should be settling down to produce grandchildren.

"He can't tell the difference between a story and a woman. Whenever he's done with one, he just moves on to the next," she groused more than once. Angus always protested, but sometimes he thought she might be right.

Angus glanced up from his steak at Thea, wondering if she might be the end to all that. She was looking at him with an expectant expression, so he delved back into his biography.

In college, Angus told her, while majoring in Near Eastern studies, he edited the school newspaper and worked as the campus stringer for WP. He figured working for a wire service was his fastest route out of the States, and at thirty, he became one of its youngest foreign correspondents.

"I always wanted to work in one of their Middle Eastern bureaus because I find the Mediterranean endlessly alluring—the history, the Byzantine politics, the ancient ruins, the food, the mix of religions, the seeming tolerance for different faiths mixed with the endless bloody feuds," he said. "And of course most important, the women, the chance to meet a wonderful person like you."

He reached for his glass of Saudi champagne to raise it to Thea again, but before he could say anything, Brandt, the general manager, stuck his head around the edge of the screen. "Sorry for the interruption, but everything okay with your dinner?"

"Splendid!" Thea exclaimed, inviting Brandt to join them. Angus hoped the guy would decline. He wanted this to be their dinner, but the manager slid into the booth. "Only for a few minutes," he said, glancing at Angus as if reading his mind. Angus wondered suddenly if Brandt used his staff to keep track of any coupling going on in the hotel.

"I know you can't turn this water into wine," Thea said, pouring Brandt a glass and prompting him to chuckle. "But could you perhaps work a minor miracle and get rid of that ridiculous screen?"

"I could," he said, grinning slightly. "But only if you both promise not to complain if the religious police make one of their little inspections of the hotel and order us all lashed for eating together without being married."

"Lashed, really?" asked Angus, thinking it might make a great story. "Does the screen make that much difference?"

"Really Angus, you sound like you almost relish the thought!" Thea exclaimed, scowling.

"The more zealous types will take the screen down to demand proof of marriage, but if you are at least outwardly respecting the religious rules they will usually leave you alone," Brandt said, sighing. He took a sip of Saudi champagne.

"Hey, that reminds me," Thea piped up suddenly. "We've also been meaning to ask you if you can do something about shutting off the call to prayer that comes through the hotel public address system five times a day. It plays havoc with us cutting our pieces. We are invariably in the midst of recording a sound track when the damn thing starts booming. Plus the first time anybody new hears it they hit the roof because they think it's an air raid siren. Can't we make the hotel a prayer-free zone?"

Brandt chuckled and patted the back of her hand. "Miss Makdisi, you want to get me not just lashed but expelled?" he asked, signaling for a waiter and ordering him to take away the screen.

"I've already had several visits from the religious police complaining about excessive fraternizing between men and women in the hotel's public spaces. I sense we are getting some leeway because the place is now filled with either reporters or American soldiers, but there are limits. Some of the rules are a little bit elastic, but the call to prayer is not one of them. Now if you will excuse me, I believe I will continue my rounds."

"No, stay!" Thea insisted, prompting a frown from Angus, but Brandt was already on his feet.

"Enjoy the rest of your meal. If I might recommend a dessert, *la poire au chocolat* is delicious this evening."

Angus and Thea watched him move to the only other occupied table, where a group of American officers from outside the hotel were being seated. They were all staring at Thea. After Brandt introduced himself, they asked him a question that prompted him to look back at her.

"They probably want to send over a bottle of apple juice of rare vintage," Angus teased. Thea waved at the officers and then shot Angus a look that made him realize he probably shouldn't needle her about her budding fame.

"Just doing my Mae West bit for the morale of the U.S. fighting man, Angus," she said. "Now wasn't the point of this dinner to talk about a story?"

A FEW days later Angus met Thea and her two-woman camera crew outside the hotel, waiting for a van to shuttle them to the airport. He always felt a bit startled to emerge from the dark, dank interior of the Dhahran Palace into the already blazing morning sunshine.

Angus stood looking at the hotel's exterior. Between the narrow, vertical rows of bedroom windows, the facade consisted of a long series of three-story, pointed arches painted the same sapphire blue as the domes out back, the paint similarly peeling. Chunky concrete crenellations, painted white, ran along the roof line. Out front, just past the canopy over the main entrance, a series of tall palm trees rooted in wide brick planters lined the concrete stairs that descended gradually down to the asphalt parking lot filling the entire space in front of the hotel. It's kind of ugly, he thought, but for the moment it's home.

Angus, Thea and her two camerawomen jumped into the van for the short ride to the low-slung Dhahran airport, a drab prefabricated structure with a chilly, fluorescent interior that stood right opposite the air base. In the few minutes it took to get there, Thea all but disappeared beneath an *abaya*, the shapeless, floor-length black cloak required of all women in Saudi Arabia.

Instead of wearing it like a hood, the most prevalent fashion, Thea covered her hair with a bright silk scarf tied at the back of her neck. She also put on sunglasses. Angus choked back laughter as she tripped over the unfamiliar garb on her way through the metal detectors.

"Laugh at me and I'll deck you," she hissed through clenched teeth. "You ought to try walking around in this getup."

"It would definitely be a new wrinkle on cross-dressing," Angus answered.

He was wearing his usual uniform—a wrinkled blue oxford shirt with the top two buttons undone and the sleeves rolled up, as well as baggy khakis spotted with ink stains. Only the back of his red hair—newly trimmed into a neat square—showed from under his slightly soiled tan baseball cap.

"Nice fuzz," Thea said, slowly running her hand up the back of his crew cut and deliberately knocking his hat askew. "Good hair, blue eyes, cheekbones, cute. You sure you don't want to do TV?"

She did it partly to tease him and partly to provoke the Saudi men nearby; the sight of a woman touching a man in public prompted them all to gape.

Angus suddenly realized she had chosen to wear the most provocative headscarf she could find, a silk print of the Picasso painting *Les Demoi-selles d'Avignon*. The grouping of five women, a couple of them with African-style masks for heads, weren't exactly clothed, and everyone staring at Thea tipped their heads back and forth trying to decipher the figures.

Although the scarf was her attempt at getting the last laugh, Angus knew being forced to navigate the modern world in that bizarre getup was humiliating. By the time the two of them settled into the first-class compartment of a Saudia Airlines Boeing 737 she let out a long sigh, closed her eyes and tipped her head back against the seat.

"The problem with walking around dressed like the grim reaper is not being covered; frankly it is kind of convenient because I can wear any old thing underneath it," Thea said, sliding her sunglasses onto her head and turning to look at Angus. "The problem is that the men don't want to see me at all; it's a negation of my presence. Modest Islamic dress my ass. In their mind, the *abaya* turns me into the equivalent of a black hole. That is what is so trying about sailing around in this thing. I am not sup-posed to be a person. Damn what I wouldn't give for a stiff shot of vodka right now."

"I'm afraid you'll have to settle for a date stuffed with an almond," he said, stroking the top of her hand and then leaving his there. Thea sighed again and looked out the window.

As the jet backed away from the gate, they were both startled when a gravelly male voice chanting impenetrable Arabic erupted from the air-plane's public address system.

"What the fuck is that?" Angus hissed under his breath.

"I have no idea. Christ I hate airplanes; how did you ever convince me to come on this trip?" she whispered back.

Angus, looking around the cabin decorated in gold and forest green stripes, could see that no one else seemed perturbed.

A Saudi man sitting across the aisle, evidently overhearing their exchange, leaned over with a bemused expression on his face to explain that the announcement was a prayer for travelers, drawn from the Qu'ran and other holy books.

"They read the invocation aloud on every flight before the plane takes off; it's quite reassuring."

After nearly six weeks in the kingdom, Angus was beginning to spot subtle differences in the way Saudi men dressed. Tradition forced everyone to wear similar white robes and headscarves, but the wealthy distinguished themselves with their watches, their shoes, their pens and the quality of their laundry. His fellow passenger's shoes were tucked up underneath the seat in front of him, but his watch was a lump of gold edged in diamonds, and his robe was so white and so starched that looking at it hurt.

"Qusai al-Gabandi," said the man, sticking out a carefully manicured hand the color of cappuccino.

"T'sharfna," Angus said. He had learned that when introducing himself, throwing out even the shortest Arabic phrase like "honored" made a huge difference in breaking the ice.

"Do you and Miss Makdisi understand the Arabic, or would you like me to translate?" al-Gabandi asked.

"The Qu'ran? That would be kind of you to translate," Angus said, ignoring the fact that the Saudi had leaned forward and was beaming at Thea, fishing for an introduction.

"Hello," said Thea, turning her head slightly and giving him a brief smile.

"I think I am the biggest Saudi fan of your work," he said, before he ran through the whole prayer bit by bit as it continued to boom through the loudspeaker: "O God, we ask you on our journey to enable us to be kind, pious and do the good deeds that you approve. Please God, make this trip easy and make it short.... And God you are our companion on the trip and the guardian of our family. O God, we shelter in you from the fatigue of the journey, the appearance of gloom and any unfortunate reversals in our wealth, our family and our children."

The recorded voice stopped as the plane retracted its wheels. Angus thanked Gabandi, who nodded but didn't say anything as he switched to muttering further supplications of his own.

"Nothing like trying to get God's ear more or less directly as your plane lifts off the ground," he whispered to Thea. "Wonder if you have a better chance of Him hearing since you are slightly closer?"

She managed a wan smile but turned her head to look out the window again. She pushed her scarf back off her hair, figuring nobody in the first-class compartment would say anything.

"I am afraid of flying, so I have to look out to see where we are every time the engine noises change," she said, squeezing Angus's hand like she wanted to break it.

She released it when the plane finally leveled off and Angus surreptitiously tried to massage some life back into it. But Thea noticed. "I'm sorry. I didn't hurt you, did I?" She took his hand in her own and lightly brushed it.

"I don't bruise that easily," he said, smiling back reassuringly, garnishing the traveler's prayer with a quick, silent, perhaps blasphemous supplication of his own.

Chapter Five

BRIGHT mountain light bounced off the coppery glass sheathing the Taif Sheraton, a seven-story circular tower, like beams from a spotlight. Equally dazzling rows of polished black Mercedes bearing Kuwaiti license plates were lined up in the front parking lot, while Asian maids chased toddlers gamboling across the lawns in miniature Arab robes.

As the battered airport taxi bearing Angus, Thea and her crew whisked under the hotel's tentlike canopy, Angus remembered a joke told by a disgruntled Kuwaiti refugee.

"How can you tell when the Kuwaiti government is on military alert?" he asked.

"They call the States?" Thea guessed.

"No, not bad, but it's when all the limousines are parked facing south," he answered.

They were laughing as they walked into the hotel, their footsteps echoing in the cavernous white marble interior. The lobby was empty. Angus figured now that Kuwait's future oil wealth was in question, the usual parade of impoverished leaders beseeching its princes for handouts had ceased.

A woman from the American public relations firm the Kuwaitis had hired to handle their press came bounding down to the front desk as soon as they called. She was a short, flat-chested woman wearing a conservative blue suit, her brown hair carefully bobbed, and she oozed North American efficiency behind her clear acrylic clipboard. She quickly ushered them up to the waiting area outside the fourth floor conference room where cabinet meetings convened.

In the softly lit corridor, scurrying aides lifting documents from a bank of whirring fax machines jostled for space with white-jacketed stewards pushing carts laden with fresh juices and silver dishes of pistachio nuts.

Arabic newspaper stories about the latest diplomatic developments were plastered across a cork bulletin board. One newspaper clipping stapled to the upper right-hand corner showed Saddam stroking the hair of a little British boy, one of hundreds of Westerners held hostage in Iraq, which called them "guests." The picture tacked up next to it showed Hitler in virtually the same pose.

"History Repeats Itself!" was scrawled underneath in English with a red magic marker.

Angus and Thea had asked to see the defense minister, but the American press liaison explained that a reporter already inside needed about twenty more minutes. She wandered off with Thea's crew to take random shots of life around the hotel.

In the more relaxed atmosphere of a hotel filled with Kuwaitis, Thea dumped her black shroud on one of the couches. No one reacted, but Angus drank in her nonchalance and surveyed the details of her body as if for the first time. She was dressed vaguely like him, except she was wearing a tailored brick red blouse with her khakis and had wound a billowy beige silk scarf around her neck.

The two walked to a tall window and stood looking out over the craggy black mountains dotted with pine trees. It was a relief to see something green after so many weeks of flat, featureless desert.

"I don't want to fly that miserably vibrating little plane back to

Riyadh to make the connection to Dhahran," Thea announced. Like most reporters, her first thought on reaching someplace was how to get out. "Why don't we ask the Kuwaiti government for a limo to take us down to Jidda. We can fly directly from there back to Dhahran on a big jet. Jidda is supposed to be the most sophisticated city in this country, the Saudi answer to Manhattan."

While talking, she distractedly buttoned and then undid the second button on his shirt, slowly, over and over again. Angus looked down and watched her strong but slender fingers, the short nails perfectly mani-cured in clear polish, working the button. It was one of the simplest, most erotic gestures he'd ever experienced, simultaneously public yet intimate. He wondered if she was conscious of the physical effect she was having; she gave no sign. He turned to the window and slightly away from her while she kept talking.

"I would definitely like to see Jidda, however briefly," Thea said. "With all those cars out front, I'm sure they have limousines to spare."

"I'm not taking any limousine provided by the Kuwaiti government," Angus told her, his face set in a stern expression. "You television types are constantly begging favors from the very people you cover just to keep the mud off your extremely expensive shoes. It's wrong. Reporters are sup-posed to be independent, unbeholden. Forget it."

She wrinkled her nose at him and was about to argue when her cam-era crew returned. "The minister is eager to see you now," the American woman purred. Angus wondered quietly when, if ever, an Arab minister might welcome foreign reporters with anything approaching eagerness.

They were ushered into the cabinet room, furnished with a long mahogany table surrounded by about forty expensive office chairs uphol-stered in bottle green leather. Thick pink velvet curtains completely blocked the windows. The defense minister, Sheikh Salman al-Sabah, a short, overweight man dressed in a white robe and headdress, rose from one end of the table, beckoning them with a sweep of his hand to approach.

As they sat down they knew immediately which television reporter had preceded them—he had left a copy of his book on the conference table. Spencer Carr was a blond American who grew up somewhere in the Rockies and made a name for himself as a macho reporter in Beirut by dragging his cameras into the heart of hijackings, Marine barracks bombings and other senseless violence.

His reputation was clouded when he turned up one day with an ugly gunshot wound in his leg, explaining that he took a bullet while slaloming his car through the no-man's land dividing the city's Christian and Muslim sectors. The few dicey crossing points were known for snipers. Carr claimed the bullets were flying so thick toward the end that he abandoned the car and crawled out on his belly.

It was not difficult to check that kind of story in Beirut, since the various militias that maintained snipers along the fault line all fielded press spokesmen ready to take credit for anything. When they denied shooting Carr, wags in the press corps suggested that some Lebanese husband likely tired of the attention Carr was paying to his wife and warned him off by shooting him in the leg.

Once Thea and Angus were settled, the Kuwaiti defense minister launched into a lengthy explanation of why the deposed government should not be viewed as a pack of cowardly bumblers. Using carefully diplomatic language, Angus suggested that Sheikh Salman seemed incompetent for failing to put the army on alert after Saddam massed troops at the border.

"We didn't want to provoke that madman, the Thief of Baghdad, into launching an attack, to provide him with a pretext to invade," the Kuwaiti prince said ruefully in his high-pitched voice. "We deluded ourselves into thinking that at most Saddam's army would barely cross the border, maybe seize a few oil fields that he could ransom to bargain down the billions he borrowed from Kuwait during the decade he fought Iran."

The Kuwaitis failed to gauge the depth of Saddam's outrage at not being hailed as the Arab savior for fighting the ancient Arab enemy, Persian Iran, to a stalemate. Never mind that he launched the war against the newly born Islamic Republic in the first place. Besides, Saddam figured he had nothing to lose. He knew most Arabs outside the Gulf considered the Kuwaitis spoiled, cheap and arrogant, calling them the Arab Jews.

"Okay, so we are rich, very rich even, but is that any reason to hate us?" said the minister, who seemed in turn embarrassed and perplexed by the disaster. "When you think about it, we paid for those tanks that came across our border," he said, adding with sudden vehemence. "But we are fighting back!"

He began prattling on about how the resistance spearheaded by a few young princes was already shooting Iraqi soldiers at random and planting car bombs. "I can't tell you all the details, that might jeopardize operations, but I promise you it is strong!" he said.

Angus was skeptical. The Kuwaiti side of the story thus far was largely that the Sabah family, which had ruled the country for 350 years, demonstrated its devotion to its people by hightailing it out of the country.

The one senior prince left behind, a brother of the ruling emir, was too drunk to understand what was happening. He was an early casualty, shot dead at the top of the staircase in the main palace as he lurched forward with a carved gold hunting rifle to stave off the tanks crashing through the elaborate front doors. The royals boasted one hero at least, however unintended.

Angus knew the Iraqis would have no compunction about slaughtering whole neighborhoods to wipe out any sign of resistance. Thea, on the other hand, was enraptured, picturing herself being smuggled behind enemy lines to bring out footage of heroic resistance fighters mowing down evil Iraqi soldiers. The TV networks were already jockeying for position about who would be the first to broadcast from Kuwait, even though the event might be months or even years away. Pulling off a report from inside the occupied city before allied troops entered would be an extraordinary coup.

"Do you think I could make a clandestine trip inside?" she asked, musing aloud how handsome and brave those princes must be. It seemed either the most foolhardy or most brazen of reporting trips, and Angus wondered if he should pursue it as well. The minister was decidedly negative, answering again and again, "No, no, it would be too dangerous. You are too important for us to risk, Miss Thea."

Thea started arguing why it was a good idea. For one thing, the sack of Kuwait lacked a human dimension, at least on camera. For another, everyone held an idealistic notion of resistance fighters, so it would galvanize world opinion against the occupation, prompting more governments to send troops.

She was interrupted by a waiter wheeling a silver cart into the room. He didn't say anything but lightly tapped on a little brass gong atop the cart. The minister explained that lunch was served upstairs and their interview was over.

"I'm not going to let this idea die," Thea said, smiling and wagging a finger at the minister. "You can't let other news take precedence over the story of Kuwait's valiant resistance."

Angus raised an eyebrow. He was beginning to understand Thea's success in charming so many recalcitrant male sources into doing her bidding. Overblown flattery played no small part.

The dining room took up the top floor, its glass windows offering a stunning 360-degree panorama of the mountains and trees. Two whole roasted sheep sitting atop massive trays of steaming rice filled the room with a delicious aroma. They were the crown jewels of two lavish buffet tables spread with dozens of salads and dips. Angus looked around the room and took a quick census, counting nearly everyone in the government except the two or three most senior princes, who remained permanently closeted in their suites.

Angus noticed several ministers lugging Carr's book. He shook his head. The book jacket was dominated by a large picture of Carr standing on the ramparts of a Crusader castle, his blond curls looking dashingly windblown. So many Middle East correspondents had envisioned themselves as Lawrence of Arabia in his classic *Seven Pillars of Wisdom* that Angus wondered if the phenomenon might not rate as a medical condition. Carr appeared to be suffering a serious case. T. E. Lawrence had started his exploits studying Crusader castles in Syria.

Thea was looking around for the real Carr, wondering if he was off interviewing the emir. "I feel cold," she said, pulling her *abaya* off the back of her chair and draping it around her shoulders. "What a disaster if Carr pulls off a scoop on the very day we are wandering around here getting nothing!"

"We can check with that American woman if you want, but I wouldn't worry about it. I'm sure we are all getting exactly the same access," he said. "Arab leaders think they are far too important to stoop to an interview with a mere correspondent. They only talk to foreign editors or anchors who fly out from the States expressly to see them. It's one of the many sublime means they use to shoot themselves in the foot by never getting their message out."

"You mean coming here was more of your print lunacy of seeking out the offbeat? Given that their country is occupied, I would think they'd want to speak once they knew we were in the building," Thea said, frowning as she stood up to go back to the buffet table.

BY NIGHTFALL both of them were antsy to leave, so Angus summoned the battered Peugeot station wagon that had brought them from the airport. They went outside to wait, drinking in the fresh mountain air of the early evening, scented vaguely of pine. The taxi rattled up, braking sharply behind a black Mercedes stretch limousine whose front doors were painted in gold with the Kuwaiti government seal—a dhow in full sail astride the waves. Angus started bargaining with the taxi driver over the ride to Jidda as Thea parted from her crew, who opted to fly back directly.

Spencer Carr suddenly emerged from the hotel and strode toward the limousine. "Hey Carr," Angus hollered, "Did you get that limo in exchange for all the copies of your book you handed out?"

"Kuwaiti ministers are rich enough to buy my book," Carr snapped back, ducking into the back of the Mercedes which then squealed away from the curb.

"TV people are such assholes," Angus growled before noticing Thea standing next to him. "Present company utterly excepted," he added hastily, but she apparently hadn't heard him.

She was too intent on watching the black limousine bear her television colleagues away. She stuck out her lower lip and said, "That could be us," before climbing into the sagging Peugeot.

Angus sighed. All he wanted to do was kiss her. Never mind that kissing an unmarried woman in Saudi Arabia might get both of them flogged by the religious police, that singular branch dedicated to enforcing public morality. It would be worth it.

Angus slid in next to the driver.

"I still wonder if Carr got anything more than we did?" Thea was saying from the backseat.

"Of course not, Thea," Angus reassured her. "It's a solid little story about an incompetent government growing even more incompetent in exile."

"I wonder if that is enough?" Thea fretted. "The one thing I dislike about leaving the Dhahran Palace is that I lose contact with people like Aaron Black. CBN doesn't have anyone with his caliber of experience. The stuff he produces poking fun at situations like these always comes out so well. I wish I could call him, although I don't think it would be quite right, somehow."

Angus made reassuring noises but wasn't really listening. All good reporters brooded constantly about their stories. He was looking at the map of Saudi Arabia spread over his knees; he never traveled anywhere without pouring over the route. He turned toward Thea to explain that the drive to Jidda would take about two hours.

But the driver kept shaking his head and repeating in broken English, "Non-Muslims no use the road Mecca, non-Muslims no use the road Mecca. Prison. Prison."

Angus wasn't sure what he was talking about. Saudi Arabia invested billions in a fantastic highway system and posted no speed limit, making travel fast and direct. Angus, like most reporters, drove around the country at maximum speed. There was plenty of evidence that it was wildly dangerous; roadsides were littered with grotesquely twisted heaps of metal. But the desert landscape proved so monotonous that the desire to escape overwhelmed caution.

In a vain attempt to lessen the carnage, all cars were fitted by law with an annoying alarm that sounded continuously after the speedometer passed seventy-five miles per hour. When Angus first rented a car in Dhahran, he attempted to disable the alarm by unplugging the fuse. To his dismay, he discovered that the same fuse powered the air-conditioning.

Speed bells were one thing, but the idea of highways that were restricted to Muslims was news. The map offered him no explanation. The direct road from Taif wended down out of the mountains and then headed straight for Jidda for a total journey of about seventy miles. The wide detour he spotted around Mecca, marked al-Sayl Road after the largest city along the route, was almost twice that. Angus used his rusty Levantine Arabic to question the driver until he understood the reason for the detour.

The city of Mecca, birthplace of the Islamic religion and a site millions of pilgrims visited every year, lay smack in between Taif and Jidda. Non-Muslims were banned from not just the holy Kaaba, the house-size black stone that is the holiest of holies, but from the city itself. To ensure against even temporary transgressions, the government constructed hundreds of miles of detour roads so that infidels would skirt the place entirely. It was like banning non-Catholics from Rome in case they got lost and approached the Vatican.

Sure enough, highway signs soon appeared marked Non-Muslim

Road, and to ensure that no one missed the detour, the signs said in equally large, reflective lettering, "All Non-Muslims Must Exit."

"An unbelievable example how this country has the infrastructure of the twenty-first century and the mental attitude of the twelfth," Angus said.

"Maybe it's the nickname for the road to hell, but who expected it to be so clearly marked?" Thea mused. "It seems too benign. One kind of wishes that they were more demanding like 'Infidels: Exit or Die!'"

Angus laughed, "Or maybe they should call it the Heathen Highway."

They dozed for a bit, awakening with alarm when the driver started screaming at them, "Get down! Get down!"

In the dark he had missed the full detour and a checkpoint suddenly loomed into view, the kind set up on the city's perimeter to weed out errant non-Muslims. The two foreigners slithered to the floor as the driver gunned the engine. He waved at the guards, who let the rundown taxi pass.

Fear of eternal damnation seemed to drive the car for the next ten miles, the full extent of their transgression. The driver, sweating gumdrops, a tormented expression contorting his face, pushed the car to well over a hundred miles per hour. Angus didn't want to look at the speedometer from his position on the floor, but he could hear the alarm pinging feverishly.

"I wonder which station of hell is reserved for infidels who die in car accidents while trespassing on holy ground?" he yelled over the din of the engine and rattling chassis.

In a combination of exasperation and fear, Thea pulled her black cloak over her head and lay buried in cloth. She was in no mood for jokes. "Let's just get to goddamn Jidda," she said in a muffled voice.

They cleared Mecca without being pulled over and the two reporters sat up. The driver stopped sweating. Angus wished it was daylight so he could see the mud brick forts perched on the hills overlooking the narrow valley that ran from the holy city to Jidda. The forts once protected the long camel caravans conveying pilgrims, the main source of Arabia's annual income before oil.

THEA and Angus pulled up in front of the Jidda Holiday Inn, stretching as they stepped out of their rattletrap taxi into the muggy night. At the end of the darkened street lay the Red Sea, where far out in the bay a brightly illuminated geyser shooting water hundreds of feet into the air marked the isolated peninsula where the king's palace sat.

Dragging themselves across the inevitable marble lobby—this one was rose colored—to the reception desk, they continued to be hounded by the bureaucratic torments rooted in the Saudi version of Islam. Thea had lost her single-woman permit. Without it, the Pakistani hotel clerk adamantly refused to give her a room. "If the religious police come to check the registry and they are not finding a letter, they will make big problem," he whimpered.

Thea and Angus groaned in unison. Saudi women needed the written consent of a father, brother or husband to travel alone. Given their lack of any handy male relatives, each female correspondent received a blanket permit issued by the Ministry of Information. Thea referred to it as her "don't call me a whore" letter.

"This country can be so exasperating," she fumed. "It looks like a Holiday Inn and it smells like a Holiday Inn, but it might as well be on a different planet. It is just fucking unbelievable that my vagina is considered such a threat that I can't travel anywhere without a chaperone or a permit explaining why I don't have one. Fuck these clowns. You should just get a room and I will find a way to sneak up there. If they want me to play the whore I will."

"You won't get an argument out of me," Angus said quietly.

Thea glowered at him. "You should be so lucky," she snapped.

Angus tried a different tack with the desk clerk. "Well, we work for different news organizations, but she is actually my cousin," he said. "So can I write the letter saying it is okay for her to be in the hotel?" They didn't look alike, but it was one of those situations where he had to try anything.

They heard a guffaw behind them and a friendly voice said, "No, you see you can marry your cousin. That won't do at all. Scandalous, in fact."

Angus and Thea turned and recognized Faisal Basha, wearing a long white robe and red-and-white checkered headdress, along with elaborately embroidered red leather sandals. A trim, pleasant man with a salt-and-pepper goatee and an impish sense of humor, Basha was the editor of the *Saudi Chronicle,* which like most of the big national newspapers was headquartered in Jidda.

He suggested that Thea call her office in Dhahran and get them to fax a copy of the travel permit or, if she couldn't raise anyone this late, call CBN headquarters in Miami to get them to fax a letter that would cover the clerk overnight. While awaiting the fax, the three sat in the coffee shop.

"You know when I travel with my wife inside Saudi Arabia we have to bring our marriage certificate to prove we are legally married, or else we can't get a hotel room," Basha said.

Angus, slightly groggy from a long day and repeated run-ins with religious rules, wasn't sure he wanted to hear more, and the expression on Thea's face indicated that she felt the same. Possible infractions were so constant and so tiring, Angus was beginning to understand one reason why many Saudis accomplished so little. With both of them looking at him in polite disbelief, Basha started to tell them a story.

He and his wife once set out from Jidda for Riyadh in the middle of the night and discovered when they arrived around 3:00 A.M. that they had forgotten their marriage certificate. Rather than wake up friends, the couple drove around looking for a mosque with an insomniac prayer leader.

"We found one and asked him if he would marry us and he agreed, waking up some guy sleeping in the mosque to serve as a witness," Basha said, laughing. "So we got married again and we took the certificate back to the hotel and got the room."

"A kind of local version of a Vegas wedding chapel!" Thea exclaimed, "or a completely different twist on a dirty hotel weekend. If it's true of course, Faisal. You're always exaggerating stuff to amuse us and half the press corps doesn't know the difference and reports it anyway."

"It's true, it's true," Faisal chuckled. "By God you can come home right now with me and ask my wife before I even say a word to her."

"The more I think about it, I'm not sure your story is amusing or horrifying," Thea said suddenly, her forehead creasing.

"Really Faisal, how can you bear living like that all the time?" Angus asked. "Forgive me, but it seems perverse to be treated like a child who must be guarded from vice at every turn. It's like the whole country is one giant boarding school. The religious police are the dorm monitors, and the people try to get away with breaking the rules as much as possible behind closed doors."

Basha shrugged. "It becomes second nature. I would rather live here than anywhere else."

"Then why not fight to make the laws less intrusive?" Angus asked, thinking he should probably be writing all this down.

"Most people like them. You guys tend to interview a very small, very educated segment of the population sophisticated enough to know that the rest of the world works differently. But the vast majority out there in the desert heartland believes in all this stuff."

"Then why do you stay?" Thea wanted to know. "You could work anywhere in the world and not have to put up with this nonsense."

Basha smiled at her. "You press Bedouins have probably abandoned the notion of having a home, but I and the others like me haven't. It's my home and drinking liquor behind closed doors or not being able to vote seems a small price to stay. Given the choice, I would rather live like that than fret about my daughter getting raped or my son taking drugs at age ten."

"Come on Faisal, you know that doesn't happen to every kid in the West," Angus argued, sipping from a glass of fresh lemonade a waiter had brought.

"No, nor does every Saudi get flogged for drinking," he said, readjusting his headscarf by bringing the ends down and then flopping them over his head again. "I would rather put up with a little less personal freedom and live in my own country than put up with all the crime and pornography and other unsavory aspects of life in the States."

After the conversation went back and forth like that for a while, Basha changed the subject and started asking them about the war, and when they thought the United States might switch to the offensive to expel the Iraqis from Kuwait. They chewed over the topic endlessly; everyone did, even though nobody could predict when the real fighting would start.

Eventually the desk clerk materialized waving a letter faxed from Dhahran and handed keys to Thea and Angus.

In the elevator, Angus watched the numbers mount with a certain dread, wondering how to propose a nightcap with just Pepsi and fruit juice in the minibar. When they got off on the seventh floor, they discovered their rooms lay at opposite ends.

"I know it's been quite a day, but how about a little hummus with an apricot juice chaser?" Angus suggested.

"I'll take a quick shower and come down the hall," Thea said. "I have a surprise for you. Order me something simple from room service, please, a salad."

Angus couldn't wait. He showered and had just put on clean pale blue boxers and a white T-shirt when he heard a strange thumping in the corridor, followed by a knock on his door. He found a figure standing outside completely covered in white, a walking shroud.

"Well don't just stand there, let me in," she said, pushing hard on his chest with her hand.

"I wasn't sure it was you or the ghost of travelers past," he said, catching her arm and pulling her into the room.

She dropped the sheet on the beige carpeting and held up a small white plastic bottle with a blue top filled with a brownish liquid. "Ta-dah! Surprise!" she grinned, shaking the bottle. She was wearing a simple flowered cotton dress and had run a comb through her wet hair, slicking it back off her forehead. Her feet were bare.

Angus looked between her face and the bottle, confused. "What? You want us to drink nail polish remover? I don't think I'm quite that thirsty for a little alcohol," he said finally.

"It's Scotch, Angus! C'mon, pour us drinks and make it snappy, please," she said, grinning broadly, proud of her contraband.

"Really!? Where did you get the stuff?" he asked. "And why the sheet?"

"Surely you don't expect me to reveal my most important sources," she answered, tapping her index finger against her lips.

Angus wondered if this was the moment to kiss her for the first time. He couldn't believe he was alone with her in a hotel room in the middle of the night. Being alone so spontaneously would have been impossible inside the Dhahran Palace.

"As to the sheet, I couldn't stand the thought of draping myself with that horrid black sack one more time after a shower, so I tore apart my bed and used the sheet, feeling my way down along the corridor by tapping on the walls with my hands. I feel so free standing here in a dress."

"You look great too," he said, handing her a glass. "Cheers. To vice."

"Ah yes, to the special exhilaration of vice in Saudi Arabia," she said, clinking his glass and holding his eyes for a minute while taking a slug. "It's amazing. A country that drives you to drink at every turn doesn't have any booze."

"Nor much in the way of food at the moment. I'm sorry but I didn't get around to ordering anything from room service. Can you make do with the roasted almonds in the minibar or do you want to look at the menu?"

"Just the drink will be fine."

"You know there is probably a divine prohibition against using the minibar glasses for scotch," Angus said, taking her glass from her and turning slightly away to set both their drinks down on the desk. "Probably worth a few lashes or a spanking or something."

"What are you doing, Angus?" she said, her voice betraying a slight uncertainty.

"Something I have wanted to do all day, not to mention the entire past six weeks," he said, drawing her to him and kissing her. It was not a long kiss, but he was glad that she pressed her body against his instead of pushing him away.

He then lifted their glasses and handed Thea hers. The fact that liquor and any form of premarital physical contact were illegal in Saudi Arabia made the wetness of the kiss and the bite of the Scotch taste even better than usual.

Angus wondered to himself if that was the only difference. Thea seemed like someone he had known for a long time. He had been through at least a dozen of these hotel relationships, thrown together with lonely colleagues in strange cities, marooned for a week or two or maybe a whole month chasing a story. Despite being virtual strangers they tumbled into bed for the duration and often never met again.

"What a day," Angus said. "The Kuwaiti government in their marbled exile will make for a fine story, we had an excellent adventure on the road and, best of all, you are here with me. Life as a foreign correspondent doesn't get much better, no?"

"I'm not sure I should have been at the end of that list," she said, pouting with her lower lip, "And surely to be a truly ideal day there should have been a little shopping in there, shoes or silver jewelry or something."

Angus laughed and hugged her. "I was doing it chronologically," he said. They sat down on the room's two-seater couch and began talking about the people they had interviewed in Taif and what might make the best angle on the story. After a while Angus tried to kiss her again, but this time Thea put her palm gently on his chest to stop him.

"No Angus, not now," she said, leaning away before tossing back the rest of her drink and setting her glass down. "It has been a lovely day, but it's so late and we have to get up early to find a flight back to Dhahran."

Angus put his glass down too and took her hands in his. "But our lives are so random, so completely unpredictable, who knows when we might get the chance to be alone like this again," he said, looking up from her hands into her eyes. He ran one hand slowly along the side of her face. "I feel so comfortable tonight. It's such a rare thing that anyone can make the rest of the world seem far, far away, even for a little while. You do it like nobody else I've ever met. Please stay."

"I know what you mean, Angus, but not tonight," she said, smiling at him while standing up to collect her little bottle and her sheet before walking toward the door. "It has been too long a day. Thanks for having a nightcap with me, though. I'll call the desk first thing to arrange our tickets. Good night."

With that she kissed him briefly on the lips, threw the sheet around her shoulders and went out into the corridor. "If any Saudis see me at this hour, well, it will just have to be the shock of their lives," she said, pausing to look back at Angus and laughing.

Angus wondered if he should tell her that he wouldn't be going directly back to Dhahran, that his editor had told him to wander around the rest of the country to find other stories, to write about how the pending war was playing with the Saudis. He sensed, though, that she wouldn't be swayed. Maybe in the morning he could convince her to stick around Jidda for a day or two to do some reporting with him.

He watched her shadowy form recede down the corridor, hoping their assignments could somehow be arranged in tandem. It was not often that he got to spend time with someone he actually liked.

When Angus first became a foreign correspondent he thought the hotel thing could go on forever—an eternal stream of engaging women and nothing to tie him down. It seemed a more interesting choice than the houses and mortgages and children that corraled his friends. At his ten-year high school reunion his classmates sitting around the table confided how they slipped their wedding rings off on business trips and flirted with everyone in sight. One especially crass guy even bragged loudly about how many stewardesses he'd sodomized. That life held no appeal for Angus.

But the trade-off was a certain creeping loneliness, a hollow spot slowly opening deep among his organs that he sometimes imagined he could find, pushing aside his kidney and his stomach to wriggle a finger in the void. On recent trips Angus had felt more alone than when he first started, and he was unsure what to do about it. Perhaps Thea was the answer, he thought, an accomplice along the route wherever it lead.

Chapter Six

A FEW DAYS later Angus strode out of the Jidda Holiday Inn and hailed a cab for the American consulate. He usually felt exhilarated on arriving in a new Arab city, ready to explore its streets on foot or roam through the hidden corners of mazy bazaars. He had read in *Jidda,* a magazine the hotel put in his room, that much of the old souk had long since been knocked down to make space for anonymous office towers and malls filled with electronics outlets. But a newly formed preservationist group was fighting to save the last surviving historic block downtown. It was built of bricks cut from the coral reefs that formed the shoreline along the Red Sea.

In pictures the three- and four-story houses exhibited a ragged charm, tilting at slightly odd angles because the coral bricks had settled differently over the years. They were blindingly white and their windows covered with turquoise *mashrabiya,* carved wooden screens that formed little balconies where the women could look out or catch the evening breeze off the water without being seen by strangers from the street below. Chunks of the screens were missing, the wood rotted in the humid air heavy with salt.

Angus knew that if he only saw pictures of those coral houses, it would not be the first time he had skipped a rare spectacle. He could not count the number of cities where all he experienced was a faceless, antiseptic hotel plus the various offices of the people he interviewed and occasionally the spot where an earthquake or other disaster had wreaked the most damage. He would sit in the taxi on the way to his departing flight as a strange city flashed past, berating himself for not taking an afternoon to get a sense of the place, for not walking through the bazaar even once despite all his eager anticipation.

Frequently events happened so fast that there was no time, but often it was empty notebooks. The lack of a story made Angus anxious, so he clogged every waking hour with interviews in hopes of finding something to write about. If an activity did not involve chasing a story, or if the story did not seem meaty enough, he wouldn't pursue it. Once his notebooks were full, he would be totally absorbed in his hotel room writing. It was a pattern he couldn't break despite countless resolutions. Every time he reached a new city he swore things would be different.

In the back of the cab moving down the broad boulevard that meandered along Jidda's seafront, Angus barely glanced at the water glittering under the morning sun or at the park where the children's swing sets were interspersed with modern sculpture by artists like Henry Moore and Picasso.

Instead he was thinking back to his last conversation with Thea. A few hours after leaving his hotel room, she had startled Angus awake with a call from the front desk to tell him she was checking out. Her bureau chief in Dhahran had phoned, ordering her back because the army was finally organizing a desert trip to cover live fire exercises and had awarded CBN a much coveted spot.

"Why don't you come upstairs and say good morning properly," Angus had said, his voice still husky with sleep. "You don't even have to bring coffee."

"I can't, Angus; I don't have time," Thea answered in a brisk tone.

"Maybe I could get the same assignment," Angus mused aloud. He knew it was impossible. His foreign editor had told him to forget about the U.S. military for a while, to leave that to the others, but Angus wanted to keep her on the phone.

"Taxi's honking," she said. "Gotta go Angus. See you back in Dhahran soon, I hope."

"I miss you already, Thea."

He liked her, maybe loved her a little, although it usually took Angus a few months to fall in love. Thea was smart and spunky and laughed at his jokes. He sensed they could be great friends and felt there could be a strong physical connection too. But he needed to spend more time with her.

Angus reluctantly tried to put her out of his mind, opening the back of the reporter's notebook on his lap to go over the questions he wanted to ask Hawkes Middleton, the American consul he was about to meet.

After Thea left, he spent a couple days in his hotel room, ordering meals from room service while reading Saudi history and waiting for phone calls confirming the interviews he sought. Jidda was the kingdom's commercial and media hub, so he wanted to talk with various businessmen and newspaper editors—who always knew far more than they could publish or even tell him on the phone—as well as one or two foreign diplomats.

In the few interviews he had already conducted, he learned that Jidda residents considered themselves more sophisticated than the desert rubes of central Arabia. They lamented King Abdel Aziz al-Saud's conquest of their city early in the century as a tragedy from which they might never recover.

The Sauds and their Bedouin loyalists returned the favor by labeling Jiddans *tarsh bahar,* or vomit of the sea. The derogatory nickname reflected the fact that many were descendants of the faithful who settled around the port after journeying from distant lands—Persia or India or the various countries of Central Asia—for the annual Muslim pilgrimage.

Angus had read how ibn Saud, as the founding monarch was called in the West, put his name on the kingdom by unleashing an army of Muslim zealots from the heartland—descendants of the Wahhabi clan that adhered to an austere brand of fundamentalist Islam. In the late 1920s, his warriors, known as the *Ikhwan*, or Brothers, had condemned ibn Saud as insufficiently devout and tried to unseat him, but he crushed their rebellion.

To forestall a contemporary uprising, the royals had moved the capital to the central mud brick village of Riyadh starting in 1954, eventually paying a lot of high-priced foreign architects and road engineers to transform it into a modern city. The idea was to create a giant patronage mill for jobs and government largesse, making the bureaucrats beholden to the government rather than their tribes. All the ministries and foreign embassies were gradually shifted to the scorching desert, away from the cooling Red Sea breezes and sparkling views.

Relief is said to have come in the form of a soothsayer. Several editors revealed that a wrinkled Bedouin sorceress King Fahd consulted before making any decision—large or small—prophesied that he would die in Riyadh. The king sought to stave off the inevitable by living in Jidda. His whim forced the entire government and much of the diplomatic corps to maintain offices and residences in both cities.

Diplomats generally cultivated the rumor mill like a subsistence farm, so Angus hoped Hawkes Middleton would give him a few story ideas or at least a few leads. Angus had been around the Middle East long enough to know that American diplomats rarely possessed the freshest news or the most zesty rumors. They tended to be caught up in who was being promoted back in Washington. Iraq's invasion of Kuwait showed their appalling lack of crucial intelligence. One in about ten proved useful, however, so Angus always checked in.

The American diplomatic compound in Jidda occupied an entire block in a residential neighborhood, surrounded by an intimidating fifteen-foot concrete wall painted yellow. From the street Angus could see just the tops of a few palm trees and abundant quantities of bright fuchsia bougainvillea threading through the coiled razor wire capping the wall. He noticed the American flag hanging limply against its pole, the humidity already stifling at 10:00 A.M., even at the end of September.

Middleton was a tall, thin man in his late fifties, with thick white hair and leathery skin from years in the sun. He welcomed Angus just inside the central building, a one-story bungalow of cement blocks painted white that could have passed for a 1950s Florida country club. The red brick walkway leading up to the entrance was lined by a short wall of whitewashed cinderblocks patterned like flowers.

In a small conference room whose walls were hung with a woven Bedouin rug and a Trans World Airlines poster advertising St. Louis, Missouri, Middleton offered Angus a cold Coke before asking him what he wanted to talk about.

Angus had heard from various Saudis and expat residents that trouble was brewing, prompted mostly by the massive influx of American soldiers. What country wouldn't become a little unhinged if 500,000 U.S. soldiers showed up all of a sudden, even if most of them were out in the desert? Angus couldn't rove the streets and ask people about it, since the traditions of Arab hospitality meant everybody would likely lie and tell him that the Americans were welcome whether they believed it or not. The anemic local press wrote nothing about the domestic rumbling, so Angus asked Middleton what he had heard.

"Well, to start with, some Radio Baghdad broadcasts have been giving us a real headache," Middleton began, his voice a smooth rumble. "Not only did they announce that American troops are stationed in the holy cities of Mecca and Medina, which is untrue but drives the ultra-religious Saudis wild. Far worse, the broadcasts said the Americans have been opening bars and brothels to serve all the soldiers."

"And have you?" Angus teased, half wishing it would prove true.

"Of course not. But our switchboard has been fielding a constant stream of phone calls from drunken Saudis demanding 'Where are the bars? Where are the whores?'" said Middleton, laughing and shrugging his shoulders. "They get abusive when we tell them there are none. You know all Arab governments use the press so often to lie to their people that your average Muhammad readily accepts anything he hears from the other side."

What the Saudi press was not reporting but was burning up the local grapevine, Middleton told Angus, was that the religious police suddenly discovered Jidda was unusually fertile grounds for their lightning raids on private homes looking for illicit alcohol and dancing.

"I keep hearing about them, but nobody has told me who they are exactly," Angus said.

The religious cops, the spiritual descendants of the Wahhabis, were extremists lacking any real education who spent all day making sure people respected religious customs, Middleton explained. They called themselves the *mutawwa*, or volunteers, but were formally known as the Committee for the Promotion of Virtue and the Prevention of Vice. Expatriates derided them as "the Promotion," Middleton told him. They were separate from the regular police but had equal power to arrest and mete out punishment. They had nabbed the king's most trusted English translator on one recent foray.

"Really? How did the Promotion get so much influence, anyway?" Angus asked, taking a sip from his Coke.

Middleton continued his abbreviated history. Over the years, the Promotion unsuccessfully fought innovations like public education for women and the telephone, arguing they were instruments of the devil. But gradual changes meant that by the late 1970s Saudi women were beginning to wriggle out of their traditional confinement, entering more difficult, more public fields such as medicine or architecture. In sophisticated cities like Jidda, they appeared outside their homes in fashionable flowing robes rather than the shapeless black tents prescribed by tradition. Everyone expected the notorious ban on women drivers to be lifted.

Instead came the 1979 Islamic revolution in Iran—with its religious leaders denouncing the Saudi royal family as too decadent to protect the holy shrines. To refute the Iranian accusations, the Saudi rulers granted free reign to the religious police.

"It's like a bunch of Massachusetts Pilgrims in their original garb were suddenly unleashed on the streets of Boston as a kind of freelance vice squad," Middleton said.

The Promotion wanted the kingdom to reflect the religion the way it was at the time of the prophet. Its invariably scrawny members even claimed that they dressed like the original converts, Middleton told Angus. They sported straggly beards and unkempt, short robes and let their headscarves fly loose around their heads rather than anchoring them with the circle of black silken rope everyone else used.

They mostly cruised the streets in big Chevrolet Suburbans, but during the afternoon and evening prayer times they swept through shopping malls on foot patrol, armed with short bamboo riding crops. They whipped Muslim men who did not shutter their shops during prayers. The religious police were not supposed to strike women but could arrest any who were inappropriately dressed.

"The fight to maintain strict gender apartheid is their last stand against all things Western and dissolute," Middleton said, shaking his head. His tan face creased with a wry smile. "They successfully lobbied for a law prohibiting movie theaters, for example, on the grounds that it would allow for the sinful mingling of the sexes in the dark. Aside from policing the country's blue laws, by the way, their headquarters periodically makes public pronouncements on matters of religious import."

"You mean like interpretations of the scriptures?" Angus asked.

"Some of that, but sermons and that kind of stuff is generally left up to mosque prayer leaders. I was thinking more of their recent position paper on science education, which said astronomy students should be taught that the world is flat."

"You're joking!" Angus said, not sure whether he should be appalled or amused.

"I'm unfortunately not. The days in the Middle Ages when the Arabs were on the cutting edge of science are...well they never really got beyond the Middle Ages, let's leave it at that."

Middleton explained that the particular problem at the moment was the Promotion's opposition to the U.S. presence in the kingdom. Many had volunteered to fight the communists in Afghanistan, where their efforts were led by Osama bin Laden, the charismatic son of an immensely wealthy Jidda clan. The Soviet withdrawal from Afghanistan left the mujahideen, or holy warriors, feeling invincible. They believed they could defeat any enemy and wanted to defend the kingdom without American soldiers.

"The ruling princes naturally supported the effort in Afghanistan largely to get the lunatic fringe out of the country, so they have no desire for thousands of them to come roaring back to fight a new jihad at home," Middleton said.

"It would be like the rise of the *Ikhwan* all over again," Angus said.

"Exactly. Some Saudis believe that if rebellious enough, some tribesmen might still try to wrest the kingdom away from a royal family grown rich, fat and complacent."

Angus, filling page after page in his small notebook, was elated. Middleton was turning into a story gold mine. His anecdotes would all have to be checked, of course, with sources other than diplomats since they all saw each other constantly and circulated the same rumors.

Middleton explained that the royals were hoping to avoid having zealots rub shoulders with foreign troops. The princes recognized that most American soldiers would be stationed off in the desert where few Saudis would ever see them. Dhahran was a potential problem, however, since U.S. troops often shopped there. The idea of a confrontation between an outraged native wielding a bamboo prod versus an American GI armed with an M-16 rifle constituted something of a horror story for the ruling princes.

The governor of the Eastern Province, Prince Khalid, headed off trouble by suggesting that all area Promotion members spend the war in Mecca and Medina, ensuring that the holy cities were not violated by foreigners. He even paid them to go.

"Naturally they found the holy cities totally boring—no vice," Middleton said. "Both are crammed with women and children because a lot of Saudi men thought their families would be safer on holy ground if Iraq invaded."

Instead the Promotion began prowling Jidda.

"They were absolutely thrilled to discover that it was as close as Saudi Arabia comes to Sodom and Gomorrah. Jidda residents love nothing more than a good bash, and the men feel free to grope all the foreign stewardesses and nurses they can find now that their wives and children have been packed off to the holy cities."

Middleton told the story of a colleague who had been partying in a villa the Promotion raided a few nights earlier. They parked their Suburbans along the outside of the compound, sealing the driveway, and then about fifty of them scaled the walls using wooden ladders.

"The guy described how they battered down the front door with an ax and told me the rest was like living through an attack of wild dogs," he said, contorting his mouth into a snarl before shaking his head and chuckling a little. "What a country!"

"They didn't attack the partiers with axes, did they?"

"No, but if anything remotely resembling a party is going on indoors, everyone is carted off to jail. We have diplomatic immunity so we get sprung quickly, but a Saudi whose breath smells of alcohol gets a two-month jail sentence and lashes. Even the women. If they are caught with a drink they can get up to two years' imprisonment. The king's hapless translator will have to cool his heels in jail until a big religious holiday when His Majesty can issue blanket pardons."

"Are they considered a threat to the government?"

"Not domestically, no, not yet, although some of them served as foot soldiers to Juhayman, the nut case who occupied the holy mosque in

Mecca back in '79. Took the government about ten days to decide to storm the place and shoot dozens of them dead. If that kind of thing spread, or if a more persuasive leader came along it could be dangerous. That's why they are so wary about welcoming back Osama bin Laden and his ilk."

Middleton explained that the Saud family could not confront the religious establishment directly; after all, their long rule and control over the nation's coffers were built on their image as staunch defenders of the faith. The most they could do was try to isolate the fringe.

"What does the party crowd want the government to do about them?" Angus asked, jotting the question on the back of his notebook to remind himself to ask a few Saudis about it.

"There has always been a kind of tacit understanding that if you get caught by the religious police you have to take your medicine. But they are harassing the daughters of the wealthy here, who are scared to death. Jidda residents think of their city as more relaxed than the rest of the country. There was an incident last week that brought the whole thing to a head."

"That sounds like a great yarn," Angus said, his earlier story anxiety beginning to dissipate. Neither the Saudi nor the foreign press had written about this stuff.

Middleton told Angus what had happened. The daughter of a prominent heart surgeon had been working out at a lavish health club that reserved separate hours for men and women, mornings for the wives of bankers, construction tycoons and foreign diplomats, and afternoons for males. The religious police, dumbstruck by the parade of women and men from the same public place, were convinced it was a brothel. So they positioned a couple of their Suburbans down the block and watched.

Frustrated after not discovering any obvious vice, they singled out a particularly pretty girl who emerged and swept into the back of an olive green Mercedes sedan with tinted windows. They gave chase, claiming later they could see from down the block that she was wearing a provocative shade of bright red lipstick.

Angus thought of Thea for a moment, with her lovely, full lips, then berated himself for being distracted from Middleton's story.

"In Riyadh women know that the thing to do is pull over, call your husband or brother or father on the car phone to tell them where you are, then roll down the window a crack and let the religious guy vent, assured that if they force you to the precinct, help is already on the way." But the inexperienced Jidda girl ordered her Sudanese chauffeur to gun the engine for home.

"Well, there is nothing like defiance to make the Promotion rabid," Middleton explained. He told Angus that the enraged religious police sideswiped the Mercedes repeatedly with their Suburban, badly damaging it and forcing it to stop on a freeway shoulder. When the girl and her chauffeur then locked themselves inside, the religious police smashed the windows, hauling out the driver and the girl. They punched the driver and made the mistake of striking the girl with their little bamboo sticks.

"Hitting a girl is a serious breach of protocol," Middleton said. "The traffic police are terrified of the Promotion, but a passing patrol car tracked the license plate of the Mercedes, called the girl's house and told her brothers what was happening. A male relative is the sole authority the religious police will listen to."

The girl's brother arrived with a bunch of regular cops who arrested the religious police for striking his sister. The family was now demanding that Jidda's royal governor sentence the religious police to seventy lashes each for sullying the girl's reputation, and Middleton thought they would likely get it.

"There is definitely trouble in the Magic Kingdom. The zealots feel impotent because so many foreigners are suddenly deemed necessary to protect them, while the liberals want to use the presence of the foreigners as a wedge to loosen things up. I've even heard some of the more prominent women are organizing a demonstration to demand the right to drive. They think the official reaction won't be too bad with all you reporters running around."

"Really? What a fantastic story! Is there a date set or anything?"

"Not yet, not that I know of."

The sole woman Angus had seen driving apart from the soldiers was Thea, naturally. She was so pissed off about the ban that whenever the vehicle she was riding in pulled up to the Dhahran Palace to unload equipment, Thea drove it down into the parking lot. The Saudi military types around the place pretended not to notice. Once she drove all the way downtown on a late-night foray with a couple other CBN women to buy falafel sandwiches, the three of them hooting hysterically throughout the trip.

"Have Saudi women never had the right to drive?" Angus asked. "It wasn't like alcohol, which was banned after a drunken prince gunned down an expatriate?"

"Some of the Bedouin tribes living way out in the desert let their women drive as a practical matter. They say their grandmothers drove donkeys so what's the difference? But in the cities every third-rate preacher rails about how letting a woman drive is degrading because it will inevitably lead to contact with strange men.

"How they overlook the imported chauffeurs as being strange men is beyond me; I know some of the women ball their chauffeurs just to get even."

Middleton grinned and then looked at his watch. Their hour was up. He picked up a telephone and dialed, checking with women involved in organizing the demonstration whether it would be okay to give Angus their phone numbers. Angus thanked him profusely and left.

Chapter Seven

ANGUS looked across the dark, deserted lobby of the Riyadh Hyatt, kicking himself for racing to his next story yet again with no advance planning. It was after 1:00 A.M. and the hotel was full.

Earlier that evening, eating a dinner of grilled sea bass in Jidda and thumbing through his notebooks, he had decided that it was time to move on, that he had written all the stories possible from the leads provided by Middleton and the rest. As he was packing, Angus came across *Jidda* magazine. He had never gone to look at the old coral houses during his two weeks in the city.

Now he berated himself for not staying in Jidda an extra day, doing a little sightseeing after making a hotel reservation in Riyadh and setting up a few appointments, rather than following his usual pattern and hurtling himself onto the first airplane he could find. His craving for a sense of momentum often overwhelmed common sense.

The Riyadh Hyatt was an eleven-story box surrounded by a sort of giant screen porch designed to ward off the grueling sun. The outer wall was about four feet from the building and consisted mostly of five-foot-wide swaths of an aluminum grid. The metal was painted gold and each strip came to a pointed arch at the top, a common architectural touch to give the building a Middle Eastern flavor.

The hotel sat across a four-lane road from the Saudi Ministry of Defense, a campuslike enclave dominated by a row of three sandstone buildings whose ribbed shapes reminded Angus of old-fashioned radiators. A high fence of metal stakes painted white surrounded the ministry, and sprinklers whapping back and forth kept the lawns green. The ministry housed the headquarters for the coalition forces—most of the top American generals worked out of there. Consequently, U.S. military personnel or news organizations occupied every room in the Hyatt.

Angus wondered whether he should try another hotel or wake someone up. He asked the clerk to check the registry for anyone from the World Press and was happy to discover that Benoni Ryan had a room. Ryan, a South African photographer, picked up on the first ring.

"Yeah, man, I'm in a fuckin' minisuite here, come right up," Ryan said when Angus explained the problem. "You can watch my home movies with me."

"Do I want to?" Angus asked. "I guess the Hyatt doesn't offer much in the way of porno channels."

Ryan laughed. "It's nothing like that—not even humping camels. You've got to see it. Come up."

Ryan, wearing jeans and a black T-shirt, opened his door engulfed in a cloud of cigarette smoke. His long brown hair was gathered into a ponytail that fell the length of his narrow back.

"Fuck," Angus thought; in his eagerness to find a bed he had forgotten that Ryan was a chain smoker. Just one night, Angus told himself, walking into the haze. The only light was coming from the TV, and he ignored the smoke when he saw that the image paused on the screen was a close-up of Thea sitting on a bus. She was wearing the same brick red shirt she had on when he last saw her, with some other reporters indistinguishable in the background.

"Such an amazingly beautiful mouth; bet she gives great head," Ryan said as he picked up the remote and sat down on the room's long, narrow couch. Angus, his eyes adjusting to the shadows, could see that the couch and the rest of the room were done in shades of mint green. "In fact the entire crew of news babes totally lives up to its name."

"What news babes?" Angus asked, dropping his bag on the floor and plunking down next to Ryan. He swung his legs up on a low glass table, pushing an overflowing ashtray aside with one leg.

"That is what the soldiers call them, 'The News Babes,'" Ryan explained, hitting buttons on the remote. "Thea brought along two women, a camerawoman and a soundwoman, on this live fire trip I was on just before coming here. Everyone else was making fun of them as oddballs, apparently no network has ever done it before, but the three completely seduced the military. Everyone from generals on down was panting to be interviewed."

Although Ryan had won all kinds of awards for his pictures covering the fight over apartheid, he had once confessed to Angus that his most fervent wish was to become a television cameraman. It was hard to aspire to big toys like the largest model BMWs on what a photographer earned; freelance television crews could gouge the networks for much bigger sums, especially during a crisis. While he was in Dubai awaiting his Saudi visa, Ryan had bought a video camera to teach himself technique. Whenever there was no action to photograph, he started shooting videos, creating often amusing footage of reporters in their unguarded moments.

"Take a look and tell me what you think of my handiwork," Ryan said as the tape rolled.

The camera panned through the bus from where Ryan had been sitting near the back. Angus spotted a few people he knew, at least in passing—Lydia Santangelo, a writer for one of the newsweeklies, and Jack Quisburt, a military wannabe who worked for a newspaper out west, Phoenix or San Jose or somewhere.

Roderick Vining, a British radio correspondent for the BBC, was also on the bus. Vining was an infamously witty crank, ready to find fault with anything, preferably anything American. He was among the few foreign reporters that the U.S. military press office allowed on its trips. Of medium build with a prominent beer gut, Vining had arrived in Dhahran sporting a short white ponytail. Everyone teased him endlessly for cutting it, accusing him of trying to curry favor with the American troops.

Outside the bus's windows, early daylight showed as a bright line of burnished salmon along the lower edge of a pale gray sky.

Angus was riveted to the screen when Thea was on camera, even the back of her head. Ryan was sitting behind her, so she was often visible in the scenes like the one on the screen right now with Aaron Black, dressed in a khaki shirt with epaulets and jeans, sidling between the seats. Angus followed his inexorable approach toward Thea.

Black had a slight paunch, but Angus thought he looked more solid than fat. Angus had been eating lunch in the Dunes a few weeks earlier when women sitting in a booth next to his table had started gossiping loudly about Black. Lydia told a wild anecdote, describing how he assaulted her during the Washington party feting a book she had written about Central America. He had pulled her off into a broom closet and was kissing her passionately and getting his hands high up her skirt before she fought him off. It was clear from Lydia's flushed face that it wasn't the attention she minded as much as the venue.

On the screen, although Ryan pulled back from a close-up shot of the two, Angus could hear occasional snatches of their conversation. Much of it was inconsequential, but he thought Black was flirting with Thea.

"So who is your talent on this trip, anyway?" he heard Thea ask at one point, and Angus knew she was likely a little nervous about the competition.

Black snorted. "Television has got to be the only profession in the entire universe where 'talent' is a pejorative term. Forget about all the other correspondents and concentrate on what you can learn from me, the senior producer, to help you escape CBN into the big leagues."

It was Thea's turn to hoot.

"The big leagues? All those senior citizens watching network news in the midafternoon and hopefully not snoring before the first laxative commercial?" she snickered, Ryan framing a tight shot on her face as she turned to face Black. "I am in the big leagues. Everybody around the world watches CBN all the time because of this war. And I mean everyone. When was the last time Saddam watched you guys on air, big boy?"

"No wonder he thinks he's winning," Black retorted off camera.

Angus watched Thea's face turn serious. She told Black she thought sitting around the hotel was a total bore and wondered aloud whether they all might be better off striking out on their own to find units in the field.

Black explained that any unit would probably welcome her. Soldiers love it when their wives or girlfriends see them on TV looking like heroes, but the problem would come the moment she filed her first story. The brass, either in Riyadh or at the Pentagon, would yank her out and put her on their shit list until the end of time.

Thea speculated that she might be better off in Baghdad rather than sitting on little yellow school buses waiting for the war to start.

"I'm sure I could suggest ways to make your life more exciting," Black answered, again offscreen, but his blurry face edged into the frame as he moved closer to her.

In Riyadh, Angus felt a twinge of jealousy. He wondered what he was doing stuck in some miserable hotel room while Thea was off on desert trips that gave other men a chance to hang out with her. He vowed to find a way to spend more time around her, but his thoughts were interrupted by Ryan.

"In this next part I was having a hard time deciding whether the close-ups worked better or if it was more effective to hang back a little so the viewers could see all the people involved in the conversation," Ryan said, squinting at the screen with a scowl on his face. "This camera angle shit is harder than it looks."

"It all looks good to me, except when Black's face suddenly poked in all out of focus, but I suppose there is not much you can do about sudden movements," Angus said, earning a frown from Ryan. "I will tell you if I notice anything remarkably great or remarkably awful, although what the fuck do I know?"

Ryan's camera, lingering briefly on the other mostly dozing reporters, returned to Quisburt, sitting opposite Thea and Black, who joined in their conversation.

"There can't be any unilaterals in this war or the whole pool system organized by the Joint Information Bureau will collapse, especially after the balloon goes up," he said in his nasal voice, adopting the hectoring tone he always took with other reporters.

"What's a unilateral?" Thea could be heard asking. Ryan began jumping the camera back and forth between the two.

"A 'unilateral,'" Quisburt explained with mock weariness, "is any dumb fuck who tries to cover the military without going through the JIB."

"Sign me up," said Thea and clearly winked at Black.

Quisburt, a tightly wound bantam with a brown crew cut, glowered.

Angus, in his few dealings with the guy, had discovered that he was one of those Pentagon correspondents who had long since gone over to the other side. After years covering generals and colonels commanding thousands of soldiers, Quisburt ardently wished for nothing more than to walk around with a couple stars on his shoulders. He loved parading his gung-ho, macho knowledge about howitzer sizes and tank guns and toxic gases and all the other stuff that the rest of the press stumbled through. He also manifested the merciless soul of a copy editor, endlessly culling other reporters' work for lapses in military usage.

Angus had never seen the guy wearing anything other than desert camouflage fatigues and he ostentatiously carted the Navy Seal fitness guide around the hotel. His backpack was crammed with military hardware—compass, canteen, plastic map file—and he eventually brought every conversation around to how much longer than anyone else he would survive alone in the desert.

Worse, Quisburt adopted Pentagon jargon, using verbs like "acquired" in their peculiar military sense, as in "the gunner acquired the target." Any conversation with him was like talking to a foreigner who had taught himself English from some wacky technical manual. He called his hotel room "my hooch" and his bed "my rack." He couldn't say "yes," it was always "that's affirmative." He even used the military's twenty-four-hour clock, so if you asked him the time in the early evening he would answer "1900 hours."

He drove other reporters crazy. But they would wind him up when they were bored, and Angus heard Black start.

"Hey Quisburt, how about that ABC story from a couple of days ago about the troops not being allowed to raise the American flag because the Saudis don't like it?" Black said. "Pretty unpatriotic rule, don't you think?"

Quisburt was habitually behind all army policy 100 percent, no questions asked, and the matter of the flag proved no exception.

"We have to protect host nation sensitivity," Quisburt answered on camera, using the army euphemism for things the Saudis didn't want reported.

Black pointed out that the Saudis didn't want much reported, notably anything military, and that countless princes paid for their mansions in Marbella or Sun Valley by skimming fat sales commissions off purchases for the ineffective Saudi military.

Quisburt, sitting bolt upright with both hands on his knees, argued that writing about soldiers flying the flag would only get the men in trouble and prompt even stricter rules, hence undermining their fighting morale.

Angus could hear Vining laughing offscreen and Ryan jerked the camera to where he was leaning on a blanket folded against a window. "Frankly speaking, I also think the American flag makes for terrible desert camouflage. I wouldn't want to be in a trench with it flapping around. The soldiers should all wait to wave it when they are back marching up Broadway. You will be in the victory parade, won't you Quisburt?"

Quisburt ignored the question but the camera's microphone picked up Thea and Black chuckling in the background.

Black started complaining that the Saudis were far too sensitive, ticking off the subjects he had been admonished not to report, like the fact that army rations may contain pork, which is forbidden under Islamic dietary rules.

Vining joked that it tasted more like dog to him, prompting laughter from both Angus and Ryan in their Riyadh hotel room.

"Hey, I forgot to ask, you hungry, man?" Ryan asked. "You want something from room service? Remember it's all on mother WP."

"Nah, thanks, I had a good dinner in Jidda," Angus told him quickly because Ryan had suddenly focused the camera on Thea again.

She was telling Quisburt that if the reporters kowtowed to every Pentagon rule, the coverage would consist of fighter jets taking off and warships churning the ocean. He responded that he saw nothing wrong with that; in general the public loved watching military equipment in action.

They were interrupted by the military public affairs officer, a skinny, hollow-cheeked man with greasy, thinning blond hair, blowing into a bullhorn at the front of the bus. He had just learned over the radio that the brigade they were supposed to visit had redeployed farther north, so they would have to go back to board choppers at the air base opposite the Dhahran Palace Hotel because it was too far to drive.

Everybody groaned. The screen showed the floor of the bus and then went dead.

Ryan stood up and asked Angus if he wanted a near beer, the nonalcoholic version, from the minibar. Angus said yes even though he didn't much like the stuff. He thought it tasted like real beer that might have already run through someone's body once.

"Quisburt is a prize dickhead," Ryan said, snapping open a can and handing it to Angus. "He like runs ahead of us to ask the chopper pilots all these complicated questions that are just meant to show how much he fucking knows. They were telling him this stuff that seemed really technical like the IFR method of flying or the IFP method, or whatever, and he was nodding like a jerk. After the flight was over, Thea asked the pilots about it, thinking we all might have missed something.

"The pilots explained that IFR technically means navigating by instrument flight rules, or flying by instruments alone when you can't see anything. But in Saudi it came to stand for 'I follow roads,' meaning the guys just flew along the highways because there are no landmarks to navigate with in the desert."

Ryan chuckled and took a sip of his near beer, falling back down onto the couch.

"The IFP method was 'I follow pipelines.' It's less obvious, apparently, but the disadvantage is that the pilots cannot tell the difference between going north or south when hovering over a pipeline. Along the highways they can read the signs. Can you believe that? They're like that guy in the mountain man movie: 'I ain't never been lost, but I been powerful confused for a month or two.'"

Angus grinned. "This is great footage. I think those tight shots on the faces as they spoke worked best, even if you missed the occasional line as you jumped from one to the other."

Ryan, pleased to showcase his efforts, placed a second cassette into the VCR.

The next shot showed a stocky colonel of about fifty with gray temples edging his closely cropped black hair. He was standing by the flap of a large khaki-colored tent pitched in the midst of a featureless expanse of desert; flat plains of tawny sand stretched away in every direction. Beyond the tent no blade of grass or skittering rodent broke the monotony. To Angus it looked like an outpost on Mars.

The camera swiveled around to where a great cloud of dust obscured a bunch of Humvees in the background. The reporters emerging from the cloud looked like someone had doused them in buckets of talcum powder.

The first person to step forward was Lydia, a tall, skinny woman, about five feet eleven. A wide, bulbous nose, slightly veined from heavy drinking, dominated her face and years of terrible reporter's hours had etched deep shadows under her eyes. One front tooth bent outward. Despite her somewhat battered physical appearance, Lydia sustained an aura of style by lavishing huge sums on her wardrobe and easily paying $250 to get her black hair trimmed, in addition to airfare. She flew from Cairo, where she was based, to a stylist in Milan.

For the desert expedition she sported large black sunglasses, a pink and white striped shirt and tan Capri pants. She had done her hair up in a turban of rough Indian silk that matched her shirt and made her seem even taller.

"When God made this country, he must have had the ass," the colonel said in a lilting Tennessee accent by way of a greeting. "Y'all go on into the tent now and I'll try to teach you how to survive out here," he said, lifting the flap.

The next shot, poorly lit, showed the colonel standing in front of a whiteboard, explaining with a blue magic marker and a rough map of the country that they were ten miles from the Iraqi border, but told them it was information they couldn't report.

"Who's the officer?" Angus asked Ryan.

"That would be Colonel Joseph Cox, the commanding officer of the 82nd Airborne," Ryan said, hitting the pause button and making a vague salute. "Most of us were calling him Colonel Coxsucker by the end. He is one of those officers who blame the press for losing the Vietnam War. He really hated Black; you'll see in a minute. He basically didn't want us around. It was the usual crap—a lot of make-nice chatter and absolutely no access to anything interesting, like the chopper pilots who'll actually go into combat. It's beginning to look like this pool system is designed so the press never spends a spontaneous moment with anybody."

"I know what you mean," Angus said, sliding down on the couch and balancing the beer on his chest. "It just sucks how all we do is sit around wishing the fighting would start."

"Fortunately Cox had this really cool public affairs officer, Captain Baxter A. Thorn III—where do they find these guys—who was fearless and tried to take us everywhere, even right smack up to the border. He was a Ranger but it looked like his unit was going to sit out the war, at least the beginning, so he volunteered to be a press officer to get right over here. That made Coxsucker and the other senior officers totally suspicious, but he's the coolest PAO I've ever met."

On the video, Vining could be heard needling the colonel about the dateline restrictions. "I'll file my dispatch with the dateline 'Somewhere in the Eastern Hemisphere.' Would that be okay, Colonel?" he said.

The press corps had been stunned by a lengthy Pentagon memo restricting what datelines they could use, and they never stopped making jokes about it. The memo said things like they could start their stories with IN NORTHERN SAUDI ARABIA but they could not say near the border, nor even IN VERY NORTHERN SAUDI ARABIA, despite the fact that everybody knew all the troops were there. A few pool reports, reflecting the general frustration with the rules, had been filed under the dateline WHEREEVER.

Colonel Cox gave Vining a thin smile and went on, detailing their desert exercises.

Black then asked a question and Ryan focused the camera on him as he explained that a couple of helicopter pilots passing through Dhahran had told a WBC producer that the newest attack helicopters assigned to the 82nd Airborne, the Apaches, were proving too delicate for the Saudi sand. The grains chipped at the rotary blades and gunked up the engines, leaving an appalling 30 percent out of commission daily.

The question provoked a look of disgust from the colonel.

At the Hyatt, Ryan hunched forward on the couch. "This next bit is great, even if there was not a lot of light in the tent. You can hear the clash between Coxsucker and Black."

The picture was indeed dim, more black shadows than actual people, but Angus could hear the voices clearly.

"Trying to relive the glory of your Vietnam reporting, Mr. Black, American boys burning down villages and all that crap?" Cox said tersely. "I'm sure you'll be sorry to hear there aren't any villages out here."

"I'm sure I'll find something, Colonel," Black shot back. "Can you answer a direct question about whether your helicopters are failing or not?"

"We are ready to accomplish the mission we were sent here for," said the colonel, suggesting the reporters move out to the tent where they would all be staying. Black did not let go, however, saying that American taxpayers had a right to know whether the expensive equipment they were paying for was actually doing the job it was supposed to do.

"Right you are, Mr. Black, and I am telling you that we are good to go," the colonel said in an icy tone. Angus could sort of make out the officer strapping on his camouflage helmet and then a sudden flash of sunshine blotted out everything else onscreen as he lifted the flap and left the tent.

Ryan hit fast-forward. "That Black guy is like a bloodhound sniffing for news. It's good that there are one or two of you like that, trying to find a way to report about something other than this endless color shit, not that it does any good. We always end up with color anyway. I am skipping this next part because the stuff will make you seasick; the Humvee was bouncing around too much."

When the video started rolling again, the reporters were gathered in front of another tent, this one olive green and sitting in a long line of similar tents facing a gravel walkway. A few yards away the camera caught a low plywood sign stuck into the sand next to the walkway, almost like a lawn ornament, that read "Kick Their Ass and Take Their Gas."

"The army guys who built the tent called it the Palace, and it really is the best place I've stayed yet," Ryan said. "Check it out."

Ryan had filmed in close-up detail the delighted looks as reporters discovered that the tent was the desert equivalent of a hotel in Vegas. The walls, floor and ceiling were lined with plywood. A dart board hung on the back of the wooden door front. Reading lamps cantilevered over the cots and there were built-in closets. The Palace even boasted its own power supply with sockets in the walls.

Colonel Cox joked that he had allowed his supply men to build it just in case King Fahd showed up and needed a place to sleep. He explained that it usually housed just four guys but was spacious enough to line up sixteen cots. The men had strung two rain ponchos in green and brown camouflage across one end to give Lydia, Thea and her crew some privacy.

The press started asking questions about why more tents weren't like this and the supply guys explained that plywood was the rarest, most highly prized commodity in the military's desert economy. Apparently someone with plywood could barter it for anything—medicine, machine guns, probably even sex.

In the next shot Ryan showed Black stretched out on his cot with his gas mask pouch tucked under his head like a pillow.

"Tired old man," Thea said, standing at the foot of his cot.

"Take a load off," Black could be heard saying, then Ryan caught him patting the cot next to him.

"I'd rather walk back to my room in Dhahran," she scoffed off camera.

A tall, strapping officer, whom Angus saw from his uniform name tag was Captain Thorn, came over and told Black not to leave his head on the gas mask. "Guy over at another unit was sleeping on his, but he rolled around on it so much that it triggered the atropine injection. Needle shot right into his brain and killed him," the captain said.

"Fortunately for Black, his brain is not in his skull," Thea mocked and Ryan had swung around just in time to catch her wide grin.

The television went blank, flickering a grainy black and white.

"This is the first time I have really screened this stuff, so I am totally cool about looking through all of it, especially since the photo editor in New York told me to stay awake for a little while because he might call," Ryan said. "But if you want to go to sleep you can."

"Nah, I'm not tired," Angus said, hoping to see more of Thea, however fragmented. "What else have you got?"

Ryan switched tapes again. "How about a little live fire?"

The screen came alive with the camera jerking up and down inside a Humvee speeding across the desert. At the firing range, under a sky almost devoid of color with the sun blazing straight overhead, Captain Thorn explained that the Sheridan M-551 tanks just delivered to the armored battalions needed the sights on their 152-millimeter main gun calibrated.

"Excuse me, sir, but they aren't really tanks, are they?" Quisburt asked. "Aren't they called armored airborne reconnaissance vehicles?"

"Get a life, Quisburt," Lydia could be heard muttering somewhere near Ryan.

Thorn then told the reporters to climb on the backs of the tanks; there were almost enough that each reporter or photographer or TV crew could have one. Ryan swept the camera up and down to show how the machines were deployed in a straight line with several yards between them; the plywood targets sat hundreds of yards away across the flat sand.

Angus could pick out some of the nicknames stenciled across the sides of the khaki-colored tanks, ranging from the simple "Sledgehammer" to the more jaunty "Merrily through the Valley of Death We Go" to the somewhat moody "Momentary Lapse of Reason."

Ryan hit pause and explained the upcoming scene briefly. "I ended up on the same tank as Black because it was at the end of the line and both of us figured there would be no dust or smoke from the other Sheridans obscuring our shots. It was called 'Arnold the Battle Pig' and of course Quisburt had something to say about that. Watch."

Quisburt could be heard yelling from nearby that Black's crew should not film the name because it was about pork and the shot would violate the rules on host nation sensitivity.

Black ducked suddenly and pointed at the sky behind Quisburt, yelling, "Omigod! Vampires inbound!" the military slang for hostile aircraft. Quisburt fell for it, Ryan yanked the camera toward him as he snapped his head around and gasped "Where?" before realizing he had been duped. The tank crews could be heard laughing.

"Fuck you, Black!" Quisburt screamed.

Ryan moved the camera back to Black, who ignored Quisburt, saying something inaudible to Thea on the next tank. Then the screen went dark again.

"I'm afraid I had to bang off some real frames while the tanks fired at the targets, so I shut down the video operation for a bit," Ryan said, a thin flame cutting through the murky room as he flicked on a plastic lighter for another cigarette.

The next shot showed Thorn standing on the back of the tank with Black next to him. Thorn's thick neck and dense body looked like it might burst out of his uniform with every movement. His black hair was cut in what the soldiers called a "zero to three," meaning the back and sides were shaved and a short, three-inch Mohawk sprouted on top.

As a helicopter clattered overhead, Thorn explained that the surrounding desert was not quite the wide open country it seemed. Most of the Bedouin in the area had decamped after the first day of live fire exercises, but some were still wandering around so a helicopter scouted the immediate area before any shooting started.

Ryan had stopped filming for a while and then started again, showing Black with a restless expression on his face, then following his gaze as he looked over to where Thea was squatting down talking to a soldier, her back toward him. "Great ass, huh? Wish I could subject that to a little live fire," he said and Angus heard Ryan laughing on the tape.

Black turned the other way and the camera panned too, slowly surveying the sand filling the entire horizon.

In soft light Angus found the desert majestic. But onscreen, under the full bore of the midday sun, it was blinding, almost painful to look at. Black took off a faded green kepi that Angus thought looked like surplus from the French Foreign Legion and mopped his brow with a red paisley bandana from his back pocket.

"Here come the camels, the money shot from Saudi Arabia," Ryan told Angus, smiling as he blew out a long stream of smoke.

Onscreen, you could hear a voice from somewhere yelling "Cease fire! Cease fire! Mine sweepers on the range!"

"What are mine sweepers?" Angus asked.

"That is what the men call the camels," Ryan said, grinning. "They've been told that if they kill one they have to eat it, so they are pretty careful. Of course, after they live on the army's prepackaged meals for a few more weeks, that might change."

Onscreen, Black leaped off the tank and said something about grabbing a few camel shots. Angus could tell that the tank maneuvers had ground the sand to the consistency of flour; each step Black took raised a little puff of powder.

"The helicopter scanning for Bedouin buzzes camel herds to chase them away, but it must have missed this little group," Thorn yelled as they hurtled across the sand in a Humvee. Ryan was having trouble holding the camera steady and only caught the lower half of his face talking. "The expression on their faces never seems to change; it's always glum. It's like they're thinking, 'There goes the neighborhood.'"

Black could be heard chuckling: "That's a pretty good line; I'll try to work it into the piece!"

In Riyadh, Ryan shook his head, his face filled with admiration. "That guy Black has a great feel for camera angles; he's a master. He directed the Humvee to exactly the spot where his cameramen could get tanks and camels in a tight shot in the same frame. My still pictures came back really fantastic too. You know how Americans equate all things Arab with camels to start with. The photo desk was coming in their pants with delight.

"Thorn also took us one night to visit a group of Bedouin who occasionally invited officers over for what he called a 'goat grab' because the Arabs grill the animal whole on a spit and then tear off chunks with their hands.

"Thorn told us that one little cluster of Bedouins had not left because the oldest members, two brothers pushing a hundred, refused to move away from a favorite shady palm oasis. Like a dumb fuck I had only brought one battery and it went dead, but the two told us about the old Bedouin wars in the days of ibn Saud. They described how the men from various tribes gathered a couple pounds of dates, a few cupfuls of rice, their rifles and ammunition, saddled their camels, and went off to war. One of those geezers said they thought of it kind of like hunting.

"So then Black asks them what the desert was like since the U.S. military arrived, and they go in unison, 'Boom. Boom Boom Boom. Bobobo-BOOM. BOOM BOOM BOOM.' It was hilarious! Two toothless men in their nineties, cackling and echoing the sounds of live fire like little boys.

"Black combined it all, the camels on the firing range and these two guys, but of course the stupid network producers back in New York tried to kill it. He told me they were whining about not wanting any more feature-y, desert-lite shit. He kept telling them that there weren't any cowboys and Indians, trying to convince them this piece was different, completely entertaining. He told me the executive producer shot him down by answering, 'It's a long way from Broadway, Aaron,' and then hanging up. Generally I sympathize with New York, but this was really fun stuff and eventually they caved. I mean what else are they going to get from here? The viewers loved it, of course, and all the other networks went batshit, sending their bureaus rockets asking why they didn't have a camel story," Ryan said, laughing again. "Welcome to covering a war, man!"

The phone rang and Angus looked at his watch. It was almost 2:30 A.M. He could tell from the conversation that it wasn't the photo desk, but a veteran WP correspondent elsewhere in the Hyatt.

A small clique of old hands Angus had never met before were starting to turn up in Saudi to report on the pending war. They reminded him of Gila monsters with their scaley skin, droopy eyes and generally poisonous attitudes. Meeting them had provided the first inkling that spending life chasing wars might prove more battering than Angus anticipated.

Ryan and the WP correspondent discussed a plan by the commanding general, Norman Schwartzkopf, to tour the northern border in two days. The correspondent had wrangled a couple seats aboard his choppers. He was calling to make sure Ryan was available and wouldn't disappear.

"So you're out of here?" Angus said when he hung up. "Guess I will just have to take care of your suite for you, air it out and all."

"I've still got another day. I'm not sure when I will be back, but whatever happens, don't give up the room. They are becoming a rare commodity. Do you want to watch more?"

"I don't know, what else you got? It all seems like pretty great stuff. I think you are ready to go make your fortune as a TV camera guy, although I would hate to lose you to the dark side."

"Well, don't worry, it's not going to happen in this war," Ryan said, again standing up to go fiddle with his tapes. "I guess it's time to grab some sleep. I am going to the bazaar tomorrow to get camping supplies and stuff, but you really should watch this one tape with Baghdad Betty on it."

"Baghdad Betty?" Angus asked, wondering whether he should ask what shots of Thea were on the other tapes. He didn't want to sound obsessed.

"She's this unbelievable chick the Iraqis put on the radio and that is the name the soldiers gave her. She is too fuckin' funny talking about stuff like how the desert will eat them. You should do a story. But whatever happens, don't lose any of these tapes. Yeah, if you have to leave this room for any reason keep them with you until I see you."

"Not unless I see you first," Angus said, reaching over to unzip his bag to find a toothbrush.

Chapter Eight

AFTER about a week in Riyadh, Angus spent an empty day making phone calls to set up appointments and frequently checking his watch. He was waiting for late afternoon Saudi time, midmorning back in New York, when the foreign editor, Edward Devon, would be getting to the WP head office. Angus steeled himself for the guy's frequently idiotic suggestions, always delivered in an aggressive tone. He never talked to Devon without feeling nostalgic for Peter Markowitz, the previous foreign editor, who had suffered a stroke at his desk and retired.

Markowitz, who bore more than a passing physical resemblance to Albert Einstein, was an infamous curmudgeon, bellowing insults like "piss pot" at his far-flung correspondents if they missed a story. He had been around the WP so long that he still answered the phone "Cables," which had been the name of the Foreign Desk when all the news arrived by telegraph. Underneath the gruff exterior was an avuncular boss, however, always primed to fight the company for his reporters. You could talk about anything with Markowitz.

Devon, a tall, skinny, pinched figure with thinning black hair plastered down in a comb over, was precisely the opposite. He was all sweetness and light on the surface, but treated WP staffers like cogs in a machine. The company came first, the reporters a distant second.

The difference was starkly evident during Angus's last home leave in New York, an annual rite that was supposed to involve fine lunches with various editors and a few extended story conferences. On the day Devon was scheduled to take him to lunch, the guy's wife mistakenly packed his briefcase with a tuna fish sandwich. Rather than waste it, Devon suggested Angus go buy a sandwich in the cafeteria.

On the way, Angus unexpectedly bumped into Markowitz.

"Isn't it about time you went someplace else?" said his former editor, leaning heavily on a cane, his infamously squeaky voice now a slur.

"You mean leave Cairo?" Angus said. "I've talked about Jerusalem a little bit, but nothing serious."

"No, I mean another news organization, Angus, a newspaper. You write too well for this place," Markowitz said. He turned and disappeared onto an elevator before Angus, flabbergasted, could respond.

Although Devon had been his boss for more than a year, Angus still couldn't fathom how a news organization ever produced such a soulless bureaucrat. Worse, Devon had spent most of his career with WP in its radio branch and basically knew nothing about working overseas. When he got Markowitz's job, he tried to advertise his serious intent by showing up in the morning with journals like *Foreign Affairs* tucked under his arm.

Markowitz was right; it was time to move on, join one of the big U.S. papers. He hoped an editor somewhere would notice his work and call. But it would take a big story for that to happen, a scoop, some battle that he alone witnessed or some Saudi government scandal he unearthed. When Angus thought about the prospect of latching onto something exclusive amid the herd of reporters milling around Saudi Arabia, he got a stomachache.

As soon as he reached Devon, the editor complimented his string of recent stories. "That Kuwaiti government piece came out remarkably well, Angus. The *Times* has done it since you went up there." Angus smiled ruefully. Nothing brought WP editors to climax faster than being copied by the *New York Times*. "The piece about the religious police was also widely used and I hope you will keep your eye on them, we could use anything you write on that subject. What else are you working on?"

"Thanks, Ed," he said, and then ran through a brief list of story ideas and mentioned the women's driving demonstration again. He pointed out that the demonstration was still a couple weeks away and proposed returning to Dhahran beforehand. He held his breath, waiting for Devon to bite.

Watching Thea on tape had made Angus realize how badly he wanted to see her. She was difficult to reach on the telephone, often away from the Dhahran Palace now that the military was laying on more trips. He couldn't quite figure out what was going on. She seemed effervescent enough when he spoke with her about stories but cut him off when he tried to discuss anything personal. He could only reach her in the CBN bureau, and he hoped her reluctance to talk stemmed from the fact that her colleagues were listening. Angus wanted one more dinner at al-Hambra or rather one more night alone with her in a hotel room somewhere.

Devon scratched any chance of that.

"There are too many reporters stacked up at the hotel in Dhahran just waiting around, Angus," he said. "I really like the stuff you are working on. Nobody else is working the Saudi angle as hard, and I think you should stay away from Dhahran at least until after the driving demonstration. We can talk about it again after that."

Angus let out a long sigh after he hung up. He had always put his reporting before his relationships, before any sort of personal life, but it was wearing on him. His life was like a large orchestra playing fortissimo to try to disguise the fact that one entire section was on strike. Still, he told himself, his priority had to be writing important war stories. Surely he would have plenty of time to get a real life after that.

Angus stared at the telephone for a few minutes. Maybe he should check in with his own bureau in Dhahran. He usually avoided it, but he hadn't been able to reach Thea for a few days and they might know her whereabouts.

Ron Vandusen picked up the phone. Vandusen, a hefty thirty-four-year-old with thick black hair, covered the Pentagon for World Press. He was referred to around the Dhahran bureau as testosteRON. He reveled in the name. He had been a home run king in college and claimed he was headed for the majors before jumping off a porch roof at a fraternity bash and badly breaking his ankle.

Vandusen didn't get out to do much reporting, preferring to sit in the Royal Suite all day, guzzling near beer and answering the phones. He got a lot of stories that way.

"Hey Vandusen, how are you?" Angus asked.

"Where the fuck are you?" he responded in his reedy voice.

"At the Riyadh Hyatt. Anything going on in Dhahran?"

"Well, let's see; what you have missed? The talk of the Dunes has been that a number of women have been having weird problems with their underwear in the hotel laundry. It either doesn't come back at all—you aren't wearing it, are you Dalziel?—or it comes back with like 'I l-u-v u' written in the bra cups in bright crayon colors or the panties completely ripped and mangled. The women are a little spooked and a lot pissed off and sent a delegation to the general manager to complain."

Angus laughed. So much for war developments. Events inside the Dhahran Palace took precedence.

"Anyone figured out the case of the savaged lingerie? Although I was actually calling to check on real news, you know, what we write for a living."

"No sleuthing has answered that one yet. It's probably because poor, sex-starved Asian laborers have never seen lace in the hotel laundry before and are out of control. But you want real news, huh? You mean that stuff we put on the wire? Well, let me see. Nah, can't think of anything. Oh, except New York is sending Callahan. He should arrive in Jidda any day now."

"You sure? I just talked to Devon a little while ago and he didn't mention anything," Angus said, thinking it so typical of the foreign editor not to share minimal information about other staff.

Adam Callahan was known as a Bigfoot, a breed of correspondent widely detested by his immediate colleagues. Every news organization cultivated one or two, invariably men with decades of experience who were exceptionally eloquent in print or on camera and were rolled out for truly major stories. Most developed egos that matched their global reach and Callahan, a Brit in his late fifties, was typical.

In the absence of a crisis, he would disappear for months on end, researching obscure stories like the importance of the sunflower to the world economy, giving him plenty of time to hunt for a country home in Burgundy or Tuscany on company time.

Once assigned to a developing story, he habitually pulled seniority to lay claim to other people's ideas, stole bylines and generally treated everyone else like a hired hand. Occasionally he was forced to do his own reporting, but Callahan usually spent all his time sitting in his hotel room, brooding about the plots surely being hatched to undermine his reputation or deprive him of important stories. He was suspicious of everyone, even translators, threatening one and all to bring the wrath of New York down on their heads if they refused to do his bidding or had the temerity to argue.

The editors in New York, never exposed to the full force of his paranoia, worshiped Callahan because he had won a rare Pulitzer Prize for WP. Devon was dismissive of junior reporters who complained about him. When doling out assignments on the phone, the foreign editor used the expression "an Adam Callahan byline" with such reverence that it might have been the hand of God punching the computer keys.

A wiry, balding guy of medium height, Callahan looked battered enough to have covered every major story since the Flood. He had started life as a tabloid reporter in London but provided so much vivid copy on the side to the WP during various periods covering postcolonial wars and coups in Africa that eventually they hired him. He had been one of their main foreign correspondents ever since.

"Oh great," Angus groaned into the telephone to Vandusen. "Soon we'll have stories about expatriate oil workers fleeing Iraq and washing ashore in Dhahran on rafts made from empty water bottles lashed together with shoelaces—rafts that nobody else will be able to find—having survived for ten days on prime tuna sashimi that they throttled with their own hands."

Vandusen chuckled.

"What is he coming to do?" Angus asked and then added hopefully, "Military?"

"No, I think he is doing Saudi stuff first, and then maybe military when we get his name on the trip lists, unless of course he wants to stay with the Saudi stuff," Vandusen said, rubbing in the fact that Callahan would be horning in on Angus's beat. "But look at it this way. Maybe it will deflect heat from you. You know the ministry minders stopped by the bureau again this morning. Your story about the Promotion whacking some lipstick babe landed on the wrong prince's desk and he thinks you deserve a big wedgy. The minders threatened our visas again. I don't think anybody has told New York yet, but hell, I say keep up the good work!"

Angus rubbed his palm into his forehead, wondering if he was screwed. This is why he avoided calling the bureau; it seemed better not to know. He wasn't too worried about the Saudis. Their outrage would surely dissipate. But New York was a different story. None of the top editors had ever spent a day in Saudi, so their imaginations ran amok.

Plus it was unlikely that Vandusen or any of the Washington types would stand up for him. They probably gleefully inflated every Saudi threat. There was no love lost in the Dhahran bureau. The Washington crowd loved nothing more than sticking it to the foreign correspondents and vice versa.

"I hope someone told the Saudis that the stories were accurate and you have no idea when I will be back in Dhahran because I am out with the military somewhere," Angus said, recognizing wishful thinking as he said it.

"Yeah, we kind of waved them off, although you know how everybody gets about this stuff," Vandusen said.

"You seen Thea Makdisi in the hotel by any chance?" Angus asked, deciding it was better to change the subject.

"She's around somewhere. She is the one who led the pantygate delegation to Wolfgang. Thea actually forced the manager to agree to reimburse them for all their underwear. Come to think of it, she did a piece about the end of the Vietnam War syndrome. It was all about how soldiers in Vietnam used to say 'sorry about that' no matter what you asked them and were ashamed to be seen in uniform, but here the dominant expression is 'good to go.' It got a lot of attention, a mood piece with a little substance."

Suddenly Vandusen cackled. "Oh, that reminds me. The TV crowd is having shit fits because Geraldo showed up and the military has been flying him around in his own chopper. They all want their own choppers now, plus all the JIB guys are wearing these cheesy yellow T-shirts with 'Geraldo of Arabia' printed across the back that drive the other TV people even more nuts."

"You mean that talk show guy?" Angus asked.

"Yeah, his producer has been swaggering around the hotel, talking a big game about how Geraldo was going to slip into Kuwait and interview the Iraqi 'bad guys.' Then he told the JIB they wanted to do a major piece about the role of women in the military. But Geraldo mostly asked the women questions implying they must be banging every guy in sight because Saudi is so boring. His questions were like, 'So what's dating like here, odds pretty good, no?'" Vandusen said, still laughing.

Angus wanted to bring the conversation back to Thea, so he switched to the direct approach.

"I need to talk to Thea, so if you see her, ask her to give me a call, would ya?" Angus said.

"Why?"

"Nothing earth shattering," Angus responded. "A group of Saudi women are organizing a driving demonstration here that might make a good story, you know 'Gulf War Propels Shocking Societal Change.' Anyway, some of the organizers asked me to contact Thea."

"Oh, people in the Dunes talk about the demo all the time."

"Like what?"

"Most guys don't think it's a story. The men have been arguing that we're here to cover tanks and armaments and blood and guts, not to chase a bunch of Saudi bimbos wrestling to liberate their Lincoln Town Cars from the oppressive hands of their chauffeurs.

"Wow, did that piss the women off. You'd think all the attention these chicks are getting—even the fat ones are offered massages every night because there are so few around—would calm them down. I thought Thea might throttle some of the guys. She kept parroting them like they were retards. Then she would let rip with one of those extended salvos of hers, arguing how disgraceful it is that the U.S. is sending hundreds of thousands of troops to prop up a regime that doesn't even let women drive. I expect Thea will be in Riyadh leading the kitty pack. Anyway, nice talking to you Dalziel, but some of us have to get some reporting done. Later."

With that, Vandusen hung up.

Angus lay back on his bed, his hands behind his head. He looked over at the television, where he had inserted one of Ryan's videotapes and hit pause on a close-up of Thea's smiling face. He tried to imagine her wandering around the room and wondered how soon she might come to Riyadh even though it wasn't November yet and the demonstration was planned for the sixth.

Angus suddenly remembered what Vandusen had told him about Callahan's arrival. Another headache.

He wished for a minute that he didn't have the Saudi information ministry, Callahan and Devon to worry about simultaneously. It was hard enough being on the road by himself all the time. Now he had to fight rearguard skirmishes with his alleged support system. He wished he had someone to talk to about it, but he couldn't think of anyone. He glanced at the TV again. Thea, of course. If only she was around, he could probably confide in her without the gossip whirring throughout the hotel.

Instead he took a practical step and dialed Basha, the *Saudi Chronicle* editor, seeking reassurance about potential visa fallout from the lipstick story. Basha giggled when Angus told him what had happened.

"Don't sweat it. You know we call the Saudi Press Agency or SPA, the Sleeping People's Association," he said. "They are not used to real news in this country and when they wake up and find someone has written something about actual events, their knee-jerk reaction is to issue a denial. You know, shoot the messenger."

"Oh great. But they are aware all this religious police stuff is happening. What exactly pisses them off, just the fact that it is being covered?" Angus asked.

"Partly that, plus you don't know what translations they may be getting," Basha said. "I'm sure Iraq pays for newspapers in all kinds of Third World countries to emphasize the most lurid details, to make it sound like decadent Westerners are desecrating Islam's holiest ground."

"But I included all kinds of context explaining why this was happening."

"You don't think the context survives, do you? I'm sure your story ended up being stripped to about three paragraphs with a big headline screaming something like 'Saudi Police Cane Licentious Woman Aping U.S. Style.' Yet it still carried that WP logo. So when it landed on the desk of the interior minister or the information minister, he was naturally outraged."

Basha explained that Misri and the other ministry guys assigned to the Dhahran Palace were probably under pressure to make the reporters write more favorable things about the kingdom, and at the same time the television crowd was pestering them to confirm the stuff Angus was reporting.

"You know how lazy those television networks are; they can't lift a finger for themselves. Anytime we run anything in the paper of vague interest I have ten television producers calling me up asking for the phone numbers of the people we quoted. I mean directory assistance in Saudi Arabia speaks English! So anyway, I'm sure the TV guys are completely clueless, asking the Saudi ministry to trot out women the police have beaten or at least confirm the stories, which they have neither the expertise nor the authority to do. Instead, the easiest thing for them to do is threaten you."

Basha's reassurances couldn't stop Angus from worrying that even if the Saudis didn't expel him, their threats might prompt New York to yank him.

"Remember it takes a prince to expel anyone from here," Basha said. "Wait until the women's driving demonstration. They will forget all about you when the scandal over that erupts."

"That's a couple weeks away. That gives them plenty of time to cause me problems."

"Forget about it, Angus. Out of sight, out of mind."

Angus had barely hung up when there was an odd banging against the door. "Someone there?" he shouted. When he couldn't hear the response, he got up from the bed to open the door, turning off the TV as he went.

Ryan was standing in the corridor laden with equipment. His hands weren't free so he had been tapping one of his equipment cases against the door.

"Yeah. Whaddya want?" Angus said, blocking the way into the room.

"My suite back, you fuck," Ryan said, trying to push his way in.

"I am afraid it's fully occupied," Angus said, before laughing and grabbing some of the equipment from Ryan.

The two sprawled on the couch again and Ryan bitched about his trip. Basically it was a lot of meet and greet with no cool pictures to show for it, although Egyptian commandos staged an amazing demonstration involving capturing and barbecuing desert snakes and hares.

"What about you, you got anything going I can photograph? I have had my fill of the military and wouldn't mind switching to the Saudi side of things for a few days."

"I don't know what to do. I still have a while until the driving demonstration and nothing to write about here and the desk won't let me go back to Dhahran. I went to the main mosque downtown for Friday prayers and stumbled across a beheading afterward, but I don't know what the fuck to do with the material. All I can do is sit around here and count the days until the demo."

"A beheading! What the fuck was that like?"

Angus explained that he had gone to the weekly sermon with the vague idea of finding a story. At least he could harvest fresh public opinion about the pending war. Hundreds of men attended prayers in the sizable Qasr al-Hukum mosque, a square, modern structure built of sandstone meant to blend in with an historic mud brick fort nearby. Public beheadings, the Qu'ranic prescription for the death penalty used in Saudi Arabia, were carried out immediately after the Friday sermon on the large plaza adjacent to the mosque. They were never announced in advance.

A murderer and two drug smugglers were being executed that day—young, slight Saudis with unkempt hair trembling slightly in their white cotton robes despite the noonday warmth. A barricade of police officers kept the crowds back, forming a circle at the center of the plaza, while the charges against the kneeling men boomed over the same mosque loudspeakers that announced the call to prayer. A few teenagers climbed onto each other's shoulders around the edges of the plaza or scaled palm trees to get a better view.

Certain aspects of the process were oddly clinical—a plastic sheet on the ground to catch the blood, an ambulance to cart the remains away. Others were distinctly from another time—the flash of the scimitar in the sunlight; the scattered cries of "Allahu Akbar!" "God is great!" that erupted as the severed heads fell; the awful red gush. For Angus, the gore tempered the excitement of catching a rare glimpse of Saudi society in action.

"That's a story, man!" Ryan enthused. "Think I could go down there this Friday and snap off a few frames?"

"Maybe, although executions don't happen every Friday and I don't know how you would pull it off without the crowd turning you over to the police. That is one thing they do not want photographed. I don't know quite what to do with the material either. It's not really a standalone story; I will have to use it as the intro to something larger, something about the inhumane aspects of this place."

"What about that Baghdad Betty story I told you about? That's worth a laugh and should eat up a few days."

Angus had forgotten about it. He did not want to admit that he had only used the tapes to keep Thea's image frozen on the screen while he was doing stuff in the hotel room, cheered to see her whenever he looked up. He avoided confessing his fixation to Ryan.

"So what does this Baghdad Betty do, anyway?" Angus asked instead.

Ryan went over and fished in one of his bags to pull out a small Sony shortwave radio. "Don't know if we can hear her this far south but we can try. She always inhabits the same place on the dial." He found Radio Baghdad but the reception was scratchy. It was a news bulletin in English, which they ignored.

After a while the volume of the broadcast increased suddenly and the announcer said that a "special report" was coming, followed by a few bars of some weird tune. Angus thought it might have been the theme song from *Bonanza,* the TV show about the Ponderosa ranch, except it was played by a forty-piece orchestra heavy with strings and slightly Arabized with a lute and drumbeats.

"This is it! This is it!" Ryan shouted. "The soldiers told us it is exactly the same program every time and here it comes. Turn it up!"

Angus did, but the announcer's voice was difficult to hear through the crackling reception. He turned on his tape recorder and positioned it on the coffee table next to the radio, then sat down on the couch and put his ear next to the speaker.

"Dear listeners," Baghdad Betty started. "This is the Voice of Peace from Iraq. Here is a special program for the American soldiers in the Sa'udi Arabia desert." She pronounced it the Arabic way, with an extra syllable in the middle of Saudi.

Ryan started laughing. "The soldiers call her the Voice of Peas because her English is a bit off the wall. You can put that in the story." Angus shushed him as he tried to hear the rest.

"My dear soldiers: It is a big fact that if the land is unknown for the soldier he will be defeated. So why do you come to a land which you are not familiar with its people and its nature?" she said, hysterically shrieking the word "why" and then calming her voice to issue a vague threat: "Fighters here do not hesitate to use anything to defend their homeland."

With that, the radio broadcast decayed into an orgy of static and Angus sat up in frustration. "There is no way I can lift quotes off that," he said.

"Wait, it's clearer on the tape from my trip; let me cue it up," Ryan said, shuffling through the unmarked tapes piled on top of the VCR and slamming one into the slot. He turned the TV on and then hit fast-forward.

As the images whirred past, Angus saw Colonel Cox sitting at a picnic table in a mess tent with Thorn, Black, Thea and the rest closely gathered around. Ryan seemed to be sitting a table away, so the camera took them all in. The reporters were trying to wolf down a spaghetti dinner as fast as possible because when they stopped, flies materialized from nowhere, landing on the food or any exposed skin. The flies were especially adroit at kamikaze-like dives onto open lips, causing more than one reporter to sputter in disgust.

"What are they talking about?" Angus wanted to know, his resolve not to stop the tape every time Thea appeared dissolving instantly. Ryan slowed the tape down so they could hear snatches of conversation.

"Live fire sound good to your ears, Colonel?" Lydia asked, gushing.

Angus shook his head. "I just don't understand these women reporters. Lydia is so tough most of the time but she loses her edge around a uniform. Maybe I ought to wear a little camouflage."

"You want to sleep with Lydia?" Ryan said in mock alarm. "Man, you really have been here too long. How long has it been since you got any?"

"Just roll the damn tape," Angus said, hitting Ryan in the chest with the back of his fist hard enough to make him recoil. On it Thea, sitting next to Thorn, was pointing at something offscreen. "Hold up, hold up. I want to hear this," Angus said.

"She is not Baghdad Betty, may I point out."

"Let's hear a little sound."

"Hey Captain, what are those things covering the rifle barrels?" Thea asked. Ryan jumped the camera between the two as they spoke.

"Don't tell me you've never seen one before?" Thorn said, winking at someone offscreen. "Remind me to keep my distance."

"What are you talking about?" asked Thea, looking perplexed.

"Well, the soldiers call it their Desert Shield, but it is more commonly known as a condom. The men slide condoms over the end of their rifles to block the sand. You slide one of those over your rifle and you are good to go," he added, making a sliding motion over his balled fist with his other hand, provoking bawdy laughter.

Colonel Cox could be heard offscreen releasing a long sigh. Ryan swung the camera around to him. "That's one thing I've found out through this thing. Old men need it more than young men. If you told the men there is beer and pussy in Baghdad, they would be there tomorrow. And I would be leading them!"

Captain Thorn laughed, prompting Ryan to swing the camera onto him. "Truth be told, a lot of guys out here never had it. They talk about it an awful lot, but they never got any."

This time it was Ryan who punched Angus in the chest before hitting fast-forward. "See guy, you don't have to worry about being the only one around here not getting any; none of the soldiers are either."

Angus wondered if he should tell Ryan that he had his sights set on Thea, but decided against it. Ryan was not a born gossip like most photographers; that is one of the reasons Angus liked working with him. But none of them could keep a secret for long. They all sat around with too much time on their hands.

The screen flickered and then showed the inside of the Palace. It was morning, with the reporters ensconced in their sleeping bags. Angus could hear a sandstorm buffeting the sides of the tent and whistling through its rope lines. The plywood walls creaked and the tent's heavy green canvas contorted in odd positions, periodically banging against the wood like a plaintive child seeking shelter.

"There was this unbelievable raging sandstorm; I've never seen anything like it. So we had to drive back instead of fly," Ryan explained as the screen went dark briefly.

Next the video showed reporters gathering behind a large army truck, its rear end covered in tan canvas, in a sandstorm. Thea and her all-girl crew appeared in long black slacks and black cotton smocks of various cuts. Thea had found a Korean tailor in downtown Dhahran who could copy any picture she brought him from *Vogue*. Soon the entire female press contingent was frequenting the guy, considering their knockoffs a fashion coup. She had wound a long cotton scarf the color of burnt sienna around her head and face, creating both a turban and a mask.

She wore heavy black sunglasses, which she lifted to see through the sand as she plunked her backpack down behind the truck. Her eyes, the only part of her face showing, were rimmed in heavy kohl—the charcoal-like makeup sold as a powder in most Middle Eastern bazaars. It was an old desert Bedouin trick to help keep sand out of her eyes. The black rim accented their lovely almond shape.

Black walked up beside her and said something. Angus was going to ask Ryan to stop again but thought the better of it. He would just remember which tape it was on and try to listen to it later. She turned and heaved her backpack up into the truck before jumping onto its tailgate and disappearing underneath the tarpaulin.

"What a total babe!" Angus said with real enthusiasm.

"Yeah, I and every other guy out here know what you mean. Plus she is a completely aggressive reporter and will beat you to this Baghdad Betty story for sure if you don't get right on it."

"Just keep the tape rolling."

Once the truck was moving, Ryan filmed the two soldiers in back arguing whether to tune their boom box to Radio Baghdad or Shield 107, the FM military radio station. It tended to play themed songs like "Midnight at the Oasis" by the Brand New Heavies or "Rock the Casbah" by the Clash.

Black was asking how the soldiers developed a taste for some caterwauling Arab diva on Radio Baghdad. Smiling broadly, they explained that Betty was the Gulf War version of Axis Sally or Tokyo Rose, an Iraqi attempt to undermine their morale that was so laughable it actually cheered them up. Each program was exactly the same but they still loved every minute.

Angus could not quite tell where everyone was sitting in the truck. The camera was bouncing around too much, although Ryan had taken close-ups of some people's faces as they listened. The sandstorm still tinted everything yellow, but the radio broadcast on the tape was easier to hear than in their Riyadh hotel room.

"To the American soldier in the Sa'udi Arabia desert: Ask your friends about what happened in Vietnam," Baghdad Betty screeched, pronouncing it Vayatnam, so it took a minute to figure out. "The American soldiers' corpses are still lost in Vietnam after they had been eaten by worms."

The announcer's accent was strangely clipped, definitely not American but not quite British either. She tossed in an occasional Arabic word, plus each report was riddled with bad translations, mangled syntax and strange theories.

"You, the American soldier in the Sa'udi Arabia desert are taking such a risk in participating in this campaign and your families suffering from the burden of life. Didn't you hear that the sand heaps in the Arabian desert are moving and they swallowed many people and they will swallow you. Why do you come to the burning desert?"

That last line was delivered at a hysterical pitch before the *Bonanza* tune resumed, and the whole segment provoked an extended round of guffaws.

"Sand heaps?" Black said as Ryan zeroed in on him, "How do the Iraqis expect to fight this war if they can't even get the translation for sand dunes right on the official radio? Why is it that Arabs are some of the most cosmopolitan people around, the educated all speak at least three languages and toss around advanced degrees like confetti, and yet their governments make the Three Stooges look professional?"

Angus had once been on a bus trip to the flight line with Black and one of his junior correspondents when the younger guy started asking questions about the region. Black explained how he loathed all sides in the conflict, like most experienced Middle East hands. He found them all equally unsympathetic: too quarrelsome, too quick to see themselves as victims while conveniently glossing over the atrocities they inflicted, too caught up in ancient slights to acknowledge they were stunting their future. "It is a region run by buffoons," he had said.

The young guy wondered why he didn't move somewhere else, and Black responded that the pursuit of good stories had kept him glued there ever since he was first assigned to cover the Lebanese civil war in 1975. No other part of the world reliably produced spectacular news year after year. Plus the idea of returning to a dreadfully dull Long Island or Connecticut suburb and working in Manhattan held absolutely no appeal, Black had said. It would be like stepping back into the conventional adolescence he had spent his whole life escaping.

On Ryan's tape, the signature tune played between each segment faded once again and Baghdad Betty's voice resumed.

"To the American soldier in the Sa'udi Arabia desert: Don't you know that you are the victims of a Zionist conspiracy to control all the land of the Middle East from the Nile to the Euphrates? The Jews control you like they control the world financial markets. Why do you risk your life to be part of their devious campaigns?"

"Uh-oh. Baghdad Betty is bad for the Jews," Black could be heard saying. The camera was showing the highway spooling away behind the truck. "I suspected she might be. Although frankly we have all gotten our hopes up on that score before and been sorely disappointed. When the communists started tottering in East Germany it looked briefly like the Nazis might return to power, which would have made a fantastic story, but it never happened. Pity."

"Cynic!" Thea said, turning to face him. Ryan swung the camera to her as she stuck her sunglasses on her head over her turban, an appalled look on her face. "You don't honestly put the story so far above the humanitarian questions, do you?"

Angus drank in her criticism of Black.

"A great story is a great story, Thea, you should know that," Black could be heard responding. "It is not for us to pass moral judgments; leave that to the United Nations or the aid organizations. Our job is to bring hard news and exciting pictures to the viewers, to try to startle them with something they have not seen or heard before. If you want to be Dudley Do-Right, get out of the news business."

Thea looked a little deflated. "Yeah, the boring stretches in Dhahran have certainly made that clear," she answered.

"That is more or less it," Ryan told Angus. "The rest of the tape just shows stuff when Thea and I managed to wrangle a ride in the cab up front, where she caught the supply guy reading this book called *Cheating Horny Housewives* and telling this mournful story about how the wife of a soldier in some unit sent him a videotape of her taking it up the ass to announce she was divorcing him. After that the supply guy started rattling on about how they couldn't get American spark plugs anymore. They were ordered to use ones made in Saudi that don't work half the time. There might be a story in that too, but don't you think Baghdad Betty will make a great piece? I have pictures of those two guys listening to it on the radio."

Angus wanted to rewind to some of the stuff showing Thea, but the point of sitting around with Ryan was to generate story ideas.

"You're right,"' Angus said. "But we'll have to try to find more soldiers who have heard her to interview."

"Yeah, let's do that," said Ryan. "Let's try first thing tomorrow. In the meantime, I'm starving. Want to go downstairs to the Japanese?"

Chapter Nine

ANGUS wheeled his white Toyota out of the Hyatt's back parking lot and onto the entrance ramp of one of Riyadh's main freeways, almost empty after the government offices ended work at 3:00 P.M. He was headed to the driving demonstration, so he popped a cassette tape of Fayrouz, a renowned Lebanese singer, into the tape deck. The heavy drumbeats and gargling background vocals were okay in small doses, as far as he was concerned, but Thea loved the stuff. Since this would be their first meeting in more than a month, Angus hoped that if she heard it playing in his car he might win a few points.

It was a silvery November afternoon, still warm enough for Angus to wear a gray corduroy shirt with a T-shirt underneath it. He lowered his window an inch to feel the desert air rushing past.

The demonstrators were gathering in a supermarket parking lot in one of the capital's newer neighborhoods, and along the way Angus drove past various ministry buildings designed by renowned foreign architects. It suddenly occurred to him that the hodge-podge of styles scattered throughout the modern sections of Riyadh mirrored the character and taste of whatever prince was in charge. Any Saudi royal appointed as a minister kept the job for life.

The Foreign Ministry, a low, square sandstone building with thin slits for windows, was a quiet, highly stylized version of the old forts in the Nejd, the central desert region of the Arabian Peninsula. The Interior Ministry, on the other hand, might have landed from Mars. It was an inverted seven-story pyramid with zigzagging edges, each floor showing as a stripe of black glass. A massive, dun-colored dome ringed by portholes topped the building. The dome resembled a mini space ship that looked like it could pop off and zoom away at any time.

A few nights earlier Angus had dined in a tent pitched in the spacious garden of one of the grandsons of King Abdel Aziz, who warned him not to be fooled by all this modernity, which the prince described as a thin veneer on a desert, tribal culture. To understand the leap, the prince told him to go visit the old royal palace, recently restored, which sat not far from the downtown bazaars. Angus had seen the building, essentially a fortress, in passing.

Al-Murabba Palace was built of mud, resembling a sharply angled beach sand castle that a child finished by carving pointed crenellations along the top and making windows by poking a few scattered finger holes into the dense walls. The prince told Angus that when he was a kid in the early 1950s, the palace's electricity consisted of a few bare bulbs and the toilet was a mud brick bench with a wooden cover. Riyadh had catapulted out from its original walled center in just thirty years.

There were still a few mud brick houses in the poorer neighborhoods surrounding the bazaars, but after that came a long row of low, concrete ministries, built in the late 1950s along the once grand, tree-lined avenue leading from the old town to the first airport. Beyond that the newer districts now dwarfed the original core, the sprawl mushrooming larger and more modern as the kingdom grew richer. Away from the government office buildings and long strings of strip malls, most Riyadh neighborhoods consisted of thickets of high walls with only the roofs and the upper stories of the houses visible. The walls allowed the women to walk around inside their homes and gardens unveiled.

The entire city was braided together by a massive American-style freeway network, decorated with millions of dollars in palm trees and other desert flora. Angus negotiated his Toyota down a six-lane thoroughfare and into the parking lot of the supermarket, which was a carbon copy of the U.S. version except "Safeway" was also written in scrolling Arabic script across the square building. The demonstrators were not hard to find, since it wasn't exactly your average Saudi woman taking to the road. Mercedes, Bentleys and other luxury sedans, all glossy with frequent polishing, clustered along the palm trees lining one side of the parking lot.

As he got out of his car, Angus noticed a maroon Toyota Land Cruiser with CBN stickers plastered all over it, the driver wiping it down lovingly with a clean rag. Angus looked around for Thea, spotting her and her camera crew in the midst of the milling women. She looked radiant. Her scarf had slipped off her hair, as usual, and she wore her *abaya* open. Angus laughed at himself. The rare sight of an open *abaya* made him react like a fourteen-year-old pulling a *Playboy* from underneath his mattress late at night to stare at the centerfold.

He stood and watched Thea, momentarily oblivious to the fact that he should be interviewing the demonstrators. It was the first time in weeks that he had felt truly happy. He waded into the crowd, eager to see her face, to look at her up close, to hear her laugh.

Thea was so intent on the women that she did not sense him standing next to her.

"Are you sure we are safe standing in front of these cars?" he whispered in her ear. "I mean, we're not sure any of these women know how to drive."

Upon first hearing his voice she swung around with an elated expression on her face and greeted him, "Angus! How fantastic…," before she registered what he was telling her.

"They can't be any worse than the men," she said, glowering. "The women could probably run over both of us and still have a better driving record than your average Saudi male."

Angus smiled. "I've missed you, Thea," he said as he opened his note-book. "Remind me to tell you a story."

"Ah, you print guys are always full of stories, aren't you?" she said, winking before she went back to asking questions.

He knew this one would make her laugh. Middleton at the U.S. consulate had told Angus that the Saudi government recently commissioned an American company to figure out how to lower the rate of carnage on Saudi roads. Their report concluded that aside from poor driver education, the most significant reason for the accidents was the way the men flopped their headscarves over their heads. It blocked their peripheral vision.

The Saudi government suppressed the study as a Western cultural attack.

Standing next to Thea, Angus wanted to wrap her in his arms, smell her, rub her back and kiss her, but he couldn't so much as peck her on the cheek. It would make people think the worst of her. Maybe there would be time for that later, in the hotel. Trying to pursue a woman in Saudi was like being permanently assigned to high school study hall circa 1950, Angus thought, or perhaps 1850.

Glancing around for someone to interview, he saw a woman he had met in Jidda named Leyla Qabbani sitting behind the wheel of a Lincoln Town Car painted a sparkly, metallic navy blue. It struck him that after nearly three months in the country, the sight of a woman behind the wheel now seemed odd. He went over to talk to her.

When Leyla tried to lower the electric window, she set the windshield wipers in motion and then unleashed some window-cleaning spray. Angus held up his arms as if to shield himself. She was laughing when she finally got the window down.

"Isn't this exhilarating!" she whooped, holding her hand up above her mouth and ululating, something Arab women did on joyful occasions. Many of the other women laughed and joined in.

"I mean, part of me knows that it is ridiculous to be so excited; I drove all the time when I was getting my doctorate in Austin. But I have never driven a car in Saudi, ever. When you write your story, Angus, remember that the issue is not driving alone. Not at all. The issue is that here in Saudi Arabia, I only exist as a person from my navel to my knees."

Saudi woman were always coming up with zinger quotes like that one. As Angus got to know more of them, he began wondering whether the men invented veiling because the women were so resilient, beautiful and smart, far more lively than the generally lumpish men. Or sometimes he thought maybe it was a Darwinian thing; after centuries of veiling only the vivacious survived, compelled to project personality from inside a tent.

In Jidda, Angus had been amazed to discover a secret side of veiling on the afternoon he first encountered Leyla, when a prominent Saudi historian had invited him to her villa for afternoon tea to meet some women activists. Angus had come early, and while waiting for the women in a low window seat just inside the vestibule, was dazzled by the scene that unfolded with every arrival.

Each guest entered completely covered, clad from ankle to neck in a black cloak, her face often invisible beneath a filmy black scarf. Before greeting the hostess, the woman swept aside her head covering and then slowly started to spin. After two or three twirls, the black cloaks filled with air, moving away from the body. A Filipino maid standing close by would grab a corner and yank, pulling the entire cloak away in a single fluid motion. One stunning, well-dressed woman after another stepped forward to kiss the hostess numerous times on both cheeks.

Angus gasped audibly when a striking, athletic woman stepped from her cloak to reveal a creamy white silk teddy and tight shorts done in black lace—kind of high-fashion bicycle shorts—along with open-toe sandals. Her cinnamon-colored midriff, legs and arms were bare, and she had liquid brown eyes that seemed to cut through him from across the room. Angus was not sure where to look to avoid staring. That was Leyla.

Now she was saying something to him from behind the wheel of her

car. "Angus, Angus, are you listening to me?" she asked, her voice petulant. He started, realizing he had missed a sentence or two.

"Of course, Leyla, I hang on your every word," he said, smiling.

"You weren't writing," she said, lifting her index finger and wagging
it at him playfully. "I want to point out that Saudi Arabia is more or less
at war now, so what if Iraq attacks? Are we expected to wait around for
our chauffeurs if we want to flee with our children?"

She stopped talking as nearly fifty women in fifteen cars tentatively
revved their engines, turned on their blinkers and edged out of the parking lot. Angus looked up to find Thea, but she and her crew had departed
to get shots of the convoy.

He was going to follow when he noticed a bunch of the displaced
Asian drivers squatting off to one side, chattering with excitement. He
went over to interview them.

"I was not believing my ears when Madame asked for the car keys
and told me to get out and then drove away with the others," said one
chauffeur, slapping his hand over his open mouth in amazement. "I was
not even aware that Madame knew driving."

Angus smiled. Another good quote. It was turning into a fine day. As he
was taking notes, he sensed Thea next to him and laughed at himself again
for being so besotted that he couldn't concentrate. But he glanced up and
there she was, asking the guy what he was paid to drive Madame around.

"What is this? A press conference?" he said.

"You want the chauffeurs as an exclusive?" she mocked gently. "The
women protesters asked us not to follow. They are sure to get arrested
and thought having the television cameras around would further rile the
Promotion."

"You mean you agitate everyone around you, not just me?" Angus
said, grinning.

"Could we have a little silence for our interviews please," she said,
making a schoolmarmish face.

They both went back to interviewing the drivers. When they finished, he slapped his notebook shut and asked, "How about grabbing a little bite of dinner while we wait to see what happens?"

"I'd love that; I'll meet you back in the hotel lobby," she said. "I bet this will unroll pretty fast, though, so it may have to wait until after we file."

Thea stalked into the lobby and told Angus that she wanted to go to her room, dump her *abaya* and make a few calls to find out what happened with the demonstration. When the elevator doors slid shut Angus was so excited to be alone with her that he tried to kiss her, but she stiff-armed him. "Don't," she said, looking annoyed.

"I can't stand waiting anymore, it's been years," he said, trying a hug. But she squirmed in his embrace and he released her.

"I'm happy to see you too, darling, but we have to get this story finished. I don't think we even have time for dinner," she said.

Angus latched onto that word "darling" for a minute, but recognized it was just one of the common endearments she often sprinkled into her speech. The exchange put him in a bleak mood, riding the rest of the way up in silence. He upbraided himself for expecting anything in the midst of a breaking story. He usually had good sense of when or when not to pounce, but it was hard somehow with Thea, especially with her standing right there after so many weeks. He wondered if she would stick around on this story long enough to really start something.

THE PROTEST lasted about twenty minutes. The parade of cars that left the Safeway parking lot broke up into smaller clusters and the women were subsequently pulled over at various major intersections. Saudi men driving past gawked in amazement, often looking back as if they had seen a phantom driver, but miraculously there were no crashes. Several husbands followed each group, ensuring there would be no nasty confrontations between the Promotion and the women as they were arrested.

Angus reached Leyla briefly on the phone. She told him that she had been stopped by a portly, bearded member of the religious police who turned crimson with anger as she stepped out of the car. He was jumping up and down screaming, "I want to kill you! I want to open the ground right underneath your feet and bury you here! How dare you, a mere woman, corrupt God's commandments?"

But evidently a senior prince had ordered the religious police not to touch the women involved. So they were taken to the regular police stations and not to the Promotion precincts where detained women were habitually lashed, slapped across the face with men's leather sandals and generally treated like scum.

Despite the calm conclusion, it was still a protest and by Arab women no less. Angus could feel the level of excitement rising like a thermometer through the hotel as reporters discovered that their editors or senior network producers back in the States loved the story and wanted to play it big. No one could remember the last spontaneous protest in the Arab world; usually demonstrations were rolled out by the government and participants had to return their "Long Live National Unity" signs at the end so they could be used for the next one.

Sitting at his desk, Angus heard occasional exchanges in the hallway between giddy reporters high-fiving each other and saying things like "The fucking Saudi women! Unreal!" For once the WP foreign desk told Angus to write long, so he braided all kinds of background into his copy.

He compared it to earlier turning points, all stuff he had found out about over the preceding weeks, like the introduction of the radio in the late 1940s, which was damned by the religious establishment as an instrument of the devil. But King Abdel Aziz won them over in one fell swoop by ordering the initial broadcast to be verses from the Qu'ran. And so it went with the telephone, public education for girls, and the launch of television. At least one person died when police fired on the mob stoning the first central television station in 1965. Any change provoked virulent religious opposition in Saudi Arabia.

Angus used Leyla's remark about her navel as the last line in the story.

He hoped the copy editors in New York would not find it too suggestive and chop it. They could be so squeamish.

After filing, Angus dialed the CBN bureau, a third-floor conference room, to find out how Thea was progressing. She was almost finished recording her voiceover and told him hurriedly that barring further developments they could share a bit of room service.

Daring to hope that things were looking up, he ordered lamb kabob and assorted Middle Eastern dips and salads—hummus and stuffed grape leaves and tabouleh—and then dove into the shower. While dressing he punched the remote to watch the 11:00 P.M. news on Saudi TV, wondering whether it would report anything he might need to update his story.

He could tell right away that he needn't bother. King Fahd flew from Riyadh to Jidda that day, and for five minutes the news was taken up with that, although he did not make a public pronouncement. First it showed him leaving Riyadh, with every member of the court, all the cabinet ministers and dozens of princes lined up to see him off. The princes stood first in line, according to age, each kissing the man who was essentially their tribal chieftain on the shoulder as he passed. Then came the chiefs of staff from the armed forces and the other important commoners. After King Fahd landed in Jidda, the entire scene was repeated in reverse when he came off the plane. The ritual stretched on for so long that the commentator ran out of things to say and instead Strauss's "Blue Danube" came on, princes bussing their monarch's shoulder to the tune of a Viennese waltz.

Angus had watched the same pageant on the news repeatedly over the past months, but he was spellbound by the ridiculous amount of time devoted to a nonevent. Naturally the kingdom's first protest involving women went completely unmentioned.

He was sure that Saudi royals ordered their comings and goings broadcast to underscore the fact that they remained sticklers for Bedouin customs—everyone turning out to salute the patriarch on his journey. Never mind that the traditional camel caravan had been exchanged for a custom-built 747 with an elevator that descended from its belly so the overweight king, who had weak knees, would not have to mount the stairs. With a war looming on the horizon, Angus thought the ritual underscored the degree to which the royals were more caught up in their own self-importance than in addressing the concerns of the rest of the population. He should write a story about it, he thought.

The food arrived just as the news ended and Thea followed within minutes. He had barely let her into the room, though, when the phone rang.

"Fuck, I have to answer it, it's probably New York," he said.

"Won't bother me a bit," she answered, wandering over toward the food. "I hope your copy wasn't so riddled with problems, so desperately needing substantial change, that all the grape leaves will be gone by the time you're done."

Angus scowled at her. "Let's face it, you television types would have nothing to say, nothing but dead air and vaguely pretty pictures, if you didn't have my copy to read aloud," he said, picking up the receiver and holding it against his chest until he finished talking. She stuck out her tongue at him.

The foreign desk told Angus that his piece was the lead story on the news wire. He was pleased, since it meant that papers across the United States would display his work prominently on their front pages. On the other hand, the story would have to run a gauntlet of several WP editors. Angus hoped the questions wouldn't take so long that Thea drifted away.

He watched her while listening to an editor rattle on about how it was a great story but there were a few minor questions, which Angus knew meant a dozen at least. Thea seemed contented enough, dipping a little pita bread into the hummus and throwing her hands in the air and doing a little belly dance jiggle of happiness every time she took a bite of something new. Once or twice he hung up and joined her for a couple minutes, only to have the phone ring again.

He cursed his luck; the copy editor was the type who started calling with questions before reaching the bottom of the story. It never paid to yell, since the editor would savage the piece in revenge.

"Were the Saudi women inspired to protest by watching U.S. women soldiers drive?" the editor asked.

"Not directly," Angus said. "Not many Saudis have seen them driving."

"Were there any American soldiers on the roads and did they react or participate in any way?"

"You don't think I would miss the chance to mention an American soldier, do you?" Angus said, but the sarcasm was lost.

"Any reaction from the king or the Saudi government?"

Angus pointed out gently that the copy said there was no official reaction. "I will update the story as soon as there is one, but don't hold your breath waiting for this government to issue a statement," he said. He rolled his eyes at Thea as the questions kept coming, making his answers shorter and shorter in hopes of getting off the phone.

"Did the U.S. embassy or the military say anything?"

"No."

"How many of the women possessed American driving licenses?'"

"Unknown and seems irrelevant."

Thea giggled.

"I think it's relevant!" the editor shouted, bristling. Angus pulled the phone away from his ear and reminded himself that tossing editorial comments into his responses would just prolong the ordeal.

Thea, intrigued by the exchange, went over to the desk where Angus had left a copy of his story in a small portable printer. She read it and then walked over to the bed and kissed him on the top of his head. "Don't let them change a word," she whispered, reaching down briefly to massage his hunched shoulders. "It's a wonderful story. You're the best."

Angus's scalp prickled with excitement. He smiled at her and shrugged. Devon got on the phone, speaking loud enough so that when Angus held the receiver out a little Thea could hear him too.

"There's a feeling here that we need more sweep up high," the foreign editor was saying. "I mean we need to say right after the description in the lead whether the presence of hundreds of thousands of American troops could eventually inspire revolution in Saudi Arabia."

"Well, I wrote that some change is inevitable, but also pointed out that everyone remains unsure if the kingdom will emerge more liberal, or if this could prompt a conservative backlash," Angus said. "I think we can leave it at that. This place is so unpredictable, I really don't want to get into extended crystal ball gazing."

"I'm not sure that is enough, Angus," the foreign editor said, curt as always.

They hammered out a compromise wording and Angus hung up. He moved over to where Thea was now standing at the window and staring down at the shimmering light of the swimming pool on the third floor, one flight down. He drew her into his arms and hugged her from behind. She rubbed her head back and forth on his chest and ran her hands along his forearms.

"I'm sorry, Thea, I was so looking forward to a little romantic dinner for two," he murmured, kissing her behind an ear and licking the lobe. "I am so happy you're here."

"Hey, don't worry about it; it's an occupational hazard," she said without turning around to face him. "I'm having the best time just hanging out with you."

Despite her reassuring remarks, she seemed a little distant and Angus wondered if she was upset.

"God this has been an amazing day! I just don't want it to end," she burst out suddenly. "Can you believe we're covering a demonstration about women driving? How *Twilight Zone* is that? It is such a fantastic story, especially after being cooped up in that damn Dhahran Palace with the damn U.S. military. Although I must admit the more time I spend in this country the more it just pisses me off, makes me less and less objective. I constantly find myself wishing I could do something outrageous, anything, to get even with these idiotic, barbaric customs."

Angus slowly turned her around and then leaned over and kissed her on the lips. She hesitated at first and drew away a little, but then kissed him back.

"Just remember the more you kiss me, the more it would outrage the fundamentalists if they knew," he said when they stopped, drawing a laugh.

"I love the way you joust with your editors and the detail you go into in your story," she said, flooding Angus with warmth by resuming her habit of toying with a button on his shirt. "The bureau chief wouldn't let me use the chauffeurs because their English was a little off, even if it was a funny scene. Other than that, though, I must tell you your story sucks compared to mine."

"In your dreams," he said, drawing her slowly toward the bed, sitting down with her on his lap and gently stroking the side of her face. She did not resist. When he tried to kiss her, though, she blushed.

"Wait," she said, pushing him away and standing up. He stayed lying on his back where she had pushed him. Thea doused all the lights, leaving the room dark except for a shadowy reflection from the swimming pool undulating through the gauzy curtains, as well as a rhythmic stab of red from a car dealer's flashing neon sign next door.

She came back to the bed and kneeled over him. He reached up and stroked her hair and they kissed again.

"You don't mind if we take this slowly, do you, you know, let me stop for a minute to look at you, maybe exchange a few words, the whole girl thing," she said, looking down at him and running her finger from the top of his forehead to his chin.

"I'd be perfectly content to spend hours just looking at you, Thea," he answered, rubbing his hands along the back of her arms and then gently pulling her down toward him to kiss her.

He talked to her, told her how extraordinary she was, how he felt completely transported in her company, that he had a sense that they were meant to be together. He rolled her over on her back and unbuttoned her blouse, languidly kissing her neck and the tops of her breasts. The phone rang.

"Don't you dare," she said, hammering on each word and grabbing his erection through his khakis.

"I'd love to ignore them, honey, but if I don't answer now they will just keep calling and calling and calling," he said. "There is no escape."

"I know you're right, the journalist in me knows you are right, but as a woman I can never accept it," she said, sighing deeply. "I want you to pay attention to me, dammit."

"I adore you," Angus said, flipping over on his back and reaching for the phone. "There is nothing I would rather do than tell them to drop dead, but I can't."

Barely listening because Thea was slowly rubbing one hand over the front of his khakis, the sensation making him buck occasionally, Angus agreed to every new change the editor wanted and then hung up, turning back to her.

They kissed slowly, delicately at first, brushing each other's lips over and over again until the tempo intensified abruptly and they engulfed each other, kissing deeply and wrestling out of their clothes.

Both were sweating by the time they finished. They lay side by side, their breath the only sound. He turned his head and blotted a few beads of perspiration off her forehead, flicking each one with the tip of his tongue and relishing the slight sting of salt.

Often in his encounters, as soon as the sex was over Angus found himself thinking about the story he had to write the next day or his interviews or whatever. But this was different, something more; he wanted to linger.

"The sweetest sweat," he said, licking her neck and then running his hands over her wet breasts.

Thea moaned contentedly, closing her eyes and stretching before she hugged him and leaned over and rested her head on his chest. He kissed the back of her head.

"God I hate to admit it, but being forced to wear that hateful black robe all day makes me feel completely untamed when I'm naked," she said, suddenly biting his bare chest sharply enough to make him wince.

"Enough of this Saudi bullshit about 'protecting their women.' I bet that is the real reason they invented the veil. Sure it's modest dress, but you don't need to walk around in a tent all day to be modest. It changes me into a rutting beast when it's off."

He laughed and ran his hands through her hair, kissing her before saying, "You might not want to spread that around; it could lead to the globalization of the veil."

They lay entangled, quiet for a while.

"If you don't mind, it's been a long day and we don't know what will emerge from all this tomorrow, so I think I will trot back to my own room to sleep," she said finally.

"No, don't," he said, going up on one elbow and leaning over to look down at her. "The last time you left like that I didn't see you for weeks. We've barely had a chance to talk tonight. I know it's my fault, but I'm pretty sure they're done. Stay."

"This story will keep us together for a few days," she said, kissing him and ruffling his hair as she pushed herself up and blocked him from pulling her back down. "It'll keep. Good night."

He stood up to hug her, nearly toppling as his pants caught around his ankles. She laughed.

"Don't hurt yourself, Angus. And don't fret. I just want to get some sleep."

"Are you sure everything is okay?" he asked, kissing her forehead, wishing now that he had ignored the phone for an hour and then called the desk back. Since it was the lead story they would have panicked, though, summoned another WP reporter to come bang on his door. Thea seemed cold suddenly, but he realized he didn't know her well enough to gauge her moods.

"I'm just tired. Everything is great, Angus. I am sure this story has legs and knowing you are going to be here at the end of every day will make all the other petty hassles so much easier to tolerate."

Chapter Ten

THE NEXT MORNING, Riyadh was in an uproar. The Saudi press reported nothing, but the city's robust grapevine ensured that everybody knew. Someone in the police, usually impenetrable, had leaked the names of all forty-seven women involved in the driving demonstration. Six of the women who were professors at King Saud University arrived at work to find their name plaques ripped off their office doors and "Infidel!" scrawled there. The government immediately confiscated the passports of all the women and most of their husbands, the standard initial punishment for subjects deemed troublemakers.

The women's names and telephone numbers were printed on leaflets denouncing them. One such screed that Angus found tucked under a windshield wiper accused the women of renouncing Islam. "Each Muslim should cut out the roots of this evil plant before it spreads to every part of our holy land!" the flyer howled, demanding that the women be divorced and jailed.

Angus, Thea and the other reporters flocked to extremist mosques to hear religious sheikhs flail the women from the pulpit, branding them red communists, dirty American secularists, advocates of vice and whores. The Higher Council of Religious Scholars, the country's leading authority on all Islamic matters, rumbled out a fatwa declaring that a woman driving degraded the sanctity of the faith.

It was exhilarating for Angus finally to have a developing story, however lunatic, particularly since it meant he saw Thea daily. Often they were busy all day chasing sources or rumors and filing long into the evening, but they spent almost every night together.

They developed a vague domesticity, at least a hotel version. She more or less moved into his room, tossing her clothes into the same laundry bag and eating breakfast there each morning. In the late evenings, she cuddled up next to him, laughing and talking over each day's events with him endlessly, probing for possible fresh angles to report. On the few nights when they finished early, they read aloud to each other or watched bad movies on the in-house television. Sometimes he brought her a spray of tulips or other flowers.

Twice they were invited to the villas of liberal princes who served sumptuous meals under the stars and whispering palms of spacious interior courtyards. At one such dinner, the prince, who held an important government post, lamented to Thea that he was about to retire from public service and, for the first time since graduating from Cambridge, did not know what to do with himself.

"Why don't you become a gentleman farmer?" Thea suggested. "You could get a tract of land near a romantic oasis and cultivate sumptuous dates or racing camels or something."

"That doesn't really appeal," the prince said, sighing. "All my cousins are forever nattering on about how camel's milk gives them special powers, but I desperately want an original project."

"Then why don't you be the first prince to grow grapes and make wine?" Thea said, raising a glass of the forbidden French burgundy they were drinking. "You could call it Chateau de la Mecque and we would willingly pay $50 per bottle to give it to all our friends."

"That is blasphemy!" shouted the prince, roaring with laughter and turning to another table to pass along to a few of his Saudi friends what Thea had just suggested. He kept laughing and repeating the conversation the whole night.

The other guests flocked around Thea, telling her stories, seeking her opinion, staring at her. Angus couldn't quite believe his luck that she would be coming back to the hotel with him.

Angus reveled in much of his job—the chase, the travel, learning languages, the characters he met in all the countries along the way, the writing. But when the long days ended, when the story was filed and all the questions answered, he often found himself sitting alone in yet another interchangeable hotel room. They were all so alike that when his alarm went off in the morning he often lay there disoriented, trying to remember what country he was in.

He saw the way his colleagues faced that problem—the affairs; shopping endlessly for antique manuscripts or the perfect Ottoman era inlay chest; calling their brokers, real estate agents, or their decorators; buying gewgaws for their various pets; reading and rereading Proust; drinking too much.

He wanted none of that. He was sure he would find someone eventually, but when he encountered some correspondent ten or twenty years older who was still single, a disturbing inkling of terminal loneliness reared up like a sudden solar flair that sent shock waves through the seemingly placid cosmos.

It also happened when some correspondent his age who had already started a family made an offhand remark like "I want my sons to learn Arabic." Angus thought that he would too. He occasionally pictured himself teaching a son or daughter to enjoy simple pastimes like snorkeling, blowing the water out just before surfacing to avoid choking on the salt water. But then he would sit in an airplane—and he spent hour after hour on planes—watching a young couple wrestling with their tired, whining, rebellious toddler and think, "Not me."

In Riyadh with Thea, he began to wonder if he could have it both ways, the excitement of the chase and someone waiting for him however long the story took.

THROUGHOUT the uproar over women driving, the royal family said nothing, so the demonstrators were organizing a second protest in Jidda and Angus anticipated covering it with Thea. Then he bumped into Middleton, the American diplomat, in the lobby of the Riyadh Hyatt.

"Hi Hawkes, how are you? What are you doing in Riyadh? And what do you know about Jidda?" Angus asked him in one burst.

"It seemed like you guys were having all the fun so I found some excuse to come here for business," said Middleton, who in his dark suit and red tie looked out of place amid the minor Saudi officials and scraggly journalists. "You are aware, of course, that every second- or third-rate prayer leader is urging that the women be flogged. The noise level has gotten to the point where the royal family will have to do something."

Middleton reminded Angus that in August, when the kingdom decided to call in American troops to protect the country from Iraq, King Fahd browbeat the Religious Council into giving him its stamp of approval. The top clerics reluctantly issued a fatwa saying that although the Americans troops were infidels, they had come to defend Islam against the devil in the guise of Saddam Hussein and were thus tolerable.

"Clearly that kind of statement requires some arm-twisting, not to mention cash, which the ruling family will do when necessary," said the diplomat. "But there is a huge difference between the threat of war and women driving. To push the religious establishment around when it comes to the threat of an Iraqi assault against Saudi Arabia is a vital interest. To push them to let women drive is not. I'm sure the family will put the kibosh on a repeat in Jidda."

He was right. Within days, Prince Nayef, the king's brother and the interior minister for around thirty years, appeared on television to denounce the protest. Speaking from the holy city of Mecca to underscore his point, he banned not only women driving but any form of protest. In the grand tradition of Arab leaders blaming any domestic headache on foreign agitators, he noted that some of the women were raised outside Saudi Arabia and "not brought up in Islamic homes."

Although the ban on women driving had been an informal tradition, he made it law, the wording echoing the religious fatwa by the leading clerics almost verbatim.

Angus had trouble reaching the protestors on the phone after that. Most of them had gone into hiding with relatives for their own safety, and talk of Jidda dried up instantly. He did speak to Leyla Qabbani, but she said religious police were keeping her street under twenty-four-hour surveillance and she was convinced her phone was tapped.

"Angus, I'm sure you've heard that our beloved religious authority also ruled a few years ago that the world is flat, right?" she said. "It's 1990, we're on the verge of World War III, and Saudi Arabia formally outlaws driving by women. It's crazy. It's sad. It's ludicrous."

Then she hung up.

In thinking of unexplored story angles, Angus realized that the conservative religious establishment could claim a significant victory. Given the hubbub, women in Saudi Arabia were unlikely to win the right to drive for a good long time. No one had sought out any zealots to gauge their thinking beyond their thunderous flyers and mosque sermons.

At the suggestion of Basha from the *Saudi Chronicle*, Angus called a weekly newspaper named the *Believer* and asked if the editor would speak about the religious perspective on women's driving. Every time he asked the question Angus prevented himself from laughing because the ban seemed so absurdly backward. The offices of the *Believer* were near the Hyatt, and the editor invited Angus to come over right away.

Walking through the hotel lobby, he bumped into Thea coming out of lunch with Omar Khazzani, a young Saudi diplomat.

"So how about these Saudi women?" Angus asked, somewhat gleefully.

Khazzani was the handsome, erudite scion of an illustrious family and could lie fluently in several languages. The wily Saudi prince who had long served as ambassador to Washington knew that no one would step forward to speak for the government in such a crisis, so he dispatched Omar and a few other telegenic aides from the D.C. embassy to fight Saudi Arabia's public relations battle at home.

When not appearing on TV, Khazzani thrived on Cuban cigars and whisky and rarely could be coaxed from his room at the Dhahran Palace except for a late afternoon tennis game. Even when he unplugged the phone and refused to answer his door, you could tell he was holed up from the cigar smoke wafting into the hallway. He scandalized his compatriots from the Ministry of Information by wandering around the hotel dressed in tennis shorts and brightly colored polo shirts instead of the long robe expected of all Saudis. Soon the younger, more daring men imitated him.

Today in the conservative capital, however, he was wearing a crisply starched headdress and a white robe fastened with gold studs.

"How much longer do you think you can keep your women in chains, Omar?" Angus asked. Although he was often charming, Khazzani exhibited the smugness endemic to Saudi officials. Angus often found himself asking questions in an obnoxious manner just to see if he could ruffle them.

Khazzani flinched. He rarely ventured from his room at times like this to avoid the ordeal of explaining the weirder aspects of Saudi Arabia's xenophobic traditions. When cornered, he would occasionally dodge by saying he knew nothing about the subject, but he usually produced a passable answer. The two subjects he scrupulously avoided were the king and the religious establishment.

"Completely off the record?" he said, his usual opening parry.

"I'll bite," Angus answered.

"I confess the king is at fault for moving too slowly on this issue," he said, prompting Angus to shoot his eyebrows skyward as he wrote. Omar passing judgment on the king! "Remember this is completely off the record. You can't even quote me as a Saudi or Arab official. Anyway, the

king should probably have opened up driving to women in the special circumstances of the crisis with Iraq, perhaps by allowing them to drive
ambulances, and then it would have spread."

"Omar, don't be ridiculous!" Thea protested. "Nobody has needed to
drive an ambulance and probably never will. They should allow women
to drive because it's 1990 and the right thing to do."

She waxed a bit soapbox-y when she talked about the local treatment
of women. Angus found it endearing but knew if he told her that she
might swing at his balls.

"They may get to yet," Khazzani said defensively. "The point is that
the women made a mistake having a public protest. They transformed
this into a power struggle with the religious conservatives that they can't
win. They should have lobbied for something huge like a cabinet post.
Then they would have gotten driving as the compromise. You can't forget that despite its modern appearance, Saudi Arabia remains an exceed-
ingly conservative country."

"Conservative? Don't you mean medieval?" Thea snorted.

"Seriously, Omar, shouldn't people like you push a little harder for
change? Aren't you acting a little too helpless?" Angus asked.

"Remember even the most cosmopolitan Saudis tend to be conservative at heart," he answered. "Even me, believe it or not. I'll give you an
example from my own life."

Khazzani told them that he had been a pious teenager, refusing to
break any religious taboos like drinking alcohol. So when he turned
eighteen, one of his more liberal uncles took him on a vacation to Swe-
den, hoping to loosen him up a bit. One night they went out dancing and
of course Omar was completely taken with the stunning, blonde
women. His uncle was off on the sidelines, nodding approvingly when
Omar started dancing with one and kissing her.

"When I came back to the table, he asked me if I put my tongue in
her mouth. I made a face and said, 'No! She had been drinking beer!'"

Thea and Angus burst into laughter.

"Yeah, yeah, laugh all you want," Omar said. "My uncle almost had a coronary laughing. But the point is that the conservative constituency in this country is everywhere. Talk to some, and you will understand better."

After Omar excused himself, Angus abruptly asked Thea if she wanted to come along with him to the *Believer*. He wasn't sure how the newspaper editor might react, but any time with Thea was worth the gamble.

THE offices of the *Believer* were on the upper floors of a pyramid-shaped shopping mall covered in blue glass. Angus had spent enough time in the kingdom to know that modern architecture outside did not translate into open-minded attitudes inside. He respected certain religious figures immensely. Most Arab countries were one-party dictatorships where the slightest hint of political activity could prompt an immediate jail sentence, if not worse. In those countries the mosque could be used to gain a little leeway; a prayer leader could denounce the venal rule of a "pharaoh" without risking arrest and everyone recognized the real target. Religion was the one place where the brave found a little wiggle room from corrupt, oppressive governments.

On the other side of the coin were the religious maniacs who really meant the bile they spilled. Angus always thought of them as the Islamic equivalent of the intolerant American psychopaths who ran around gunning down abortion doctors, claiming a divine mandate.

He had learned that all young Saudis are drilled in school with a religious doctrine known as *al-war'a wa al-bara*, loosely "loyalty and distance." In practice, it meant that a good Muslim should be loyal to his fellow Muslims and shun everyone else. Under this doctrine, young pupils were taught stuff like saying "Merry Christmas" to a Christian was a grave sin.

There was a broad spectrum of interpretation, and the most extreme inevitably emerged out of the Wahhabi sect unique to the Arabian Peninsula. Saudis hated anyone calling it a sect, claiming it was pure Islam, but much of the Arab world recoiled from Wahhabism. Some extremist

Wahhabis used the *war'a* doctrine to justify violence, including killing any non-Muslim. Angus was appalled occasionally when the real thinking of the conservatives bobbed unexpectedly to the surface. He had recently been at a gathering where a university law professor trying to reassure him said, "Of course I hate you because you are a Christian, but that doesn't mean I think it's right to kill you."

So Angus took it as a good omen when the editor of the *Believer*, Ajeeb al-Oteibi, a frail-looking man with a neatly trimmed beard sitting at a desk awash in newspaper clippings, letters, pens and pencils, graciously accepted Thea joining the interview. Zealots would not even look at an unfamiliar woman, much less talk to one.

Oteibi served them thick, syrupy coffee in thimble cups and happily launched into a discussion about the evils of women driving. "Most Saudis are not zealots, but they do believe in God, prayer and keeping women behind closed doors. I think you will find that the country largely supports this ban."

Angus pointed out that there were something like 1.1 billion Muslims around the world and only Saudi Arabia, with merely 12 million natives, banned women from driving. "Even neighboring countries that ban alcohol, like Qatar and Kuwait, have allowed women to drive. Why is it seen here as such a threat?"

The editor's face lit up at the mention of Kuwait. "Yes, I am glad you mentioned the Kuwaitis. Look what happened to them!"

Angus and Thea exchanged a quick glance, wondering what was coming.

"Allah has instructed all of us that those who ignore him too often will suffer terrible punishment. We Saudis must look at these Kuwaitis and never forget to observe Allah's teachings—may Allah will it."

"Surely you don't truly believe Saddam's invasion is a form of divine retribution?" Thea asked.

"Of course it is. Let me try to explain. Most of the problems that arise in society are because of women, and what happened to Kuwait is a perfect example of the result of giving them too much independence. We don't want to deny women here their freedom, but we want to protect women from their own danger—their gossip, their scheming. A woman will use her power of beauty and power of sex to corrupt men."

Angus knew the man was serious and it was not the moment to interject a comment like "Bring on the corruption!" He bit a knuckle to prevent himself from smiling. He couldn't wait to repeat the editor's line when he was next in bed with Thea.

Oteibi went on to point out that Saudi Arabia differed from other countries because the religion started in Mecca. "You can't expect to have whorehouses, liquor and striptease in the capital of Islam. Would there be a nightclub in the Vatican?"

"There probably are," Thea said in a confrontational tone, prompting a frown to wash across Oteibi's face. "I mean at some point in the Middle Ages there was even a disguised woman pope, for crying out loud. But we are not talking about unchained vice here, just driving."

Noting Oteibi's expression, Angus interrupted.

"We understand why you would want to maintain a certain moral standard here, even if it's hard to understand that women driving is part of that," he said. "But what about the American soldiers? If Islam is so strong, why do you need a foreign army to protect you?"

"Our princes have spent billions on weapons that we cannot use so they can steal the commissions. It is a scandalous process that will change one day, although you can't quote me on that. But what I can say is that while we are all grateful for the assistance of the American army, what we are really waiting for is the interference from the real superpower, which is God, or at least his holy warriors."

"What holy warriors?" Thea asked.

"The mujahideen."

Angus recalled that Middleton at the consulate had mentioned them briefly and nodded his head, but Oteibi explained anyway. The editor told them that the young leader of the mujahideen, Osama bin Laden, had recently returned from Afghanistan, hailed as a hero. But no sooner had he reached Jidda than Iraq invaded Kuwait. The young bin Laden had written an open letter to Prince Sultan, the defense minister, begging him not to allow infidel soldiers to defile the holy land of Islam. Osama vowed that he would bring thousands of fighters back from Afghanistan and they would expel the invader instead.

"How did the prince respond?" Thea asked. Angus also knew the answer to that one from his briefing by Middleton.

Most Arab governments had encouraged their zealots to go to Afghanistan, hoping to speed them on their way to meet their maker and thereby prevent them from fomenting trouble at home. No doubt the royals would rather have the U.S. Marines running around than a bunch of wild-eyed fundamentalists. They would not welcome them back.

"The proposal is under serious consideration," Oteibi said.

"Where can we meet this guy Osama?" Thea asked.

"He has returned to Afghanistan to begin organizing the forces," Oteibi said.

Angus found himself doubting Oteibi for the first time. Everyone he had spoken with said that the Saudis were acceding to an American-run operation with the fig leaf of one three-star Saudi general, naturally the defense minister's son, being given the official title of Joint Forces Commander.

But once Angus voiced his skepticism, the interview seemed to go flat. The editor started to invoke God's name in response to every question, no matter how many times the two reporters tried to get him to admit that religion might not hold all the answers to the crisis. So they thanked him profusely and left.

Back at the Hyatt, the concierge handed each of them stacks of little pink messages. Angus frowned. Saudis rarely returned phone calls, so it could only mean the office was chasing him.

Sure enough, some English tabloid was reporting that three of the women drivers had been shot dead by their male relatives to restore family honor. Both WP headquarters and CBN had unleashed brusque messages demanding that their reporters match the story immediately.

"Christ, this seems unlikely," Angus said, crumbling the messages into a ball. "But I suppose traditional males sometimes dispatch women for more obscure reasons of family honor, so we'll have to check it."

They went up to the third floor, where all four U.S. networks filled various conference rooms wedged between the hotel restaurants. Outside NBC they found Basha trying to calm a Saudi woman.

"She's a moron, Faisal!" the woman, fully veiled, hissed. "They are all morons! I just don't know why we bother. It's impossible to get through to these American television reporters. Maybe all the blonde hair dye seeps into their brains or something. And it just pisses off the government here. I'll end up being hauled in for questioning and having to sign yet another confession."

Faisal greeted Angus and Thea effusively. The irate woman pulled off her barely translucent silk head covering and they were elated to find that it was Leyla Qabbani. They asked her about the shooting story.

"God damn you Western reporters! You're all alike," Leyla barked, startling Angus and making Thea laugh nervously. Neither had heard a Saudi woman swear before.

"You all have a preconceived notion of who we are and massage the facts until they fit that image," she said. "I thought the NBC ditz I was talking to was particularly thick but you are all awful. Of course none of them have been shot; what kind of barbarians do you think we are? That may happen in backward countries like Jordan or Egypt, but not here, or at least extremely rarely and certainly not in the educated class that organized the demonstration."

Thea wanted to know more about what her competition was up to. "Who were you talking to at NBC?" she asked.

"For some unknown reason I agreed to talk to their morning TV Barbie doll to fill in a little context and background," said Leyla, who was always in demand. She had been the first and for a while the only female reporter at the *Saudi Chronicle* and had a knack for knowing what reporters sought and explaining things in simple terms. The fact that she was a sultry beauty with sculpted cheekbones and a thick mane of curly, jet black hair didn't hurt either.

"They just don't seem to get foreign countries," Leyla went on. "She kept asking me over and over again to say how my veil and my *abaya* are symbols of my oppression. They are not. They are part of my liberation. The *abaya* and the fight for equal rights are totally separate issues."

Thea and Angus shifted uncomfortably. After an hour with the religious editor, they were not quite ready for convoluted logic, especially from someone bright like Leyla.

"Listen, you have to start with the fact that you are dealing with a completely different religion, a completely different culture," Leyla said, her brown eyes flashing. "As you have surely heard hundreds of times by now, despite all our wealth and fancy freeways, this remains an incredibly uptight country. Most men are uncomfortable with their women so much as leaving the house. But this outfit allows me to go out and mingle freely in public with whomever I want."

"Yeah, but prisoners have uniforms too Leyla," Thea said.

"I'm not a prisoner. The opposite, in fact. Without this, I couldn't walk out the front door. That NBC ditz kept saying it was degradation," Leyla growled. "I tried to explain that a woman wearing a bikini on a billboard was true degradation, because men all expect their women to look just as sexy. She couldn't grasp the concept that oppression comes in different forms, or that the veil can be liberating."

"Western women reporters are used to being independent, Leyla, but here they can't even drive themselves to an interview or to the airport," Angus said. "I think the level of frustration is pretty high, so they are prone to lash out at anything they find binding."

"Yes, I agree with Angus. It feels like being a really pampered poodle," Thea interjected. "Every time a Saudi male tells me that 'women are our jewels, we have to protect them,' I want to belt him."

"I understand it is frustrating when you are not used to it, and God knows there are areas where Saudi women do face unbelievable

THE SAND CAFÉ

discrimination, but our dress is the wrong symbol for that," said Leyla, beginning to dig in the large Louis Vuitton tote bag she was carrying. "You have read Lady Montagu, right?"

Both Thea and Angus shook their heads no.

"Lady Mary Wortley Montagu was a famous British travel writer who went to Turkey in 1716 and discovered that she liked Muslim clothing when she tried it on. This is what she wrote," Leyla continued, pulling out a page photocopied from a book. She read aloud: "'Tis impossible for the most jealous husband to know his wife when he meets her, and no man dare either touch or follow a woman in the street. This perpetual masquerade gives them entire liberty of following their inclinations without danger of discovery.'"

"That makes veiling sound like a license for adultery," Angus said.

"You're a big help," Thea grimaced, smacking him on the shoulder and shaking her head toward Leyla.

"Whose side are you on, anyway?" Angus asked, rubbing his shoulder.

"Obviously I'm not saying all veiled women running around in the streets are sluts," Leyla said. "But the point that still remains valid almost three hundred years later is that the veil allows us to do as we please without being bothered.

"I'm so tired of talking about this," she added, folding the paper back into her bag and pulling her black scarf over her head. "If you will excuse me, I would like to go home. You all must come around for lunch after this excitement blows over."

Thea and Angus walked the two Saudis to the elevator. Before he got on, Basha told them that the conservatives in the royal family and the government were suggesting that the Western press was to blame for all the hubbub about women driving. The police had immediately raided the homes and offices of the Saudi photographers present and confiscated their film, but naturally word got out through the Western press reports.

"They are saying that if no one paid attention to the protest, if it had gone unreported, then there would be no controversy and the government would not have been forced to choose between the conservatives and the liberals," Basha said.

"Shoot the messenger!" Angus said.

"Exactly," said Basha. "Anyway, everybody will lie low on the domestic side of things for a little while, but I'll call you if there are any developments."

After they were gone, Angus turned to Thea and asked, "So which form of oppression would you prefer, the bikini or the *abaya?*"

"God, the bikini, I'm sure," she said.

"Then let me be the agent of your liberation and take this *abaya* off you," he said, hoping she would agree to at least a brief encounter. It seemed like a light news day.

"Christ Angus, you are like a sixteen-year-old. Think about something else for five minutes, would you?" Thea shot back at him.

"I can only think about you, Thea. This has been such a fantastic twelve days it hardly seems real," Angus said. He wanted to tell her that given the pace of their lives, an hour in bed was the closest he ever felt to having a day off, but he was not sure how she would take it. Sensing he would have difficulty convincing Thea of the merits of a quickie, he dropped the idea. She wasn't exactly a feminist, but she had a streak of it that emerged at odd moments. She had apparently been influenced by a professor of a sophomore women's literature course who kept driving home the point that women should be in control of their own orgasms. Thea laughed about it the first time she described it to Angus, but sometimes the way she regulated the tempo of their sex life made him think it had affected her more than she let on.

Thea looked at her watch. "I have to see what the film crews have gathered on tape so I can put some kind a piece together. I'll see you later."

"When later?" he asked.

"Don't get petulant," she said, looking around quickly before kissing him on the lips and heading into the CBN office.

Chapter Eleven

No story intervened and late that night, after a couple of hours in bed together, they lay on their backs talking, skipping from topic to topic. After so many days covering the plight of women in Saudi Arabia, Angus was suddenly curious about the degree to which Lebanese women, the women whom Thea had grown up around, ran their own lives.

"So is there even a vague echo of this kind of stuff in Lebanon?" he asked. "For example, did you lose your virginity there or was that considered a horrible stain on the family honor and you waited until you were far away in college in L.A.?"

Thea giggled and leaned over and stuck her tongue in his ear. "You're joking, right?"

"No, I'm serious, tell me," he said, looking earnest.

"Oh, I think I learned pretty early that guys being so horny all the time gave me a certain amount of power as a woman," Thea said, rolling onto her back, pulling the sheet up to her chin and staring up at the ceiling as she talked. "I don't think I used it to corrupt anybody, though; I am sure our Saudi editor friend would be disappointed."

She told Angus that the first guy who ever made a concerted effort to get into her pants had been her downstairs neighbor in Beirut, a girlhood crush whom she outgrew. He joined a militia early in the civil war partly, she was sure, because he thought the swaggering and the gun would win her over.

After she had fended him off for months, he came pleading outside her door one night, rasping his gun along the wood and threatening to shoot himself if she did not relent. So she told him to go ahead but not make too much noise because she wanted to sleep.

"You were saving yourself for true love?" Angus asked.

"I guess, vaguely, although I didn't think of my hymen as some great prize. The war took care of it in any case."

"What do you mean?" Angus asked, wondering if he was dredging up the memory of a wrenching incident.

"Oh, my first sex was almost brutally casual."

She told Angus she had been on her way to Beirut airport, hoping for brief summer respite from the war, when one of those periodic firefights caused a gridlock that made her fear she would miss her plane. She was standing next to her mother's car on the road to the airport when an older guy from her neighborhood happened along on his motorbike.

He offered to weave through the traffic, so she kissed her mother good-bye and hopped on the back of his bike. When they reached the airport they waited for a while, but the firefight had spread and the planes, to avoid getting hit, scrambled skyward empty. All flights were eventually canceled.

It was dark by the time the two of them began the trip home; Thea was hugging the guy and trembling as random bullets whizzed out of the squalid neighborhood by the airport—the tracer bullets hissing past them like long venomous snakes. The fighting got so bad that they sought shelter in an abandoned four-story apartment building along the way and spent the night there.

"Sex was the easiest available means to block out the fear," Thea said, adding in a distant voice, "the harder the better." She told Angus how the shattered glass, broken plaster and other debris cut into her back as she first lay in the burned out apartment with her skirt pushed up and the guy mounting her still wearing his black leather jacket, barely pulling his jeans down. She remembered almost enjoying the sensation of crying out with the initial burst of pain, then biting the guy hard on the neck whenever the pace slowed and a shell or mortar exploded nearby, willing him to continue pounding away at her so she would lose all sense of the carnage outside, lose all hearing, all smell except that of the rough physical act.

"It was the first of a lot of nights like that, Angus," she said, rolling on her side and hugging him but not looking at him as she went on. "As you may have guessed, that is one of the reasons I got to like playing a little rough. It also made me far less sentimental about sex than most women. Relationships were so unpredictable. Men would be killed or leave the country or find some other chick who lived next door. Or when the shelling started you would be caught all the way across town at a friend's house and just grab the first guy sitting next to you.

"It made me uncomfortable at first, but soon it became like everything else, part of the unholy tempo of war. In a way it was the only thing that could disguise the fact that we were utterly helpless. I never want to be that helpless again, ever," Thea said, sighing and quiet for a bit.

"Just be careful before you fall in love with me, Angus," she added.

"Might be too late," Angus said, stroking her hair over and over again, trying to bring her back into the room from wherever her mind had wandered.

"Can we talk about something else?" she said after another lengthy silence.

"Yeah, sure. What about reporting? Did you do any reporting then?" Angus asked, thinking as he said it that he should probably have found a lighter subject.

"No," Thea said, pulling a strand of her hair straight and looking up at it. "Although I think I took it up at USC partly because I did have this older cousin who worked for one of your competitors, Reuters. She had been engaged to a French diplomat, but toward the beginning of the war he and his ambassador were shot, assassinated, after being dragged from their cars at a checkpoint. She behaved like a nun after that. She never fucked anybody; she had a completely opposite reaction to events. The experience made her kind of fearless though; she was forever jumping into her little VW bug to go report on another battle. I thought she was cool.

"And speaking about journalism," Thea said, rolling over and stuffing a pillow under her chest, wedging herself upward to look at Angus. "What story are we going to work on next? I hate the idea of going back to Dhahran to work on more fucking mood pieces about how to dig a foxhole. This driving demonstration was a relief, no question, but I want something of substance, something with an edge, an exposé. Can I tell you something that you swear you won't tell anyone else or steal it?"

"Kind of a tall order but I guess I'll manage," said Angus, trying not to look too curious and scare her off.

"Promise you won't breathe a word of it to anybody?" Thea said, grabbing his testicles and squeezing just hard enough to make him flinch. "On pain of losing these?"

"Oww," he said, nodding and gently shoving her arm away.

Thea started going over something that she said had been bothering her since she first heard it toward the end of the live fire exercise. She told him how she had befriended a supply sergeant, and on the way back to Dhahran he had stopped to get out and inspect a stripped U.S. Army truck left next to the side of the highway.

Angus thought he remembered Ryan mentioning the guy, something about getting laid for plywood and lousy spark plugs, but he decided it was not the moment to interrupt.

"So anyway the supply sergeant picks up this conversation that we had when he and his buddies first lent us their fancy tent," she said.

Riding toward Dhahran, the guy kept telling her all these stories, lore among the quartermasters about big barter deals that had gone down like the medical evacuation unit trading some of its extra body bags for women's tampons.

"To tell you the truth, I was kind of dozing behind my sunglasses and not paying attention to every word," Thea said, still hugging her pillow. "If I don't smell a story, I don't focus. But the guy kept talking."

Thea remembered him telling her they were having problems with auto parts. They used to requisition everything from the States, but recently they were ordered to buy from Saudi suppliers. Suddenly parts like spark plugs were showing up with Arabic writing on the packaging, and about a third didn't work. The supply guy was worried that they would all leap into their vehicles one day when the war started and the trucks wouldn't start.

"'Some soldiers may end up dead while a bunch of Saudis must be getting rich,' is more or less what he told me," Thea said. "Isn't that intriguing?"

She told Angus she had been making sympathetic noises, but all that stuff about spark plugs not working sounded like vaguely technical guy talk and she was thinking about the stories from the trip that she would glue together once they reached the hotel.

"Ever since, of course, his comments have been eating at me," Thea said. "It is almost like he was trying to tell me indirectly that the supply system was corrupt or something. It is so hard to interview soldiers about equipment problems, though. The military minders usually cut them off, say they are helping the enemy. I thought about putting in a request with the JIB to interview Saudi suppliers, but it is hard to think of a way to make that sexy, and I would probably be better off finding them by myself. Although it's not likely they are going to come right out and tell me anything that might jeopardize the way they are all probably minting cash. What I really need is a whistleblower. What do you think?"

"It would make sense given the amount of stuff flowing through here that someone is skimming a buck or two," Angus said. "God knows no deal ever goes down in Saudi Arabia without a prince with his whole hand in the pie. I did hear something thing from one of those Jidda conglomerate lawyer types related to this; I put it on my list of things to check when I got back to Dhahran, but I had forgotten about it because of everything else that happened. You, for instance," he said, putting one hand under the sheets and running it slowly down her back to her buttocks.

"What?" she said, rolling away from his hand. "Tell me!"

"I am not sure I should, Lois Lane," he answered, amazed anew each time he mentioned a possible exclusive story how her mood completely changed. She was like a woodpecker hammering on a tree; there was no escape until she completely excavated the topic. Often she would focus on it to a degree that he felt he could walk out of the room and she wouldn't notice.

He told her that a lot of those Jidda businessmen and lawyers were part of the "liberal opposition" against the royals, so everything they said against the government had to be weighed carefully. They had told him that the war was generally popular because it had turned out to be a golden egg. Between the Kuwaiti refugees and the U.S. soldiers, there were something like a million extra mouths to feed in the kingdom.

"This one lawyer told me a strange little fact, which might help us pursue this story," he said.

"What did he tell you? And why am I even considering letting you horn in on my story?" she asked.

"Because you love me," he said, pushing her over and lying on top of her and kissing her.

She turned her head sideways. "Come on, big boy, tell me what the guy knew," Thea said, squirming a little and shoving him off.

Angus put his hands behind his head and told the rest. The lawyer said that no successful business went on for long in Saudi without some princes horning in on the action. With everyone trying to bag as big a chunk of the supply market as he could, various princes had pressured the few Saudi companies involved to give them a piece. The competition got so intensive, the lawyer claimed, that the Saudis, in a strange reversal of the usual order, were also beginning to bribe the senior U.S. supply officers.

"The guy had no proof; he had only heard about it. But since you mentioned spark plugs, he said that the arrangements were that every time the U.S. Army orders something like a spark plug from a local distributor, the Saudi company deposits a quarter in a Swiss bank account.

"I told him that didn't sound like much money, but he reminded me just how many vehicles were in the country, given the fact that we are looking at 500,000 U.S. soldiers. It's like the entire population of Cleveland is moving to Saudi. It means hundreds of thousands of dollars."

"Wow!" said Thea. "I wonder how we could prove that? It would certainly be a scoop."

"Well, it's going to take a huge amount of work to prove it. I'm sure there are Saudis who would say anything just to dump on the princes, not to mention the United States," Angus said. "But I think it's important enough to devote time to. I hope my editors agree."

They were both aware that in a few days, on November 29, the U.N. Security Council was planning to vote on a resolution authorizing war against Iraq if it did not withdraw from Kuwait. The resolution was expected to include a deadline, which would inevitably become the deadline for war. The countdown would become the overwhelming story.

"If we head back to Dhahran, that would give us time to work on a supply piece before the shit hits the fan with the U.N. vote," Angus said. "Although we would have to work out a deal where we both reported it on the same day."

"I guess we could," Thea said, distracted.

"C'mon, where's that enthusiasm from a few minutes ago?" Angus asked, shaking her. "At least it will give us a reason not to sit around the Dhahran Palace writing about the weather."

Thea's face clouded further.

"I don't know, it's so hard there. I have to do live shots and all kinds of unplanned stuff," she said, running her fingers through his crew cut and looking somewhere past his head. "It will be difficult to spend time with you like this."

"That's why working on a story together would be such a great thing," he said, kissing her body again.

Thea didn't say anything.

"Thea?" Angus said, looking up from her belly button to her face. He couldn't fathom her mood. She appeared to try to physically shake it off, though, looking at him and smiling while stretching luxuriantly, pulling his face up to hers and bowing her body sideways along the length of his.

"I can see I better keep you in a good mood so you will tell me every-thing you know. Just call me Mata Hari," she said, kissing him.

Chapter Twelve

ANGUS stared down into his empty spaghetti plate in the Dunes, where he had just eaten a late lunch, sitting by himself in the glass extension to the coffee shop that stuck out toward the pool like a screen porch. He was in a glum mood. It was usually quieter back there, not least because the revolving door leading out back was locked for security reasons. Of course, given the pace of news developments around this hotel, I might as well be idly rocking on a porch someplace, he thought to himself.

Thea had been right when she said spending time together in Dhahran would be difficult; since their return two weeks earlier he had barely seen her. Nor had he made any progress reporting the supply story. He assumed she hadn't either. Desert trips or live broadcasts from the hotel roof monopolized all her time.

He looked out the window and watched Lydia walk across the pool deck, lighting a cigarette. A thin layer of steam hovered over the heated pool in the cool December air. Lydia stood at the edge and started to talk to someone. Angus, his view blocked by one of the thick aluminum struts holding up the coffee shop's glass extension, couldn't see the other person. He leaned up out of his chair to check. It was Aaron Black.

Angus sat back down and signaled the waiter to ask for a cup of coffee.

He toted up almost four months in the kingdom—no big story and a girlfriend now more or less AWOL. The U.N. had set midnight on January 15 as the deadline for Saddam to withdraw his forces from Kuwait, and Angus had no clear idea how he was going to fill the time until then. The fact that the haggling had started between Devon, the Washington bureau and Dhahran over war assignments only multiplied his unease.

As one of the more junior correspondents among the seventeen WP reporters assigned to the war, he had yet to figure out how to ensure himself a good slot. The WP bureau chief in Dhahran, Wanda Nachman, was a short, ample woman with spiky gray hair who wobbled around the hotel in a white blouse, combat fatigues and black patent leather spikes. She got the position only because she was the most senior correspondent there, but she was hopeless at refereeing the turf battles. Angus knew he was her least favorite among the younger guys because the Saudis complained to her at length about him. She hadn't obtained all the visas WP wanted, and she blamed him. She had never said anything to him directly, but word filtered back to him because of Wanda's phone calls to New York from the bureau. She didn't raise her voice, she screeched.

"Everything okay, Mr. Dalziel?" a friendly voice said next to him.

It was the beefy German manager, his thinning blond hair combed impeccably and his navy blue wool suit sharply pressed.

"Fine, Mr. Brandt. Join me for a cup of coffee?"

"I would be honored," he said, taking a seat. "You know, if you are worrying about the war, you are not alone. Many people have started confiding in me about survival."

"What do you mean?" Angus asked, pouring milk from a little stainles steel pitcher into his coffee cup.

"Some of your colleagues are worried about dying. The U.N. deadline seems to have made the idea more tangible. They don't want to confess it in their offices or to the military bureau in case it affects what kind of assignments they get. But they come sit in my office and tell me how concerned they are about chemical attacks, about desert warfare, about how many casualties there are going to be and how surely some of the dead will be reporters. With that long face of yours I thought maybe you were thinking the same. I am of course ready to listen at any time; my office door is always open."

"Thanks, Mr. Brandt, but to be honest I haven't spent a lot of time fretting about death, at least not yet. I have more immediate issues, like stories and girls. Who is so unsettled?"

"Mr. Dalziel! You surprise me. Surely you don't expect me to reveal such confidences, particularly to a reporter. Somehow this hotel still does keep one or two secrets, even if it often seems like the walls not only have ears but mouths."

"Really? Like scandals?" Angus asked, leaning across the table, paying attention now.

"I was thinking about recent events like the unfortunate incident of the orange stickers," he said.

Angus leaned back, disappointed. He had been in the hotel for that, although it was funny. WP served as the photo lab for all pool film from the still photographers. They kept film from different photographers separate with different colored stickers on the negative rolls. Benoni Ryan suddenly realized he had been using too many orange dots, so he distractedly took one already on his finger and stuck it onto a corner of the press pass hanging around his neck. When the photo bureau chief pointed it out later, Ryan joked that it was a special new combat sticker that the JIB was distributing after the U.N. vote. No orange dot meant you could not go onto a battlefield.

The WP photo guys thought it hilarious and put orange dots onto their press passes, figuring panic would spread among the press corps within a few days. About two hours later, a huge herd gathered outside the newly expanded military press office on the third floor, everyone bellowing for stickers.

Colonel Nate Fletcher, head of the JIB, had stood on a chair with a bullhorn to be heard over the bedlam, knocking down the rumor. Watching it all unroll in the giant open lobby area outside the WP suite, Angus thought that a mob of reporters had nothing on cults that committed mass suicide by drinking Kool-Aid.

"That was quite a prank," Angus said. "But what are those hidden stories you referred to? C'mon, just one. I won't tell a soul."

"My lips are sealed," Brandt said, "although here comes Colonel Fletcher himself. Perhaps you can drag one out of him."

Fletcher, dressed in his desert camouflage uniform and tan boots, was crossing the Dunes, striding purposefully toward their table. The colonel was forty-seven but looked younger, exuding an air of trim efficiency. He got the job running the JIB partly because had been among the first generation of American expatriates to grow up in Dhahran. The Saudi minders were a little in awe of him after he told them that King Abdel Aziz once visited his first grade classroom around 1950. Before running the JIB, he had been chief naval liaison to Hollywood, helping negotiate the deals when a movie production company wanted to film on the deck of a destroyer or, failing that, advising them on the right shade of gray to paint the mock-up if no real ships proved available. Even if he knew something about Saudi culture, the reporters figured the appointment of an entertainment specialist spoke volumes about how the Pentagon viewed press coverage.

"Drag what out of me?" Fletcher asked, having overheard the last line.

"The secrets of the hotel," Brandt said.

"I know plenty," Fletcher said. "But right now I need to divulge just one. I should probably tell you this in your office, Wolfgang, but I am a bit pressed for time. Dalziel, try not to broadcast this throughout the hotel before I make the official announcement, okay, even though I know asking a pencil to keep a secret is wishful thinking."

In military shorthand, all writers were called pencils. Angus was convinced it was a sly anatomical slur.

"Sir, I will do my damnedest, colonel, sir," Angus shot back, hoping he did not sound too mocking.

"I get no respect," Fletcher said, smiling, before turning to the manager. "There are all kinds of new regulations streaming in from the Pentagon now that we have a deadline, but the one you should be aware of is that we expect to be more or less on lockdown from the day after Christmas to the January 15 deadline or whenever the war starts, if it does. Pentagon wants the troops to have a little respite from the press to get ready, and it will give us a chance to whip the reporters into something resembling combat preparedness. I want you to know early so you can order extra food or whatever you need for a full house."

Brandt nodded and was about to respond when shouting erupted outside. They all turned to look. Aaron Black, wearing black swimming trunks with a yellow plastic Walkman headphone visible around the back of his neck, was sitting on the edge of the pool. Lydia, her pants rolled up and her legs in the water, was leaning into him, her white blouse clinging to her skin slightly where he had dripped water onto her. A young Saudi, dressed in a short robe with a straggly beard, was yelling at them, although it was impossible to make out the words from inside the Dunes.

Angus recognized him as one of the guys usually seated behind the new religious affairs table in the open area outside the JIB on the third floor. While Angus had been traveling, the table with its shiny brass sign had been set up right next to the one where the minders for the Saudi Ministry of Information sat. The religious affairs guys were ostensibly there to answer reporters' questions about Islam.

"Uh-oh, trouble in my little empire. Better go see what's the matter," Brandt said, scurrying off.

Fletcher shook his head in disbelief and said good-bye to Angus. Angus took his check to the cashier and signed it, bumping into Lydia on his way out the door. Her black wool pants were still rolled up and she was carrying a pair of woven black leather flats.

"What was that little ruckus all about?" he asked.

"You saw it? Fuck if I know. That little monster just kept screaming 'haram, haram; shame, shame' at us," Lydia said, her tone angry. "Public Display of Affection infraction I would guess, probably a misdemeanor worth thirty lashes. Wolfgang just took Black with him up to the ministry desk to have a peace powwow. No women need apply, naturally. Where are you going, Angus? Would you please stay and have a piece of chocolate cake or something with me?"

Angus wanted to say no. He had spent enough time sitting around yakking, but beneath her feisty remarks Lydia looked frazzled. As he turned to go back into the coffee shop, however, he saw that it was being pulled apart. The waiters were running around with sombreros on their heads, climbing ladders to hang piñatas from the ceiling. Mariachi music blasted inside the glass walls.

Every night had a different theme in the Dunes, and tonight was the weekly Mexican night. The buffet table had temporarily been cleared while the decorations were being put up. This place makes a nuthouse seem sane, Angus thought.

"Go sit on one of those couches over there, Lydia," Angus said, pointing to the sunken area of the lobby in front of the Dunes. "I'll get a waiter to bring us some stuff."

The sunken area was called the Palm Court, even though the few palm trees scattered around were plastic. Nothing living could survive in the permanent twilight, although the central court was slightly less gloomy than the rest of the dim, cloistered lobby. Plump, speckled orange carp swam circles in a small fake stream along one edge. In a few weeks we are going to be even more like those carp, swimming in endless circles in our confined space, Angus thought as he walked over to where Lydia was sitting. She had rolled down her pant legs and put her shoes back on.

"So what were you doing carrying out an affair with Black in the pool and besides, aren't you a little old for him?" Angus asked, grinning.

"Honestly, Angus, how can you be a reporter in this hotel and know so little about what is going on? It has been years since Black and I were an item."

"You and Black were an item?" Angus asked, surprised. "You seem too smart; I mean, you wouldn't seem the type drawn to him considering all that Cro-Magnon macho bullshit of his. I figured it was only the little bunny rabbit gopher types awed by him, by his power to make them stars."

"Ah, that macho crap is just a charade he puts on around the guys. Underneath that and despite the philandering, he's just a big romantic softie," Lydia said, using a fork to slice off big chunks of the chocolate cake a waiter had brought. Angus had ordered orange juice for himself and took a sip.

"A softie!?" exclaimed Angus. "Like how?"

"Well, for one thing, he listens to poetry all the time. Just now out in the pool he was listening to a tape of T. S. Eliot, one of his favorites. When I was a young associate producer, he was always urging me to do the same, saying the spare language and the cadence helps craft better television scripts, makes each word count. Although I must confess I always accused him of using it as just another means to compete with people. He is forever challenging everyone at WBC to see who can recite the most stanzas from 'The Waste Land' or 'Byzantium' or something."

"Such a romantic. Bludgeon them with poetry," Angus said. "Since when did you work in television?"

"You men always forget one thing: that you still own this business," Lydia said with a vehemence he had not heard from her before. Angus had been around Lydia on countless stories in the region but did not know her that well. She had always struck him as slightly aloof, although she loved a good anecdote, even at her own expense.

"Women are tolerated as décor. To really make it, you need someone with the power to protect you. Lacking that, you reach the point where all the men try to tear you down, not to mention literally fucking you in the process. Most of us can only avoid that if we pick one as a kind of guardian, or at least that is the way it worked back in the mid-1970s. Then everyone else left you alone. It's a small world, the news business, so that is all it takes, a mentor with power; it is a fairly simple trade.

"But you need to pick a good one, someone with a little bit of heart who is not just out for the lay. God knows Black comes across that way, and there are many of us who through bitter experience found that despite his vague promises and hints he was not in the least bit interested in the long haul. But he was an excellent, generous teacher."

Lydia finished her cake and lit a cigarette. "The one thing I love about this dungeon is that we can smoke anywhere in it, well, anywhere except the JIB," she said, tipping her head back and blowing a stream of smoke into the air. She looked at Angus for a moment, as if considering something, then started talking.

"Just so you know, Angus, Black and I were an item back in the days when I was still working in television as, how did you just put it, one of those little bunny rabbit gopher types."

"I'm sorry Lydia, I didn't mean…"

She cut him off, chuckling. "It's okay, Angus; it was true to a certain extent. I'll tell you the story, although it is ancient history now."

The two met in Vietnam not long before Saigon fell in 1975. Black eventually told Lydia that he took up with her because she reminded him of the first woman he ever slept with, a French woman with thick red lipstick and a dark tomboy haircut who looked like a heroine from a noir film. He had encountered the woman during his junior year in Paris in the late 1950s, escaping from his suburban Long Island home like so many kids from that era to chase Hemingway and *The Moveable Feast*.

"He always described her as his landlady's niece, although I bet she was a hooker. He denied it whenever I tried to drag it out of him, but I think he was just trying to spare my feelings about fulfilling his nostalgia for some French floozy," Lydia said, laughing again, before going on with the story.

Black had gone back to the States and tried to be the good son, getting engaged to his high school sweetheart, Miriam, and working on

Wall Street. But he was restless, his mind constantly whirring back to his days in France, sitting in cafés reading *Paris-Match,* whose pictures from far-flung conflicts or alluringly exotic locales taken by master photojournalists like Cartier-Bresson had set his imagination reeling about the chances of wandering the globe.

The summer before going to business school, in 1965, he had taken a trip around the world and pitched up in Saigon just as Washington was ramping up the number of U.S. advisers with the Vietnamese army. He talked his way into helping in the offices of WBC with translation work and periodic radio reports about the gradually expanding struggle for Indochina. He never made it back to graduate school.

Lydia told Angus that Black failed to become a correspondent in the exciting new medium of television—the network bosses said he didn't have that all-American, boy-next-door look they wanted—but he blossomed as a producer.

Fearless about hauling his cameras and his correspondent into dark corners of the country, he exposed many flaws plaguing the U.S. effort.

"He won his first Emmy with a series of short spots showing how the villages were growing ever more hostile to the pathetic U.S. effort to win hearts and minds, and with those pieces came the enduring enmity of the U.S. military brass. Rumors linking Black to Zippo lighters and thatched roofs started circulating right about then."

Lydia explained how Black went back to marry Miriam and she joined him in Vietnam, making a show of liking it for a few years. But she got fed up with everything, from the need to make her own mayonnaise to the giant cockroaches slithering up from the drains to all the hundreds of small adaptations required to live overseas, not to mention the frightening, random violence of Saigon. So she retreated back to New York to pursue a career of her own in counseling and had stayed there ever since.

"She does good works for all sorts of noble international causes to try to keep up with Aaron on the whole overseas thing. There's this running joke in the network that 'Black's wife works for world peace, while he works the world for a piece,'" Lydia chuckled—her deep drinker's chuckle. "Not that I want to denigrate the woman. She really is a saint for what she tolerates. I could never do it.

"But anyway, that's another story," she added. "After that lengthy introduction, this is where I come in."

Lydia said she arrived in Saigon as a young associate producer for the network, awed by the assignment of working for such a legendary figure. One thing lead to another, she told Angus, until the city fell in 1975.

"If you had ever asked me if I would have an affair with a married man, I would have said no and I think that is probably true for most women journalists," she said, stubbing out her cigarette in an ashtray. "It's not like the odds aren't in our favor, especially when we are younger, but again, having a mentor helps enormously. Black is smart and charming and good at what he does and has a certain magnetism. Not that anything lasts, of course."

Angus could tell Lydia was still smitten but didn't say so. "What happened then?" was all he asked.

Lydia told him that after everyone fled Vietnam their affair gradually petered out. She stayed in New York and became a producer in her own right, thanks in no small part to what she had learned from him, whereas he went to work out of London. They were rarely assigned to the same story after that.

"I guess I always had dreams about rekindling it, but you can rarely go back. The one thing I have learned over the years is that romance in journalism is like what I imagine shipboard romances were in the days of ocean liners; part of the allure is the fleeting nature of it all. He did save my ass periodically, although even he couldn't rescue me from the biggest disaster I brought down on my own head, which I like to blame him for, anyway."

Angus, amazed that Lydia had such a complicated past with Black, encouraged her to complete the story.

"Well, I must confess I got a little reckless after our affair ended. Nothing else seemed to have quite the same edge, although I was never completely clear whether it was Black or just the circumstances, I mean all the excitement of being in Saigon as it fell."

In the days before satellites became universal, Lydia explained, important film was often hand-carried back to London to be beamed across the Atlantic. During the mid-1980s, Black shipped rare footage of the Afghan mujahideen downing a Soviet helicopter, sending it from Pakistan to WBC's London bureau with a young male producer. Lydia bumped into the guy at Heathrow and in their shared car into the city tried to grill him about which neophyte Black was seducing. Enraged by his refusal to tell her and belligerent with the countless Scotches she had downed during her own lengthy airplane ride, she flung the red net bag holding the two tapes out the window into the traffic, destroying them and her career in television.

"Black was furious although he did try to defend me, but there was no placating the network anchor and I was doomed," Lydia said. "So that's the sordid path which brought me to print journalism. Not that I regret a moment of it."

"You seemed like pretty good pals out there by the pool. I guess Black eventually forgave you for the tape incident?"

"Oh, we became good friends again after he more or less saved my life."

"You are pulling my leg, making stuff up as you go along just to win the argument that he is a softie," Angus said, shifting a little on the couch, thinking it was no good hanging around gossiping when he should be chasing stories. "I really need to get back to work, but I have to hear this one."

"This is all true. Just ask him yourself at some point; he loves this story," Lydia said, looking off in the distance and smiling before she went on.

In the spring of 1989, after the Soviet withdrawal from Afghanistan, the two of them found themselves a few rooms apart in the Hotel Kabul, a four-story, yellow brick pile left over from a more graceful time in the city's history a century earlier. It stood across the street from the walled complex housing the equally grandiose presidential palace and foreign ministry.

Most of the press corps opted for the modern shoebox atop a hill on the outskirts of town, a former InterContinental where they could survey almost the entire city, which was built in a bowl surrounded by black, arid mountains. The hotel served as a kind of bird's nest that allowed reporters to pinpoint the explosions from the crude rockets that the anti-government rebels fired from the foothills.

But Lydia and Black and a few others found it more interesting to live in the middle of the low, sprawling, dun-colored city. It was the first time she had spent any time around him since the tapes incident and he had never entirely forgiven her. But around 11:00 P.M. one night in early spring, a few days after they arrived, Lydia was filing from a telex in the hotel lobby when one of the country's notorious warlords spotted her.

"Normally those feudal types were kept safely away from the capital in their mountain redoubts," she told Angus. "But periodically when one switched sides away from the rebels to the Russian puppets still nominally running the country, he was summoned to the capital to receive large gifts of cash and weapons, invariably handed over at banquets soaked in very un-Islamic booze."

The burly warlord, having just spent the evening at one such feast, pounced on Lydia. Not bothering to say hello, he grabbed her by the hair from the back and like a caveman began dragging her upstairs.

Black, awakened by her screams, emerged just in time to see the lower half of her body disappearing into a room down the hall and the door slamming shut. Without even thinking about it, he ran down the threadbare carpet and launched himself against the high door, crashing through it and immediately engaging in a tug-of-war with the astonished, outraged warlord.

The bearded Afghan, still swathed in his turban and a floor-length sheepskin coat, held on with such ferocity that he was left clutching a tuft of Lydia's hair when Black finally wrestled her away. Before the wild-eyed chieftain could recover and reach for one of the many Kalashnikovs stacked along the walls, Black grabbed Lydia by the hand and they fled down the hall to his room.

He piled all the chipped, lightweight furniture in the room against the door, doused the lights, and then called down to the desk. But the hotel staff had fled out into the chilly night from the moment the ruckus erupted.

When the warlord commenced battering on the door, Black led Lydia out onto a three-foot-wide ledge that ran around the hotel, figuring they could find an open window to sneak back inside and flee.

But Lydia had a different idea. She had seen a bottle of brandy in Black's room on their way out the window. After they had crawled a hundred yards along the ledge and were safely out of sight around the corner, she insisted on going back for it. He was adamant that she not go, but she suddenly whipped around and teetered back. He followed at a distance, reluctant to try to stop her lest she lash out at him and they both plunge two stories.

Naturally, just as she was getting the bottle, the warlord had gathered sufficient men to knock down the door and they caught a glimpse of her scampering out the window when they rushed into the room. By this time they had loaded their Kalashnikovs and fired wildly as they too stepped onto the ledge, starting a chase that lasted a good hour before a unit of the Afghan army arrived to investigate the source of so much shooting near the presidential palace.

Black and Lydia managed to escape during the ensuing gun battle that erupted between the warlord's men and the army. The errant warlord was felled inside the hotel with a tranquilizer dart, and the next day the two journalists left the country for their own safety.

"We have been the best of friends ever since, although I really hadn't seen him much until we all pitched up here," Lydia said.

Just as she finished, Black, still in his bathing suit and a T-shirt, came walking down the stairs with the hotel manager. Black waved to Lydia to come over as the two men reached the lobby and turned away, heading toward Brandt's office at the back of the hotel.

"I have to go find out what happened," Lydia said, standing up. "Sorry about that long trip down memory lane but thanks for sitting with me for a while, Angus. It's just so maddening when one of those Wahhabi psychos invades what we have come to consider our own space."

Chapter Thirteen

I T   W A S   E A R L Y   evening when Angus joined Thea and five of her CBN colleagues gathered in front of the Dhahran Palace. He was relieved to be getting out of the building after spending over an hour on the telephone overnight thrashing out his problems with Devon, the foreign editor, who hinted that Angus might have to leave Saudi soon. Devon typically woke him out of a sound sleep around 2:00 A.M.

The guy would never come out and tell Angus anything directly, but he intimated that someone had told New York that WP's Dhahran operation would have far fewer problems, both internally and with the Saudis, if Angus was replaced. Angus knew someone, likely Wanda or Callahan, had been dripping poison into Devon's ear.

This time the Saudis had apparently complained about his coverage of the women's driving demonstration and blatantly suggested that WP might get extra visas if Angus left. Angus convinced Devon to let him stay on the grounds that Saddam might pull some nutty stunt now that an invasion seemed more likely and only about half the team WP wanted on the ground for the war was actually in the country. Plus the older, married types wanted to get out briefly to spend Christmas with their families.

But there was one concession. Devon vetoed the idea of Angus doing any further reporting on the corruption story. The editor thought it would take too much time and cautioned him against alienating the U.S. military.

"If both sides turn against you, Angus, you will definitely have to come out," Devon warned. Angus agreed halfheartedly, thinking he would argue about it later when he had more material. He found himself wishing yet again that he worked for a newspaper. They had more balls than the wire services.

His spirits lifted now that he was leaving the Dhahran Palace with Thea, who had unexpectedly materialized that morning. The strange tempo of the place and the lack of communications with the field made it impossible to know when anybody was coming or going.

He had lunch with her in the Dunes, recounting the conversation with Devon, which had left him completely demoralized. Thea's attempts to reassure him were interrupted by her bureau chief, Sam Kosakowski, a tall, rail-thin man who plastered his few strands of brown hair across his scalp with Brylcreme and constantly chewed nicotine gum to try to stop smoking. He told Thea that he had gotten a call a few days earlier from a wealthy Saudi inviting them all to dinner once she was available, and the bureau chief wanted to know if she was game.

"He said all I had to do was give him a few hours' notice and he would give us some down-home barbecue," Kosakowski said in his Alabama drawl. "Not sure if he meant down-home southern or down-home Saudi, but hell, barbecue is barbecue. Today seems kind of an easy day so I thought we might as well jump on the chance. He said he knew you, was a friend of yours."

"Who is it?" Thea said. "Someone we've interviewed before?"

"Odd name, not Mohammed or anything normal. I had to write it down," Kosakowski said, fishing in the pocket of his blue Oxford shirt for a piece of paper torn off one of those little hotel notepads. "Qusai al-Gabandi."

"Doesn't ring any bells," Thea said.

"Hey, he was that guy on the plane when we were going to Taif. Remember, the guy who translated the prayer for us. He didn't invite me, just Thea?" Angus, frowning, asked the bureau chief.

"Well, he said she could bring as many people as she wanted and we just had to call him back to tell him how many cars we might need. You know, this shit happens to us all the time. You ought to think about working for CBN. The free meals alone are worth it."

"I think I'll pass, but thanks," Angus said.

"No, come," Thea insisted.

"I meant I would pass on working for television. The dinner sounds great."

Two identical powder blue Rolls-Royce convertibles with white leather interiors rolled up to the entrance of the Dhahran Palace with unusual punctuality, precisely at 8:00 P.M. as promised.

Thea whistled as she jumped over the door and sat sideways next to the driver, leaning over the seat to talk to her boss in the back.

"Sam, did you ask our host what he does? I could definitely get used to this."

"He told me he owns that chain of Arab fast food restaurants modeled on McDonald's, Abu Falafel, you know those places. Also said he does all kinds of import-export, some of the things you and I have talked about, auto parts and stuff."

"That's intriguing," she said, waiting a minute before Kosakowski glanced at something outside the car to wink at Angus.

They drove to a neighborhood south of Dhahran, to a street edged by high walls surrounding villas facing the Gulf. Angus had begun to notice that you could tell richer neighborhoods by the extra height of the walls. Some compounds also included several houses. Islamic law permitted Saudi men to marry up to four wives, on condition they be treated equally, so if the guy was rich enough he built each wife a house.

The two Rollses stopped in front of a set of heavy wooden gates—the only opening in a long span of whitewashed brick walls about twenty feet high with crenellations along the top. Servants swung open the gates, and the convertibles glided gently up the driveway and stopped near the smaller of two villas on the property.

Much of the area within the walls was taken up by an exquisite garden, carpeted with a dazzling array of exotic flowering plants. Palms or cypress pines arched high overhead and the scent of jasmine held a slight edge over the salt air. Sporadic spotlights hidden among the plants cast a patchwork of shadows throughout the yard.

Their host, wearing an immaculate white robe and ochre ostrich leather sandals, walked through the garden to greet them. He was a man of medium height with short black hair, brilliant white teeth and a neatly trimmed black goatee. Most middle-aged Saudi men used their robes to hide considerable paunches, but Angus thought Gabandi appeared to be in good shape. He wondered if the Saudi dyed his hair.

"Welcome, welcome," Gabandi said, encasing the hand of each guest with two hands.

"Mr. Dalziel! What a pleasant surprise, I had no idea you were still here," he said when he got to Angus.

Nor did you likely try to find out, Angus thought, but all he said was, "The pleasure is all mine. So nice of you to free us from the shackles of that hotel."

"I thought we would have our modest little dinner in the pool house," Gabandi said, indicating with a sweep of one hand the smaller building behind him.

Both the main villa and the pool house seemed inspired by an Arabian fairy tale, all domes and arched windows. They were constructed from mustard-colored brick. The bricks of the pool house, just like those of the compound's exterior walls, had been whitewashed.

Angus stepped through an arched doorway to find himself in a large white room decorated with obvious taste. It was edged on three sides with carved wooden couches—more like raised platforms—overflowing with embroidered cushions and expensive silk Persian carpets. Antique Caucasian kilims covered the earthenware tiles on the floor.

The fourth wall was all glass. A floodlit swimming pool glimmered just outside and spotlights illuminated the low surf beyond. Small Japanese lanterns hung on lines strung between a series of arches that ran around three sides of the pool. A throng of servants was fanning a barbecue and arranging buffet tables outside.

"What an extraordinary palace!" Thea said. "You have some nerve calling this your pool house."

"Well, it is," Gabandi said. "But I confess it was an extravagance I allowed my American wife. It was designed by the famous Egyptian architect Hassan Fathi. Surely you know his work? He wrote this long attack against Western architecture as ill-suited to the climate and poverty of the region, arguing that we should return to our mud brick roots. The book was called *Architecture for the Poor*."

"The joke is that the designs were immediately adopted by the rich," he went on. "But they wanted his simple, highly refined shapes executed in stone. It costs so much that they still call it architecture for the poor."

The guests laughed and Thea asked about the other house. Gabandi said it was built around two central courtyards. One was a communal area for his children to play, and the other a kind of refuge from the winter winds where he could sit with his friends under the stars around a charcoal brazier, smoking water pipes and playing backgammon.

"Maybe I can show you a little later, but now, please help yourselves to drinks," he said, indicating a sideboard. The knot of reporters snapped their heads around in unison, expecting a glittering array of illicit liquor. Everyone craved a drink. Being denied the stuff made it all the more enticing. But they were disappointed. Various juices and soft drinks were lined up next to a bucket of ice and heavy crystal tumblers. There wasn't even any near beer.

"I hope you were not expecting alcohol," he said.

Angus looked at his abbreviated smile and couldn't decide whether he was genuinely sorry or deliberately tormenting them. He decided it was the latter with the Saudi's purposeful use of the word "drinks." Gabandi must have known that Westerners considered rich Saudis a decadent lot, cramming their houses with booze and pornography. Their host was either different or determined to put on a respectable face.

"This is a Muslim household, of course," was all he said, reading their minds.

"Of course, we've all practically converted," Kosakowski said. "We are living so danged healthy you could market Saudi as this really spiritual spa. I hope it don't do me in."

"Well, I'm not sure the rest of the meal will help in terms of dieting. Please, join me outside," their host said.

The display proved staggering. An elaborate spread lay before them, starting with a table overflowing with small Middle Eastern mezze that included hummus, bitter olives, stuffed grape leaves, baba ganouj, little pizzas spread with thyme, heated fava beans with tomatoes in olive oil, falafel, yogurt steeped in garlic, chicken livers in pomegranate sauce, dewy goat's cheese, radishes, tabouleh, potatoes in coriander and various pickled vegetables. The platters multiplied seemingly without end.

Beyond the groaning table of mezze sat another table laden with the main meal. There were several kinds of fish, including grilled tuna steaks, a fish curry and a Lebanese specialty, a whole sea bass cooked in a thick sesame paste sprinkled with pine nuts. There were heaping platters of shrimp and chicken kabob roasted over the coals.

"Oh my God," Thea said, clapping her hands on her cheeks like a child getting exactly what she wanted for her birthday. "What bliss! This food is so much like home."

"I wish you would consider yourself at home, Miss Thea," their host said. Angus stopped filling his plate and glanced warily at his host. Expressions of piety my ass, he thought. The guy threw the party just to get into Thea's pants.

Once they were all seated at little tables under the arches, Sam wanted to talk about whether the Arab countries that dispatched soldiers to join the coalition forces protecting Saudi would participate in attacking Iraq.

"You have to remember that Saddam was the one Arab leader who seemed to be a real threat to Israel," Gabandi said. "We thought of him as our protection against Israeli expansionism. The Zionists inflicted so much humiliation on the Arabs that we readily worship any demagogue claiming to restore Arab pride.

"Saddam was our hero. We still think of him that way, despite what's happening. So Arab leaders have to be careful that any participation with the coalition does not threaten their own control at home, bring protestors into the street."

"What if he attacks Israel and the Israelis respond, what will happen to the coalition?" asked Sam, kicking back on a wicker chair, sipping a Coke in a heavy crystal tumbler, his long legs and cowboy boots stretched out in front of him.

Gabandi shook his head. "I don't see any Arab army fighting on the same side as Israel, except maybe the Jordanians if the West buys them as usual with promises of aid or something," he said, pausing occasionally as he spoke to direct his servants to replenish a water glass here or take a plate there.

"So what would be the consequences?" Thea asked.

"If Israel enters, the coalition will crumble and Saddam may find a way to keep Kuwait."

The Americans had gradually pieced together an international consensus that supported evicting Iraq from Kuwait militarily. The conversation turned to a debate over the chances for any last-minute diplomacy averting a war.

Thea summarized an off-the-record briefing she had attended with the U.S. secretary of state during his swing through Saudi earlier that week.

"He told us, 'We are not interested in saving Saddam's face, or any other part of his anatomy,' which was a great quote, so Texas, although of course I couldn't even paraphrase it on the air," she said, giggling. "He expects war."

Their Saudi host pointed out that certain Islamic nations on the Security Council that month, like Yemen and Malaysia, wanted the resolution to include a statement saying that if Iraq withdrew from Kuwait, then Israel should withdraw from Palestinian lands occupied for decades. It was something Saddam had suggested.

"Saddam has really tapped a nerve on the street with that one," Gabandi said, listing all the Arab countries where street demonstrations had erupted.

"That is beyond belief," Thea said, pausing over a forkful of white fish, the light from a blue Japanese lantern overhead dancing across her skeptical face. "How can they possibly support such a brutal thug, Mr. Gabandi? Don't they know they would be gunned down in droves if they tried a demonstration like that in Iraq?"

"Call me Qusai, please. You know not much is published about him in the Arab press, except what a hero he was for fending off our barbaric Persian enemy, Iran," said Gabandi, clipping a Cuban cigar and then lighting it. "Absolutely nothing is ever written in the Arab world about how brutish a regime he runs—it's not like any government around here has a stellar human rights record."

"But he invaded another country. Surely that must disturb them?" Thea asked.

Angus, watching Thea and marveling at how earnest her questions were, told himself that he should not spend yet another evening in a Saudi home fixated on her. He should participate in the discussion.

"Well, first of all, nobody really likes the Kuwaitis—they are far too arrogant," their host said. "Second, everyone remains sort of shocked at the idea that there could be a war among Arabs. That counters forty years of preaching about Arab unity started by Nasser, you know, the Egyptian leader who remains a hero as the first guy who stood up to the West."

Gabandi said he expected the same thing to happen with Saddam, even if he lost badly. He could still emerge a hero. Just looking defiant helped him gain stature.

"But Nasser was a disaster for Egypt," Angus interjected. "The country suffered a stunning series of military defeats; he destroyed private industry and encouraged a staggering population growth that may cripple it forever. And who really believes that Arab unity crap? Sure the governments mouth platitudes about it, but nobody accepts it. They mostly pour scorn on each other."

Angus knew all the mocking stereotypes. Other Arabs called the Egyptians beggars, buffoons and sycophants; the Palestinians rabble-rousers who never stopped whining about their cause; the Lebanese amoral pimps forever putting on airs by saying they were actually not Arabs but Phoenicians; the Syrians and Iraqis dullards or thugs; the Libyans clowns just like their ruler. The Saudis and other Gulf Arabs were dismissed as spoiled simpletons whose unbelievable oil wealth was a terrible joke that God played on all civilized Arabs.

There was even a rhyming expression in Arabic that they used to describe each other, *al-Arab gharab*, "the Arabs are mangy dogs."

Angus was surprised that their host, with his degrees from Tulane and Berkeley framed on a wall inside the pool house, seemed to have the Nasser bug. But the Nasser era was the last time any Arab could remember having a sense of self-respect, of dignity.

"He may have been a disaster for Egypt, but he is still a hero," Gabandi said, flicking cigar ash into a china ashtray decorated with flowing Arabic script on a small brass table next to his chair. "His anti-American ideas are gaining currency again, you know, but oddly among the religious types who were his worst enemy. That whole technology, chocolate and chewing gum love affair with the United States is going out the window. Arabs basically believe that Washington does whatever Israel wants and since Israel is our enemy, Washington must be too. It's a gradual thing, but it is increasing."

His guests sat there quietly, not wanting to attack their host too openly. It was such a typical Saudi attitude to curse the very hand that was keeping Saddam at bay. Gabandi apparently sensed the mood shifting away from him and made a dismissive wave with his hands.

"Anyway, I don't think any of us can conceive of the idea that there will be a war, Arab unity or not. Arab psychology tends toward bluffing, so everybody thought that was Saddam's game when he threatened Kuwait. We still do."

"Well guess what," Angus shot out, beginning to argue more vehemently than he intended. But Gabandi interrupted him by clapping his hands for dessert before Angus could finish his thought.

The servants in their long iridescent white silk caftans materialized bearing a new set of trays, laden with Middle Eastern pastries and American specialties like cheesecake. Behind the dessert trays came a man carrying a high, curved teapot. He stopped at each guest, handing out a little hourglass-shaped tea flute with no handles in a small china saucer. He held the spout of the teapot over the glass and then lifted it two feet while the tea poured.

It demanded a certain artistry not to miss the glass and everyone oohed at this display; plus it cooled off the boiling tea. The ceremony never failed to remind Angus of pissing outdoors while cross-country skiing, the steam rising off the arc of liquid. He kept the comparison to himself.

Thea started telling a joke. "A German, a Frenchman and a Saudi were sitting around discussing whether making love to your wife is work or pleasure," she said. "The German says, vel I vake up, go to vork, come home and have dinner with my wife and ve go to bed. No ze sex it's part of the day and it's definitely work."

The Frenchman responds, "Unbelievable! Cela n'est pas croyable! It ees totally a different realm. Think of the smell of your wife's skin, her natural perfume or the touch of her hands on your back, the whole thing is completely in the realm of pleasure. There can be no question."

"The two Europeans looked at the Saudi to break the deadlock. He thought for a while and then finally said, 'Well, it must be pleasure. If it were work, we would hire Filipinos to do it.'"

The reporters all laughed. Their host smiled too, but the next words out of his mouth almost made them choke.

"Surely you understand that is why we hired American soldiers to do our fighting for us. You don't think I want my young nephews at the front lines getting killed by Iraqi soldiers for the sake of freeing Kuwait, do you? It's not worth it."

Thea jumped on him. "You can't be so spineless," she said, leaning out of her chair, looking a little stunned. "After all this is your holy land, the very source of your faith. That must mean something?"

"Of course, if it came to Saudi Arabia, we would defend it. I was talking about that hideous little strip of sand called Kuwait. There are plenty of more useful things for Saudi men to do than defend it," Gabandi said.

"Like what?" Sam barked, but their host responded by clapping his hands again and demanding in a loud voice that the servants circulate again with the dessert trays.

Angus noticed that Sam turned red at Gabandi's suggestion that American soldiers were no more than paid mercenaries. The bureau chief abruptly stood and said he had to get back to the Dhahran Palace for an important phone call immediately. The others jumped at the idea, putting down their plates and scurrying for the cars.

On his way out Sam growled, "Sometimes I think if we fight for Kuwait we ought a keep it."

Angus moved toward the cars with the rest but did not see Thea and went back. He returned just in time to hear Gabandi say, "I hope you will stay so I can show you the other house. It really is a jewel."

"How kind," Angus said, stepping from the shadow of the arcade. The offer had not been extended to him and their host looked irritated. But Angus knew that the rules of Arab hospitality meant Gabandi would not refuse.

Thea asked if his wife was home or left because of the war.

"No. I divorced her," he said. "She insisted on riding around in the

Rolls without anything on her head. Of course everyone stared. It was an embarrassment."

"But what do Saudi men do for women, I mean, can you date? Aren't you terribly lonely?" Thea asked, taking a final sip from her tea glass.

"I find strength in my religion," Gabandi answered. "Now shall we go to the main house?" Angus and Thea glanced at each other, wondering if it had been a mistake to linger.

After walking through the two courtyards and a few rooms in the main house, Thea asked to use a bathroom. Gabandi told an Asian maid to escort her to his former wife's bathroom deep in the labyrinth, and then he turned to Angus and winked.

"Follow me. I want to introduce you to some friends," he said. "But you must swear that this is completely off the record."

Angus wondered what it could possibly be but nodded his agreement. Gabandi led him down a set of stairs to what looked like a basement. Angus could see a heavy wooden door and he tensed, preparing to make a run for it. He heard that some Saudi royals kept personal dungeons and supposed rich commoners might too. But when the guy pulled on a wall lighting fixture and the door swung open, Angus laughed at himself.

The pulsing beat from a new Whitney Houston song, "I'm Your Baby Tonight," blasted through the open door, and the two men stepped into a room lit mostly by flashing red, green and yellow disco lights.

The tableau of vice inside was incredible, especially in view of the pieties Gabandi had been spouting all evening. A full bar took up the entire left wall and the middle of the room consisted of a circle of plush sunken couches facing a bank of televisions.

On one side stood a raised dance platform, where a petite woman with brown skin, wearing black spike heels and nothing else, was gyrating to the music. Down below, on the low couches covered in red velvet, two women in differing states of undress with absolutely no body hair were kissing while a couple guys dressed in white robes sat watching them, a fifth of Johnny Walker Black Label opened on the circular black table in front of them.

The most astonishing sight, however, was on the long black strip of polished oak that might have once graced an Irish pub or a Parisian bistro, behind which mirrored shelves held a stunning variety of liquor bottles. A slim Asian woman with her head lolling backward was astride what looked like an American officer with short cropped salt-and-pepper hair. He was lying on his back, with his shirt off and his desert camouflage pants pushed down around his knees.

When he opened his eyes and saw he had an audience, he growled "goddammit, get the fuck outta here," and sidled off behind the bar sideways, like a snake, holding onto the woman as he went over the edge. There was a thud when they landed. The woman yelped once and then the sounds of intercourse continued.

Gabandi pulled Angus by his shirtsleeve back out of the room and slammed the door, grinning as he walked back up the stairs. Angus was disoriented; he kept looking back as if he had imagined it all.

"Well, that was interesting," he finally said. "But how can you claim this is a pious house, Qusai, and then maintain a brothel in your basement?"

"Well, I learned how to party at Tulane and I just wanted to show you that I hadn't forgotten everything the States taught me about having a good time. What nobody else can see won't hurt them. There is a phrase in the blessed Hadith, the sayings of Prophet Mohammed, peace be upon him, that if you catch a man peeping through the keyhole of your house, you have the right to poke out his eye."

"That pretty much sums up the way the country works, doesn't it?" Angus asked. "Why don't you just get it out in the open and live like the rest of the world?"

"Because we can't. There aren't enough of us."

Angus wanted to avoid the whole conservative backlash explanation again, so he changed the subject.

"What's the story with that American guy?" he asked as Gabandi, still smoking a cigar, led him to the interior courtyard.

"That is what you might call a business expense," Gabandi answered, grinning again. "You don't think I get contracts to supply the U.S. military just because I'm a nice guy, do you?"

"That's a sweetener?" Angus asked, incredulous.

"Well it's not sex alone," his host said. "Even off the record I probably shouldn't be telling you all this, but I must say you won't be able to find any written evidence. You can't legally look at any banking records in Saudi and there are none in the States. Let's just say the U.S. Army, or at least a few of the most senior officers in charge of supplies, have adopted the Third World style of doing business. They expect a commission for everything they buy on the local market. But everyone can pay that, so the entertainment I provide gives my company a little edge."

"A commission?" asked Angus, remembering what the Jidda lawyer had mentioned about deposits in Swiss bank accounts. "You mean a bribe?"

"We prefer to call it a commission."

Thea materialized suddenly and asked, "What commission?"

"We were discussing how cutting-edge art and architecture in the Arab world come solely through government commissions," Gabandi lied boldly.

Angus thought about telling her what they had really been discussing and decided against it. Maybe later.

He hoped he could use this little nugget to convince Devon to let him work on the supply story. He had promised to keep this off the record and he would, but there had to be another route. His immediate instincts, though, told him to get clear of Gabandi's compound. The Saudi, who had appeared cosmopolitan at first, if a little on the religiously conservative side, now seemed like an egotistical, sleazy hypocrite.

BEFORE they pulled into the Dhahran Palace, Angus asked Thea to come to his room and she startled him by saying no. But she said he could come to hers as long as they went separately.

"It's practically one o'clock in the morning," Angus objected. "What the hell difference does it make if we are alone or not at this hour? I mean, we have been out to dinner together after all."

"At this hour there is all the more reason to be separate. The sight of us together would not only intrigue our nosy fellow reporters, but who I really want to avoid are those guys from the Promotion up on the third floor. They can be ghastly."

"You've got to be kidding me. The guys at the religious affairs table? They aren't those vice squad nut cases. Maybe one or two overdo it a bit, but they are from the conversion wing, vainly trying to get someone, anyone, interested in their religion."

"Don't be naive, Angus. You may not be aware of it, but ever since that table was erected it has completely changed the way women move around the hotel. We all use the back stairs and cross from one side of the hotel to the other on the second floor so we don't have to go near that table. They are religious police and they track us night and day."

Angus, suddenly remembering the scene with Lydia and Black by the pool, did not argue.

"Okay, I guess it would be preferable that you not be publicly castigated as an adulteress," Angus said, smiling. "Stoned and all that."

Thea frowned as she slid out of the car.

They worked their way separately up the back stairs to her room. As soon as he stepped in the door, Angus doused the light and held her in a long kiss. The phone rang. Thea sighed and turned the lights back on and went to answer it.

"I'm sorry," she said before picking up. "I'm on call after midnight you know, which is why I wanted to come to my room. Please excuse me, Angus."

He went into the bathroom to urinate and brush his teeth. He missed part of the conversation but kept his ear trained on it while he was brushing.

"Welcome back, but I'm too tired," she was saying. "And our Saudi host kind of put me into a funk with his attitude, although the feast was to die for." She listened for a minute. "No, I don't think that would help and please don't even think about coming up here to try it. I'll be fine. Really. I can't wait to do it tomorrow."

Angus wondered who could possibly be offering to visit at this hour. The suspicion crossed his mind that he might have had trouble finding her in the hotel at times because she met someone else while she was traveling or while Angus was away. A couple of his WP colleagues were juggling somewhat fluid liaisons as they came and went from the Dhahran Palace. But he dismissed the thought as a ridiculous way to torment himself. They were a good, solid couple. She did overnight shots all the time to get herself on the air during prime time.

The telephone conversation went for a few more minutes before Thea said good night and hung up. She came into the bathroom and stood next to Angus, leaning her head on his shoulder while he brushed his teeth and wrapping one arm around his waist. Both of them stared into the mirror.

Thea held up both her hands and pulled the skin around her eyes.

"Am I getting wrinkles?" she said, as much to herself as to Angus. "How many years do you suppose it will take me to make it in this business—and then how many more before I start having a plastic surgeon carve me up so I can desperately hold onto my spot on the air? Guys get away with wrinkles—they seem more distinguished. Women are expected to be flawless, and at age thirty-four I am already starting late."

She moved her jaw back and forth a few times before she went on. "I have this recurring nightmare, more a vision really, of myself as a wrinkled old hag at fifty sitting alone in one hotel room after another, drinking and calling former lovers or my plastic surgeon."

Angus was always taken aback by how strong Thea seemed in public yet how lacking in self-confidence she could be in private; the breadth of that gap was one of his most surprising discoveries about her.

"You are flawless, if not quite as youthful as I am," Angus teased. "Maybe you should spend the rest of your life with me and then everyone will always be impressed that you attracted such a handsome young buck. Who was that on the phone? Anything happening?"

Thea took the brush from him and looked away. "Oh, one of the producers wanting to go over the scripts on some advance pieces we are doing for Christmas," she said, ramming the brush into her mouth.

"At this hour?" Angus blurted out before he could stop himself.

"The guy works on Miami time." Thea gurgled and went back to brushing.

Angus shrugged it off. He nuzzled her neck and turned the lights off in the bathroom, but she shrieked through the toothbrush and turned them back on. "Silly, I can't brush without light," she said.

Angus walked into the bedroom and took off his clothes. He lay on his back in the dark with the sheet over him. She emerged from the bathroom wearing a towel.

"She comes, a torch in the shadows, and it is day," Angus said.

Thea smiled, letting the towel drop. She pulled back the sheet and slithered on top of him before raising herself up and running her hands over his shoulders and down his biceps. She sat up across him and he reached up and kissed her and then bit her gently on the throat before flipping her over on her back.

When they were finished, Angus turned onto his stomach. She pulled the sheet up over both of them and snuggled.

"Angus, where was that line from?" she asked.

"What line?"

"The one about the light in the shadows."

"That was no line. Besides, you are a torch, Thea, no mere light," he said, kissing her full on the mouth, happy to be alone with her.

"But where was it from?" she asked again when they stopped. "Stop trying to distract me with those kisses."

"I made it up myself, inspired by the beauty of the moment."

"Liar," she said, slapping him on the ass.

"Oww, how can you be so sure?"

"It sounds like something old," she answered, leaving her hand on his buttock and rubbing. "By the way, if no one has ever told you, you have a really nice ass."

"Where is that line from?" Angus said, smiling.

"I'm trying to talk a little literature here."

"As long as you keep rubbing my ass I'll confess to anything. It's from one of the *Tales of 1,001 Nights.*"

"Which one?"

"The one about the seller of asses!" he answered, laughing loudly. She lifted her hand to slap him again and he defensively rolled away. He had memorized the line when he read it but forgotten the specific tale.

She raised up and tried to shove him off the bed. "Half of them are about ass sellers," she said, laughing too. "You probably got it from 'The Book of 1,001 Lines.' Get away from me."

He pulled her back down on top of him and she snuggled down and sighed deeply.

"That was a long sigh," he remarked.

"Oh Angus, I don't know, I was just thinking, do you suppose we'll ever have 1,001 nights together, or even 101?"

"Honey," he answered, wrapping his arms around her, "nothing would be nicer, but I must say I doubt it, what with the war and everything. Our lives are so impossible to predict."

She rolled off him and turned her back and he could tell by her stony silence that he had upset her.

"What's the matter?" he asked, stroking her shoulder.

"How can you possibly say we are never going to spend any time together?"

"I didn't say we aren't going to spend any time together; I said what with the war and all it was unlikely to be a lot of time," Angus said, groping to find a diplomatic way to argue that she was willfully ignoring what he said.

"C'mon Thea, be realistic. Would you prefer that I flat out lie to you and say 'Of course, darling, I think we will spend the next 1,001 nights together.'"

She turned to face him. "Yes Angus, on some days I would rather hear a lie about the future so that I can trust there is one, or at least one different from this hotel," she said, a squall of tears erupting.

"You know that is the test, Angus. Sure, we can hang onto each other in this hotel. I can let you fuck me when we have a few hours together and then we just bury our feelings the rest of the time. But what comes next after this war? Another story? Another hotel? Another man?

"Okay, so I might be a little single-minded about making it in television; I dumped a guy in Los Angeles who really loved me to get here. But why should I have to chose? I want to know that I can be a success in television and move one of these relationships out of a hotel, move it into real life, wherever that is."

She wrenched away from him again.

Normally this kind of scene would have prompted Angus to think about exiting. Hotel relationships were supposed to be untroubled, with few tears and no worrying consequences.

At times like this when confronted with questions about the future, he recognized that his mother may have been right when she said he treated women like stories. He was totally immersed in the one he was working on but never stayed long, always daydreaming about something larger, better, more important, funnier or more interesting waiting around the corner.

He wasn't quite sure what to do. The thought that this might end with Thea at some point had, uncharacteristically, not even occurred to him. But he hadn't talked about the future with her either. He didn't want to promise her a rosy picture of the days unrolling in front of them, a promise he couldn't fulfill. Yet he deeply wanted to be with her.

"Thea," he said softly, trying to pull her toward him. She resisted, so he nestled his body along her back and wrapped his arms around her. He sensed from the way she was shaking that she was sobbing silently. He stroked her shoulders and her upper arms and kissed the back of her head.

"Thea, honey, you know this is important," he began, stumbling over his thoughts, and was relieved when she stopped him.

"Don't say anything else Angus, just hold me," which he did, hoping she knew he would hold her that way forever if he could, until they both fell asleep.

Chapter Fourteen

ANGUS spent another entire day distracted, looking at his watch, anticipating calling New York as soon as Devon was due in the office. He
couldn't wait to describe the basement bordello, sure the editor would
eagerly assign him full-time to a corruption story.

He felt a little guilty about not telling Thea since they had agreed to
work together and she had invited him to Gabandi's. But there hadn't
been time before her outburst and afterward seemed hardly the moment.

Devon squashed the story flat: "Dalziel, I am going to say this just
once loud and clear: I want you to drop this."

"What?" Angus said, his jaw dropping. "Perhaps I wasn't clear enough,
Ed. I think American officers are taking payoffs for supplies. I don't have
the sense it is widespread but there are clearly a few rotten apples."

"I heard you," Devon answered, sounding exasperated. "And I don't
want you to do the story. There is already a quorum here that thinks you
have gotten us in enough hot water with the Saudis and that we should
pull you out. On a number of occasions I have been on the verge of picking up the phone and ordering you to leave but reconsidered because of
the quality of your work."

"Ed, this would be real news instead of that namby-pamby stuff about the guy who cooks hamburgers just like Mom's," Angus sputtered, his mood plunging as he realized that not only had he lost the argument but the threat of being pulled out of the country remained painfully alive.

"You should know, Angus, that the *Philadelphia Inquirer* recently splashed an exposé across its front page that certain frontline units did not have enough ammunition to fight a war. Instead of the kudos they expected, they were buried under an avalanche of reader mail complaining that they were abetting the enemy. I don't want to put World Press in a similar position," Devon said.

After a few more comments in a similar vein, he allowed that the only way Angus could do any work on the story was if the U.S. government itself announced it was pursing a corruption investigation.

"Until that moment, no more telephone calls, no reporting, nothing, do you read me loud and clear?" Devon said. "The military is on the verge of assigning slots on the combat pools for the war, and the last thing we need to do is piss them off with half-baked accusations. If I get one single hint that you are working on it, Angus, I will pull you back to the desk and you won't see another war for ten years. Do you understand?"

"I hear you, Ed, but just think about it for one more minute. An American officer was screwing a hooker in Saudi Arabia. We just don't read about that every day," Angus said, still hoping to hit some journalistic nerve.

"Perhaps you can find a way to mention the fact that some U.S. officers appear to be enjoying unusual extracurricular activities and leave it at that. I don't want to put a vivid description of fornication on the wire," the foreign editor said, his tone frosty. "I hope I have made myself clear."

Angus agreed halfheartedly and then hung up, damning his luck at being stuck with a weasel of an editor at such a time.

Angus had imagined being a foreign correspondent for almost as long as he could remember. It was the fulfillment of the dreams of derring-do that started when his father read Kipling to him. It was not Kim's spying career that appealed to Angus as much as the ability to mingle seamlessly amid any local population.

Even the smallest details about the Middle East and its complicated language delighted Angus. Soon after he was assigned to the region, he learned that the Yemenis had an Arabic greeting, "May you always have teeth," which echoed the Pathan ones from Kipling that he and his father had used since Angus was little. Father and son had laughed heartily over this new variation in their long-standing exchange.

His father had been largely responsible for planting the journalism seed as well. Dr. Dalziel subscribed to both the *New York Times* and the *Wall Street Journal,* and when Angus was in high school, assigned him to pick one story each week to discuss at length over Sunday lunch.

His months in Saudi Arabia, however, were the first time Angus had been exposed to a lot of older newspaper reporters. When he sat around at dinner and heard grizzled writers for the *Times* or the *Post* boasting about how they were going to bring down this or that government policy, he sometimes wondered if he had the right stuff for the newspaper business. He doubted he would ever suffer from the illusion that he was a policy player.

With Devon, Angus had to face a reality he never imagined—an editor who did not want to do the right thing. If he tried to report anything about the story, Wanda or Callahan or someone in the office would inform Devon and deny him his first chance to cover a major war.

He glanced around his room, feeling suddenly like the four walls were closing in. His eyes fell on the fruit basket sitting on the small table next to his arm chair, the weekly offering that arrived with a signed card from Mr. Brandt. The fruit was perspiring inside its cellophane wrapping, untouched since it had been delivered a couple days earlier. Even the fruit is trapped in this hotel, he thought, knowing he had to escape the Dhahran Palace for a while, get away from editors and telephones and the constant backbiting. The first step was to check the trip board outside the JIB for anything new. Angus slammed the door as he raced out of his room.

Now that war was imminent and more journalists were arriving each day, the JIB had outgrown the tiny Mecca Banquet Hall and had moved into a far larger third-floor conference room adjacent to the giant ball-room at the rear of the hotel that WBC and CBN subdivided as their bureaus.

Much of the third floor was a huge, empty area that included all the floor space around the square central well plus an enclosed area above the roof of the hotel's front canopy, which was called the Peninsula Ball-room. Its tall, unshaded windows faced the air base across the hotel park-ing lot and beyond that the desert, making it the only room inside the Dhahran Palace flooded with natural light.

Several Saudi ministries had set up tables for their newly formed press offices along the windows at one end of the Peninsula Ballroom, not far from the entrance to the JIB, but much of the space had been turned into a lounge, with two giant television sets turned on all the time faced by a few couches and armchairs. Along the glass wall at the oppo-site end from the Saudis ran another row of tables crowded with fax machines and computers for the hundreds of reporters who needed to file from the hotel but lacked rooms.

The JIB grew like an amoeba, dividing and redividing as it gradually ate a big chunk of the open area along one side of the central well with a maze of plywood partitions used to create desk space for each new pub-lic affairs officer. The reporters milling around the trip board outside were rarely allowed past the entrance. It was blocked by a red velvet rope hooked to two brass poles—the same kind of barrier bouncers outside trendy New York City night clubs used to keep the crowds away from the door. In the Dhahran Palace, as at the clubs, only a select few gained entrance to the JIB's inner sanctum; most of the envious horde was left begging at the rope. Reporters stood outside for hours hoping to catch Colonel Fletcher or one of his top aides.

Angus was in luck, though. Just as he entered the open area and headed toward the JIB, Colonel Fletcher himself swung his legs over the rope and walked straight toward him.

"Hi Colonel! How's it going? Hate to delay a man on a mission, but any decent trips going anywhere that haven't been announced yet? I really want to get out of this hotel for a few days before the lockdown."

"A trip, huh? Let me think," Fletcher said, looking down at the bright orange carpet for a minute. "We are going to lay on a bunch of stuff for Christmas, but nothing in the next couple days. Come to think of it, though, the Saudis said something to me yesterday about taking reporters out to see their navy. I think the sign-up for that is going to go up this afternoon, so why don't you hang around the trip board and grab a spot; that is, if they'll let you."

"What do you mean, Colonel?" Angus asked, thrown off balance, wondering if the entire hotel knew things that he didn't about his troubles.

"Nothing, Angus, I just remember that Khafji imbroglio. I don't know if I ever told you this but I helped calm the Saudis down when they wanted to boot your ass out of here as a spy. I'm not sure they've forgotten. So on the sign-up sheet, don't put your name down too clearly. Just put a scrawl with WP next too it. They will probably be too lazy to check with the bureau and just assign WP the slots. But whatever happens, don't do anything stupid that could jeopardize your chances of staying for the war."

Angus wanted to ask more, but by now the inevitable knot of reporters had gathered around Fletcher like metal shavings drawn to a powerful magnet. Angus figured they had probably heard enough already and didn't want anything else buzzing through the hotel grapevine.

"What advice did he give you, Angus, something about combat slots? Huh, did he?" two or three of the jostling reporters asked worriedly, while a few others peeled off and pursued Fletcher into the bathroom to petition him there.

"Nothing important, technical stuff," Angus said, shrugging.

He went and sat sideways in one of the armchairs so he could watch TV while keeping an eye on the trip board. When he saw a Saudi military officer posting a sign-up sheet and then wandering off, Angus hurried over. It was the trip to a Saudi destroyer, the first such visit to the country's rather obscure navy.

Angus glanced around to ensure that none of his Saudi foes were watching and then scrawled his name illegibly, as Fletcher had advised. He wrote WP clearly next to it and put a generic "WP photographer" under his own name.

THINGS went well with the Saudi navy, the trip evolving into an interesting look at the cultural problems faced by a desert people trying to go to sea. Toward sunset, the Muslim call to prayer boomed out over the destroyer's loudspeaker. About two dozen men, the ship's wake churning behind them, threw their individual prayer rugs down across the ship's fantail and bowed in prayer toward the invisible shoreline and Mecca. Angus had never seen Muslim prayers at sea before and that clinched the material he had gathered for a good, quirky feature.

Back at the Dhahran Palace, before sitting down to write, he went to grab a bite in the Dunes, hoping to bump into Thea or someone from CBN who knew where she was.

He found the entire press corps in an uproar. Everyone in the coffee shop seemed to be shouting at once. Angus saw Lydia sitting alone and went over to ask what was going on.

"Where've you been?" she asked.

"Out with the Saudi navy," he answered.

"Saudi navy?" Lydia giggled. "What? Is that a joke about camels, a border patrol on ships of the desert or something?"

"No. They really have a navy, destroyers and everything. But what's happening here? Why is everyone so agitated?"

"You haven't heard?"

"Heard what?"

"Omigod!" Lydia shrieked, her eyes widening. "They offered us guns!"

"Who offered you guns?" Angus said, annoyed. "What's going on?"

Lydia told him, barely pausing for breath. The Pentagon spokesman, Pete Williams, and a pack of colonels who directed public information had arrived from Washington unannounced, like a sudden gale marking the abrupt change in seasons. Last-ditch diplomatic attempts to avert war were gradually petering out. Everyone in the Dhahran Palace anticipated that war would change their lives, but not quite how. This visit was the first inkling; the Pentagon wanted to finalize the rules for combat reporting.

Lydia told Angus that a couple colonels dropped in on a press pool meeting, where the various news organizations dickered so ruthlessly over dividing up combat pool slots that it practically disintegrated into hand-to-hand combat. The meetings convened every other night to allow smoldering tempers time to cool, but the fights raged on like a fever.

"So this colonel steps in front of the room and tells us that among other things the military will issue us all 9-millimeter pistols!" Lydia said.

"What for?"

Quisburt, eavesdropping from an adjacent table, butted in. "So we could join in with the soldiers in defending our positions in the trenches. It's a fine idea and I don't understand how all you guys can possibly think of it as dangerous or weird. Any reporter with an ounce of common sense would want to carry a gun."

Angus was taken aback. "Come on, Quisburt, reporters with guns? That goes against just about every neutrality rule in the book, doesn't it?"

Lydia added, "Plus what could be worse than a bunch of unstable reporters stalking around the hotel with loaded weapons?"

Quisburt scowled.

"So did they put the choice to a vote or what?" Angus asked.

"The guy was almost laughed out of the room," Lydia said. "Vining stood up and said, 'Colonel, there are two good reasons why you shouldn't give us guns. First, we would use them to shoot each other, then we would use them to shoot ourselves!' I mean everyone was rolling on the floor."

Lydia interrupted Angus's laughter to say that the colonels were distributing a draft of the wartime reporting rules and had announced that a physical fitness test would be mandatory.

Quisburt, wearing his usual hotel getup of neatly pressed desert camouflage fatigues, grinned at the mention of the test.

"I was standing next to the bulletin board when they posted the physical fitness rules and I am telling you people turned white when they read them!" he crowed. "I bet some of these older, fatter guys, not to mention the women, are about to learn that they don't have the right stuff."

"I know what you mean," Lydia confessed. "I'm actually a little nervous about it. The most exercise I get is walking across my hotel room to the minibar. And sometimes I dial room service from bed to avoid that."

Angus laughed again, then noticed that Lydia was eating fried chicken and coleslaw while Quisburt had spread out in front of him a whole series of brown envelopes and little cardboard boxes.

"Has the food gotten so bad in the Dunes that you are resorting to military rations, Quisburt?" Angus asked.

"Naw, I always eat them; I kind of like them. I have a huge stack of them up in my hooch if you ever want any. Plus now that some of us are going to be going into combat we better get used to them."

Angus was about to argue that the salad bar would probably make one far more fit for combat than the weird, freeze-dried rations, but he didn't want to provoke a lecture. Besides, he was a little concerned about the fitness test. His own workouts had been intermittent over the months despite the drudgery of the hotel.

"Is the fitness test anything tough, Quisburt?"

"I'm certainly ready for it!" Quisburt answered with enthusiasm, hurling himself out of his chair into push-up position on the floor and then pressing himself up and down vigorously.

Angus and Lydia simply stared at him in disbelief.

"Don't pull a muscle, Quisburt," Angus said, remembering suddenly that he was looking for Thea and not seeing her as he glanced around the restaurant. Quisburt kept going. Angus looked at Lydia and rolled his eyes before saying "later" and walking out of the Dunes. Sometimes the place was too much of a zoo to even contemplate eating there. Thea wasn't in the CBN bureau or her room.

Angus decided to order lunch from room service while he banged out his Saudi navy story, to escape the draining clamor of the hotel, at least mentally. Unlike a lot of reporters, he actually liked the writing, playing with the sound and texture of the words.

Up on the third floor, he found the double doors to the WP's Royal Suite locked, something that had never happened before, and knocked loudly.

"What the fuck…," he started to say when one door opened just enough to let him squeeze inside. Vandusen, the WP's Pentagon correspondent, stood there with his finger to his lips, pointing to the suite's combination living and dining room just beyond the vestibule. The sectional couch in butterscotch leather dominating the sitting room was overflowing, holding at least twenty people, with more gathered around on folding chairs and all around the dining table. The dusty red velvet curtains were pulled shut and the low lamps on the black lacquer side tables, their shades flared to look like Chinese pagodas, turned on.

Williams from the Pentagon and the colonels were talking to the bureau chiefs and senior producers from all the networks, as well as the top still photographers. Angus was irritated; the gathering meant he couldn't sit down in there to write. Instead he set up one of the WP's crude laptops on a rickety sideboard in the dark, cramped vestibule, under two dusty drawings of old Arab houses. He closed the inner doors to block out the noise from the meeting.

It did not take long for him to sense a growing rumble on the third floor outside the suite.

"We know they are in there," he heard someone say angrily, over and over again.

Soon people began pounding on the outer door. "Let us in god-dammit," someone raged. "You can't hold meetings without print reporters. Open the door!"

Angus tried to ignore it, hoping they would go away. But the clamor grew more insistent, then some of the men threw their shoulders against the suite's double wooden doors. He wondered how long they would hold.

Angus also began to wonder if maybe the reporters were right, that they did deserve to attend. He opened the door to the main suite to listen and heard Williams say, "We really must insist. Your reporters will have to wear military uniforms. The intelligence guys have explained in no uncertain terms that Russia's spy satellites will be able to detect nonmilitary clothing. Then they can probably figure out which unit has which reporter with it and give the Iraqis the coordinates if they want to."

There was a moment of silence from the television producers. Angus expected them to launch into a tirade arguing that the Russian spy satellites were probably tracking more important things than individual reporters. But no, they objected on fashion grounds.

"Our reporters don't really want to wear uniforms," Black said. "If they are wearing uniforms and reporting on people in uniforms, then the audience might get confused—our audiences rely on rather simple, not to say childish, visual cues, you know. They might think that the people doing the reporting have enlisted or something."

"Is there something wrong with enlisting, sir?" one colonel barked.

"Well," Black said. "Let's just say it could raise questions about our credibility."

Others weighed in like a Greek chorus: "It's true, it's not the right look."

Black went on. "Most TV reporters shop at Banana Republic. They really like that store, so we all own various kinds of khaki-colored clothing already. We could wear our own clothes and still blend in with both the desert and the military units."

The others all chimed in behind him. "Yes, yes, Banana Republic." "Khaki," they said repeatedly, as if it were a mantra that would get them off the hook.

"There's a Banana Republic store near ABC, right up Columbus Avenue, in New York," a senior producer from that network added helpfully. "So many of us shop there at lunchtime that the place seems like a newsroom meeting. We could get safari jackets sent over for any staffer who doesn't already own one."

Angus couldn't believe what he was hearing: the military's top spokesman was talking to the nation's most powerful television networks. War with its terrible carnage was likely just weeks away. And what was the burning issue? The color of their clothes! For this the print reporters were baying outside the door like a pack of wild dogs! Angus was eager to tell them, expecting they would all leave in disgust.

He was nearly thrown off balance by the force of the reporters pushing against the door when he unbolted it. There were thirty or forty swirling around outside who all started bleating "Let us in" as soon as Angus appeared. He tried to calm them.

"Guys, guys, there is nothing going on; it's Williams talking about combat clothes. Don't waste your time. It's TV nonsense."

"You fuckin' candy-ass liar, Dalziel!" someone near the front screeched. It was a fat, self-important reporter from *U.S. News & World Report*. Angus had forgotten his name. "Open the door and let us in. We know Williams is distributing combat pool slots."

"It's a meeting about clothes, I swear to God, about khaki as camouflage. I know it's hard to accept but I couldn't make it up if I tried," Angus said. "Now please go away. I have a story to write," he added, still hoping reason would prevail.

More cries of "Liar!" erupted from the mob, which kept growing. Angus tried to close the door but couldn't. The chubby guy wedged his foot in it and shoved his face into the crack. Angus tried to push him out. "Grow up, for Chrissakes!"

"You're an asshole, Dalziel. You've been an asshole since you stepped off the plane and you will always be an asshole," the guy said, saliva dribbling down his red face as he spit out the words. He looked like an overweight version of a crazed Jack Nicholson trying to come through the door in *The Shining*. "It's our right to be in this meeting. Open this goddamn door!"

Angus had enough. He stomped on the intruder's foot with the heel of his boot and shoved his face out of the door, yelling, "Get the fuck out of here, all of you. This hotel is an insane asylum!" He was too agitated to concentrate for a while at his little desk.

ANGUS filed and then trudged back to his room, disgusted with his day. Damn this hotel, he thought. It just saps your morale.

Four months and nobody had been anywhere near a battlefield nor seen a Stealth anything, not even close. Instead they passed day after day in this dump, waiting, growing so paranoid about missing the action that when it did come they were gnawing on each other like proverbial rats in a cage. Every conceivable angle about preparations for the war had been written about, not once but two, three, four times.

When he paced the hotel corridors, Angus sometimes thought he caught a whiff of the old mildew in the carpets, the mildew that smelled so strong back in the early days when he first checked in. Now he wasn't sure whether the fungus still flourished, merely tamped down by the heavy foot traffic in the jammed hotel, or his senses were playing tricks on him because he felt his life was so stagnant.

How many more days like this would he have to endure, he wondered, how much more waiting. If the war started, could it continue like this, all manufactured activity and no action? Would he be stuck in the hotel for the war? He shuddered at the thought. Angus vowed to get a slot on a combat pool.

In the meantime, where the hell was Thea? Was she avoiding him after the scene the other night? Something was not quite right. Sometimes when he looked down into her eyes, she just wasn't there. With many women he wouldn't have given it much thought. With Thea, though, the distance bothered him.

Thea had told him of a night she spent drinking with a bunch of American women on one of those expatriate compounds, the gated communities that allowed Westerners in Saudi Arabia to live as they did back home, with softball leagues, community theater and family-friendly bars serving homemade brew. The conversation turned to love, and one of the women asked Thea about her boyfriend.

"I told her that I was in a relationship with a reporter and do you know what happened?" Thea had related in a voiced tinged with sad frustration. "She cried out, 'A reporter?! You are not going to develop any real feelings for him, are you?'"

Angus wondered now if she blamed their separations on him. If she brought that up again, he would lie and say he expected they would spend many nights together during the war. Maybe he should also promise to take her someplace exotic, someplace where they could share their own little island or something equally romantic, when this was all over.

He wondered, though, as he had numerous times before, whether that is what she wanted to hear.

Chapter Fifteen

IT WAS Black who tapped into the really big Christmas story, the story that horrified the Saudi government and ruffled the complacency of the reporters idling in the hotel.

Black reveled in the clamor, of course, particularly the fact that the other networks received furious demands from their New York offices that they match the piece. When they couldn't, they had to broadcast Black's footage. After weeks of drudgery, of not a single remarkable story from Dhahran, he emerged once again as master of the game.

His scoop was to film the holiday pageant that the huge American community in Dhahran staged for the U.S. troops.

Most of the expatriate Americans worked for Aramco, the oil giant born around World War II as the Arabian-American Oil Company. It gradually became a wholly Saudi-owned enterprise, but the expertise of a couple thousand American engineers remained crucial to maximizing the production from each oilfield. As one Aramco man after another explained to Angus, if the expatriates departed, the production and hence the revenue needed to pay war bills would suffer. Consequently no official evacuation materialized, even under the threat of Saddam's chemical weapons.

The affable local governor held periodic press conferences to reassure everyone. "I feel safer in the Eastern Province than I do in New York," the prince would say. "There are fewer people with guns."

The joke was funny back in August, the first time he used it, but had worn thin by December, with every family ordered to seal one room as a chemical weapons shelter and tens of thousands of new soldiers streaming through the Dhahran air base.

The Aramcons, as they were known, lived on a massive compound that Angus thought resembled an idyllic southern California tract suburb with cute, low-slung bungalows buried under heaps of vivid bougainvillea blossoms the color of jewels. The bungalows lined orderly streets with names like Lemon and Lime, which actually intersected, and the compound boasted strip malls, schools, public swimming pools and a communal dining hall rather like a college cafeteria. Women could even drive within its confines.

In the months since Saddam invaded Kuwait, the nightly ritual in almost every home was an extended discussion about the chances for the evacuation that never came. Even in the best of times the Saudi rulers recognized that life under their harsh Wahhabi brand of Islam could be trying—the Aramcons stayed mostly because they earned three and four times what they could at home, got free housing and paid minimal U.S. income tax. The Saudis, experts at ignoring unpleasant details, turned a blind eye to the fact that the Aramco compound fired up more stills than West Virginia.

Angus and a few other correspondents learned that every garage on the Aramco compound came with a special room designed for a still with its own water supply, gas and ventilation. The compound became one of the few steady sources of liquor for the reporters, so many developed a few friendships there.

Lydia discovered that an American wife working as a hair stylist snipped away while serving her clients what she called "plonk"—the British word for wine of dubious vintage. If the hairdresser was in an especially good mood she would even blend up a pitcher of margaritas. As the months of waiting dragged on, Lydia and some of the other women got shorter and shorter hair. They did not write a single story about their stylist.

It did not take long after Black filmed his Christmas piece in the compound for Angus to hear the story swirling through the Dunes of how he landed it.

Black, unlike most of the press, tried to do a story about illicit stills but never convinced an Aramcon to let him film one. An associate producer of his learned that the stills were a tradition dating to the early 1960s, when a group of unusually gifted engineers wrote a how-to manual called "The Blue Flame." The name came from the low burner needed to heat the mash.

Although written in dry, technical language, the pamphlet was considered one of the great treatises on making moonshine. It was lovingly handed down from generation to generation in the compound like a sacred text. Black figured that a few lines from "The Blue Flame" and a shot of a still would easily make for an engaging story.

The Aramcons, however, figured a television piece would prompt a crackdown. The pamphlet had become hard to find in the 1980s after an engineer was arrested for distilling vast quantities of bootleg. The Saudis' willful blindness did not apply to wholesalers. Liquor trafficking carried a minimum sentence of three hundred lashes and expulsion.

Black and his WBC team were told again and again that the expelled engineer sued Aramco for damages in a U.S. court, citing the widespread distribution of "The Blue Flame" as proof that the company condoned homemade hooch. After he won a hefty settlement, Aramco seized all the copies it could find and forced everyone to be more discreet. On the phone or in other conversations, Aramcons called the stuff "sideeqi," which meant "my friend" in Arabic, as in, "Why don't you come over around 6:00 to meet sideeqi?"

Black, on one of his expeditions to the Aramco compound, had met the wife of an engineer, one of the few women who stuck around. She explained that for Thanksgiving members of the Aramco Women's Association invited soldiers to their homes by the dozens, but they wanted to reach many more for Christmas. So they put together a holiday review worthy of the Rockettes.

A WBC producer who relished telling the story over and over in the Dunes suggested that Black considered the story pure fluff, but figured there was no harm spending a little time with bored Aramco housewives. So he trotted his cameras to a dress rehearsal and the first performance.

The pageant turned out better than anyone had imagined. The audience, hundreds of soldiers freshly emerged from the desert after months of tedium, spent the entire performance on their feet. They were clapping, stamping, punching their fists in the air and bellowing "Hu'rah," the half cheer, half grunt U.S. soldiers use to express enthusiasm. The climax was a medley of Broadway show tunes like "I'm a Yankee Doodle Dandy" complete with a line of women wearing leotards kick-stepping their way into the footlights.

To the Americans, it was good clean fun. Some camera shots showed men and women soldiers hugging each other as they jumped up and down, singing along with the show tunes. A few cried. Black produced a piece of dynamite television; you couldn't dream up a more patriotic, heartwarming holiday story.

To the Saudis, who didn't even want to hear the word "Christmas" whispered, Black's footage played like a wanton pagan orgy. It didn't help that Iraqi television broadcast the show repeatedly, especially a close-up of a woman kicking that showed ankle socks printed with the Stars and Stripes. The announcer intoned that infidel women were defiling the holy land of Islam.

The Saudi government scrambled for damage control, announcing some new measure practically every time Baghdad aired the footage. First they closed the show, then they canceled all visas for the women accompanying Bob Hope on his holiday tour. Then they banned all musical shows, period.

In the press corps, Black was the hero of the moment for working the Saudis into such a tizzy.

Angus finally ran into Thea just outside the entrance to the CBN bureau, where she confessed that she was torn between admiration and envy. She said she had spent days locked in the bureau, still editing her pieces from the field, but was feeling deflated because of the buzz about Black's story.

"My stuff is not bad, but hardly an exclusive like that," she told Angus. She said that she had been avoiding the Dunes, not only because of the chatter but because the endless rounds of "Jingle Bells" and other aggressively cheerful carols playing on the Muzak loop just reminded her of his triumph.

"Would you like to see what I have done so far?" she asked, the question tentative, laced with insecurity.

He quickly agreed and she led him back into the long bureau. There was a desk immediately to the left of the entrance, where a cheerful Aramco housewife sat working as a receptionist. On the wall behind her hung a square whiteboard with a calendar drawn on it in black magic marker. A huge mushroom cloud erupted out of January 15, the U.N.-imposed deadline for Saddam to withdraw from Kuwait.

The rest of the room was divided into five editing bays, with a conference table and the bureau chief's office at the far end next to the windows overlooking the swimming pool. Shelves holding hundreds of tapes lined the walls. Thea lead Angus into one of the editing bays, which held three director's chairs and a long table stacked high with electronic equipment.

Her first story was about the men facing the wall of sand that Saddam's forces had bulldozed all across southern Kuwait and Iraq, the initial line of defense, marked on maps as the Saddam Line. In the voice-over, Thea explained that right over the wall the border fortifications bristled with razor wire, land mines, trenches to be set ablaze with crude oil and a ghastly array of battlefield chemical weapons. But it was the wall that the soldiers would have to breach first.

The soldiers called the wall the berm. It stalked them.

"Every day, I can feel that berm breathing down my neck," one private told Thea on camera. Some of her footage showed the men slithering forward on their bellies like salamanders, grasping long, thin wooden sticks with one hand as they wriggled underneath barbed wire. Every foot or so they would stop and push the stick gingerly into the sand, probing for mines. The camera followed the stick rasping slowly down and back out. Sweat dribbled off the nose of each soldier as he anxiously tracked his stick with his eyes. It was nerve-racking to watch.

"For all you Rambos with Bowie knives dangling from your leg, if you are with me and one of those knives hits a mine, remember I'm going to crawl out on my bloody stumps and choke you out," said the sergeant directing the exercise. "The reason for doing all this again and again and again is so that when your buddies disappear in a big pink mist and body parts are flying everywhere, you'll know what to do and you will continue doing it."

Thea told Angus that she thought the war coverage had been fairly antiseptic thus far, not stark like this footage. Occasionally death was mentioned when someone asked a general about expected casualties. Otherwise she could not remember any piece focused on soldiers talking about their fears.

"The army likes it that way, of course, dreading any dire news that might awaken the ghosts of opposition to the Vietnam War," she said, and Angus nodded in agreement, happy to be shown her work. Although he hated to admit it, the technology involved in television production sometimes made it seem cooler than a mere pen and a pad of paper.

Thea closed the piece with a young, handsome guy who looked haunted. Desert grime encrusted his blond hair and was smeared across his pallid cheeks. His blue eyes seemed caved in behind deep black circles. When he turned slightly away from the camera and pointed to the berm, about a hundred yards away, black streaks of dirt running down his neck were visible.

"We used to sleep in body bags out here," he said in a monotone.

"They were warm, but Sarge took 'em away, told us body bags were meant for people who couldn't get back out." His voice dropped to a whisper before he added, "Sometimes that's how I feel about the berm, that once we get inside her, we'll never get out."

"Don't you love that?!" Thea exclaimed to Angus as the piece ended. "I finally feel like I got something a little dark, a little closer to the truth. But I am having trouble with the navy stuff; basically I just keep looking at the raw footage. Maybe you can help spot a theme?"

He enjoyed watching her in action. It was the first time they had done this.

Thea turned to a stack of tapes on the table, all numbered and labeled USS *John F. Kennedy,* and slapped raw footage into the editing machine, grimacing as she scrolled through it.

"This was my worst experience with the navy ever because the public affairs officer proved to be Major Control Freak, as we called him, mostly behind his back," she said with a mischievous grin.

When they first landed, he greeted them with a list of recommended questions for the men on board. "How do you feel?" was the first one.

"I wish you had been there, Angus, since even I would have confessed that my thickest television colleagues could have figured out that one for themselves."

The major then informed the pool that no pilots would be available, they were too busy in briefings and none wanted to talk, anyway. Thea guessed immediately that the navy wanted to prevent reporters from pressing the pilots for details about sensitive topics like possible targets or techniques for rescuing men behind enemy lines. She was determined to get around the major, knowing that to most women, the pilots exuded a kind of randy heroism that would keep them glued to their television sets, even skipping their favorite soap operas to ogle the muscular young men.

Major Control Freak's first suggestion, however, was to interview the men in the boiler room.

"I told him, 'God bless the men in the boiler room, but women across America want to see fighter pilots,'" Thea said.

The major ignored her, dragging the reporters all down to the boiler room first and then traipsing throughout the ship's bowels, stopping to have them shake hands with hundreds of sailors. It went on like that for three days. Tired of being the morale officer, Thea was chafing to break free. Her moment came when a group of pilots whistled as she walked past the open door of their briefing room. She spun around and was introducing herself on camera before the press officer could react. That was the footage she had slapped into the machine:

"Where have you been?" the pilots asked in unison.

"I thought you didn't want to talk to me," she answered, putting her hands on her hips.

"Are you kidding? We've been waiting for you all our lives," one of the men said.

"I've been washing my hair special every day," another added, running his hand over his closely cropped head.

The camera caught Thea giving the public affairs officer an I-told-you-so-you-idiot look.

From then on the pilots were in almost every shot. Thea knew the viewers would drink it all in, particularly when intercut with dramatic footage of the fighter-bombers, whether they were zooming off the deck into the clear blue sky or wobbling down out of the inky night.

In the CBN bureau, Thea scrolled back and forth through the footage, saying it lacked an edge somehow. She stopped fast-forwarding through the tape at one point, suddenly distracted by what seemed like five minutes when the camera focused solely on the tight butts of navy pilots in their one-piece jump suits.

"What is this stuff?" she said, slowing the tape. "The camera crews make a cult out of collecting sexy souvenirs for the greatest-hits videos they spin together to rock music, but that is an awfully long shot of male ass."

Thea turned up the sound on the editing machine.

It was the soundtrack her crew was after, Thea talking to the men in one long girlish rush: "We love to interview you guys, absolutely love it. It's really fun, it's really interesting talking to you. There is absolutely no one we would rather interview. It is pretty universally acknowledged that what you guys do is pretty neat, I mean *Top Gun* movies, the heroism associated with what you do. You are my heroes, you really are…" She prattled on and on.

"That's all it takes for you to start gushing like a schoolgirl, some goon with straight teeth squeezing his ass into one-piece pajamas?" Angus asked.

"Well really, Angus, you're just jealous. But is it of me or the footage? I'm not quite sure."

Thea thought the best footage was from the night landings, which one pilot described as "hitting a postage stamp in the dark." The shots were taken from the angle of the officer on deck who talked the pilots down. One minute the jet fighter was a tiny light wavering in the sky, and the next a trembling beast caught by a wire on deck, its afterburners a roaring inferno. The men were graded on which of four wires they hooked, and missing the wire was the one thing that made them more nervous than flying over Baghdad.

"I don't know. It's pretty enough, but everything still feels goddamn tame. I need to get a reaction, to get the viewers talking. I've only got a minute or two on air but it should be like I'm reaching out of the television and slapping them.

"Someone suggested I do a little package about navy fears, army fears and then maybe go find some air force fears, although I am not sure how to ask the JIB to interview people in the air force ready to crap in their pants," Thea giggled. "What do you think?"

"I think it's great stuff, certainly different from anything else," Angus said. "Besides, your mere presence is enough to capture anyone's attention. You captured my attention in less than two minutes, and you didn't even have to slap me."

"Yeah, whatever, Angus. I know you never watch television, that you basically look down on us all, so you are just trying to cheer me up," she murmured, knitting her brow and glancing at her stack of tapes.

"I am sure something really strong about soldiers' fears is the kind of piece I would have heard about in the Dunes, and I haven't," Angus said. "It's a great idea, something new. Speaking of the Dunes, I'm hungry. What about grabbing some lunch?"

Thea looked pleased but shook her head, turning to the machine and ejecting the tape they had just looked at and feeding it another. "No thanks, Angus. I think I will just sit here and work on this stuff for a while. I'll see you soon, although I have overnight duty for the next few nights."

Angus looked at her back for minute, weighing whether he should revisit the issue of how much time they spent together. It didn't feel like the right moment.

AT THE Dunes, Angus slid into a booth with Ryan, Callahan and a few other WP staffers. Black and colleagues of his from WBC were at the next booth and the two tables were bantering loudly together about who had come up with best scam on expenses. The WP guys were astounded because the WBC office made a collective agreement that each of them would charge for at least two hefty, round-trip cab rides a day to the JIB, even though the bureau was twenty feet away in the same hotel. Nobody at WP would have dreamed up such a simple, lucrative scheme.

Then a newly arrived correspondent asked Black if he was getting any in Saudi. "I don't know what you are talking about. I'm a married man," Black answered, grinning like the Cheshire cat.

"Married? Yeah right, Black," Callahan shot out. "What, you signed one of those temporary marriage contracts like the Shiites across the water in Iran use—I think they call them pleasure marriages? You agree to be married in the eyes of God for an hour or a month or as long as you both want and then the marriage ends. Did you sign up for the whole war, or is that too long for you and you are just doing it in monthly installments?"

Both tables laughed.

"Okay, so maybe I'm getting some, but it's rough work," Black said, drawing groans of envy from the other men. "I ought to get combat pay for some of the feats she expects. Sometimes I know how Rockefeller must have felt dying of a heart attack while screwing his secretary on his desk."

Angus wondered who he was talking about. He would have to ask Ryan or Callahan or someone later, although the personal gossip in the Dunes usually went in one ear and out the other. It was the story stuff that Angus latched onto. The others had long since finished eating, but Angus kept taking large bites out of his club sandwich.

"What I fail to understand, Aaron," Callahan said, "is how after all these years Miriam lets you get away with it. How did a billy goat like you ever land such an understanding wife? Not to mention how all the other women put up with you. I'll never forget one time when you were changing girlfriends—I can't quite remember which war this was—and I watched you put the new one's picture in that damn scuffed leather frame you keep on your desk all the time. You tossed the picture of the old one in the garbage can, right underneath the desk. Don't the women ever see stuff like that and know what fate lies in store?"

Angus sensed that beneath the needling, Callahan was jealous. Both men were about fifty, but Callahan looked it—scrawny, lacking most of his hair, his skin a strange pallor, his overall appearance pockmarked by decades of strange hours and stranger food. Black seemed exceptionally robust in contrast.

"Oh I don't know, most of them are so young," Black answered slowly, drawing more groans. "You have to catch them while they are still patient and appreciative and don't know enough to bother you with petty nagging about stuff like putting the toilet seat down. I must say the one benefit of turning fifty is that I can legally sleep with any woman half my age in any state in the Union—if I ever make it back there, that is.

"As for Miriam, well, I have never probed too deeply for the source of her leniency, lest I damage it in the process. I think she tolerates me because I don't embarrass her around New York, although she has never confronted me over the issue. In her own sly way though, she sort of lets me know she's onto me."

"Like how?" Ryan asked.

"I'll give you one example. Just before I left for Saudi, I had this vivid dream that I thought confirmed my loyalty. I wake her up all the time with my dreams. The one great thing about sleeping next to a psychotherapist is that you get instant dream analysis.

"Oddly enough, the dream took place in a hotel bathroom," Black went on, drawing doubting hoots from all the men listening.

In his dream Black and his wife were stripping when two other voluptuous women, naked, walked into the bathroom. They left as fast as they appeared, drifting off to other bedrooms, but Black stayed with his wife. The dream showed that in his subconscious he was a loyal husband, which is why he woke her up and blurted out the sequence to her.

"Miriam had a completely different take," Black said, grinning. "She told me that the rooms all represented me, and the fact that there were other women in them indicated that I felt a need to expand, to reach out to other women. Like I said, I never know when she says something like that whether it is real analysis, or her subtle way of telling me that she knows what I am up to."

At that point Colonel Fletcher walked in and all the chatter quieted immediately. "Any more news about the number of combat slots, Colonel?" Callahan sang out.

"We're still working on that, guys," the colonel answered. "But we just pinned the sign-up sheets for the Christmas trips on the board, the last trips until at least January 15. They have been up for about three minutes, so there might be one or two slots left."

With that, the tables cleared.

Chapter Sixteen

ANGUS was watching camels gorge on Christmas cookies.

As an opening scene for a holiday story from Saudi Arabia, it had promise. It might not be how he imagined life as a war correspondent, but Angus consoled himself that hundreds of newspapers depending on WP for their war coverage would use it.

Even the camp's name fit the theme. The Marines dubbed it Camel Lot, the pun painted in green letters on a huge piece of plywood at the entrance.

The press pool arrived around noon on Christmas Eve just as a five-ton truck piled high with mail came bouncing along the rutted track from the highway. As it roared across the sand, individual letters flew out, spinning off into the dusty wake. Beyond the cloud, a camel herd that had been grazing on low shrubs several hundred yards away loped in pursuit.

"Are those letters flying away?" Angus asked the public affairs escort officer, a wiry man with short red hair named Major Paul Schuyler.

Schuyler groaned. "It seems like everyone is writing the troops, trying to wash away the collective guilt about the shabby treatment given the Vietnam vets," he said. "To make amends the women of America are determined to cover the desert in junk food and perfumed, morale-boosting notes."

"Really, all the mail is supportive?" Angus asked.

"Well maybe not every blasted piece," the major said. "I opened up a letter the other day from some peacenik in Berkeley who referred to all the U.S. troops as 'baby killers.' But to answer your first question, those are not personal letters flying away."

Schuyler explained that even small units like his got an entire truck-load every day of general stuff addressed to "Any Service Member." It didn't matter if a few letters winged off into the desert. The personal mail came separately.

"And you see those camels frothing toward the trucks?" the major asked, chuckling. "The men open the packages right on the truck to divvy up the spoils. The troops have become so particular that if the cookies aren't homemade or are a store-bought brand they don't like, they throw them to the camels. The camels now recognize the truck and come over for a feeding frenzy."

The officer paused, looking offended. "War is hell," he said.

Angus, along with the other reporters on the trip, including Beau Riggs from CBN and Lydia, all walked with Schuyler to where the mail truck parked. The camels lumbered within twenty yards and stopped, grunting and spitting impatiently, their wooly, sweaty smell hanging over the gathering.

About thirty men formed a rough semicircle near the back of the truck. Like all soldiers living in the desert, they looked like they had been dipped in flour, the dirt on their faces cracking when they smiled.

First came the mail sacks, tossed to the various platoon leaders. Then the men concentrated on dividing up the packages, ripping them open to check the contents. The first contained a big sack of popcorn. The circle of men waiting booed and it was thrown to the camels.

"Gets stale in transit," Schuyler explained. The next package contained Chips Ahoy and Oreo cookies. The men cheered and the packets were divided up. The third package contained deflated basketballs.

"Where the fuck do people expect us to play with these?" one of the soldiers said, the gift bringing home their isolation.

"Some people are clueless," Major Schuyler said. "One guy in L.A. sent us a couple electric exercise bicycles. I mean, where did he think we could plug them in, not to mention hauling them into battle?"

Suddenly a package tossed off the truck fell to the ground. The crunch of breaking glass, a loud shattering pop, sent a stricken look over the faces of the men. A dozen rushed forward, their hands cupped to catch the brown liquid that began seeping from one corner. "Jack Daniels!" one of them cried and everybody swore.

The reporters went with different platoons to watch them open mail sacks. Angus ended up in the same tent with Riggs and the CBN crew. He cursed his luck. Working in tandem with TV was impossible. They were forever screaming about camera angles and making snide remarks about his head blocking their perfect shot. During mail call, the platoon squeezed into one tent around the letters dumped in a pile on the sand. One clown tried to claim the entire pile. "I've legally changed my name to Any Service Member, so you guys are shit out of luck," he said to laughter all around. A few started ripping open envelopes.

"Hey, this one says 'I'm single, 26, with no kids and attractive.' And she included a picture. She is pretty! I could sell this one," hooted a Marine. The guy sitting next to him looked crestfallen. He tried to snatch the picture and missed.

"How come I always get the letters from third graders?" the second Marine groused.

"Because you can relate," the first Marine shot back.

Angus asked if the letters to Any Service Member were better or worse than the personal letters they got from actual family members.

"I don't know, I've gotten letters from people I never heard from in a long time," said one soldier. "Like my cousin wrote me and said, 'Gee, it must be scary for you knowing that you can get killed any day.' I was thinking, like, 'Gee, thanks a lot,' so sometimes I guess it's easier to get strangers telling you that you are a hero or someone showing a little skin."

"I don't get personal letters from anybody," said another Marine. "I would write myself a letter, but it would probably take twelve days to get here."

Angus laughed. It was not only a great quote but a dig at the vaunted distribution system, which the Pentagon liked to advertise as flawless.

AT BREAKFAST the next day, Christmas morning, Major Schuyler explained to the reporters that too many holiday events would make the men homesick, so the regular schedule did not change much. The one big difference would be morning and evening church services, but they were closed to reporters because the Saudis were sensitive about non-Muslim prayers.

As compensation, the major told them, after the turkey dinner they could join various low-key holiday activities the men themselves planned in their air-raid bunkers, away from the camp and underground, where they could make more noise than in their tents.

Angus and Lydia decided they would go to separate bunkers and share their notes. Angus took the bunker where Schuyler had said the men were composing their own Christmas carols while Lydia went off to what she later described as the Vespers Bunker. The TV and radio guys hit the sack.

Angus slid his way down into the song bunker using the red gel on his flashlight. It was a tight space about four feet underground with four-by-fours holding up a packing crate for a roof. There were seven men sitting shoulder to shoulder against each wall, facing each other, their knees touching in the middle. One guy worked the tape recorder playing background music and another the machine recording.

They were singing along, karaoke-style, to rap Christmas tunes, and when the song ended they interjected messages to buddies back at their base in Hawaii. Most of the messages were stuff like "Don't fuck my wife." It wasn't anything that could be printed in a Christmas story, and Angus wondered out loud if he wouldn't be better off in another bunker.

"Shit no, man," one soldier said. "All they do in that other bunker is beg God every night to find a way that they don't have to pull the trigger, to kill people. You want something nice, like Christmas carols? We've written a bunch."

They launched into a medley of famous Christmas tunes adapted to their peculiar environment.

"On the first day of Christmas George Bush said to me, you are going to old Saudi," one man started, but he was shouted down by a couple of men wanting to sing the carol normally about grandma's house and snow.

"Dashing through the sand, with an M-16 in my hand, terrorizing the land, looking for Hussein," they sang. "Treads on tracks will ring, giving troops a fright, open up the door, we get out and fight; Oh ring their bells, ring their bells, ring their bells all night, push them back to Iraq so we can win the fight, hey!"

That wasn't exactly the Christmas spirit either, so after writing some of it down Angus slid up out of the bunker and found his way back through the still camp to the press tent. He ran into Lydia outside, smoking, and he paused to survey the night sky.

He had never experienced anything like the dazzling array of stars visible in the utter blackness of the Saudi desert. The light showered down undiluted. It felt like being in one of those medieval paintings where the saints are encased in radiant splendor.

"Strange, but this is the first time in my life I think I've really experienced silent night, holy night," Angus said.

"Merry Christmas," Lydia sighed. "I must say it is on nights like this that I wonder if I have made the right choices in my life, that maybe I should have had a family. Those fifteen or sixteen years since I first started working in Vietnam have just gone by so fast. Take my advice, Angus, don't let all these stories pile up one after the other until you suddenly discover that real life has passed you by."

Angus was already feeling somewhat glum and didn't want to engage in this particular conversation, which he'd had with himself repeatedly since meeting Thea. So he asked about the other bunker.

"It was just a group of irksome Holy Rollers," Lydia said. "Like there aren't enough in this country. I don't think I can use any of it. What a day! What a Christmas! Remember earlier when we discovered it was all guys here and there were no latrines for women?"

"Not really," Angus said, looking up at the stars again.

Lydia told him that the women did not relish sharing the men's outhouses—they were built with two adjacent seats and you could see through the screen. Instead the women pulled Desert Shield T-shirts and ball caps out of their backpacks and traded them to the operator of a small bulldozer in exchange for digging a trench and putting a little sand wall around it. The women then had their own, exclusive bathroom. Unfortunately none of the Marines on guard duty knew about it.

After leaving the prayer bunker, Lydia had ventured out there with her red flashlight. She had barely balanced herself on the cardboard ration box that served as the toilet seat when a Marine with a blackened face appeared at the entrance. He pointed his rifle right at her.

"Who are you?" he asked gruffly.

"I'm a reporter," she squealed, trying to arrange her camouflage poncho so that her underwear and legs weren't showing.

"Don't you know that you are less than two hundred feet from the perimeter and you can't have any lights?" he barked. Then he inexplicably relaxed, lowered his gun and squatted down as he launched into an amicable conversation. "So," he said politely, "Merry Christmas, ma'am, what's your name? I'm Corporal Byrne."

Lydia laughed as she told the story, sending puffs of cigarette smoke into the night sky. Angus smiled.

"I explained to him that it was not the moment," she said. "It's a good thing that I wasn't wearing my new pilot underwear. I think I would have peed the insignia right off out of fear when he first showed up. This may go down as my oddest Christmas ever."

"Pilot underwear?" Angus asked. "Did you sleep with some guy on a carrier and steal his boxers?"

"Of course not, Angus, how could you even think such a thing?" Lydia said. "Although those pilots were soooooo cute."

She told him that one squadron the press pool visited sold their own line of underwear, condoms, all sorts of stuff printed with their logo. "Well, that underwear was a must-buy. Between me and Thea and her two women, I think we wiped out their entire stock. Sure all those T-shirts from Dhahran are great, but navy panties are the best war souvenir yet."

The mention of Thea made Angus feel even more lonely. It had been three years since his last normal Christmas, the kind with a tree and a fireplace and eggnog. He wished he was in a ski resort, snuggled under a big eiderdown with her. He would even trade this chilly, forlorn desert camp for Christmas night back at the Dhahran Palace Hotel in her company.

"Maybe Thea will model hers for me," he said wistfully, not meaning to say it out loud, wondering why she hadn't mentioned panties to him when she showed him the tapes from the carrier.

"Thea will what?" asked Lydia sharply, snapping Angus out of his daydream. He was aware that other women didn't like Thea much. Behind her back, the other women reporters rolled their eyes or put their fingers down their throats when she made kittenish remarks to the soldiers. Angus figured they were just jealous of her budding fame.

"I don't know, maybe Thea Makdisi will model her underwear for just anybody," Lydia snapped. "But I suspect the one guy getting that particular pleasure is Aaron Black. You can take a number, but I hear it might be a long wait."

Angus hoped his shock did not show. He could barely choke out a question. "How long has that been going on?"

"Months. I mean since the beginning, I think. You must be the one person in the Dhahran Palace who hasn't seen them slinking in and out of each other's rooms at all hours," she said, snorting and dropping her cigarette into the sand.

"He's helped her develop her on-air persona, those damn trademark scarves of hers and everything. It's 'My Fair Lady' all over again. They should remake the movie and move it from London to the Saudi desert. This is Eliza Doolittle reporting live for CBN."

"It's one of those hotel things?" Angus asked, his mind reeling, trying to remember if he had ever seen the two of them together. Nothing obvious came to mind besides that one embrace back in late August or early September at the chemical weapons lecture.

"No one remembers Black sticking to one woman for this long, and he's told me he's changing. But I suspect his true colors will emerge eventually. It's a crying shame that so many smart women are so damn insecure as to want a man like Black, but God knows I've been there. Anyway, I'm going to bed. No sense rehashing tired gossip on this of all nights. Good night, Angus, and Merry Christmas," she said, tramping back toward the tent.

When she was a few yards away Angus remembered to mutter, "Merry Christmas, Lydia," and she wriggled her fingers over her shoulder at him.

Angus stood looking up at the stars, dazed. Why hadn't he realized that his nights with Thea had become more sporadic all through December? Even when they were together he sensed she was adrift, but he chalked it up to the war.

"Damn her," he said, angry and more than a little confused. Given the circumstances of life in the Dhahran Palace, he and Thea didn't have a perfect relationship, sure, but evidently he was alone in thinking of them as a couple. The woman Black had been talking about fucking a few days ago in the cafeteria had been Thea! It hurt, hurt deeply, leaving him disoriented and breathless, like being back on the soccer field when a high-speed collision knocked the air out of him, his chest heaving as he gasped for oxygen that did not come.

Should he have been more open with her, or at least more optimistic? It was probably not a good idea to sidestep every conversation about life outside war, but Angus had convinced himself he was doing it to protect her, to save her the disappointment if their assignments pushed them to opposite sides of the kingdom for weeks or if something unforeseen went wrong.

But she didn't want to hear the practical thing. She wanted to hear he would hike across hell to be with her. She had even told him she wanted to hear the lie. Did Black promise women the earth? Did Black lie? Of course he lied.

The average run for any story that Angus had covered since becoming a foreign correspondent—a major earthquake, the death of a long-ruling king—was about two weeks. His affairs had generally followed the same trajectory: Caterpillar to butterfly to dust in two weeks. Afterward everyone scattered. Occasionally, when the sex proved unusually magnetic or he was otherwise intrigued, there would be a follow-up rendezvous in Paris or Istanbul or some other exotic locale. But nothing ever jelled. Usually they just disintegrated into a series of recriminating faxes and phone calls.

He had started to think differently about Thea, even if they had not reached the point of defining what they shared. She had made a scene when he referred to it aloud as an affair. "It's so tawdry, so transient," she had said, weeping. Could her tears have been prompted by the fact theirs was a sideshow of her main event with Black?

"Don't be an idiot," Angus told himself, suddenly cold. He walked a few paces away from the tent, pulling his military parka closer and crossing his arms over his chest.

The war distorted things, no question. Sleeping with someone kept away more than just the usual loneliness. It kept away fears about death; it staved off thoughts about coffins shipped home as air freight and untimely funerals. But over the last few weeks he had begun to comprehend that his feelings toward Thea were not governed solely by the nature of this peculiar assignment. It was something he probably should have told her.

Why Black, Angus wondered again. To help her career? That was the easiest explanation, of course. CBN was a joke before, but now everyone watched. She would be noticed if her pieces were good, had been noticed already in fact. Was that Black's doing?

Angus knew the answers would not come by pacing up and down in the desert by himself all night. He slouched into his tent, took off his boots and swung his legs onto his cot, determined to find a way to persuade Thea that Black was not worthy.

HE DIDN'T sleep much, so the sharp squawking alarm of an early chemical weapons exercise came as a relief, a chance to think about something else. He jumped into his boots and stumbled out into the desert, everything around him shadowy in the ghostly predawn light. The air smelled wet.

It turned out to be a short exercise and soon the entire camp assembled in the mess tent, drinking hot chocolate. Angus opted for watery coffee instead, hoping a little caffeine might override his doldrums, push him to do some reporting.

The commander, a lieutenant colonel, told Angus that he had sounded the chemical alarm to get everyone pumped up, alert. Now that Christmas was over and war loomed, he wanted them to prepare mentally. The officer, a black man of medium height with a barrel chest, had gathered all 150 men in the battalion to talk about fear.

He stood up on a table and gave a long speech:

"I want to talk about fear. You will be afraid. If you're not afraid, there's something wrong with you. It's okay to be frightened. It's natural. Fear is not a bad thing. It can be used to your advantage. I want to tell you about the things that happen to your body when you are afraid, when you are really afraid. I'm not talking about being scared. I'm talking about no shit you believe you are going to die afraid. I have experienced it a few times, and each time is seared in my memory. I will tell you about one of them. I was in a tank, and my tank, which was filled with combustible ammunition, caught fire. My gunner said, 'Sir, we have a fire on board,' and I looked down and saw flames licking between my toes. It wasn't a fire, it was a fucking ape-shit conflagration, you know what I'm saying. We were burning to the goddamn ground. And I stepped from the bottom of that tank to the turret in one step. It was not easy. But I was strong. Fear pumps adrenaline into your system. That does two things. It decreases the blood supply to your extremities, to your arms and your legs. That is a good thing, because if you get shot there you won't bleed as much. Second, it gives you the strength of ten men. It took me one step to get out the turret and another to get on the ground. When I was on the ground I realized my driver was still stuck in the tank. So my third step was in front of the tank. I yanked him right out of the hatch and set him on the ground. I could not have done that, no matter how strong I was, if I had not been afraid. So do not worry about fear but learn to cope with it, to grapple with it, to harness it.

"You will know when you are afraid, guys. You'll feel a need to urinate, you will taste metal in your mouth like you are biting down on a half dozen nails, and you will find that you cannot slam a nail up your ass with a sledge-o-matic."

The men, following the officer's speech with quiet intensity, laughed. The officer continued speaking, telling the soldiers that letting fear rule them would get them killed.

"Fear is going to happen. Understand it. Cope with it. Talk to each other about it. Understand with each other that all of you are afraid. Men don't like to admit stuff like that. That's like admitting that maybe you're not a sexual athlete. But it's okay to be afraid. Now cope with it. Talk about it. Deal with it. Face it. Take it out, look at it, examine it and then put it in its place. Recognize it for a useful thing, but do not let it dominate your mind. If you become frozen with fear, that is when you become susceptible to bad shit happening, when you are unable to act. That's not good."

It occurred to Angus, writing the speech down as fast as he could, that he might apply the advice to his own life. Somewhere buried in himself he knew he had feared moving on, had feared what it meant exactly to become an adult. It had seemed far easier just to float from story to story, woman to woman, and never have to make a decision.

But the sudden risk of losing Thea now forced him to recognize the consequences of that. He refused to end up sad, lonely and bitter like so many of his single colleagues, or married to a pretty woman from the Third World who could provide companionship but could not navigate the West by herself, who wouldn't get his jokes. Angus snapped his notebook shut and stood up. It was time to get back to Dhahran, to find Thea and to fight for her if necessary.

Chapter Seventeen

By the time New Year's Eve rolled around, Angus had yet to share so much as a cup of coffee with Thea. Despite his attempts to force a showdown, she remained elusive, always somewhere around the hotel or leaving messages under his door, yet not there either.

She gave him the usual plausible excuse; she was the reigning queen of overnight live shots. It meant she stayed out on the hotel roof all night transmitting updates to the States every thirty minutes or so. There was no news, but CBN's novel method of bringing a correspondent on live near the top and the bottom of every hour lent even the most mundane reports a sense of urgency that kept viewers watching.

Besides, Thea was getting her face on the air back in the States during prime time. Angus knew that in television, face time like that mattered the most. But it meant that whenever Angus passed by her room during the day, a Do Not Disturb sign barred her door. Waking her up to accuse her of cheating seemed like a poor strategy.

Nearly a week had passed, a week Angus spent brooding how to fight for her or alternately wrestling with his old self, questioning whether he was ready for a tectonic shift in his own easy-come, easy-go habits. Independence, after all, seemed like a key asset for a reporter. But whenever he wavered, a gut feeling proved stronger and Angus knew that he had to make Thea drop Black. She didn't need the guy; she was good enough on her own. Her fame was already spreading with no war to report yet. Why was it that a woman who seemed to exude confidence like a natural musk needed constant reassurance?

He managed to reach her just once in the CBN bureau. She picked up the phone by chance and had sounded overjoyed to hear from him but put him off. "Can't wait to see you darling, but I am on the most desperate deadline. Crashing a piece actually in the next few hours. Crashing, crashing, crashing. We'll have a meal soon. I've got so much to tell you! I miss you terribly. Got to go, bye."

"Dammit Thea, this just can't continue," he started, but she was already gone. He didn't call back. It was an unwritten rule that you did not keep other reporters on the phone when they were working against a deadline.

Given the circumstances, Angus anticipated a blue New Year's Eve. He realized how quickly he had adapted to the idea of spending free time with Thea, of no longer having to steel himself to sit through holidays alone or, worse, to fake cheer with whatever colleagues happened to be around. Now his loneliness reasserted itself in a more virulent strain. The military ban on reporting in the field, which meant he could not immerse himself in work, made it worse.

Much of the press corps drew special passes from the Ministry of Information for the forty-minute drive across the causeway from Dhahran to Bahrain, where they could drink, even if it meant rubbing shoulders with countless intoxicated Saudis in hotel bars featuring seedy floor shows. Angus, still hoping to find time with Thea, opted instead to join a few other reporters gathering in the WP suite to share whatever rare foods they had been hoarding.

A subdued mood infected the suite as the group spread its meager supplies over the low square cocktail table in front of the sectional couch.

Little pots of pâté and caviar as well as a few slabs of smoked salmon and a bit of dill sauce dotted the table's black lacquer surface. Not exactly the raw material for a feast, Angus thought. It didn't help that Callahan was there, recounting endless tales of previous New Year's Eve exploits—in Vietnam, in the Congo, in Salvador—all fraught with mortal danger. Worse, Wanda was whining her way through a protracted fight with New York over some tenuous news analysis about how Saddam might back down at the last minute.

Vining, the BBC guy, had produced a tuxedo jacket from somewhere and sat on the couch, mocking her journalistic zeal.

"Tell them to make the headline: 'War Hopes Fade, Peace Looms!'" he said, grinning mischievously.

Angus gave a short, rueful laugh. It exactly reflected the mood in the Dhahran Palace. Major wars were rare and the press remained impatient for this one to get going. Frustration tormented the press corps like an itchy shirt.

It was unseemly to confess that relentless boredom had become the major occupational hazard for a war correspondent. Nothing truly momentous had happened since Saddam invaded Kuwait, which all but two or three reporters missed. There had been no fighting, no violent demonstrations, no significant flood of impoverished refugees, no fireworks. People like Callahan lectured Angus endlessly that war reporting was like an ocean crossing in a small boat—extended periods of calm punctuated by flurries of abject terror. But so far it had been waiting and more waiting, the press corps spinning in circles like a boat caught in a relentless if not dangerous eddy.

Like most reporters, Angus needed a continuous stream of bylines to buttress his spirits. Part of the reason for the restrained New Year's was the common feeling that nobody present had generated an important story in months.

Thom Hawxhurst interrupted Angus's thoughts, dancing into the WP suite and transforming the mood. Hawxhurst, an ex-Marine middleweight boxer who wrote for *USA Today*, had been tantalizing Angus and the others for days with hints about a "secret date." Everyone figured that he had scored some serious liquor. Whenever they asked for more details, his enigmatic response was, "If you think Operation Desert Shield is big, wait until you meet my date."

His date turned out to be an anatomically correct blowup sex doll with buoyant breasts and several strategic holes.

Hawxhurst called her Desirée Shield.

"You can call her Desirée too, although I would prefer if you all addressed her as Miss Shield," he said, delighting in the hesitant laughter and bewilderment of the others. Desirée was both funny and unbelievably sordid.

Hawxhurst brought the doll slightly deflated so he could shove her under a camouflage parka and not attract attention walking through the hotel. Once seated on the sectional couch, however, he inflated Desirée to her full ripe proportions and proceeded to dress her in a red-spangled bikini and a gold conical party hat. It said "Happy New Year" across the front in red glitter. Since she was designed to lie flat, she couldn't really be bent into a sitting position and kept slithering onto the floor. Finally Hawxhurst pushed one arm over the back of the couch and she lay half across it, her prominent breasts poking skyward and her mouth open in a permanent O.

Hawxhurst then flourished a canteen of vodka, demanding that everyone toast Desirée by drinking a shot.

"How did you get a full canteen?" Lydia asked, her eyes wide and suddenly sparkling.

"I probably shouldn't reveal my sources, but I confess to filling it with contraband the last time I went to Bahrain," Hawxhurst said, bursting with pride. "I carried three canteens, one filled with water and two with vodka. I dumped all three right there on the Saudi customs counter. It was like a game of Russian roulette—which one would the guy open. But he ignored them. Anything camouflage, you know?"

The gathering filled paper cups with about an inch of vodka each. "To Desirée," they sang in unison before gulping the shot.

"Hawxhurst, you been fucking that plastic broad all this time?" Ryan burst out, asking the question that everyone had been thinking.

Hawxhurst swore that the doll was a Christmas present from a female editor back home with a wry sense of humor. Everyone snapped pictures whenever Hawxhurst embraced Desirée or waltzed around the room with her after Lydia put on a Sinatra CD.

Angus swung dangerously between glee and despair. It was not a bad party, given the circumstances, but Thea's absence tortured him. She couldn't be working. Everyone in the States would be partying and waiting to watch the ball drop on Times Square, not wanting live shots from some joyless Saudi hotel, especially since nothing was happening.

He kept rebuffing the idea that she might love Black. If Angus could just see her, if he could confirm that she had not been play-acting during their time together, he could convince Thea that he was the better choice. He had run the argument through his head enough times that he was sure she would be won over. But as the minutes ticked toward midnight, it started to feel like a foolish mirage.

Angus looked around at the group of laughing, joking reporters and suddenly felt like he was sitting there all by himself.

With fifteen minutes to go and the small vodka dosage long consumed, everyone decided a quick delivery of Saudi champagne was required. While Angus was haggling with room service to ensure that the fizzy fruit juice cocktail was delivered within minutes, Thea waltzed into the room with a breezy, "Happy New Year, everybody."

She was wearing an orange silk shirt with the collar turned up and tight black pants. Her lipstick, which she rarely wore, flamed like her shirt, and a heavy line of black kohl underlined her eyes. She looked great.

Angus marveled how quickly she could alter his mood from dejection to elation merely by showing up, whatever the situation with Black. He found himself wanting to hug and curse her simultaneously.

The degree to which her affair with Black seemed common knowledge was immediately apparent. "Where's Aaron?" Wanda asked at the same time that Lydia said, "Is Black coming to drink a toast with us too, if you can call it drinking?"

Angus clenched his jaw, waiting for the answer.

"He's out in the field, doing a piece," Thea answered, darting a quick look at Angus but neither holding his stare nor acknowledging the relief flooding his face.

"I thought all trips were off," Wanda said, abruptly concerned about getting beaten on a story.

"Yes, it's a sort of 'Last of the Mohicans' thing," Thea said. "They asked specifically before the lockdown was announced to spend New Year's with a particular medical unit and the JIB had already approved it. Some medical unit built a disco tent on a chemical warfare theme. Since real war is two weeks away, I hardly think it's appropriate to film a kind of MASH holiday piece, but cute is apparently all they could find."

Angus held onto the hint of criticism about her supposed mentor. The others wanted to know more about the story. They suffered a collective spasm of concern that they should be out interviewing soldiers, worried that the WBC piece might generate middle-of-the-night calls from New York asking for something similar.

Thea rolled her eyes. "It's pool stuff and they are due back tomorrow at the latest, so don't fret. You can steal whatever you need."

"Tell us exactly what it is," Wanda protested.

"Can I have a drink first?" Thea asked, looking exasperated and picking up a white plastic cup from the table.

Angus, somewhat shell-shocked by her sudden appearance, had remained quiet. But her question woke him up. He grabbed a pitcher and poured her a glass, quietly murmuring, "I've missed you," as he handed it to her. She winked.

Thea sat on the couch next to Angus and gave a brief summary of the party story, knowing that the pack would give her no peace until they could denigrate the event entirely.

She told them that a medical company stuck two tents together and put in a plywood floor, dubbing the whole thing MOPP Level 4, the name the army gave the highest level of chemical warfare alert. The hottest DJ called himself Scud B and the most popular dance, the Gas Mask, mimed the steps required to put one on.

In the dance tent, Thea said, nobody was allowed out on the floor without a helmet, flak jacket, rifle and gas mask in case there was a real alert. "With that attire, it might even catch on," Hawxhurst said, drawing laughter by dancing with Desirée while trying to shove a gas mask on her.

Thea went on, saying Black had been debating whether to film a group of nurses who did a dance routine named the "Stealth Bomber." They covered themselves in the black *abayas* that Saudi women wear and swooped across the disco tent imitating the low-flying aircraft allegedly invisible to enemy radar. At the last minute they ripped open the *abayas*, exposing their push-up bras and caroling "Bombs Away!"

"Typical Black," Lydia snorted, much to Angus's delight. Thea ignored her.

Vining chortled. "Tits in Saudi Arabia! Bloody hell! If Black shows them on TV, they certainly will go off like bombs."

The laughter was interrupted by Radio Bahrain, whose English-language station was playing in the background, announcing that it was time for the countdown. Everyone raised their Saudi champagne glasses and then hugged and kissed. Angus moved to hug Thea but felt strangely awkward.

Wanda screeched that it wouldn't be a true New Year's Eve celebration without singing "Auld Lang Syne" and started warbling out the tune, beckoning the others to join. They declined and the party broke up lest she perform an encore.

Angus followed Thea out of the suite. All he wanted was to whirl her around and kiss her. As soon as they got a little way from the others, he told her that he wanted to give her a Christmas present in his room.

She turned to follow him and then hesitated. For a few agonizing seconds he thought she might tell him to wait until tomorrow.

Instead she said, "A present? Really? How fantastic! You spoil me mercilessly, Angus. But as usual I need to be in my room...I am on duty for any live shots after midnight. You know, in case Saddam stages a preemptive raid or anything. It would be just like me to miss my moment."

She giggled before continuing, "Can you imagine? So come to my room. I'll leave the door slightly open so you don't have to knock or anything."

Angus was a cautious shopper. He rarely joined the hordes of reporters who descended on the malls like locusts just to amuse themselves. Everyone was collecting staggering numbers of ball caps and trashy souvenirs such as alarm clocks that emitted the call to prayer.

He had been drawn to one shop, though, run by a wizened old man named Abu Ali with a white beard and frayed robe. Abu Ali sold old brass coffee pots and other battered relics of desert life and never seemed to have any customers. The last nomads had long since settled down and if a Saudi bought a coffee pot now, it was likely a gold-colored Thermos shaped to resemble one. Stepping into his dim, dusty shop, wedged between various brightly lit electronic outlets, felt like stepping back in time.

Abu Ali was a Shiite, a minority Muslim sect whose Saudi adherents lived in the Eastern Province. Once he grew to trust Angus, he explained how hard it was being a Shiite in Saudi Arabia ever since the 1979 Islamic revolution across the waters of the Persian Gulf in Iran.

Iran was the only overwhelmingly Shiite country in the region and the Saudi royals, convinced that all Shiites were scheming to overthrow them, subjected their own domestic minority to random arrests and beatings. Abu Ali told Angus that the Shiites had been vilified, fired from jobs at Aramco, their children denied entrance to the local university and their slightly different call to prayer banned. Their prayer halls were largely shuttered, and they met furtively in darkened basements.

Angus, wanting to learn more, returned repeatedly to drink endless small glasses of overly sweet tea.

Occasionally Abu Ali showed him pamphlets that fanatical Sunni opponents produced attacking the Shiites because they worshiped Ali, the fourth caliph and Mohammed's son-in-law, as the prophet's rightful successor. His death during the late-seventh-century struggles over the succession had caused the first major split among the faithful, Angus knew, with the very word "Shiite" enshrining the difference because it meant "partisans": they were the partisans of Ali.

One of the pamphlets the shopkeeper showed Angus discussed the possibility that Shiites grew tails. Abu Ali told him that Osama bin Laden, the mujahideen leader, paid for a roaming band of proselytizers who traveled from town to town in the Eastern Province, seeking to convert them all to the Sunni branch of the faith. No Shiites had been allowed to join him as fighters in Afghanistan.

An afternoon spent with Abu Ali reminded Angus that there were bigger stories to pursue out there in the local population, but even suggesting it to the foreign editor as the war loomed would sound like heresy.

When the conversation lagged, the shopkeeper wandered around the cluttered store, extracting interesting tidbits from the heaps of junk, raising a cloud of dust that further dimmed the weak light emitted by the store's few brass lanterns. Abu Ali had stuff tucked away like an antique flintlock rifle ostensibly used during the Arab revolt led by Lawrence of Arabia, its stock decorated with delicate arabesques carved in silver filigree; he also had small silk prayer rugs, scraps of parchment bearing pre-Islamic poetry and Angus's personal favorite—large shark teeth collected from the desert, left over from the days when it was an ocean.

Angus considered having a shark tooth mounted in gold for Thea. It seemed an appropriate symbol for a television reporter, especially one so competitive, but he was uneasy about how she would react.

One day Abu Ali produced an old rolled up newspaper. He took it out so stealthily that for a minute Angus thought it might be a political tract about deposing the royal family. But it was ordinary newspaper wrapped around a series of small, uneven, donut-shaped beads. The shopkeeper put a few in Angus's hand. Some were cloudy round plugs, the color of butterscotch or toffee, some clear droplets like frozen honey. The second kind appeared to glow with inner light. Insects or little bits of leaves lay inert inside a few of them. One cradled a tiny scorpion.

Angus kept holding the scorpion up to the light. It was among the simplest, most beautiful things he had ever seen. The shopkeeper explained that it was amber, which Bedouin women knotted onto necklaces to ward off the evil eye.

Angus had a pair of earrings made out of the scorpion piece and another drop of amber. It was expensive, almost a month's salary, but he was convinced Thea would be enchanted. Given the way their relationship started, not to mention her work habits, he thought a nocturnal creature a fitting memento.

He had bought the amber before he found out about Black. After Thea's appearance at the New Year's fete, however, he decided that the gift was another way to prove himself to her. He grabbed the flimsy little cardboard box and headed to her room. He wanted to run, but that might attract unwanted attention in a hotel full of journalists.

After he bolted the door, her voice sang out from the bathroom. "Is that you darling or is it you, Mr. Misri, abandoning your Ministry of Information desk for yet another midnight ramble to bang on the doors of all the women reporters?"

"*Salamu aleykum*," Angus intoned.

"Won't be a minute," she giggled. "Doing my ablutions."

Bathing: a good sign. He looked around the room. It was a wreck, though Angus was relieved that a quick inventory of both the bed and the chaotic desktop revealed only female detritus.

Thea, like many reporters, had asked the hotel to remove the second bed and erect a plywood desk in its place. He grinned. He couldn't quite imagine a television reporter, no matter how good, spending any real time at a desk. What for? But they all flaunted the trappings of serious intent.

Her desk overflowed with magazines like *Vogue, Cosmopolitan, People* and *Spy*. He picked up an issue of *People* and skimmed through it, wondering if this is what she spent her time reading.

"What is all this junk?" he asked, raising his voice to be heard through the bathroom door.

"Don't be so judgmental," she said, emerging in a yellow terry cloth robe and toweling her hair. Silently he damned himself for opening up with an implied criticism; no point in putting her on the defensive from the start.

"Miami sends them to me by the bushel, and I glance through them before carting them out to the women soldiers in the desert, who devour them, of course. As do I. Call it escapism, but how can I cover a war in Saudi Arabia if I don't know who is canoodling whom in what hot New York bistro?"

Angus thought the canoodling line was an opening large enough to drive a tank through, but he was reluctant to initiate an argument just minutes after he had walked into the room. To stop himself he leaned over and kissed her. He tried to make it a long kiss, but she backed away.

"Let me catch my breath a minute," she said, putting him at arm's length. "I haven't seen you for so long I feel like I barely know you. What have you been working on, anyway? Somehow I don't have time to read the wires."

The last thing Angus wanted was to be drawn into a discussion about work. But in the hopes of making her laugh and relax he sat in her armchair, describing the camels eating cookies and the rest while she sat on the bed combing out her hair. He looked into her eyes occasionally as he spoke and the old sparkle was there. It seemed real enough. He hesitated asking about her pilot underwear and decided not to, instead telling her to close her eyes so he could deliver a surprise.

When her eyes were tightly shut, he extracted a small flashlight from her cluttered desk and doused the rest of the lights in the room. He walked over to the bed and stroked her cheeks and her hair. An uneasy look flitted across her face.

"What are you doing, Angus?" she asked, her voice shaking slightly.

"Wait just a second," he said.

He put the box into her hand and shone the light on it. She giggled with delight after she opened her eyes. "Angus! You shouldn't have." When she opened the box, she looked perplexed and slightly disappointed with the brownish lumps until he pointed the flashlight through the one containing the scorpion. A shadow of the rich golden amber and the cradled scorpion fell across her cheek. She couldn't quite see it, so Angus moved the flashlight to project the golden outline onto the wall.

"It's real," he said softly.

"Oh Angus! How beautiful! Wherever did you find them? Let's turn on the lights so I can see them clearly."

"I have a better idea." He unscrewed the top of the little black flashlight. The top, when inverted, formed a pedestal that held the rest of the flashlight, its tiny bulb glowing like an electric candle. Angus set it on the bedside table. She held the magic beads up to the little light, the room filling with a diluted reflection of their honeyed glow. She sat on the edge of the bed next to the bulb, slowly twirling the earrings, while he stretched at full length behind her, watching.

"If the war starts tonight I will have to tell them to put someone else on live," she said. "I have to lie here and look at my little scorpion."

Suddenly she furrowed her brow. "Angus, there isn't any bad symbolism or evil omen in a scorpion, is there? Don't they devour their mates?"

"No, you're thinking of black widows. Sometimes male scorpions sting the females when they are mating, but there is no message. I wanted to find you a unique souvenir of the desert," he said, rubbing his hands down her back.

He knew this might be the time to broach the subject but dreaded the idea. He didn't want to be the one to bring it up. Hadn't she just heard the others talk publicly about Aaron in front of him? Surely if it was important to her she would say something.

Angus could feel her warmth through her robe and he rose up to nuzzle his cheek against her neck. The delight he felt in simply feeling her skin was tarnished, though, clouded with the knowledge that it was not just his to caress. "You deserve something unmatchable," he added, hoping he sounded sincere.

"You are too good to me, you know?" she said, turning to face him, her naked thigh sliding out from her robe. He caressed her inner thigh and then pulled her over on top of him and she came over, slowly.

He wondered whether it was hesitation or whether he imagined it. He held her for a while, but when he tried to kiss her and slide off her bathrobe at the same time, she stopped him.

"I usually detest New Year's, but this has been dreamy and I owe it all to you," she said, searching his eyes as she spoke. "I think, though, that it would be better if we broke this off and that you didn't sleep here tonight."

"Why, is someone else going to?" he blurted out before he could stop himself, wishing he could haul the words back even as he said them. Yet he felt his anger cracking open like a tiny fissure in a dam suddenly bursting, unleashing in one giant gusher all of the emotion he had kept pent up inside himself for these many days.

"Maybe," Thea snapped.

"Don't play coy. You know damn well exactly who," he shot back.

"Goddam you, Angus. If you knew there was something else happening in my life, if it bothers you so much, then why didn't you say something? What did you come here for? You just came here to get laid, to buy my favors with your little trinkets. If that is what you wanted, sailor, then take your precious little earrings and shove off now."

She picked up the earrings and flung them at him, the amber bouncing off his chest and rolling across the floor. Angus watched them roll as if it was his life rolling away from him.

"You haven't exactly been a paragon of honesty yourself, have you Thea?" he yelled at her. They were shouting loudly enough to be heard in the hallway, so Angus lowered his voice to an angry, clipped tone.

"Why all the subterfuge? The avoidance? I have to go out and stand in the middle of the fucking desert to discover from someone else that all this time together when I thought something was growing between us, something important, you were off screwing another man the second my back was out the door."

"What are you talking about?" she asked, weeping, caught off guard by his ferocity, defending herself by laying into him. "We've kept each other company, shared some good laughs. I admit we get along, that maybe this is more than the usual fuck in some strange hotel to keep loneliness at bay. But whenever I tried to talk to you about it, about anything longer term, you pushed me as far away as you possibly could."

"I hope you are not implying that I chased you away, forced you to seek solace elsewhere. You know exactly what you want and you always have and you think that Black can help you get it."

She flinched when he said Black's name but did not concede an inch. "I've worked damn hard to get where I am, Angus, and if someone powerful like Aaron Black thinks I'm talented and can help me get a little farther, well, what's wrong with that?" she hissed.

"Then why the hell did you drag me into it?"

As they argued, the sour mood filing the room like bile rising in the throat, Thea drew her robe more closely around her and Angus retrieved the earrings from the floor. Thea ended up leaning against the headboard, hugging a pillow, while Angus sat on the foot of the bed, not really wanting to look at her but not wanting to leave either, staring down at the two little plugs in his hand, at his lost hope.

Thea went on, "I remember standing next to that hotel window in Riyadh, listening to you argue so passionately with your editors yet trying to make a lark out of it for me. I remember feeling so content with your arms around me, loving even the short red hair on your hands. I know I felt something initially, something big, perhaps. But it just doesn't feel big enough any more. I kept hoping it would grow as the weeks passed, but it hasn't. I am afraid in a blissful moment I reverted to my old, wartime pattern of 'Love the One You're With.' I'm sorry."

Angus wanted to lash out, to make Thea suffer so that in salving her own wounds she would be forced to see her callous mistake.

"I am sure Black thinks you're talented, Thea. Anyone who has been to bed with you would find you immensely talented," he started, and she gasped. "But how can you delude yourself, or even respect yourself, for fucking your way to the top? Do you really think if you weren't sucking his dick he would be there, praising every piece you did as a work of art?"

"How dare you!?" she cried in outrage. "Ten years ago I was a gopher and now I'm one of the network's main correspondents reporting the biggest story in the world. And I haven't, as you damn well know, been with Black all that long. Besides, I can learn from him. But it's more than that. He and I make a great team. I sense it and he does too. He loves me, Angus, and thinks we would be good together anyplace and you don't. It's that simple. We've even talked about marriage!"

"Marry him!?" Angus snorted, cutting her off before she could say anything else, not wanting to accept it as true. "Come on Thea, how blind can you be? You know his past. He's been fucking any associate producer with two legs and probably some without for at least two decades.

"I am sure undiluted attention from a famous producer is flattering, but get a grip. Do you really think you will get loyalty from a man who doesn't know how to spell the word? I thought you were smarter than that."

"He loves me; even he is surprised that this thing between us has proved so different from the rest," Thea said vehemently, as if trying to convince herself. "Besides loving me, if Black has the power to make me a better, more visible television correspondent, what is wrong with that? CBN is changing television news, Angus, and I am going to be there to make sure everyone notices the change. I think I can have the man I love and the job I want at the same time, and why shouldn't I grab it?

"I doubt you saw it, but *People* magazine just did a story from the hotel, a 'Women at War' piece that allowed them to use their famous old photographs from legendary correspondents like Margaret Bourke-White. When the reporter asked me about marriage and children, I told her that if I found a husband, I would also find an armor-plated baby carriage. I meant it, Angus, in terms of the fact that I think with Black I can have it all."

"Christ, Thea, *People* magazine? Who gives a fuck what *People* magazine says? What matters is that I love you, I really do," Angus said, his ebbing rage replaced by a waxing tide of sadness, knowing the sentiment might sound false, like he was grasping at any straw in desperation.

"Oh Angus, you are just saying that in the heat of this moment. You are happiest when you are off alone, skulking along the streets of Khafji or digging through the local bazaars," Thea said, her voice also losing its edge. "Sometimes I think of your heart like that Baskin-Robbins ice cream store down at the Dhahran Mall, you know the one with the little wooden sign that says 'No Women May Sit in this Shop.'

"You don't need me. I'm not convinced you need anyone. Maybe a newspaper job, that's it. But I know I need someone. I need hugging. I want someone there all the time for me. I want him to be thinking about me as the most important event in his day."

Angus regretted that he had not made his thoughts clear earlier. He had been too slow to recognize that she occupied his mind far more than anything else. So he tried to say it now: "You are the most important event in my day, Thea."

When she didn't respond, he went on the offensive again, "Besides, do you really believe Black is going to be there for you? Why do I doubt it? He loves the chase as much as everyone else. Hell, we all love the chase. And remember he's been here four months without his wife, although we all clearly know how he has been able to endure that."

She ignored the slight, her face becoming earnest. "Aaron makes it seem so easy, Angus, he takes the stress out of it for me. You know before I met him, I used to throw up before I had to do live shots, I was so nervous. But he has given me the confidence to know that I am good, a step above the others."

"Okay, so you needed to boost your confidence and you have. Now forget about Bluebeard."

"It's love, Angus," said Thea, still hugging the pillow, speaking in little more than a whisper. "I have been trying to tell you that my relationship with Black works on both levels where it doesn't with you. I don't get the sense of an emotional connection all the time, that you are really there, that this is something big, something for the long run. I am beginning to think about my future life a lot, not just my reporting. I mean I was joking about that armor-plated baby carriage, but deep down I worry if I will ever have that kid.

"You know when I was still in L.A. I went to a national journalism convention where I met this wire service reporter, Maureen something, who has covered every major story for the past twenty years. I mean a real veteran.

"After the seminars ended each day she used to plant herself in the bar and get soused and growl at any man who came near, spitting stuff at them like 'I've forgotten more than you'll ever know.' You could see that she had been quite beautiful once, dark and sparkling. But it was gone, all gone, like a Renaissance wall tableau where the rich colors have faded and great chunks are missing.

"That woman is my nightmare, Angus. I felt like the journalism version of Ebenezer Scrooge being visited by the ghost of stories future. It is a fate I am determined to escape. Black promises me that. He builds me a dream palace for the future, while you don't even try. Besides, by working next to him, I can make sure he doesn't stray."

Angus was lost for words. Her decision was beginning to feel like a brick wall he could not budge, couldn't so much as loosen one brick. He looked down at the earrings that he had been gripping tightly in his hand and sadly slipped them into the pocket of his dark blue flannel shirt. He would find a better occasion to give them to her again. "So I am doomed, huh? You've made up your mind?"

She came up behind him and hugged him and then sat next to him, taking his left hand. A few of her tears dripped into his open palm.

"Don't get me wrong, Angus, you are incredibly important to me.

We are tremendous pals, more than that. I admire you wholeheartedly. You are different from the rest of these hotel Lotharios, I know that. You have not been tainted by marriage and infidelity and divorce, you are a good writer, you know what you want. I love the stories you write. You find topics or angles that nobody else does. Sometimes I think I started sleeping with you just to try to steal your ideas."

"I always suspected as much."

"But something else happened to me that is more important. I should have told you at the outset. I think I did try to warn you in Riyadh when I told you not to fall in love with me. I don't know, there's so much uncertainty about what this war will bring. You felt like a pretty solid rock for me to cling to. You still do. I almost didn't want to choose."

Angus saw a glimmer of opportunity and tried one more time.

"I am sure Black is very good at whatever he does, Thea, but stop kidding yourself. Aaron Black? Important? Is there any woman working in television..."

"Don't, Angus, please don't. I know what I am doing," she cut him off. "You are a good man; you make me laugh and the sex has been wonderful. Maybe you and I could make it work if we had to. I really did hope to find a way to avoid hurting you with this. I thought maybe if we could get to the war, then a natural separation would come about and it would all end without rancor, the way these things so often peter out.

"You have to accept the idea that I want to build my life in a way other than what you imagined. Think of it in simple terms. You're print. I'm TV. We don't mix."

Angus stood up. He was feeling grainy in the head, abused by the conversation. He didn't want to be a good sport. He wanted to break things.

"You are a beautiful, talented woman, Thea, and you deserve whatever you get. I can't really stand the thought of being separated from you forever, but hell, it may be a long war and who knows what might happen?" he said, trying to summon buoyancy when all he felt was apprehension. "I can't accept the idea that you and I are completely over. I'll think of it as a kind of hiatus, leave it at that. Good night."

"Hiatus? I don't think so, Angus. I just have this incredible sense that this war has started something rolling for me and nothing can stop me. Don't live with any illusion that there will be any more nights like before," Thea said without anger.

"I'm done with the illusion business for a while," he said, fighting back tears again as he stepped toward the door. "Happy New Year, Thea. Don't get up. I'll let myself out."

He closed her door and walked down the corridor, despair oozing through him. Before he reached his door he stopped a moment and leaned his head against the wall in the hotel corridor. Tears glistened at the corners of his eyes. "How could she?" he grunted, kicking the wall with such force that his boot went right through the plaster with a resounding crack. His foot caught and he jumped backward with his other leg to keep himself from tumbling.

"Hey what the hell was that?" he heard someone in the JIB shout. "Get the bomb squad!"

Angus stared mutely at the gaping hole in the wall and then stumbled into his room. As he lay fully clothed on his bed, not sleeping, he could hear the officers from the JIB assigned to the bomb squad rooting around in the corridor. They cursed the fact that they had been hauled out of bed for a hole kicked in the wall.

"Some dumb-ass reporter probably didn't get the pool assignment he wanted," one of them groused.

Chapter Eighteen

ANGUS stood by the swimming pool and considered whether there was a worse day for a fitness test than New Year's Day, particularly one administered by the military.

The JIB had ratcheted up the intimidation factor by scheduling practice sessions before the main event. Angus, wanting to make sure he wasn't missing anything, had gone to one run by Colonel Fletcher a few days earlier.

The lean colonel ran a few laps inside the back fence to establish the acceptable pace and then demonstrated proper military form for push-ups and sit-ups.

"Many of you, and many of your colleagues, have quite a ways to go before you will be in physical shape for combat," Fletcher said, his face stern, provoking a little nervous toe shuffling from the assembled hacks. "Being out of shape will not only jeopardize your own life but the lives of the soldiers serving as your escorts."

Angus found it a little heavy for a motivational speech. It provoked giggles, though, from a cluster of flabby British tabloid reporters hanging around the edges of the practice in order to mock it in print.

"Must be the only escort service in the world which forces the push-ups before you get the escort," one of them cackled and the rest joined in.

Fletcher ignored them, starting his push-ups. "Lower your body until your arms are parallel to the ground, an almost ninety degree angle at the elbow," he said, augmenting the chagrin of the assembled group by talking in the middle of his exertions. "Rest while you are up and your arms are straight, not in the down position."

He maintained a rigid flatness throughout that made him seem like a human coffee table. Most of the reporters groaned, although a few of the valiant set about mimicking his style.

Fletcher's sit-ups were old school, naturally, not the abbreviated crunches developed by modern gyms where you barely lift your torso. He pulled his entire upper body all the way to his bent knees, making it seem effortless. As he executed one after another Angus noticed reporters rubbing their stomachs doubtfully.

NEW YEAR'S DAY turned out sunny and dry, free of the intermittent light rain that had marked the previous week. Angus felt like he was back in junior high, or maybe even third grade, waiting to be picked for a dodgeball team. Those who didn't pass would be left on the bench for the entire war.

Through endless conversations at the Dunes, the men had previously agreed they would not give the military press officers the satisfaction of seeing them compete. They would not play Spartacus, slaves fighting each other to the death for the titillation of their Roman owners. Instead they would all do the minimum requirements and not one iota more, not one extra push-up or sit-up, and no unnecessary speed for the running. A few reporters even showed up in street clothes, a way of saying, "I do not intend to break into a sweat for this."

Angus wore gray sweats cut off at the knee and a long-sleeve T-shirt that had once been white. He looked around to see who was taking the test with him, finding both Black and Quisburt, among others. Black was wearing navy blue running shorts and a yellow WBC network T-shirt, while Quisburt somehow acquired a sweatshirt and something like spandex bicycling shorts in desert camouflage. Angus didn't want to be around Black. He was curious whether the guy had the slightest inkling about their little connection. Unlikely. If he was Thea's mentor, she would have kept her secrets.

The gathered reporters were suddenly distracted by the guy from *Stars and Stripes,* the military's newspaper. He made it abundantly clear that he was not like everybody else. He had cut the sleeves off his military-issue, olive green T-shirt because they constricted his biceps, and dense leg muscles poked out of his olive shorts like primed warheads. Worse, he started jumping rope and stretching vigorously as a kind of warm-up, making all his muscles flex at once. The other reporters tried to ignore him but couldn't help assessing what he was doing out of the corner of their eyes.

The three military press officers running the test arrived smirking. One smoked. After taking attendance, they lined everybody up for the three laps around the back lot. The lieutenant holding the stopwatch growled, "On your marks, get set, *go!*"

The *Stars and Stripes* reporter bolted away and with that everyone's resolve to complete the test in a laid-back style evaporated. Testosterone triumphed. They scrambled to catch up with the guy, elbowing each other as they jockeyed for position. The ones wearing street shoes cursed themselves aloud for lacking foresight.

The military reporter completed the mile and a half in less than nine minutes, well under the required fourteen minutes. The first runner in the rest of the pack was a good three minutes behind him, everyone wheezing and leaning over with their hands on their knees just over the finish line.

Then they tottered to the pool deck for part two.

"Okay, which one of you iron men wants to go first?" growled the brawny black drill sergeant imported uniquely for this segment. The

Stars and Stripes guy volunteered even faster than Quisburt. He did at least 120 sit-ups and 60 push-ups in flawless form. He gave an extra push and clapped his hands every ten push-ups.

Angus watched those ahead of him. Sit-ups were executed more or less as advertised, except with lots of groaning. It's hard to fake a sit-up. Sometimes when a reporter barely got off the ground, though, the monitoring officer counted it as half.

The real art of cheating emerged during the push-ups. There were several methods that Angus had not seen since he was thirteen. Some guys would move their shoulders up and down vigorously while the rest of their body remained virtually immobile. Some bent their elbows a bit and then came back up, which allowed for a high yield in numbers but barely any motion. And the third method was a kind of contortion, where the feet and shoulders didn't really move, but the cheater would bow his back and bend his neck downward, trying to create the appearance of vigorous movement without doing any.

Quisburt was livid. He had already annoyed everyone by shouting out his own numbers as he did his test. Now he kept saying things like "That's not a push-up" or "You are not counting that one, are you?" to the supervising officers. They were enjoying the mere fact of the test and not being sticklers for form.

Angus watched, spellbound, as Black verged on failure. He seemed in pretty good shape for his age. He knocked off the run in the required time and did twenty-nine sit-ups. But on his way to the minimum twenty-six push-ups his arms started to quiver at number eighteen and he slowly squeezed out two more before he went down and couldn't push himself up.

Quisburt hastily rendered judgment. "War is not an old man's game. Leave combat reporting to the young and the fit."

Angus smiled. Maybe his problem was solved: Black would have to go. He wondered how Thea might react to her teammate failing to pass muster, but his hopes were short-lived.

"When the shit hits the fan, it's the running that will matter," said the drill sergeant. "I guess you producers don't really hump much gear anyway, so I'm passing you. I think you'll find that under fire you'll move faster and hump more crap than you ever have in your life."

Some of the other TV types started mocking Black amiably.

"What's the matter, Black, too many push-ups last night?" one guy said, pumping his pelvis. Black grinned.

Angus felt oddly alien. He pushed through the twin glass backdoors of the hotel, still taken aback after all these months by the sharp contrast between the dazzling sunshine outdoors and the tomblike interior of the Dhahran Palace. Even with all the reporters milling there waiting to be mobilized, the hotel felt like a rest house on the River Styx. Busy, certainly, but somehow lifeless.

As he headed for the stairs, Angus caught sight of Thea and Wanda wrapped in an urgent conversation with Brandt and a Saudi man at the far end of the reception desk. Angus couldn't tell who the Saudi was because his face was blocked by his headdress. As the man turned slightly, Angus realized it was Qusai al-Gabandi. He decided to find out what the peculiar huddle was about, not least because he felt a burning curiosity about how Thea would react to him after the storm of the previous evening.

"So did ya pass?" Wanda asked as Angus approached, putting her hands on her hips.

"Yeah, with flying colors, Wanda. They even told me I should reconsider my life and maybe become a Marine," Angus answered. He hoped she would take the hint that he was lobbying for the pool slot with the Marines expected to land on Kuwait, a prime assignment that would surely go to a senior correspondent like Callahan, or if he didn't snatch it, one of her pets like Vandusen.

Angus shook hands with the two men and smiled uncertainly at Thea before asking, "But what is this little powwow about? Staging another barbecue, Mr. Gabandi?"

After the foreign editor stopped him from doing the supply story, Angus had described for Thea the sleazy scene in Gabandi's basement, skipping the part about the U.S. officer, and he was surprised that she would associate with the guy again.

"No, we need his help with a fatwa," Thea said, looking straight at Angus, all business. Angus wondered to himself why he expected anything different. She had always been like that with him when others were around.

"A religious edict? I did not realize you were a learned Islamic scholar too, Mr. Gabandi," Angus said, trying and failing not to sound overly caustic.

Gabandi laughed. "I am not going to write it myself, Angus, but of course I know many of them. And as I have repeatedly promised Miss Thea, I am always at her service."

"And what sin has Miss Thea committed that she needs absolution from an Islamic sheikh?" Angus asked, tipping his head slightly and holding her eyes until she looked away, deciding that being morose would get him nowhere. "Or perhaps I already know."

Brandt answered, reminding Angus of the scene a few weeks back that they both had witnessed of a Saudi man from the religious affairs table berating two reporters out by the pool. Ever the diplomat, Brandt did not mention any names. The Saudi complained to the head of a local chapter of the Promotion who came to inspect, horrified to find men and women using the pool simultaneously. He ordered the hotel to bar women from the pool. In the ensuing ruckus, Brandt advised the female reporters to wait until the whole thing blew over. But now that they were all trapped in the hotel and everyone had to pass a physical fitness test, the women wanted their access to the pool restored immediately.

"So I called Mr. Gabandi," Thea said, picking up the thread of the story, "and he graciously offered to help us by making sure a large check lands in the hands of the right religious authority, who can issue an edict overruling the Promotion. Isn't that great!"

"It's amazing what a donation to the right mosque or charity can achieve in this country. It's basically the route to whatever decision you need," Gabandi said.

"But are you certain it is going to work, sir?" Wanda asked. "I mean the rules against women seem so strict!"

"The beauty of Islam is that there are so many different texts that practically everything is negotiable," Gabandi said. "Obviously there were no women swimming in Prophet Mohammed's time, but I am sure the sheikhs can find something, perhaps a reference to Aisha, his favorite wife, who led men into battle during the succession wars after his death. They will surely decide that all you women in the media need to use the pool a couple hours a day because you will play a similar, crucial role. I am just guessing, of course; we'll have to leave it up to them."

He then excused himself, turning to Thea and telling her as he left that he would be in touch just as soon as the deal was struck.

After he exited the revolving front door, Wanda let out a yelp of delight and both Brandt and Thea grinned. Angus alone was perturbed. He realized he probably shouldn't start, but he did anyway. "Honestly, though, why stoop to their level, to bribes and religious chicanery?" he said, frowning. "Why not just force open the pool because it is the right thing to do. How are they going to react, kick all the foreign women reporters out of the country? It's not like they can treat you guys like pariahs like those unfortunate Saudi women drivers. By doing it their way you are becoming complicit in the system."

Both Thea and Wanda scowled and Angus sensed his chances for a slot on the Marine pool fade even further.

"Oh Angus, as if we could," Thea shot back, looking annoyed. "You can be so exasperatingly moral. It's all just Saudi bullshit and if that is what it takes to get things done, so be it. It's just the fucking swimming pool we are talking about. Right, Wolfgang? Back me up here; tell him he's wrong."

"I really must defer to you Miss Thea, you are precisely right. It is not for nothing that they call you 'the thinking man's sex symbol,'" he said, bowing slightly from the waist in her direction.

"Oh!" Wanda exclaimed, a look between admiration and envy flitting across her pillowy features. Thea giggled with delight, asking, "Who calls me that?"

Thea's reaction evoked for Angus her unwelcome explanation from the previous night about how he had no place in her life, how Black was advising her, helping her create an image on air. Before he could hear the answer, he backed away, saying, "If you will excuse me, I really need to take a shower."

He turned and took the stairs two at a time, trying to lift the heaviness he felt inside.

Once all the PT tests were out of the way and the pool slots distributed, the reporters confronted a further series of hurdles, a sort of bureaucratic assembly line that mirrored some of what soldiers went through.

They were told to gather at a series of long tables outside the JIB one morning to fill out various forms and waivers before collecting the equipment they would need.

The trick question on the forms was about religion. The answer would be stamped on their dog tags and various other documents. A discussion erupted around Angus about what to declare.

A young WBC producer asked loudly, "Hey Black, what are you doing about the religion thing? Did you put down Jewish? Should I? I mean if we get captured by the Iraqis or even have a car accident in Saudi, it might not be the greatest label to have hanging around your neck."

"I don't think Christian would do much good either, so I'm cutting to the chase and having my tags stamped 'infidel,'" Vandusen offered. Everyone around the tables laughed.

Wanda, sitting next to Angus, bristled. She was so indignant that she stood up, shaking on her high heels, and launched into a brief, pointed sermon. "I damn well put down Jewish and everyone else who is should too. First of all, there are hundreds of Jewish soldiers in the army defending these Saudis and they damn well better learn to live with it. Secondly, my ancestors didn't suffer through pogroms in Russia and elsewhere for hundreds of years so I could come along one day and deny my faith."

"Imagine. First Queen Esther saved the Jews from the marauding Persians and now Queen Wanda is rescuing us from these brutish Arabs," Black gibed.

"Damn you Black, you would probably put down Muslim if you thought it might get you a story," Wanda shot back. "This is no time to be a self-hating Jew."

"I'm not a self-hating Jew, Wanda, just not a self-advertising one. Hmm, Muslim. I hadn't really considered putting that down, but it's not a terrible idea. Unless, of course, they captured you and suggested you go through the prayers with them. I would get all the bowing wrong and they might behead me for blasphemy."

Just as Angus was about to indulge himself with the image of Black being beheaded, his thoughts were interrupted by Ryan, the WP photographer, sitting right next to him.

Ryan had brightened visibly when the possibility of writing down "Muslim" was first broached, but he rejected the idea. "If you think about it, they treat their own much worse in all these countries than they ever treat outsiders, so it would probably work against you," he said, and everyone nodded.

"Remember if you die on the battlefield, the faith stamped on your dog tags will determine your prayer service," Wanda said, looking around with a stern expression.

"I expect at that point I would be beyond caring," Angus remarked drily.

"I don't think the religion thing is really a problem on this round," Black said. "It looks like the Saudis are pretty much bowing to the Americans about who is working here anyway, and it's not like the Iraqis will be pleasant to anyone captured. To be a little bit safe I'm going to put down 'Lutheran.' Nobody will know what it is."

"You've always taken the easy dodge, Black, ever since Vietnam," Wanda snarled. "You have no scruples."

"One of these years you are going to have to forgive me for never wanting to take you to bed, Wanda," Black said, staring right at her while she reddened and started muttering.

The other reporters looked away, concentrating on the rest of the forms that proved even less inspiring. Each reporter was required to sign a copy of the ground rules, agreeing to a host of limits on what could be reported. Angus had seen the rough draft, but the eleven pages of minutely detailed formal guidelines seemed daunting.

Reporters couldn't interview anyone with the rank of brigadier general or above without prior clearance. It meant if Angus jumped out of a helicopter and found a commanding general standing there, he was not supposed to ask questions. There would be no reporting of religious services. They could not write how many soldiers were in a unit. Any reporting about special operations was specifically forbidden, as were all tactical methods.

The form gave a few examples of tactical information that could not be written about, like the speed or altitude of airplanes. It said you could describe the planes as being "fast" or "slow" and flying either "low" or "high" and that was it. Nothing could be written about what the United States discovered about the Iraqi military—like whether their camouflage was effective.

The list of barred things went on and on, but the one that made Angus cringe was the sweeping limitation on reporting what happened on any battlefield. That included details of any battle damage or casualties. If the Iraqis slammed a chemical weapon into a group of U.S. soldiers, the reporters couldn't really describe it, nor could they write about a ship being sunk by a missile. Casualties were to be generalized as light, moderate or heavy.

Angus could hear muttering about that one. The Washington bureau chiefs had agreed to the Pentagon's demands for these picayune controls, so there was nothing the correspondents could do now. One ground rule even barred reporting the ground rules. "This would identify to the Iraqis and to terrorists the limits of what can be reported," was the explanation on the form.

"I am surprised there isn't a ground rule barring us from reporting the color and texture of the sand we are standing on out in the desert," Angus said to Ryan. "I'll bet those wily Bedouin trackers on the Iraqi side, armed with an image of a few grains of sand, could pinpoint the location of any unit."

"We're in the army now," Ryan sang out as he signed. "We're fucked."

"Don't get me wrong, I wouldn't want to report anything that got a U.S. soldier wounded, much less killed, nor draw fire on my own head," Angus said. "But this seems like we are signing away the right to do our jobs."

"Yeah, I know, all this stuff about our copy and pictures passing through a 'security review' is sugar coating meant to disguise the fact that we are swallowing military censorship," Ryan said. "But they have all the toys and he who owns the toys, makes the rules."

They were interrupted by a grizzled British veteran who had covered Suez and Vietnam and every Third World conflict since for a rival wire service.

"I feel like I am a goddamn government contractor," the guy spat. One front tooth was missing and spittle dribbled onto his gray stubble every time he launched into a tirade. "The line between me and the PK is pretty thin."

"I'm sorry, PK?" Ryan asked.

"The Propaganda Kompanie, the German reporters assigned to glorify the battlefield exploits of the Hun," the guy growled before moving on to pick up his equipment.

Angus looked at the guy and remembered what Thea had said about her own vision of the ghost of future stories. He wondered if he would be rattling around at age sixty, trying to close flak jackets over his paunch and earning a miserable sum with no one around to care whether he made it back or not.

"The sight of that guy is almost enough to make one go into television, grab the money while I still have all my teeth," Angus said.

"I know what you mean," Ryan said. "But remember even by the elastic standards of this profession I think PK over there is a little nutty. Sometimes with these old wire service guys who have never moved on, you get the sense that they want to die in a war. They figured out long ago that bylines don't really mean anything, so it's almost like they want their name on a plaque by the elevator in New York, saying they exited reporting. It's the one route to immortality left."

"A bleak thought," Angus said.

"Yeah, well, while we're in the mood, let's go draw our equipment," Ryan responded.

Once their paperwork was stamped, they proceeded down a long line of large cardboard boxes set up in the Peninsula Ballroom and were handed some forty pounds of battlefield clothing and equipment. Among the things soldiers standing behind the boxes handed Angus was a new heavy-duty chemical weapons suit in forest camouflage and a new set of pills and injections.

"These pills won't do anything, big guy, but eat them anyway when you're told," said the soldier handing them out, next slapping a little olive green canvas sack of syringes on the stack of stuff Angus was holding with both arms. "Remember that a massive jolt of atropine can save you, although it also might kill you," he added, laughing.

"Geez, I appreciate that," Angus said, but the guy had already turned to the next reporter and was repeating the same lines.

The last station along the equipment trail was where you picked up your newly minted dog tags. They listed Angus's name, his news organization, blood type, social security number and religion. He swung the metal chit on a chain around his neck, feeling almost like a soldier despite the white Oxford shirt and thin black fleece he was wearing. But the woman sergeant handing them out advised him to secure them through his boot laces.

"If you do that, even if you get blown to tiny bits, the graves registration guys will probably find your boots, and then they will be able to inform your editor that he can just forget all about that next scoop you promised for the front page," she said, grinning.

Angus, swaying a little from the load of equipment in his arms, stepped off to one side to try it all on, to make sure it fit. The entire third floor was crowded with the 120 or so correspondents and cameramen who had been assigned to combat pools, gradually transforming themselves from civilians into something resembling soldiers.

Angus and Ryan were standing near the television sets, and as they were taking the plastic wrapping off their equipment, a report came on about a speech Saddam had made the night before, yet another tirade against the infidel invaders expected to force their way into Kuwait within days.

"The great duel, the mother of all battles between victorious right and the evil certain to be defeated will begin soon, God willing. Death is better than the humiliation that comes with the subordination to the foreigner. The blood of our martyrs will burn the invaders or they will all drown, choking, floundering in a sea of American blood, pleading for mercy that will not come."

As with most broadcasts from Iraq, the flamboyant rhetoric—not merely that favorite phrase "mother of all battles"—provoked peals of laughter.

"One thing about Mr. Moustache, he really knows how to turn a phrase," Ryan said.

"Yeah," Angus responded, half listening.

He had finished donning his uniform and at that moment slapped his new Kevlar helmet onto his head with both hands, a strange tremor running down through his body when he did it, like he really had become a soldier. He felt he had physically removed himself from the realm of being an independent observer, signed his life away to God knows what. When he was little, imagining himself slipping into local garb like Kipling's Kim to pass unnoticed among the native population, he had never conjured himself up as G.I. Joe. Was this anything remotely similar?

Colonel Fletcher was walking past and must have caught the look on Angus's face as he strapped his helmet under his chin, because the officer stopped and inspected him up and down.

"Well Dalziel, you could pass for the real deal. That helmet really brings it all home, doesn't it? You know it is serious when you put that on," the colonel said in an avuncular tone.

"I thought I was the only one feeling that," said Angus, sweeping his hand across the mob of other reporters. Many of the TV correspondents had ordered their associate producers to bring them mirrors and were admiring themselves. "Everyone around me seems ready to stagger out onto some fashion catwalk."

"That will all change. Once you get out of this hotel in this stuff, everyone will feel different, more sober, more serious."

"I'm not so sure. They'll probably compete over who has the hippest accessories."

Fletcher laughed. "Anyhow, don't worry about it. The novelty will wear off, you'll get used to it," he said, moving away.

After he was gone, Angus caught a brief glimpse through the crowd of Black holding up a mirror so Thea could look at herself.

Long before, when he had imagined this moment, he thought he would draw courage and comfort from doing what the soldiers did—lodging a pair of Thea's panties in the interior webbing of his helmet.

She had laughed uproariously when they returned from a desert trip and he confessed to her how the men had been spying on her and the other women in the showers. He also described how he discovered that soldiers stuffed lingerie up into their helmets for good luck. She plucked a pair of his boxers stamped with little tropical fish off the permanent stack of clean laundry on his chair and vowed to implant them in her helmet. Then she stripped off her jeans and handed him a confection of peach-colored lace.

That had been one of their best afternoons, one of those treasured moments when Angus felt like he had life, that what they did every day was normal. He had used the panties in the various helmets the WP kept for its reporters to wear on maneuvers, carefully removing them each time. After he learned about Black, when he saw her helmet in her bedroom he speculated whether she had grabbed a pair of his underwear too, switching pairs back and forth as she changed beds. He had resisted the temptation to check.

Evidently using hers was no longer an option for Angus. He didn't know the etiquette for retired fetishes. Should they be burned? It was not the kind of question he could ask Colonel Fletcher or the others. He'd have to wait until he was interviewing some soldier who had received a "Dear Joe" letter. Then he kicked himself for being so pessimistic. He would win her back and the peach panties could go back where they belonged, lodged inside his very own helmet.

Chapter Nineteen

THEA, assigned to a press pool covering an aircraft carrier in the Gulf, departed the hotel early on January 15, the morning of the U.N. deadline. Anticipating war, the JIB mustered all pool reporters well before dawn by telephoning their rooms. There was no prior warning.

Angus awoke to the commotion caused by correspondents lurching down the hallway, wrestling with unfamiliar helmets and flak jackets and web belts, their attempts to quell their fears audible in their strained voices. He wouldn't be leaving the hotel immediately, having been assigned to a rapid reaction pool. He hoped it meant missile attacks and other major events. But their role remained uncomfortably nebulous.

Someone dropped a helmet against his door with a resounding thud. The guy retrieving it launched into loud rant about the lack of room service, not bothering to lower his voice despite the hour.

"Goddammit. I need some coffee. Right after the wakeup call I tried to get room service but there was no answer. How are we expected to go to war if we can't get a decent cup of coffee? This sucks. I hope one of the associate producers bought a cappuccino machine for the office or I'm going to fry all their little asses."

Angus groaned. He was fully awake now. TV nitwit, he thought. He knew he might as well get used to it. Once the war erupted, the place would be humming twenty-four hours a day. He stumbled out of bed, thinking maybe he could talk to Thea before she left. There was no telling when they might be in the same place again.

The scene downstairs was not what he anticipated. He had conjured up a gathering of hardy battle correspondents modeled on Ernie Pyle, men sporting dirty, rumpled fatigues, a two-day growth of beard and a dangling cigarette like the famous World War II reporter.

Instead, the lobby of the Dhahran Palace Hotel looked more like a Japanese tour company gone haywire. Roughly ten pools, or one hundred reporters, were departing simultaneously. The JIB escorts carried long skinny sticks with their pool number tacked on them, waving the numbers in the air at various points in the lobby in the vain hope that everyone would line up and march out to the buses idling in the driveway.

No one was lining up. Everyone drifted over to the Dunes to rattle the doors, expecting a Filipino staffer to materialize with a coffee pot.

Angus didn't see Thea at first. Most reporters were wearing their helmets and lumpy chemical suits, making it hard to distinguish one from another. He wondered if she might have changed her mind and was staying.

It was too early in the morning for the brown marble fountain near the entrance to be switched on. Without the distraction, Angus noticed for the first time that the large urns stamped with Arabesques were actually tin, their surfaces painted a dull gold to look like brass. Here and there a chip of silver showed through. He hadn't really thought about them before, but suddenly plastic palms and phony urns for a desert press corps posing as artificial soldiers seemed entirely appropriate. He quickly admonished himself. This was the wrong moment to turn bitter. The war was finally starting, the day he and everyone else had been waiting for all these months had come. He shouldn't let what was happening with Thea color the whole experience.

Thea's accent tended to carry, so Angus finally located her amid a knot of CBN reporters and cameramen off to one side, partly obscured by piles of their gear. On the brown marble wall behind them hung a row of large woven portraits of the late King Abdel Aziz, the current king, Fahd, and Crown Prince Abdullah. Pictures of the three were mandatory in every hotel lobby, in fact every public building, but the Dhahran Palace had opted for a remarkably hideous set done as carpets. The men's headdresses, flaring hooked noses and goatees were executed in thick pile in various shades of red, tan and black.

Angus walked up behind Thea and squeezed her shoulder, half wishing that he could stroke her butt instead. She tipped her head to the side, sighed and said, "Good morning Angus," before turning around and smiling at him.

"How are you, Thea? Marching as to war?" he asked.

She giggled. "I feel more like a kid in a snowsuit."

"You don't seem like one, you seem…," he started, but she cut him off, giving him a quick look and glancing toward her colleagues before changing the subject.

"You don't come bearing coffee, do you? You would think that sorry JIB might arrange morning coffee for their traveling clientele."

"I have some up in my room," Angus said, forcing himself to sound playful and weighing how he would explain the absence of coffee once they got there. "Want to go?"

She held his eyes for a minute before taking the easy out. "I'd love to, Angus, but you know we might leave any second now. Then again, we could be here all morning. What are you doing gadding about at this hour anyway? Come to absorb the aura of real reporters before you are stuck with the company of your fellow hotel warriors?"

He hadn't spoken to her at any length since New Year's and considered whether this was their future—empty banter. He didn't relish the thought, but then again plunging into a serious exchange as she was about to depart for the war seemed excessively melodramatic.

[257]

"I actually feel like a mental patient watching my fellow inmates bust lose," Angus said and Thea laughed. He basically said anything that came to his head that was as far removed as possible from a conversation about the two of them, speculating aloud about problems like filing at sea, until finally he couldn't help himself: "Surely I am not the lone fan among your legions coming to bid you adieu?"

"Who else wou...oh you mean Aaron," she said, stepping away from the other CBN staffers. "You must be kidding, a mighty television bureau chief emerging from bed at this hour for anything short of nuclear war?"

Angus winced. He wondered if she had just risen from the same bed.

"Did you tell him?"

"Tell him what?"

"About us."

"What us? There isn't any us anymore, Angus, so of course I didn't tell him and please don't you either," she said, reaching up out of habit to toy with his shirt button. He let her at first but then lightly pushed her hand away.

She looked up at him. "Promise me you won't engage in any kind of stupid mountain goat head-butting either. I am sorry that you and I didn't work, but don't try to wreck my life as a consequence."

She went on, "I have broken maybe ten hearts in my life, Angus, and turned down at least three marriage proposals. I told myself before this war started that I wasn't going to live that way anymore, that I was only going to chase the one that felt real, felt big. You came along—cute, funny, talented and I let myself do it. 'Why not?' I said. But it was wrong. It was fun, comfortable, but it wasn't big. Still, I don't think I've broken your heart. But if I did, it's only because something overwhelming came along."

Angus felt a sudden drift, like a giant glacier shifting, creating a crack that might one day prove unbridgeable. He remembered the grizzled wire service reporter stumbling about the day before and brooded again if that was where he was headed. If Thea was aware of his volatile mood, she gave no sign, still talking.

"You'll mock me when I tell you I was reading a magazine about dating in New York which said women usually hold out until the third date before sleeping with a guy. Third date! I'm lucky if I get three nights in a row with any guy. Look at us. We've been in the same country for months and still not managed to spend much time together."

Angus was perplexed. Was she blaming him somehow? She seemed to sense his thought.

"It's not your fault, Angus. Our life is so disjointed. So many of my days are peopled with passing friends. I am not even sure they can be called friends. Sure we spend a lot of time with Lydia or Vining or even Quisburt, and they can all be charming in their weird way.

"We are forced together by necessity and when the necessity wanes, so do we. Once the stories are filed, once the headlines diminish, we all go our separate ways until the next catastrophe. I just can't bear it; it is all too fleeting. I have to find continuity." She quieted for a few seconds, looked away, then looked right at him. "As to your first question, I didn't tell Black about you because I want him to trust me."

"You mean you are being honest with me about being dishonest with Black—have I got that right?" Angus said, still hoping to find a chink that Thea was not confessing.

"Maybe I am deluding myself that I can change him, that he wants me enough to stop being the patron saint of wandering mates. But he promised me he will. I want to give it a chance, Angus, so please don't do anything angry or confrontational or stupid. Let this be our secret, okay?"

Angus didn't know how to respond. He was a little stunned that it all came pouring out of her given the surroundings and he felt even more constrained that he couldn't touch her.

"Pretty long speech for a woman who says she is coffee deprived," he said, beginning to wish he had stayed in bed. But Thea seemed to labor to explain why she wanted Black. She was rationalizing, Angus felt, so he decided to make one more appeal before she walked out of the hotel and possibly out of his life.

"Despite what you said, Thea, I want you to know that I adore you and every moment with you in a way that Aaron Black never will. Maybe that sounds corny, perhaps even insincere considering that I never really said it clearly before. But I want you to think about that while you are on that aircraft carrier and know that when you return I will still be here fighting to get you back."

An affectionate look crept across her face and she was about to interrupt him when Angus held up his hand and continued, "Before you even suggest it, no, I don't want to be friends. It would be too frustrating.

"What we had was more than just staving off the lurking solitude of another damn hotel—we laugh at the same things, we like the same food, we have great sex, I thought we had a similar sense of integrity, although I am not quite sure about that anymore.

"Oh yeah, plus we both hate sleeping with the air conditioner on," he said, feeling that he had to lighten the tone. "A love of the same climate is hugely important."

Thea frowned and was about to say something when a JIB guy by the door started shouting through a megaphone for everyone to board the buses. There was a scramble for gear and too many reporters bending underneath new backpacks tried to squeeze themselves out the revolving doors at once, prompting a large scrum and widespread swearing.

"I have to go, Angus," Thea said, looking at him, holding his stare for a minute and then looking around for her gear.

"I'll be waiting."

"Once this thing gets started you'll forget all about me."

"No I won't. Not possible," he said, shaking his head and realizing that it was the wrong moment to say anything else. "C'mon, you wouldn't want to be late for war," he added, lifting her backpack so she could slip her arms into it.

Her camerawoman, standing nearby, quipped that Angus had all the makings of an associate producer in training.

To try to dissipate the gloom that descended as he watched Thea turn and slowly walk away, Angus pulled out a notebook and started interviewing departing reporters.

He approached a bleached blonde who wrote a column for a paper in Texas somewhere, likely Dallas. The woman was infamous. Angus overheard her once in the Dunes describing a column she had filed detailing the fact that her favorite brand of enchilada sauce was not available in the Saudi version of Safeway. She asked her desk to send some, claiming she couldn't write without eating the stuff first.

"How about a quick synopsis of your feelings for posterity?" Angus asked. He hated interviewing other reporters and a little sarcasm inevitably crept into the questions.

"It's really scary now," she said, opening her blue eyes wide. Angus wasn't sure whether she was putting him on.

"I'm determined to get this whole warrior thing down," she went on. "I even tried to do a few push-ups when I got out of bed this morning. I did three but I couldn't concentrate because I was thinking about all the stuff I needed to pack.

"At the moment I'm a little frustrated because I can't even get my stupid chin strap fastened and even if I could the helmet smushes my bangs. Every time I try to adjust the thing one of my earrings falls out. I'm not sure I'm ready to go to war."

Angus was grinning as he wrote and glanced up expecting to find her laughing, but she looked deadly serious. She even lifted the helmet to show him her battered bangs.

Angus sighed, flipping his notebook shut as the last line of departing reporters threaded its way out the revolving doors. He wished that he was in a country where he could get a stiff Bloody Mary.

The lights inside the Dunes finally snapped on. A big plate of scrambled eggs would have to do.

Chapter Twenty

AROUND 2:00 A.M. on the morning of January 17, the entire Dhahran Palace trembled and the windows shook in their frames as wave after wave of jet fighters hurtled into the night sky. The world outside became one continuous roar.

Angus turned on the television in the WP suite and watched the first live reports from Baghdad, tinted acid green by the eerie light of cameras operating with night vision equipment. On screen, bombs plummeted down—long sequences of menacing black dashes answered by extended fusillades of ineffective antiaircraft fire that erupted like popcorn in emerald, incandescent bursts.

Angus walked out of the WP suite, took one look at the mob of three hundred reporters milling outside the military press office and decided against joining it. The third floor, the war's great information bazaar, was in turmoil, clearly not working as envisioned. Every time an officer emerged from the JIB the journalists would quiet and press forward, straining not to miss a single historic crumb. From their solemn looks, Angus surmised that they were all convinced they were positioned in exactly the right spot to file an exhilarating, perhaps prize-winning description of the outbreak of what was being billed as the biggest conflict since World War II.

The officer invariably ignored all questions, instead barking, "Dictation, dictation, I need someone to take dictation from a reporter in the field." All the reporters recoiled, horrified at the idea that their war might start with such a menial task, a real memoir killer. Lacking a volunteer, the officer latched onto the shirt of the first reporter within range and hauled him bodily into the JIB, despite sputtering protests.

The clamor began anew when the dictation was over and the report printed and xeroxed. The crowd surged forward like fledglings waiting for their mother to shove food down their gullets.

Angus felt downright queasy reading the first report. It was a fine piece of color reporting, all about the soldiers anticipating the fighting. The problem was that the anticipation was months old. They had been doing nothing but anticipating since August. Now that the war had started, where were the reports of what the soldiers were doing?

Worse, at that point the soldiers in the desert were a mere sideshow. What the correspondents really wanted to know was how successful the air raids were, what was targeted, whether any allied pilots were shot down and the nature of any Iraqi counterattacks. Each time a volley of questions erupted from the mob of reporters, it was met by an unquotable shrug from the JIB officers.

NBC News had shipped its star Pentagon reporter to Dhahran aboard a special, last-minute flight. The guy was known for two things. Behind his back, his colleagues made fun of his remarkably inanimate, cinnamon-colored toupee. But he was famous for being able to project a question fifty yards. No matter how far official Washington tried to hold back the press, the lobbed question was always loud enough that ignoring him made them look intimidated.

Angus, standing all the way across the third floor, could hear the veteran newsman seething. "I ask them for news of the war and they tell me to contact the Pentagon!" he bellowed. "What the hell did I fly 7,000 miles for if all the news is back in Washington? They can't even tell me whether the drizzle falling here is also falling in Iraq. Tom Brokaw will ask me what I know about that and about the oil fires that Saddam's forces ignited in Kuwait—news reported on Radio Baghdad—and guess what I will have to tell him? 'Tom, I don't know a thing.'"

The shouting and complaining was abruptly drowned out by a deafening squawk, as if a gaggle of panicky geese had been unleashed somewhere in the hotel.

It took the mob of reporters outside the JIB a minute to grasp that the horrible racket was the hotel's air raid alarm. Suddenly they had to think about survival.

Major Fergus K.W. Ramsden, a ramrod straight, fifty-two-year-old ex–Special Forces type the hotel manager had imported from Britain as the security consultant for the war, goaded them along. He stood in the hotel's central well with his megaphone on full blast, braying over and over again, "This is a gas warning. Please put on your gas masks. Please move calmly down to the shelter."

The horde descended to the basement, unable to move at speed because the entire hotel went simultaneously. One of the television crews created a bottleneck by standing on the landing just before the entrance to the bomb shelter, obstructing the stairs, until they were shoved aside by an ashen-faced reporter who snapped at them, "Find another place to get your fucking footage."

Once inside the sepulchral shelter, nobody knew what to do. They were all standing around, craning their necks to look for telephones to call their desks to explain why they weren't filing or answering the phones upstairs.

The shelter consisted of the hotel kitchen, the employee dining room, a food preparation room and a storage room. Dozens of cases of bottled water were stacked in every corner and large Persian carpets covered the floors. The walls, white tiles, reflected a faint light in the otherwise darkened rooms.

With everyone standing around in their odd assortment of clothes and gas masks, combined with the flashlight beams bouncing off the tiles at crazy angles, the whole place seemed to Angus like an intergalactic disco. It was the Star Wars bar with strobe lights and no alcohol.

Water and free cookies were on offer from a table the hotel had set up in one corner. Some Kuwaitis camped in front of it, complaining.

"Orange juice!" they snapped at the Filipino waiter. "And fresh! Nothing from the carton."

The polite Filipino made no headway trying to explain they were in the midst of an air raid.

"What kind of second-class hotel is this?" one Kuwaiti raged. "Why don't you have fresh juice?"

The Kuwaitis created such a ruckus that Brandt had to intervene, placating them by promising them fresh juice for free in the Dunes as soon as the air raid was over. In the meantime would they please find a comfortable place to sit along the walls.

Angus was debating whether to escape the hot, stuffy basement and head to the roof to watch any missiles falling, but Ramsden made a great production of sealing the shelter. He turned from the doors transformed into a petty despot, lifting the megaphone and snarling through his gas mask in a voice heard through all four rooms: "Sit down or you will be tried!"

Everyone slowly pressed themselves up against the walls and groped downward in the half light. Angus found himself next to Hawxhurst and tried to whisper to him, although it was difficult through the air filter.

"Maybe if we were court-martialed they would punish us by exiling us upstairs, where at least we might escape this bedlam and find out what is happening."

Ramsden must have overheard because he started to proclaim, "Remember there will be no exit. We must maintain the integrity of the seal."

"'The integrity of the seal!' We've got to impress Quisburt with that one," Angus muttered.

The basement grew increasingly stuffy as the minutes clicked past.

The hotel's air conditioning system had been switched off to prevent the circulation of chemical agents. Perspiration soaked the hair and crept down the faces and necks of everyone wearing gas masks and they were all tense, quietly bracing for whatever came next.

"I wish we were upstairs watching TV so we could find out what is happening to us," someone said loudly.

"I will tell you what is happening to us," Angus said. "We are sitting in the basement hoping we don't get blown to flinders by an incoming Scud."

"I know, but it's better on TV," the other guy said. "It seems more real."

"I hope this is about as real as it ever gets," Angus answered.

He watched in stupefaction as the Filipino cooks, Pakistani cleaning staff and other hotel workers pulled either paper surgical masks or black plastic garbage bags over their heads, their eyes wide with fear. It was like encountering a homeless person in New York City—wasn't there someone to provide for these people who lived around you all day? Some of the Saudis too lacked masks, but that turned out to be a different story.

"I put my trust in my God and I am not afraid," said one of the Saudis when Hawxhurst asked him about it. "There is no need for masks. If God decides this is the moment, then I have no choice."

Angus noticed that Lydia, sitting opposite him, had no mask either and had broken into her neighbor's chemical agent kit. She was gobbling the white antidote pills meant to be taken daily for twenty-one days as if they were candy. Lydia was wearing pink Capri pants and a mauve long-sleeve T-shirt. Ramsden materialized from somewhere and wrapped black plastic garbage bags around her bare ankles.

"There is still the possibility of gas," he intoned several times through his megaphone.

Lydia began to cry.

"I'm feeling fucking naked here," said a women from the *Los Angeles Times* wearing a paper mask, commiserating. "I bitched at the foreign editor today about not getting us chemical suits in time for the war and do you know what he said? He said confidential Pentagon sources were assuring them that Saddam would not use chemical weapons so there was no need to panic. That made me feel just great because it was probably those same fucking bright-eyed, bushy-tailed confidential Pentagon yahoos who predicted six months ago that Saddam wouldn't invade Kuwait."

"I can top that," Vandusen shouted from his mask. "Our dingbat foreign editor suggested that we share the suits because they cost so much."

"What did you do?" asked Lydia, sniffling.

"I wrote back and said that although I've lost fifteen pounds since the invasion, I didn't relish trying to get the zipper of a suit closed around two people if the sky was raining chemicals. The shmuck finally relented."

"You would think the guy had never been in a war," Lydia remarked.

"That's the problem," Vandusen said. "He hasn't."

There was radio reception in the shelter, and just then the news announcer said that previous reports of an air raid against Israel had proved to be a false alarm. There was no word of any attack against Saudi Arabia, and several reporters realized suddenly that an attack against the kingdom had never been mentioned, prompting them to pepper Ramsden with exasperated questions.

"Hey Ramsden, are you sure there was an air raid?" the NBC Pentagon reporter wanted to know, his singular voice not muffled by his mask.

"There is still the possibility of gas," Ramsden chanted by way of a response, walking around the basement with a little handheld chemical agent monitor clicking away in his hands. The noise was like one of those blue outdoor lights that zaps bugs in summer and was putting everyone even more on edge because they didn't know whether the tempo of the beeping signaled a higher or lower likelihood of gas.

Then the hotel manager started circulating, asking everyone if they were comfortable.

"Hey Brandt," another voice called out through a gas mask, "who signaled this air raid anyway? Did the Saudis tell you to turn on the alert or the Americans?"

It was Black's voice. Weird, Angus thought, for the two of them to be jammed into the same basement a few yards apart while Thea was off on a ship in the Gulf. He didn't have time to dwell on it though, because the manager sheepishly admitted that neither the Saudi civil defense nor the U.S. military had issued a warning.

Brandt said that he and Ramsden were sitting in his office drinking coffee and discussing whether the hotel was ready for an air raid. The television was tuned to CBN, which interrupted its newscast to say that Israel had just declared an air raid warning. Ramsden instantly assumed that if Iraq was firing toward Israel, it was firing in all directions and urged the hotel manager to hit the alarm.

"Fucking great, a TV air raid for a TV war," Hawxhurst groused. The reporters began peeling off their masks as word spread. Ramsden, sensing mutiny, opened the sealed doors and the crowd edged back upstairs.

Soon afterward, a bellhop in a red fez began circulating with one of those chalkboards on a stick with a little bell attached, the contraption used to page people in the lobby and the restaurants. The large white capital letters on the chalkboard read, "RAPID REACTION POOL 4." The bellhop trilled his little bell as he walked toward the Dunes.

Angus slowly wandered back up to the JIB to find out if anything else was developing and came across a small knot of network bureau chiefs, including Black, gathered around Colonel Fletcher, arguing about broadcasting live from the roof for the first real air raid, despite the threat of chemical weapons.

"Okay," an exasperated colonel finally relented. "You reporters will be our coal mine canaries. We'll run a cable for television down into the basement and when we see you guys foaming at the mouth and collapsing, we'll know the danger is for real."

Angus went back to the bureau and announced he was volunteering to do the same thing, telephoning the WP radio desk in New York. He had barely retrieved his chemical suit from his room when the bureau suddenly echoed with the alarming music a local TV station used to signal an air raid.

It was a few bars from de Falla's "El Amor Brujo," which sounded like a flamenco dancer pounding across a stage. The staccato notes were at once deafening and riveting, jangling the nerves of anyone within earshot.

The notes were fading when the voice of Ramsden again erupted from his megaphone in the lobby. "This is a real air raid," he trumpeted. Realizing that he was getting a sluggish reaction after the previous false alarm, he stepped up the warning level. He sent hotel waiters running from room to room along all the corridors, slapping every door with their open palms and crying, "Scuds! Scuds!"

That triggered the flood again.

Angus donned his full chemical suit in the WP bureau, working under the emergency light beams because the hotel doused the electricity once more. Vandusen hung around the office offering to help, but Angus sensed the guy was hoping he would bail out.

"You sure you want to do this?" Vandusen kept asking.

"Vandusen, you have a wife, maybe kids someday soon. It doesn't matter if I pollute my DNA with a little mustard gas, but you have more important concerns."

Vandusen laughed and the two of them headed out of the bureau. Lydia walked past, this time carrying her gas mask and dressed in her chemical weapons suit. "I don't know how many more of these I can take tonight. I think I would rather stay in my room," she said before disappearing down the stairs.

The hotel was almost deserted, although in the WBC bureau near the top of the stairs, a few television technicians in their gas masks and protective suits were huddled around a television monitor, watching the Buffalo Bills batter the Los Angeles Raiders in a playoff game. The two reporters walked downstairs together.

A few technicians in similar garb were also watching the game in the ABC studios on the second floor.

Vandusen and Angus moved through a fire door onto the back white marble stairs. While Vandusen descended toward the basement with half a dozen other stragglers, Angus stepped outside.

Chapter Twenty-One

ANGUS had been too caught up in his deadlines to venture outside much, so the hubbub startled him.

The roof of a one-story rear hotel wing that housed administrative offices had been transformed into a television shantytown, densely packed with satellite transmission dishes, klieg lights, generators, television monitors, computers and nylon tents crammed with beeping electronic equipment. Thick braids of coiled wire ran everywhere like the umbilical cord of an unseen giant.

The various TV networks had built raised wooden platforms, with roughly the proportions of a king-size mattress, to serve as alfresco studios. Plywood walls on two sides plus a roof provided a little shelter from the whipping sand or occasional light rain. Every platform sported a couple of comfy chairs for the correspondents and at least one palm tree in a brass pot.

Angus couldn't tell if the plants were real or not, but he knew instantly why the hotel staff called the place Little Hollywood. It looked more like a series of cheery living rooms than a combat zone, with woven Bedouin rugs nailed to the walls and the chairs invariably covered in a kilim pattern. The decor screamed "Middle East!" in case any viewer was uncertain about the war's location.

Sand surrounded two of the platforms. Angus figured the insta-dunes had been lugged up onto the roof so when the camera pulled back, the correspondents seemed to be sitting in the desert.

It was hard to see across the roof because of a steady drizzle, although each broadcast platform was bathed in light. They were strangely silent, not just because of the potential danger but because the networks were venturing into the unknown. No one had ever done live war broadcasts before, the portable equipment being relatively new.

Angus walked over to an area where the print news organizations had set up their phones, well away from the narrow, heavily trafficked pathways between the broadcast booths. The print area was a forest of small satellite dishes, but he quickly located one bearing the round, dark green WP logo.

The best technology of 1990 had whittled the apparatus down to a fat, ninety-pound suitcase with the unlikely name of the Ultra-lite. Once opened, its most visible component was the mesh satellite dish—which looked like a small beach umbrella blown out in a windstorm. The dish was attached to a three-foot pole planted in the middle of the case.

Angus picked up the thick dialing pad. The numbers glowed yellow. He opened his notebook and followed the directions. He hoped the call to WP Radio would go through on the first try because the drizzle made the inky instructions bleed. He was thankful for the warmth of his heavy charcoal chemical suit, but he found the thick rubber gloves too clumsy for dialing and removed them.

The radio news desk in New York rang busy.

"Fuck," he said.

He hit redial, praying that Saddam would hold off the missiles until WP answered. The call failed a second time and then a third, but Angus stayed in a crouch, punching redial and watching the manic broadcast activity.

At ABC, Spencer Carr was holding up a mirror, testing different looks. He turned the collar on his leather bomber jacket up and down and then up again, tousling his shoulder-length, curly blond hair to make it sit differently. The producer kept telling him to put on a gas mask but Carr argued that it would make his hair look weird on air if he took it off later.

"I mean, I know it's an air raid and everything, but if my hair is weird then everyone will focus on that," he whined.

The ABC cameraman rolled his eyes and said, "Plus if your hair was squashed you would make a fairly ugly corpse." Carr scowled and went back to the mirror.

Angus, still having no luck, envied the networks their ability to talk via their satellite links. He hit redial again and while the telephone emitted its series of beeps like erratic musical scales, he suddenly realized that Black might also be on the roof.

WBC's broadcast booth sat closest to the glass door that led into the hotel stairs. Peering through the drizzle, Angus discovered Black was there, barking orders. As he watched, a Marine in full battle regalia stepped through the doorway. The soldier urged Black to evacuate the roof and bring the other network guys along.

"We're not going anywhere," Black said, crossing his arms over his chest. A day's growth of beard shadowed his face and he was wearing a bright white shirt. From a distance his face was darkened while his shirt glowed, which gave Angus the eerie feeling of watching a headless body speak.

"This could be extremely dangerous," the Marine argued. "None of y'all are wearing protection and there could be gas all over the place."

Angus saw the cameraman, the soundman and the correspondent exchange nervous glances behind Black. The cameraman crooked his head toward the door and raised an eyebrow as if to say maybe they should go indoors. The soundman shrugged and nodded toward Black, who was saying to the Marine, "Look, I know you're concerned for our safety, but this is what we do: we broadcast. We always broadcast."

Black must have sensed the edgy stirring behind him because he turned to his crew.

"You yellow?" he asked the cameraman. The guy, cowed, said no, and the soundman also shook his head. Black asked the same thing of the correspondent, a pretty woman with long auburn hair named Larissa Tyler. She looked like she wanted to argue but instead shrugged and said, "Sure, I'll be a hero."

The Marine made one last attempt. "I know I can't order y'all around, but all I'm saying is there could be twenty dead bodies out here in about five minutes," he said, his eyes surveying the other broadcast booths before he pivoted and disappeared inside the hotel.

The collar of Larissa's blue-striped shirt was visibly torn. "I've got to change before we go live," she said. "When the alarm sounded I stood up a little too quickly and my shoulder caught the corner of one of those damn plywood desktops."

Larissa was holding another shirt in her hands. She whipped the torn shirt over her head and was suddenly standing on the well-lit WBC platform wearing a satin lavender bra. Angus could see a reddish scratch and slight bruise on her lightly freckled shoulder.

"Oooohhh does that hurt?" Black asked, stepping up onto the lighted platform and standing next to her. He ran his fingers along the bruise and then slid his hand down toward her breast.

"Don't touch me Black, you aging pervert," Larissa said sharply, slapping his hand away. "I am not one of your news bimbos. Christ, there's a war on."

"Isn't it exciting?" Black answered.

Angus was riveted, finding the little drama revealing. Black's mind was evidently not quite as focused on Thea as she wanted to believe.

Before Angus could further mull over how he might exploit Black's peccadilloes, a vicious explosion split the night sky in half. The powerful detonation jangled the roots of his teeth and made the entire hotel quiver.

Angus, who had no idea what was happening, turned his head rapidly from side to side trying to locate the explosion. In the small-scale guer-rilla battles he had covered previously, it took practice before anyone could distinguish between the noise made by incoming versus outgoing artillery. Smaller ordnance was sometimes difficult to distinguish from a car door slamming. But this was stupendous.

Immediately afterward, a red line arced across the sky. Angus realized that the noise had come from a Patriot antimissile missile fired from the base next door. Everyone had been waiting for one of those to go off. The arc of the thing terminated with another eruption in the sky, the giant echoing boom caused by a Scud missile being demolished. The hotel rattled again and in the distance, air raid sirens shrieked to life across Dhahran.

Angus closed his eyes in supplication and hit redial. It didn't go through. He opened his eyes, watching controlled pandemonium unroll on the broadcast side of the roof. NBC evidently lost its line to New York.

"What the fuck happened?" the producer yelled. "We can still hear them, but they can't hear us. They just said on air that the line to Dhahran went dead, not a good sign. Oh Christ I hope my mother isn't listening. Everyone will think we're dead."

The bang and whoosh sequence happened again—a second Patriot. Angus was glad to find that his nerves remained steady. The bangs made his adrenaline work overtime and his hands were shaking, yet he felt no desire to escape the roof.

He poked the redial button furiously but the call stubbornly refused to connect. "Come on, come on," he said to himself. "Goddammit, I am not going to die in a missile attack without even filing a story. "

Angus took solace from the fact that the networks weren't doing much better.

He gathered that ABC Sports was reluctant to let the news division cut in because the Buffalo Bills were still trouncing the L.A. Raiders in the Super Bowl playoff.

Spencer Carr was frantically waving his hands and a gas mask at the camera in case anyone in New York could see him, screaming, "Get us on camera! This is not a drill, New York. Get us up in audio. Hello New York. This is Saudi Arabia. *This is not a drill!* Let's go! Let's *go!* We're firing Patriots, we've got flares and we've got sirens. Let's go live."

The percussion from another Patriot rent the sky and Carr's body jerked involuntarily. That explosion was enough to convince New York, but they switched to Saudi Arabia so fast that Carr was standing with his back to the camera and twirling his gas mask, waiting to see the Scud explode as the ABC producer yelled, "You're on, you're on!"

Carr pirouetted quickly, explaining that he was standing underneath a Scud attack and pointing toward the glowing red arc that the Patriot missile drew across the sky. "Peter, we are balanced out here on the edge of a knife," he said.

Angus groaned, hoping he could avoid tainting his remarks with self-aggrandizing drama once he got through. The correspondent was pointing upward and saying that the midair explosion they heard was the sound of a Scud missile being blown apart.

"We heard a loud boom, the report from a firing of a Patriot antimissile missile. Then sirens. We perceived that we were under our first intense air raid. Tonight there have been four different Patriot launchings and all in different directions. This last one seemed to hug the earth and intercept a rocket right behind us, very close to our position here. Others went off and seemed to get lost in the sky. We haven't heard any incoming and of course the explosive power of these Scuds carrying a 1,000- or 2,000-pound warhead is great. There is no evidence yet that any of these rockets can carry a chemical charge."

Angus was sure viewers would be spellbound by the drama. Carr's head twitched from side to side and he interrupted himself every few sentences to point at a minuscule dot of light in the clouds that he thought might be the exhaust of a yet another Patriot.

Angus was appalled by what happened next.

Carr turned to the camera and said, "That last one looked like it was

about two miles down range, two miles east of us. The Iraqis are probably aiming for the main air base next door or maybe even this hotel, but
the Scud has a notoriously crude guidance system."

Great, Angus thought. It's bad enough sitting under attack without
these TV morons calling in the missiles like sports announcers calling
plays. There was no need to act as forward spotters for the Iraqi military,
nor give it ideas about smacking the hotel.

All the correspondents were guilty of the same indiscretion to some
extent, but most weren't as specific as Carr. The drawn look of fear and
uncertainty etched on the correspondents' faces, combined with the
noise of the explosions, was enough to convey what was happening in
Dhahran without being so detailed. Angus hoped Baghdad wasn't adjusting its sights.

He looked at his watch. Although it seemed like the attack started at
least an hour ago, only seven minutes had passed. He punched redial
endlessly to no avail.

Carr suddenly interrupted himself and intoned, "I am being told that
the military guys are putting on their gas masks," which made Angus feel
cold and apprehensive.

From his subsequent remark Angus surmised that Carr's anchor in
New York asked if maybe he and his crew should head for shelter.

Carr puffed out his chest and pulled on the collar of his leather
jacket. "In all likelihood that would be a wise course of action if we were
not more concerned with making sure that we are broadcasting to you.
We feel that we should stay at our posts and deal with this as we so often
do in the field, a field always ripe with risks and threats. I must confess
that the advisers in the U.S. and British military are upset, but we have to
do what we have to do."

Angus didn't know which was more nauseating, the air raid or the
arrogance. Carr put on his gas mask and it became harder for Angus to
hear what he was saying.

To his immense relief, Angus finally got a ring. A woman's voice chirped,

"WP Radio Network," but before he could blurt out that he was calling in a Scud attack, the operator said, "Hold, please," and went off the line.

"I don't fucking believe it," Angus muttered.

The operator came back and transferred him to the news producer, who told him that the anchorman was a guy named Robert who would introduce him in fifteen seconds. The producer told Angus that missiles bearing conventional explosives had already hit Israel and asked him to mention that fact as soon as possible in his remarks.

The producer counted down the last seconds, "And in five, four, three, two, one," in the midst of which Angus could hear the anchor saying, "And now we are going live to Dhahran, Saudi Arabia, where a missile attack is under way, for a report from our correspondent Angus Dalziel. Tell us what is happening in Dhahran, Angus."

Angus hated live broadcasts, although he did not stutter and was able to supply trenchant, vivid descriptions. But he did not do it enough to relax; the beats of his heart sounded louder than his voice. Sometimes he forgot to say the anchor's name at the end of his shpiel, the signal that he was finished.

He began by explaining that everyone in Dhahran had been braced for Iraqi retaliation from the moment the first planes launched toward Baghdad. "There is a sense of nervous anticipation mixed with dread here as everyone either huddles in bomb shelters, praying, or ventures outside, scanning the sky for incoming Scuds. Of course everyone is anxious about chemical weapons, but since Iraq hit Israel with conventional weapons, residents here hope no gas is aimed at Saudi Arabia either, Robert."

In the few seconds it took the radio anchor to phrase his next question, another explosion ripped through the sky. Angus was both nervous and relieved. They still didn't know what was in those warheads being destroyed overhead, but a little action would enliven the broadcast. God was acting as a fine executive producer.

The New York anchor was talking to him. "We could hear that explosion. Was it on the ground near you, Angus?"

Angus took a deep breath and forced himself to sound calm.

"That was the launch of a Patriot missile, which looks like a Roman candle on steroids," he said, explaining the whole choreography of the Scud–Patriot death dance before describing what was happening on the ground. "There haven't been any explosions on the ground as far as I can tell from here. The whole idea of the Patriot is to destroy an incoming missile in midair. It is designed to blow them up high overhead, although they can go off on a fairly low trajectory if they get the warning late. We didn't get a good look at that explosion up there because of the weather —it looked like fireworks in the fog, a kind of red glow in the clouds. But so far I haven't seen any explosions on the ground, although of course various chunks of the Scud and the Patriot will scatter beneath the explosion, Robert."

"Are you in any danger, Angus?"

"There could be some risk if the warhead was armed with chemical weapons, but I don't think the explosion was close enough to present any danger from falling debris here. I am a little uneasy about telling you exactly how close it fell lest the Iraqis improve their aim, Robert," Angus said, hoping that it sounded casual, that his voice was not shaking like the rest of him.

Robert chuckled a little and then said, "At the moment we are getting reports of another missile attack on Israel, so if there is nothing more on your end, we will go to them. Please stay on the line in case there are any further developments, Angus."

Angus breathed a sigh of relief. One report out, and he might get another. About thirty minutes passed without anything happening. A few reporters trickled out of the basement, saying they preferred the threat of Scuds to the shelter's stale air, but most stayed put. The all clear had not sounded.

Suddenly the night filled with another roar, longer and more sustained. Again, everyone on the roof tensed.

They soon grasped that this was not the bang of an outgoing missile, but the long, continuous roar of jet fighters and bombers taking off from the adjacent runway. Several squadrons of American F-16s and British Tornadoes zoomed into the night sky, headed north toward Iraq. The hotel sat right in the flight path of the main military runway, so the fighters streaked low overhead as they lifted off.

Angus was startled by Beau Riggs of CBN, a short correspondent with brown hair and the chiseled good looks of a shirt model, describing the scene. "There go fourteen British Tornadoes, heading toward Baghdad, about an hour flying time from here," he said. Riggs seemed oblivious to the fact that any of Saddam's minions watching could organize a nasty welcoming party.

Angus's nostrils began to burn from the heavy cloud of jet exhaust settling over the hotel like a blanket, which even the light rain did not disburse. The exhaust also left a bitter, slightly numbing taste on his tongue. He covered his nose and mouth with his jacket.

Across the roof, Riggs panicked. "Gas! Gas! Gas!" he yelled, dropping completely off camera, his hands quivering as he struggled with the straps on his gas mask. Everyone on the roof froze. If a reporter was saying live on air that there was gas, it had to be true. Most people were wearing regular clothes. In a gas attack, they would perish in the time they needed to retrieve their chemical suits.

It took everyone an excruciating thirty seconds to understand that Riggs had mistaken the jet fuel exhaust for chemical weapons. His CBN team struggled to limit the damage. The military reporter who had been standing next to Riggs talking about Scuds stared down at his colleague, dumbfounded.

"Say something, say something," CBN's producer hissed frantically, knowing that extended silence would convince millions of viewers that the reporters were keeling over dead.

"Reports of gas are unconfirmed at this point," the military correspondent said laconically, slowly putting on his helmet.

Riggs popped up next to him with the gas mask on, saying breathlessly,

"I can still taste that bitter tang from the gas but my body seems to be functioning okay. I think I will live through this attack, but I cannot be sure of the safety of those around me."

Angus figured that CBN cut the live shot, since the producer stepped up onto the broadcast platform and started yanking at Riggs's mask. He fought her off, shrieking, "Are you crazy? Are you crazy? It's a gas attack. I can still taste it. It's gas. You're losing your senses. Save yourself!"

"Riggs, you shmuck, you fucking blue-eyed nincompoop," the producer yelled back, whacking him on the head repeatedly with her clipboard. "You are tasting either the jet fuel or the rubber tube for breathing. Look around you, you jackass, all of us are still standing. Now if you don't take that mask off and go back on air to say you made a colossal mistake, I am going to ram that rubber tube down your throat so that you taste it for the rest of your miserable life. I hope the fuck that you didn't give anyone watching a coronary."

Riggs did as he was told, looking around at everyone staring at him like a man emerging from a trance. Dazed, he stumbled off the platform just as the long wail of the all clear sounded.

Angus figured there was no reason to stand out in the rain and try to communicate to New York when he could do it from indoors, so he headed for the main staircase only to find it blocked by a fight.

A guy Angus recognized as a retired army colonel who still looked the part but was now writing military analyses for the *Chicago Tribune* had grabbed Riggs by the lapels and was shaking him like a rag doll. "You will not scare the fuck out of my family again," he snarled, tersely describing how he phoned his family after the erroneous gas attack report to reassure them and found his wife in tears, convinced that after years of sleepless nights wondering how her husband was faring in Vietnam and elsewhere, he might be dying on a journalism assignment.

"I can't believe an incompetent fuck like you is even allowed near this place, much less on the air," he spat, grabbing the press credentials hanging by a chain around Riggs's neck and yanking them off. Other reporters took advantage of his loosened grip to pull the guy back and Riggs scuttled away.

Angus bounded upstairs to the WP bureau. As dawn broke, a few reporters were diligently typing, while a bunch of others showed up for the large urn of coffee delivered to the WP suite first thing every morning. Hawxhurst walked in, drew a cup and started telling Angus about what had gone on in the bomb shelter. He had spent the air raid sitting next to a stammering radio reporter filing from a phone down there.

"How come WP isn't using one of those phones?" Angus complained. "What the hell was I doing up on the roof dodging Scuds if there are enough phones to do live radio from the basement?"

"No, you're not getting it," Hawxhurst said. "What I'm trying to tell you is that the guy was making the images up wholesale. I mean we are all sitting down in the basement with no idea what the hell is happening over our heads and this guy is spewing out this you-are-there stuff."

Hawxhurst said the radio reporter spoke in a loud whisper, as if making noise might bring the missiles down on his head: "The air raid sirens are sounding all across Dhahran," he told his listeners, shoving his microphone under the wailing hotel alarm to give them the full effect.

Hawxhurst continued, "There was this very low boom every few minutes that did not seem far away and really gave the hair on the back of my neck an erection." The radio reporter then informed his listeners that six Scuds were approaching Dhahran and that the muffled explosions heard inside the hotel indicated a major missile attack outdoors.

"When they announced the all clear, Armed Forces radio said the Patriots successfully downed all the Scuds," said Hawxhurst. "The whole place erupted in applause. I mean, you would think the Patriots were their team in the Super Bowl."

Prowling around to grab quick quotes for a story, Hawxhurst learned that hotel staffers who lacked gas masks or chemical suits had taken refuge in the basement's meat locker, since the air was filtered and a bomb would have to penetrate its heavy metal door.

"But it was too cold in there to stay for long, so they were running in and out. Every time they went in either direction, they slammed the door. And do you want to guess what it sounds like? I'll tell you what it sounds like. It sounds like a dull, distant boom."

"You mean the boom the guy was describing as a Patriot missile firing was in reality a large refrigerator door slamming?" Angus asked, incredulous.

"Yeah, don't that beat everything?" Hawxhurst said, looking disgusted.

The words barely escaped his mouth before the alarm sounded, the piercing screech again echoing through the hotel. The reporters in the WP suite reflexively grabbed their gas masks and headed out the door. But when they emerged into the main part of the hotel something was amiss. The lights blazed and Ramsden was not downstairs barking into his bullhorn.

The alarm stopped abruptly for several counts and then started again. Angus suddenly understood what was happening. The television networks, their in-house monitors on loud, were feeding tape of the last air raid to New York. The taped rerun of the earlier attack sounded like a new air raid.

"Christ," Angus said, trudging slowly back into the WP suite. "We'll be lucky to finish this war with our sanity intact. Welcome to Club Scud."

Chapter Twenty-Two

THE PRESS pretty much ignored Radio Baghdad after Betty quit the airwaves. She took all the fun with her.

"We've been calling her 'Bombed-Out Betty' because the air force boys must have hit her transmission towers or something," one sergeant told Angus when he asked about her. "She's nowhere to be found on the dial."

The task of monitoring Radio Baghdad's Arabic service fell to the WP Gulf bureau in Dubai. Farida Sharqawi, a forty-eight-year-old Egyptian woman, ran the office there single-handedly.

Farida had been a beauty in her youth, a tall, sensual woman with long, straight black hair and luminous black eyes. But she stubbornly resisted her family's attempts to marry her off, choosing to assert her independence by working for one Western news organization after another.

Her beauty gradually faded, with the exception of a husky, flirtatious voice. On the phone Farida could give a guy goose bumps just by saying "good morning." She worked the phones several times a week, patiently dialing over fifty numbers around the Gulf—various police and government ministries plus local reporters and newspaper editors. Her voice always elicited a response. In countries where the sexes cannot mingle, men would gossip freely just to keep that voice on the line.

As much as WP correspondents admired her tenacity, she also drove them crazy. Farida was incapable of editing herself. She was trained early in her career by *Time* magazine, whose New York editors showered her with praise for lengthy memos even if they lifted just three paragraphs. Reading one gave them something to do all week. Wire service staffers, on the other hand, needed the news fast, and no one relished wading through 3,000 words to find it.

So Angus reacted warily when he answered the phone in the Dhahran Palace bureau one morning in late January and found Farida on the line. Her conversations were rarely shorter than her memos.

"What's up Farida?" he said, resigning himself to the inevitable.

"Well the oddest thing just happened, Angus," she answered. "You know how you added the Khafji Beach Hotel to my list of numbers to call?"

"Yeah," he said, leaning back in his chair and stretching his neck from side to side while making a mental list of things he should do that day.

After the Saudis had warned repeatedly that Angus would be expelled if found in Khafji again, he reluctantly abandoned his trips and asked Farida to check in periodically by phone. Everyone had pretty much deserted the town anyway in anticipation of war. But the Beach Hotel staff stayed, welcoming occasional Kuwaiti refugees or American troops savoring a hot meal. In addition, a few British and French television crews who couldn't get spots on the U.S. combat pools had holed up in the hotel, making clandestine forays to the front lines just a few miles away.

Farida explained that she had dialed the hotel in Khafji as soon as she heard a bulletin on Radio Baghdad that morning announcing that Iraqi forces captured the Saudi border town. Angus was half listening. Arab radio stations invent shit all day long, he thought. Why is she bugging me about yet another cockamamie story?

Farida had developed a congenial relationship with the man who worked the Beach Hotel's front desk, a fellow Egyptian who alerted her to border developments and guests she might want to interview. At one point the Kuwaiti princess who ran the national museum snuck over the border, describing for the first time the looting of its exquisite art collections. "I'd like to take Saddam's eyes and heart and boil them," had been one of her best lines.

On the telephone, Farida was saying to Angus, "Well the most unbelievable thing happened."

"What, Farida?" Angus answered, trying to sound interested.

"An Iraqi answered the phone!" she said, giggling in her excitement. "I could tell by the accent."

"Are you sure?" Angus said, still stretching and considering how to exit this conversation. "Kuwaitis and Iraqis have nearly the same accent. And besides, he must have been a contract worker. I don't think the Saudis expelled Iraqis already working here."

"No Silly Billy, it was an Iraqi officer, he told me," Farida said.

Angus banged his chair down on the floor and leaned into the receiver. Farida had his complete attention now. Could the Iraqis possibly have moved south, crossed the border and occupied a corner of Saudi Arabia without anybody announcing it? The allied forces had said nothing about an Iraqi incursion and of course the Saudis, embarrassed, would be unlikely to admit any such thing.

It never ceased to amaze Angus how major news in the Arab world slipped in through the side door. Every leader in the region spouted wildly exaggerated rhetoric and rarely backed it up with the slightest action, so real news came as a surprise. The invasion of Kuwait was a stellar example; given Saddam's incessant blustering, no one thought he would make good on threats to smite the place.

"Farida! Are you completely sure? It wasn't your Egyptian buddy pulling your leg? You know Egyptians are born pranksters."

"I'm positive, Angus. When I remarked on his accent the guy said he was an Iraqi, that they controlled the town and that after freeing Kuwait, this was Iraq's second step toward liberating Jerusalem. He said he could tell I was an Egyptian from my accent, and he started insulting President Mubarak, calling him a donkey and a tool of the West and that whole shpiel. I tried to interrupt him by asking how many Iraqi troops controlled the town but he cackled and said, 'See you in Jerusalem!' and hung up."

"Do you think they really control the town?" Angus said, his heart thumping while his mind raced at the thought of the Iraqi Republican Guards inside Saudi itself. Could it be a feint or were they heading south to grab the world's largest oilfields, not to mention entering into the fiercely welcoming embrace of the U.S. military? That could mean an ugly ground war.

"It seems Radio Baghdad isn't exaggerating this time, at least if Saddam's men are confident enough to be answering the phones," Farida said. "There hasn't been anything reported by the combat pool up by Khafji, has there? I want to put the story on the wire but I thought someone should check it out first."

"Yeah, you're right Farida. I will go read the pool reports and call you right back," Angus said.

He hung up and sat staring at the phone for a minute, trying to think clearly. If Iraqi troops had crossed the border and the pool wasn't being told, he wanted to be the first one up there.

But he needed to find a way to do it without raising the Saudis' hackles. Even the unflappable Colonel Fletcher had warned Angus that the JIB could do nothing to protect him if the Saudis busted him for going to Khafji again, and the Saudis were clearly not ready to forgive him. Major Raad from the Saudi military press desk had made that abundantly clear when Angus bumped into him a couple days earlier at the buffet table in the Dunes at lunchtime.

"How nice to see you, Mr. Dalziel," lied the major, a short, slight man. "I haven't heard anything about you recently. I hope you are staying out of trouble."

"Come on, Major, all that was months ago. Don't you ever forget anything?" Angus said, glancing around with relief to see that neither Wanda nor Callahan nor anybody else from the WP bureau was within earshot. He wanted to finish the conversation quickly to avoid any possibility that someone might report back to New York.

"Don't you know the famous story about Abu Hassan?" the major asked.

Oh no, here we go, thought Angus, expecting to hear the usual story about a tribal leader who informed a neighboring clan that the first tribe finally killed off an enemy who slighted them fifty years earlier. "You acted hastily," the leader of the neighboring tribe admonished. The story was a staple in countless U.S. embassy briefings and analyses by green reporters about how ancient enmities thrive in the region.

But the major related an entirely different tale: "Abu Hassan was a wealthy Arab trader in the Gulf who had never married. After turning forty he met the most beautiful woman he ever saw in his life and decided on the spot to wed her, throwing the most lavish wedding feast his country ever witnessed.

"All the mulled date palm wine, the fruits and nuts and other rich foods worked on Abu Hassan, however, so right in the middle of his wedding toast he let rip with a colossal fart that his guests tried but failed to ignore, peals of laughter echoing through the wedding tent. It was all anyone at the party could talk about and Abu Hassan was humiliated by the giggling that subsequently dogged his every footstep. The melancholy groom figured he would go live in India until the whole thing was forgotten."

The major recounted how Abu Hassan grew even wealthier but always pined for his Gulf homeland. After about a decade, determined to find out if the embarrassing incident was now buried, he disguised himself in the rags of a common seaman and returned. Roaming the streets and coffee shops for a few days, he eavesdropped on one conversation after another, and no one mentioned his colossal fart. He was understandably ecstatic.

[*287*]

Then one day, as he was resting against the wall of a house, he heard a little girl asking her mother about when her birthday was coming and the mother replied, "Don't worry, everybody remembers it clearly because you were born near the date of Abu Hassan's fart."

"So you see, Arabs celebrate their long memories, even for things that others might consider trivial," Major Raad said, grinning fiercely. "You may think we have forgotten your trips to Khafji and your lies about the religious police and all your slights against Saudi Arabia, but we haven't."

Angus forced a thin smile and said, "Did you make up that story yourself, Major?"

The major, not laughing, answered, "No, it comes from *Tales of 1,001 Nights*. I thought I saw you reading the book and figured it had inspired your love of fairy tales about Saudi Arabia."

"And here I always thought it was the official version of events that reflect the local penchant for fairy tales," Angus said.

"Watch yourself, Mr. Dalziel," the major said sharply and stalked off.

Angus told no one about the exchange, which had left him distinctly uneasy.

Now that he knew the Iraqis were in Khafji, he weighed relinquishing the trip to another reporter, although he hated the idea of Callahan or Vandusen getting to Khafji first. This was the type of story he had been waiting for since the invasion, hell, since becoming a journalist. Angus looked at his watch. It was noon. He could cover the two hundred miles to Khafji in a little under three hours, if he drove eighty miles an hour and managed to sail through all the checkpoints. Daylight started to fade around 4:00 P.M., so to really see what was going on he had to arrive by then. That gave him at most an hour to organize a plan.

He walked over to the JIB, where Lieutenant Brett Swain was at his usual station Xeroxing overnight pool reports. Swain, a black-haired, muscular Marine, was a favorite of the press corps because he organized trips to obscure units near Iraq.

Angus lifted the latest pool reports from WP's mailbox and leafed through them. "Anything from up around the border?" he asked casually.

"It's a mighty long border, Dalziel. Where exactly?" the Marine officer said.

"The border with Kuwait, around Khafji," Angus answered. "Isn't there a pool with the Marines up there?"

"Khafji? Yes, there's a pool stationed just south but we haven't heard anything from them. Why you asking? Something happening up there? Didn't the Saudis evacuate that town?" Swain said, pausing suddenly and narrowing his eyes. "Hey, you aren't thinking of busting out of here I hope. I seem to recall you getting your ass in a sling a couple times already over Khafji."

Angus sidestepped the questions. He did not want to tell Swain that there might be news, big news, so he mumbled something about being bored with the usual reports about Mr. Scud.

"That was an awfully specific question," Swain said, suspicious because the press often worked faster than official channels. "What's going on?"

"Nothing lieutenant, trust me," Angus said, backing away with the pool reports. "Fishing for something to write about. Got to go dig through these. See ya."

Angus glanced toward the Saudi military desk. Should he ask them? He laughed at the very idea. He might as well go wave a red flag. Instead he walked back to the bureau to decide what to do.

Much to his relief Benoni Ryan was the only person there. Half visible behind a screen of cigarette smoke, the photographer launched into his favorite theme as soon as he saw Angus, bitching about the narrow profit margin on his expense accounts. Angus, always glad to work with him in bad situations because the guy never panicked, interrupted Ryan's grumbling and quickly explained what Farida told him about Khafji. Ryan was instantly game.

"I can't wait to escape this dump and it's my week with the Range

Rover." The WP rented an odd assortment of vehicles but the Range Rover, the color of a bruised and battered plum, was considered a prize worthy of strict sharing because the Saudis awarded them to all top American generals. "That should help us get through the checkpoints no problem."

There were five Saudi checkpoints between Dhahran and Khafji, all with express orders to turn back reporters lacking a government escort. Angus and Ryan agreed that if they were driving the right vehicle, wearing uniforms and saluted, the Saudi soldiers would likely wave them through. No Saudi would dream of pretending to be a soldier by putting on a uniform, so the guards would likely assume that any American uniform was legitimate too.

"Is the story worth getting thrown out of here for?" Angus said aloud, a little nervous about airing his doubts lest someone else grab the assignment.

"If there really is fighting, it's big news and everybody will pour up there and no one will remember that you shouldn't be there," Ryan said, grinning. "On the other hand, if there is no bang-bang and you get busted, well, there will be other wars. Think of it this way. Anything is better than dicking around this hotel being Scud bait. Let's go."

Just as they were about to leave, Vandusen, Callahan and a few others walked into the bureau, so the two explained where they were going in case anything went wrong. No one thought it was a real story, especially after a few phone calls to U.S. military sources inside Saudi Arabia elicited firm denials about any fighting up north. Despite that, the bureau consensus was so strong that the two of them leave at once that Angus briefly condsidered whether they wanted him to tie his own noose—to get busted for being in Khafji without permission and thrown out.

It was odd that Callahan did not try to assert seniority, Angus thought, although the tacit rule that whoever gets a tip first runs with the story worked against a last-minute attempt to wrestle it away—particularly since Angus and Ryan were on their way out the door. Squabbling might lose the WP precious lead time on other news organizations. The fact that Callahan didn't try probably meant that he didn't think the story was true, Angus realized. He thanked God Wanda was not there to kick up a fuss. Angus was gleeful at the possibility of landing a scoop, outracing the entire press corps. Even the big shots like Black would have to sit up and take notice if Angus broke this story.

He had been a foreign correspondent for almost five years, but he had never been assigned to a major story. When the Palestinian uprising against the Israeli occupation would flare up, he found himself dispatched to an Arab capital to write a summary of the reactions, not sent to cover the main events. Through a combination of either bad luck or ill-timed vacations, he also saw more senior correspondents assigned to big stories like Saddam using chemical weapons to slaughter the Kurdish town of Halabja in 1988 or the funeral of the Ayatollah Khomeini in Iran the next year. Inevitably Angus was assigned to the editing desk, making sure everybody else's copy read well and flowed smoothly to New York. The task left him seething with frustration.

Khafji, he vowed to himself, would be different.

Angus and Ryan departed in their own clothes, but as soon as the Dhahran Palace was out of sight they pulled onto the highway shoulder to don military uniforms. Angus put on the fatigues and helmet issued to him for pool duty. Ryan fished a clean desert camouflage uniform still wrapped in its plastic dry cleaning cover out of his small duffel bag.

"Where did you get that?" Angus asked.

"I borrowed it," Ryan chuckled, slipping it over his shirt. "I grabbed it as the hotel guy was delivering laundry. He only left the trolley unattended in the corridor for like thirty seconds, but I think I got a pretty good fit," he said, laughing louder. "I'm sure the captain it belongs to won't mind. It's for a good cause."

Ryan rolled up his ponytail and tucked it inside the helmet, the only head gear that allowed him to hide it all, then steered the Range Rover north at full throttle under a pale winter sky. They were listening to the soundtrack from *The Last Temptation of Christ*, an edgy combination of traditional rock with Middle Eastern instruments, the pounding drumbeats occasionally interrupted by a drifting flute. It seemed fitting for both the landscape and the miracle they needed to pull off.

Ryan barely slowed the boxy vehicle for the checkpoints manned by the Saudi National Guard, giving a vague salute through the somewhat muddy windows and then gunning the engine.

As they got within thirty minutes of Khafji, more and more sand-colored Humvees or armored personnel carriers thundered south on the other side of the road. That was a bad sign. If there was a major battle on just ahead, why were the soldiers leaving?

Ryan spotted the black stencil of a palm tree over two crossed swords painted on the door of a series of vehicles. "It's the Saudis, not the Americans!" he shouted happily. "They have the same damn equipment. If the Saudis are ready to bugaloo the hell out of there at speed, I bet the Iraqis really have crossed the border."

The Range Rover lurched suddenly and a loud "phwap, phwap, phwap" drowned out the roar of the engine. It took a minute of stunned silence before they both realized they had a flat. Swearing, Ryan veered the Range Rover over to the side of the road and Angus got out to look. The back left tire was in ribbons, pancaked on the ground.

They had stopped to fill the tank at the last gas station, and it was too far to drive back. Angus had run inside the station during that pit stop to phone Dhahran to check on developments. Vandusen had told him that the first pool reports saying there was fighting around Khafji were released around 3:00 P.M., but they were sketchy and confused. Given the ground rules on naming troop positions, no one could figure out if various pools were describing the same skirmishes. Plus no reporter included a time line, so it was impossible to tell when the fighting took place.

"You wouldn't believe these pool reports," said Vandusen. "Some of them are complete mumbo jumbo, some little more than impressionistic pictures. We are desperate for basic news—time and location and the number of troops involved—while the reporters in the field seem to think they were sent out to paint little Persian miniatures. It is un-fuck-ing-believable. If you guys get up there and get a basic nuts-and-bolts story, we'll scoop everyone."

Vandusen also said that the officer at the Riyadh briefing, after repeated prodding, finally admitted that allied troops skirmished with what he termed "Iraqi reconnaissance units in force."

"They are sitting on this one so heavily I get the feeling that the entire Republican Guard could be pouring over the border and they would call it 'Iraqi reconnaissance units in force,'" Vandusen said.

Angus knew the flat tire was costing precious time. Given the confusion, other reporters were probably heading north and the military would be on alert for them. He and Ryan needed to get moving again, and fast. He rummaged around in the back of the car and thanked God quietly when he found the Range Rover had a full spare tire.

But where was the jack? It was not with the tire and he couldn't see it under the smelly heap of soda cans, old french fries, dirty blankets, books, magazines and newspapers that filled the back of the vehicle. Rummaging around with his hands, he felt something metal about the right shape and pulled it out.

"Fuck!" he shouted. It was a jack all right, but from some little Suzuki jeeplet. Reporters were constantly cannibalizing each other's cars for parts and someone had switched jacks. It was far too small to lift the Range Rover, so Ryan got out of the car to help.

Angus prayed that nobody from the U.S. military came along and stopped to ask what a couple guys wearing half military uniforms and jeans were doing within striking distance of the front. They tried various ways to get the jack to lift the Range Rover, including balancing it atop a stack of three flat rocks. But it was too small to even budge the heavy vehicle.

"Our only chance is to flag down one of these Saudi Humvees and hope they lend us their jack without asking too many questions," Angus said.

"Don't use any of that Arab talk of yours. It will just make them suspicious," Ryan said. "Play the dumb foreigner."

"What was I, born yesterday?" Angus answered, running to the other side of the road and waving his arms. A Saudi Humvee slowed and parked a little beyond him. The driver leaned out and saw the flat tire, turning to speak to someone inside. Before Angus could even approach, a jack sailed out the backdoor and the Humvee spun back onto the highway with a squeal of burning rubber.

"Thanks!" Angus yelled after them, putting up his forearm to ward off the shower of sand and gravel.

"Love that Arab hospitality," Ryan said.

"Didn't seem too intent on expelling us," Angus said and they both set to changing the tire, adrenalin pumping. They were back in the race.

The two went silent as they approached the last checkpoint about eight miles south of Khafji, this one manned by American soldiers. Angus turned the music off. It was their last hurdle, but the most important. He had been through this particular checkpoint enough times to know that it was an abbreviated obstacle course: a series of three sand embankments that forced all vehicles to negotiate a tight S shape.

Reaching it, they no choice but to slow to a crawl. Ryan wheeled the Range Rover expertly around the first embankment while Angus glanced out the window, looking for signs that someone was going to try to stop them, his heart whacking against his ribcage.

Clustered along the side of the road he saw the seven or eight reporters in the Marine combat pool, all gesticulating and shouting at the soldiers standing in their path. Although he couldn't hear, it was clear from the body language that the pool was stuck. Angus snapped his head forward. If they recognized him, someone would surely rat to the public affairs officer that a reporter was crossing the checkpoint.

Several American sentries stood on opposite sides of the road after the final embankment. Ryan kept his foot on the gas, neither slowing so much that the soldiers could look inside nor speeding up to make them suspicious. Both he and Angus briskly saluted through the window and the soldiers, thinking they must be officers, automatically stopped approaching the car, returned their salutes and waved them through.

It was a little too easy.

"I didn't like the fog of war inside the hotel so much, but the phenomenon is beginning to grow on me," Angus said and Ryan laughed.

Past the checkpoint a confusion of tanks, heavy trucks and self-propelled artillery pieces criss-crossed the two-lane highway going in all directions except north toward Khafji.

The elevated roadway stood about twenty feet above marshy sand flats that lay just south of the town, flats that flooded after heavy winter rains. The road's steep, rocky sides would be highly treacherous if they went off the shoulder too fast. Ryan kept the Range Rover flying along at speed anyway, the tires squealing as he swerved through the maze of moving vehicles, wanting to put as much space as possible between them and the checkpoint.

The road from the checkpoint toward Khafji was a long, gentle curve, and soon they found themselves within a mile of the town. It had grown quiet outside, the clanking of the heavy machinery receding, the only noise the growl of their own engine. The gray late afternoon sky blended seamlessly with the wet, gray sand, making it difficult to discern the horizon.

Off to the right just ahead of them, a few hundred yards from the town's southern edge, Angus could see a Marine platoon deployed across the sand flats in one long row, most of the soldiers hunkered down inside their vehicles. The vehicles were lined up perpendicular to the elevated roadway, with the first one at least sixty yards from it. One man in each Humvee, wearing full battle armor, stood up through the roof, leaning into either the antitank missile launchers or the 50-millimeter machine guns mounted there. The soldiers were motionless and intense, looking neither left nor right, riveted on the town.

Ryan slowed the Range Rover to maneuver around a four-foot crater gouged in the roadway by an artillery shell. It proved impossible to tell from inside the vehicle whether there was enough room, so he stopped and got out to look. He left the engine idling. Angus got out too.

The distant thump of heavy artillery boomed ominously across the flats and the clatter from a helicopter or two ebbed somewhere behind them.

About five hundred yards ahead a belch of bright red fire and a pillar of oily black smoke obscured a wooden triumphal arch, built in the shape of castle turrets and painted lime green. It marked the entrance to Khafji. From past trips Angus knew that it said "Hello and Welcome" in sinuous Arabic script, but through the smoke he could no longer make out the letters. Between the place where he and Ryan were standing and the arch sat an armored vehicle of indeterminate nationality. They would have to drive past it if they decided to enter the town.

Angus grabbed the binoculars out of the Range Rover and focused on the tiny flag flapping off the vehicle's antenna, but he could not identify the country.

"I don't like it," Ryan said flatly, staring ahead.

"It's awfully quiet. Do you think maybe we should edge up to that armored vehicle and ask them what is going on?" Angus asked.

"I don't know. Look at how the Marines are lined up, facing in, not making a sound. Something's wrong," Ryan answered. They stood for a few more minutes looking for signs of activity in the city. From this vantage point it seemed normal enough, even peaceful. But the Marines were too coiled.

Angus suddenly felt cold. He reached inside the Range Rover for his bulletproof vest and put it on.

"I think I will bang off a few frames here," Ryan said, walking up to the front of the vehicle before raising his most powerful lens and snapping half a dozen exposures of the billowing smoke. It was a nervous moment. The biggest camera lenses resembled a grenade launcher, and in the midst of a firefight few soldiers bothered to stop long enough to check. But nobody shot at them.

"Well, do you want to go in?" Ryan asked aloud. They talked it over for a few more minutes and decided it would probably be safest to totter down off the highway and ask the U.S. soldiers what was happening. If they ran into an officer who went strictly by the book, they might be expelled before getting any information, but it felt like the better gamble.

The Range Rover slowly lumbered down the sides of the embankment and across the wet sand. Angus leaned out the window to talk to the Marines in the first Humvee, bracing for the reaction when he told them he was a reporter.

They were thrilled. It was often like that with the men on the front line, what the army called the pointy end of the spear. The guys facing enemy fire didn't give a damn about pool rules or JIB escorts; they were gratified that somebody was there to record their story.

"What's all that black smoke?" Angus asked.

"The Iraqis just bought a whole lot of whoop ass from those two Cobras that were here a couple minutes ago," one soldier replied. "You must have just missed 'em. They blasted an armored personnel carrier that is sitting alongside that blue warehouse you can see not far from the arch. Saddam's boys have infiltrated the entire city down to that row of buildings. They have been firing at us sporadically, but hopefully that Cobra nailed one of those motherfuckers."

"I can't put 'motherfuckers' in the story; this is for family newspapers," Angus said while writing down the quote, and they all laughed.

He locked eyes with Ryan and held his grin for an instant. As reporters they lived for moments like this; the uncertainty, the big gamble paying off in a guaranteed front-page story, the intensity of it all. The swift decision to talk to the Marines probably saved their lives and opened the door to what could become a major exclusive.

The platoon commander, Lieutenant David Castaldo, told them over the radio to come to his Humvee near the middle of the lineup. Like most Marines he had a husky build, making him look shorter than his five feet, eight inches as he leaned against the back of his vehicle. His black eyes were bloodshot, but he was clean shaven. Even in the middle of a battle Marines were under orders to shave every day. It was considered a morale booster.

"I'm sorry if I seem a little groggy, but we've been on this vigil for nearly twenty-four hours," he said after they shook hands. "We fire at anything that might be an Iraqi."

He told Angus that the previous night had started out quiet, a little cold, with thousands of stars visible despite a yellow, almost full moon that made the waters of the nearby Gulf sparkle. Just after 10:00 P.M., about eighty Iraqi tanks pulled over the border, which lay six miles north of Khafji. Their big guns were rotated backward in the international military sign for surrender.

"Defections have been increasing up and down the lines, so no one was suspicious at first despite the large number of vehicles," he explained. But when an escort party from Arab forces stationed nearby arrived, the Iraqis launched their attack, the night erupting in a staccato of small arms fire. Within less than a minute, Iraqi artillery back across the border opened up on Khafji, pulverizing the communications tower and the governor's empty palace.

Castaldo said he had been close to the border and called in a strike by navy A-6 bombers against the Iraqi artillery positions. He lingered to watch the outcome of a hit through his thermal sight. A fireball briefly framed the black silhouette of the gun barrel and the four or five Iraqi soldiers around it.

"One soldier was fully out of his foxhole, in the middle of taking a piss when the bomb hit," Castaldo said. "I sat there and watched because I could tell from the thermal sight as death gradually embraced him and the other soldiers. I saw their bodies slowly change color from bright orange to blue to nothing at all."

The officer went quiet for minute.

"Not the kind of thing I practiced at Annapolis," Castaldo said finally, scowling and shaking his head. He then explained that with eighty tanks lumbering around Khafji, the Marine and allied forces had regrouped south of the town, hence his soldiers lined up across the sand flats.

Angus wrote it all in his notebook as fast as he could. It was night now, the sky overcast, so no moonlight illuminated the scene. Occasionally the Marines watching the town through thermal sights would discern something and a machine gun would discharge a few rounds.

"I guess they control the town for the moment, but it is only going to be for a moment," the lieutenant said. "Feel free to stick around as long as you want."

Ryan and Angus huddled for a minute. They had urgent news—Iraq had seized a Saudi town—but now the question was how to get it out. Angus could file from the nearest phone, but Ryan needed to drive all the way back to Dhahran to process his film. It was too important to entrust to anyone else.

Crossing checkpoints would be a problem in the dark: they could not expect to brazen their way through with a salute. The soldiers would want them to roll down their windows and would shine flashlights into the vehicle. Heading south toward Dhahran would probably be fine, but it would be impossible to turn around and come back to the front.

"Write a story quick and I will phone it in from that first gas station," Ryan urged.

"You sure?" asked Angus, knowing Ryan was being generous, too generous. The cardinal rule of war reporting was that you never let your buddy go anywhere alone. No matter what kind of trouble you encountered, there were two of you to help each other.

"Yeah, I really mean it," he said. "All the danger is north of us. On the highway south all I'll need to fear is getting tailgated right up the ass by the retreating Saudis. I mean you saw what we just went through—nothing. But write something fast so I can get a move on."

Angus sat in the Range Rover, balancing a little red flashlight on his lap while he filled about fifteen pages of his small notebook with a roughly coherent story, enough to break the news to the world. He hoped against hope that his report would hit the wires before television, certainly before Black, and it would contradict the official reports of minor skirmishes. He could practically taste the boldface headlines: "Saudi Arabia Invaded!"

He tore out the pages and handed them to Ryan, who folded them in half and buttoned them into the pocket of his borrowed military tunic. Toward the end of the line of Humvees someone fired a wire-guided missile that whined across the sand toward Khafji. They both watched until the missile exploded against the wall of a building right above an armored personnel carrier, a bright orange fireball in the pitch black. Then they turned and shook hands.

"I'll see you when I see you," Angus said.

"Not unless I see you first, mate," Ryan responded. They smiled. It was an old routine lifted from the movie *Gallipoli,* which they had watched together something like twenty times when they had been marooned on a slow story in Damascus. It had been the only thing playing on the hotel movie channel.

Angus wondered if the exchange might bring bad luck in the middle of a battlefield, given that both characters in the movie died, but it was too familiar a ritual to stop. He watched the tail lights of the Range Rover recede across the sand and into the darkness, hoping that he had made the right decision. Then he jumped into the back of Castaldo's Humvee and began to inventory the scene around him.

The vehicle, sealed against the winter chill, smelled like stale sweat and perfume, a symptom of soldiers living for weeks with only Babywipes for a bath. It was crammed with the men's rucksacks plus cases of water and boxes of army rations designed to withstand nuclear explosions.

The rations were the stuff Quisburt elected to eat instead of the food at the Dunes. They came in pouches made of thick, chocolate-brown plastic and were called MREs, or "meals ready to eat." The soldiers called that "three lies in one" and often referred to them as "meals rejected by Ethiopians." The menus stamped on the outside were distantly related to what was inside—omelet with ham, tuna with noodles. Angus had eaten enough to grab for one marked chicken stew, which always contained a small package of M&Ms. He could live off those.

He tuned his short wave radio to the Armed Forces network for the late briefing from Riyadh, carried live. The Saudi military spokesman up first told the reporters that a reconnaissance patrol occupied Khafji briefly but had been "completely liberated" by Saudi forces.

The Saudi officer had barely finished describing the brave exploits of those forces when a series of explosions erupted around the Marine platoon. The Iraqis had launched a sudden shower of rocket-propelled grenades. One of them hit the mud flats just in front of Castaldo's Humvee, the impact sending dirt clattering down on the vehicle like hail and rocking it slightly.

All three soldiers inside ducked instinctively and Angus did too. What the fuck did I volunteer to stay here for, he thought to himself, burying his fears as Castaldo turned around in the front shotgun seat to talk to him.

"Seems like some Iraqis haven't gotten the word that the town has been completely liberated of them," the lieutenant said. Angus chuckled. From the chatter back and forth between the military units on the Humvee's radio, he could tell that the Americans were having trouble getting the Saudis to rally. The lieutenant gave him the background:

"Word came down from on high—the king himself, apparently—that it must be Saudi forces who liberate the town, with at most the backing of other Arab units, mostly Qataris, bivouacked nearby," he said.

The Marines were to provide heavy artillery, but not too overtly. It was a nearly impossible set of limitations. The American officers at the front were tensely waiting for a plan to take shape, while keeping the Iraqis bottled up in Khafji.

Lieutenant Castaldo explained that although the wiry Qatari soldiers were raring to go, the local Saudi commander was balking and so were his men. The commander had argued for weeks before the bombing campaign started that there would be no war, and after that derided any suggestion that the Iraqis might invade. Now that it had happened, he was in shock. Hence evasive statements were pouring out of Riyadh while everyone waited for him to rally.

"They should court-martial his ass and bring in a commander with some zeal, but apparently removing him would insult his whole tribe and they would all go home in a sulk, so here we sit," Lieutenant Castaldo said with disgust.

Angus stepped out of the Humvee and walked up and down the line for a while, harvesting quotes from the soldiers about what it was like being in a real firefight after months of waiting. A series of loud cries drew him to a slightly larger Humvee, an ambulance used by two medics parked a little behind the rest. The medics let him stand outside their bright headlamps while they bandaged an ugly shrapnel wound that made the inside of a guy's arm look like so much strawberry jam spilled from a broken jar.

It was the first time Angus had seen a truly stomach-wrenching battlefield wound and he stood there for a while, testing himself by not averting his eyes and wishing he could get a quote out of it somehow. But the soldier was too shot up with morphine and the medics too busy fixing the guy for Angus to get much detail about what happened. He wished Ryan was still around to take a picture.

By the time he got back to Castaldo's position, a plan was afoot. The lieutenant said the original estimate of 2,000 Iraqi soldiers in the town had been revised sharply downward, with the Saudis and Qataris now asserting there were only a few hundred left. The Arab allies, set to launch an assault to drive them out, were waiting for American air support before rolling.

While the officer spoke, the rumble of the heavy armor collecting on the raised highway intensified suddenly and Angus saw the column of tanks and armored personnel carriers lurch forward, clanking toward Khafji.

"What the fuck?" Castaldo exclaimed, firing questions into the radio about why the mechanized assault was advancing before the air support or the heavy Marine guns got the chance to soften up the Iraqi positions.

"The Saudi lieutenant colonel in charge of the force has decided to act immediately on his orders to retake the city," came back the crackling voice of a Marine liaison officer with the Saudi forces. "The king's pride obviously takes precedence over military prudence, not to say planning, over."

Angus watched the Arab force trundle up the highway. A Marine passed him a pair of night vision goggles and he followed the line of armor as it set out on the mile that separated them from the entrance to the city.

When it reached the "Hello and Welcome" arch, the night erupted with chaotic explosions. Angus saw red machine gun tracers streaking from the buildings all along the southern edge of the city, punctuated occasionally by the brighter flash and bang of a rocket-propelled grenade exploding against a piece of armor.

Even without the goggles, Angus could tell that the Arab force was taking withering fire from all sides. At the same time, rocket-propelled grenades and heavy machine gun fire raked across the Marine position where he was again sitting in Castaldo's Humvee.

"A couple hundred Iraqis my ass," Castaldo said, spitting chewing tobacco out the window into the dark and putting his helmet back on. Angus did the same.

He was scribbling furiously into his notebook in the dark, hoping he could read it later and, more importantly, file it somehow. He felt calm under fire, since the Marines around him were so steady. No need to agonize about getting the copy out while the battle is raging, he told himself, just write everything down and worry about what to do with it after the shooting stops.

When the gunfire intensified, Angus heard division headquarters come on the radio and tell Castaldo to pull the platoon back. The Saudi and Qatari forces, in complete disarray and shooting at each other as often as at the Iraqis, shambled out of the city too. It took them a while to get their machines turned around and to retreat back along the high-way. After a few hours, once everyone got out of range, the fighting petered out to sporadic machine gun bursts.

ANGUS jerked awake in the backseat of the Humvee just before dawn to witness Arab forces regrouping in the shadowy light. This time they waited for the Marine Harrier jets and 155-millimeter artillery to pound Khafji before edging forward. Behind that barrage the Saudi and Qatari armor began pushing the Iraqis out. Lieutenant Castaldo's platoon crept forward as far as the warehouses on the perimeter, but much to Angus's disappointment they did not enter the town.

Castaldo was listening to radio reports from a small Marine recon-naissance unit that had hidden on a rooftop after being trapped in Khafji. The guy on the radio described the Arab forces, while dogged, as firing blindly at each other, in part because some units used the same kind of vehicles as the Iraqis.

"No point in getting our butts shot off in that stew," the lieutenant said after confirming that a few wounded Marines inside the town could hold out.

After the months spent in the Dhahran Palace or on press pools where he couldn't go to the bathroom without tripping over at least three other reporters, Angus found it hard to believe that he had this major battle, or at least this key American position, all to himself.

He occasionally listened to news on the radio. U.S. military broad-casts out of Riyadh weren't saying much and reports on the Arab stations kept repeating that the Iraqi troops were isolated. The American military, evidently besieged by the press, finally released a statement that the Armed Forces station read out in full:

"There was contact with enemy forces at three or four different loca-tions along the border. The contact began last night and continued until early this morning when contact was broken off. Preliminary reports indicate heavy losses of both personnel and equipment on the Iraqi side and light losses to U.S. Marine and other coalition forces. As soon as we can develop a more complete account of the engagement, we will provide additional information."

Angus was relieved that there were no other reports about the battle, but the lack of any mention of a WP story about the invasion made him wonder what had happened to Ryan.

"Must be the fog of war," Castaldo joked. "What they really need to do is talk to you."

"Now that you mention it, I need to find a way to get this stuff out of here," Angus said. "You don't think the fighting will come back this way, do you?"

"Nah," said Castaldo. "I'll see what I can do to help you out."

The firing advanced farther into the city all day, the explosions growing fainter as the Iraqis either surrendered or withdrew northward. Angus hung out with Castaldo's platoon, hoping another reporter or someone from the WP would materialize so he could feel comfortable leaving the area to file his copy.

The pool was nowhere to be seen during the fighting, but somebody would surely brief them anytime now. Finally a Marine captain offered to run Angus to a telephone at a nearby gas station, where he called Dhahran and filed, not lingering on the phone except to say he was returning to the platoon.

The captain drove the Humvee back on the highway, passing through that final checkpoint before Khafji. Right after the checkpoint, Angus saw a small group of reporters interviewing Marines who had taken part in the battle. He recognized a couple of colleagues who were not with any pool and wondered if he could now rove a little more freely without running the risk of being expelled.

The captain driving Angus pulled up on the shoulder opposite the reporters and was hanging out his window, talking to another officer. As they chatted, Angus saw the designated Marine press pool arrive. He watched in disbelief as a heavily freckled television correspondent wearing full battle regalia, including a helmet and a bulletproof vest, walked up behind a reporter in the middle of an interview, grabbed him by the shoulder and spun him around.

"You asshole, you'll prevent us from working," he yelled at the guy, who looked like he was ready to swing at the TV correspondent. "You're not allowed here. You are breaking the ground rules. Get out now! Go back to Dhahran and tell everyone there not to come. I'm telling the minders."

The TV correspondent then stomped back toward the vehicles where the rest of the pool reporters were standing around looking sheepish, kicking their toes in the sand and trying to pretend they weren't part of the same group. He hauled forward a press escort officer, who told the small group of reporters, "You're not allowed to talk to U.S. Marines and they're not allowed to talk to you and you will have to leave this area immediately. The pool can provide all the coverage you need."

"Take their notes! Take their notes!"

The Marine officer shook his head, saying he would not.

"But you confiscated the video footage from those French guys!"

"The French guys filmed wounded Americans and dead Iraqi soldiers and carried no press credentials," the Marine escort officer replied. "Besides, they were French."

Eavesdropping from his perch across the road, Angus pulled his head back deep into the Humvee. No point in attracting the attention of either the correspondent or the press officer and face being expelled after what he had just gone through. The captain at the wheel finished his conversation and turned to him, "Hey, buddies of yours are across the way. Do you want to go talk to them?"

"They're no friends of mine," Angus answered. "One guy thinks all war news is his exclusive, not that I saw him around during the actual shooting. Let's get back to the platoon."

"Good to go," the captain said, spinning the vehicle away from the roadside.

Chapter Twenty-Three

THE BATTLE reports Angus filed drove the hundreds of reporters stuck at the Dhahran Palace into a frenzy.

Already sensing they had missed something, it was only when they read his vivid descriptions of the fighting that they realized they had been sidelined during the war's most dramatic land battle thus far. If not exactly the invasion of Normandy, Khafji was a key first step toward forcing Saddam Hussein to abandon the annexation of Kuwait.

The entire press corps in Dhahran and Riyadh verged on insurrection as it became clear that both the pool system and the briefings failed to provide a timely version of events.

Adding to the professional insult, a couple European television crews who had escaped from the Khafji Beach Hotel just ahead of the Iraqis and had remained on the town's outskirts to witness the fighting provided footage, which arrived back in Dhahran shortly after Angus's story hit the wire. It showed American jets streaking overhead and heavy guns hurling shells into the city—spine-tingling pictures the U.S. networks lacked.

The frustration was clearly audible as reporters barked their questions during the daily briefing in Riyadh, broadcast live.

"How is it possible you know so little, General?" one snapped. "This all started three days ago."

The general gave a rote response about protecting operational security.

"Well the Iraqis clearly know by now that they have been routed, and we did see some footage of the action, General, so why can't you tell us about the Marine engagements?"

"The Marines were not engaged," the general answered. "In military terms, engagement is defined as involvement in maneuver and combat action. The Marines at Khafji were simply bringing in support artillery fire."

"Goddamn," the reporter cursed before the general took the next question.

At Khafji, Angus had been listening to the briefing on a short wave radio held up to his ear but set it on the hood of Lieutenant Castaldo's Humvee after a small cluster of other platoon commanders who had been holding a meeting gathered around. Most left when the broadcast ended, but the lieutenant stayed leaning on the vehicle.

His eyes were heavily bloodshot—the whites all but disappeared after three days without sleep—and his short black hair was matted to his skull. Long streaks of dirt ran across his forehead and down his temples where he had been rubbing his face with his hands. It looked like someone had been drawing on Castaldo with a burned cork. Angus knew his own face probably resembled the lieutenant's, except he hadn't shaved his red stubble.

"No one want to throw my ass out of here yet?" Angus asked.

"You kidding, you're making us look like heroes. The next time Congress dares discuss cutting funding for the Marines, the commanders can wave your articles at them. And you don't think those wusses in the JIB are going to come to a war zone to look for you, do you? They might soil their uniforms."

Angus grinned. "Any news from your powwow?"

"What started out looking like a skirmish is turning into a rather pivotal battle. We are beginning to look at this as a kind of dry run for how to plan for the assault on Kuwait. Everybody figures if the Iraqis do badly here, it will be a real morale blow for them later when they try to defend Kuwait, so this could be a real turning point."

"That's big," said Angus, writing furiously again in his notebook. "Any action today?"

"There's been a whole series of little Iraqi incursions all along the border. Nobody can quite figure out what is happening, but the Republican Guards have been either firing at isolated vehicles or grabbing them and taking prisoners."

"Really, people killed or captured?"

"Well it's about a dozen killed, and the captured aren't fully known so far because there are a bunch of recon units who don't always check in regularly, but six people remain unaccounted for."

"Is there still fighting? Anything worth describing?"

Lieutenant Castaldo caught the gleam in Angus's eye.

"Listen, we are not going near the place and there is no way I can get you to a unit that is. And if you find another reporter or another vehicle, don't strike off on your own, Dalziel. I mean that. These guys said the Iraqis are hiding right on top of the border, behind dunes or whatever, and when they see a vehicle coming along solo they pounce before anyone has a chance to summon help. You want to end up dead or a prisoner of war, go ahead. But I'm telling you all this so you stay the fuck away from the border.

"And another thing," Castaldo went on. "There have been reports of a large Iraqi force gathering on the other side of the border, which is complete and utter bullshit. The Saudis have their hair on fire about it, and we don't know where it is coming from, but there are no tanks. So don't go looking for phantom tanks either; that will only get you snagged by one of those ambush patrols."

"Okay, lieutenant," Angus nodded. After sheltering him for nearly three days, letting him stay through all the combat, Castaldo was treating him like one of his own men. If he was saying there was genuine danger, he meant it.

"I have to get to another meeting over at brigade headquarters about where my platoon will deploy next," Castaldo said, jumping into his Humvee. "Maybe when I get back we can take a spin through Khajfi together."

Angus debated what to do. It had turned into a cold day. The clouds were gone and the sun was out, but a frigid breeze smelling faintly of salt blew across the sand. Leaning against another Humvee to get out of the wind, he wrapped his military parka more closely around himself and pulled down his black wool cap. He never thought he would miss the heat stroke from the previous summer, but he did.

For almost the first time since the entire Khafji escapade began, he wondered about Thea, if she was back at the hotel and whether she had seen his articles, whether she was admiring his work. Maybe that would win her back, he mused before he caught himself, dismissing the idea as utterly foolish. She would not jump back into bed with him because he got an exclusive. She was focused on her own career.

It was time to get busy with something else, to drive through Khafji and look at the mopping-up operation perhaps. He hoped that before Castaldo got back a WP photographer would materialize—Ryan or one of the others could be counted on to pop out of the ground like a genie just when you needed one most. They could cruise through Khafji, get a few details about the state of affairs there and haul back to Dhahran.

His spirits lifted when he looked back across the sand flats in the direction of the checkpoint and saw a forest green Jeep Cherokee racing toward the Marine line. When the Cherokee skidded to a halt, Angus was startled to see Aaron Black step out, his crew and a WBC correspondent emerging behind him.

"Hey congratulations, you are all over the front pages," Black said, smiling and pumping his fist in the air. "I figured you were where all the action is, so I came to find the same position."

The elation that Angus had been feeling about getting the Khafji story ebbed sharply at the sight of Black. It took a certain amount of self-control not to just turn on his heel and walk away. Angus ignored the compliment and stood stock still.

Black was wearing neatly pressed chocolate chip battle fatigues, as were the rest of the WBC crew. He reached into the Cherokee to pull out a sheaf of faxes.

"Here are the clips," he said, handing them to Angus.

"Thanks," Angus responded, trying to sound relaxed and failing at the last minute. "Cute uniform."

He searched Black's eyes to see if there was another message there. He didn't see any. The first faxes were the pool reports from the Khafji fighting that Angus scanned quickly, reading leads.

"Any reason to go through these?" he asked, hoping to drive Black away as quickly as possible. "I don't expect there is much in here that I don't know already."

"No, it's junk mostly, although there is a Quisburt classic," Black said. He explained that Quisburt filed a pool report saying that ten Marines were killed in action but did not say where or when. Since everyone in the hotel knew there was fighting in Khafji, they assumed the deaths happened there and ran with it.

"Quisburt fired off a screed against the entire press corps, implying that we're all dangerously incompetent," Black said.

Angus found it in the stack. It started: "Radio and television reports monitored extensively here in the field despite the trying conditions have erroneously and egregiously placed the Marine deaths in the Khafji area. This is wrong. I repeat, this is completely wrong. According to the staff officers with the 1st Marine Division headquarters, only small numbers of Marines have been involved in the fight to retake Khafji. I would like to underscore that I have worked hard to gain the credibility and trust of the 1stMarDiv soldiers who now treat me almost as one of their number. After pool reports are edited inaccurately, it hurts my standing at this end when broadcast reports come through with the bum scoop."

"Bum scoop?" Angus snorted, a little incredulous that Quisburt managed to slip in his beloved military slang. "Can you believe the hectoring tone of this thing?"

"Yeah, it's like having your wife on a pool," Black said.

Angus looked at him hard for a moment before lowering his eyes to read the remainder of the report, hoping to learn more about the Marine deaths, but there was nothing, merely a few more paragraphs decrying the mistake. In his writing about the actual fighting, Quisburt included only Marine officers describing how well their new equipment performed.

"He didn't go into the deaths at all?" Angus said without looking up at Black. "Nothing on who they are or how it happened despite being treated as one of their number?"

"Nothing," said Black, shaking his head. "It is sort of a pool report version of 'Aside from that, Mrs. Lincoln, how did you enjoy the play?' The only way to avoid using this garbage is to thrash around up here on our own like you've been doing."

Angus ignored the praise again. The guy obviously wanted something, but Angus would be damned before volunteering anything. He looked at the clips once more, rifling through the ones underneath the pool reports. After the fear and tension of the previous days, seeing his work in print made him feel good. Ryan's picture of the burning armored personnel carrier and Angus's story were splashed across front pages in Europe and the States. That ought to make a few editors at the *Post* or the *Times* take notice, he thought.

A few pieces in the stack from the British tabloids read curiously like his own copy but carried other bylines and datelines reading "With Allied Forces South of Khafji."

"Hey, I didn't see any of these guys around here," said Angus, holding up the offending pieces. "What unit were they with?"

"Oh yeah, I asked Vining about those because I wanted to find out how they sneaked in," Black answered. "He said all those reporters filed their dispatches from their lounge chairs around the pool at the Meridian

Hotel and they used that 'with the soldiers' bit because a few American and French soldiers were swimming."

"At a hotel! But they were two hundred miles south of Khafji!" Angus protested.

"I pointed that out to Vining and naturally he cited Churchill," Black said, quoting the line: "'It's not a lie, of course, but it is a bit economical with the truth.'"

Angus felt robbed, his exclusive tarnished. He had barely slept for two days, he was tired, his body itched from all the old sweat and dirt clinging to him and here was Black once again the catalyst for undermining what Angus thought was going to be his moment. Handing back the clips, he wished he could lash out somehow.

"Tell us what is going on here," Black said, trying to sound friendly but obviously impatient, wanting to find an important story of his own. "I've had the feeling since the first day I was in that infernal Dhahran hotel that the only way to get any news around here was to jump in the Cherokee and drive north, but every correspondent in the bureau said I was just trying to get him killed. You know television reporters only really believe the news if they hear it from print. So your example helped me kick a little ass around the bureau."

Angus looked at Black's hands rolling up the stack of clips and his mind flashed back to the first time he watched them kneading Thea's butt at that chemical weapons lecture, his mind retracing the night when Thea told him it was over because she wanted to spend the rest of her life with this guy. The last thing he wanted to do was help Black.

"I'm sure you'll figure out something," he said, hoping Castaldo would not show up right then.

Instead, a Toyota Land Cruiser totally covered in mud came racing across the sand, executing a quick hand brake turn on the wet sand, sliding 180 degrees and looking almost like it was going to slam into the group.

Ryan hopped out laughing. "Damn, war hero Dalziel in the flesh!" he hollered. Ryan sported a three-day beard and no longer felt constrained to keep his ponytail in his helmet. Although unwashed and greasy, the desert wind blew it in all directions. He had replaced his purloined uniform top with a faded jeans shirt with one pocket torn away.

"I hope I look more alive than you do," Angus shot back, walking over to Ryan and putting his arm around him, drawing him away from Black and the others so they could sketch out a plan. "What happened to the trusty Range Rover?"

"Not so trusty. Couldn't find a new spare," Ryan answered. "Generals must have them all."

Angus told Ryan about the reporting he wanted to do in Khafji and started to brief him about what the Marine officer had told him.

"Listen, Castaldo told me about a couple reports, stuff about little Iraqi incursions all along the border and another one about more tanks massing on the other side." But before he got any further, he heard the lieutenant calling his name.

"Dalziel! Dalziel! Where are you? I want to talk to you about Khafji," he yelled.

Angus looked up, surprised. Castaldo must have driven up and parked someplace else while he was distracted by Ryan.

"Damn," Angus said quietly. "I don't want fucking Black barging in on our unit. Distract him and I'll talk Castaldo into taking the two of us into town."

He walked back past the line of Humvees to find the Marine lieutenant and then stood in such a way that Castaldo was facing Khafji and Angus could watch over his shoulder to see what Black and the others were doing. He figured if they approached he could change the subject or draw Castaldo away.

The whole WBC crew in their starched uniforms were huddled around the shiny hood of the Cherokee, looking at a map. Ryan had walked over to them and they were tracing their fingers along something. Angus frowned. He knew his photographer wanted to become a television cameraman to earn better money, but he did not want Ryan kissing Black's ass at his expense.

"You listening to me, Dalziel?" Angus heard the lieutenant say. He berated himself for getting so distracted by Black that he was not concentrating on reporting from inside Khafji. Castaldo described his plan to take a quick reconnaissance trip inside with a few Humvees and was offering to bring Angus along.

"Ryan's back; okay for him to come along too?" he asked.

Castaldo grinned and said, "Sure. Good to go."

Angus looked over the lieutenant's shoulder just in time to see the Cherokee shoot away across the sand, which took on a faded yellowish hue in the winter sunlight.

"Where the fuck are they going?" he asked Ryan, watching the Cherokee bump up onto the divided highway, its brake lights brightening suddenly as it reached the opposite lip before it disappeared over the other side.

"I told him what you told me about the tanks and he had already heard some of it on the radio, so we figured out the best route to the border," Ryan said. "The scoops around here just don't stop coming, do they? I told him we would link up with them just as soon as we took our leave from these Marines, without being too specific about Khafji. That is what you want to do next, right?"

"You what?" Angus almost shouted. He realized that Ryan had passed on his half-completed briefing, the one that Castaldo's arrival had interrupted. Ryan had given Black the impression that the next story was along the border, without knowing the lieutenant's dire warning about the risk of small groups getting kidnapped by the Iraqis.

He quickly explained the situation to Ryan; the photographer's face gradually darkening with a deep frown. "Oh shit."

"Should we chase after them?" Angus said slowly. "Or tell Castaldo to alert the units up near the border?"

Ryan thought for a moment. "You know, Black's a pro. Think of all the shit that he has gotten himself out of all these years. He's a survivor. If we tell the Marines to be on the alert for journalists, it gives them the incentive to start flagging all of us down. We won't be able to move around at all once we break away from these cats. Right now, we kind of have the run of the place. You positive you want to spoil our freedom to roam? I'm sure Black will stop to talk to any U.S. soldiers he encounters toward the border and they will warn him."

Castaldo yelled that he didn't have all day, that if they wanted to get into Khafji with him it had to be right away. That settled it.

"Christ I hope you're right, Ryan," Angus said as the two men jogged to the command Humvee.

KHAFJI had little to recommend it. Like most provincial Saudi towns, it was a mile-long strip of one- and two-story concrete buildings, some with a shopping arcade on the first floor, all painted a drab gray or flat yellow.

Iraqi tanks had destroyed the larger structures. They'd shot up the massive telecommunications tower, turning it into a blackened heap of twisted metal that ignited the post office underneath as it collapsed.

The first place where Castaldo got out to walk around was the local governor's palace, which the Iraqis looted. They'd even detached all the bathroom fixtures but fled without carting them off, a stack of pink toilets and sinks with gilded edges lying in a jumbled heap just inside the wrought iron front gates.

Castaldo walked stealthily through the palace ahead of them with a 9-millimeter pistol drawn. But all they found inside were the remnants of small fires for teapots, a nasty smell and hundreds of flies buzzing around because the Iraqis had smeared their own shit on the walls.

After wandering around on the streets for a little while, they turned a corner and ran smack into the official Marine pool. The same TV correspondent Angus had watched at the checkpoint immediately raised a ruckus.

"This is our story. You guys don't belong here! This is pool territory. Officer!"

In the years since he had become a journalist, Angus couldn't remember a similar incident of turf hysteria, discounting the tension within any news organization over who got what assignment.

"You're a prick," Ryan snarled. "You don't belong in a combat zone."

Nikki Vassos, a waif with curly black shoulder-length hair and appealing décolletage under her flak jacket, came up to Angus and said hello. He was grateful for the distraction and smiled broadly.

Nikki was his neighbor in Cairo, the Middle East correspondent for the *Los Angeles Times,* but he had seen little of her during the war. He had bumped into her a couple times at odd hours slinking out of the room of a stocky young Saudi, the spokesman for Aramco assigned to the hotel who lived a few doors down from Angus. She always claimed that she was checking one last fact before filing to meet various West Coast deadlines. He was convinced that was not the whole story but never teased her about his suspicions.

"Our TV friend is from another galaxy," she said. "It's bad enough that he treats people outside the pool this way, but he treats everyone inside the pool exactly the same."

She told Angus about an incident which supported his prejudice that all television reporters were lightweights bent on wrecking what was once a worthy profession. In Nikki's pool, the Marines gave every reporter a ration of one bottle of water per day. They left a pile of bottles outside the pool tent before dawn each morning so the reporters could grab one on the way to breakfast. The day after the TV reporter arrived, all eight bottles were empty when the reporters emerged and nobody could figure out why.

"I asked the guy if he had seen anyone drinking the water," Vassos said. "And do you know what he answers? 'I used it to wash my hair.' That was our drinking water! Everyone was screaming at him about how he had been there for one day and would never last the war. But of course he complained to the Marine public affairs officer who caved and got him an extra ration of water. Then the PAO moved him into his far more comfortable tent."

A Humvee pulled up to the curb just then and a Marine major hopped out, so Nikki stopped talking and both of them turned toward the officer. He had come to order Angus and Ryan to leave, confirming that only official pool reporters could be in Khafji.

"You've gotten a lot out of here, writing for days without us doing anything, but it's over, time to revert to the rules and to leave this to the Marine pool," the major said.

Angus glanced at Lieutenant Castaldo. He shrugged, so Angus figured it was no use arguing. He had enough stuff to describe the town anyway, and a confrontation with the major might reflect badly on the lieutenant. He didn't want that to happen.

Ryan growled but Angus put his arm around his shoulder and, addressing the officer, said, "Okay Major, we'll leave, but I'm afraid we'll need a ride back to our vehicle on the flats." He winked at Ryan to signal they could do what they wanted once they got to the Toyota.

"He winked!" the correspondent screamed. "They're not planning to go anywhere!"

"We would be happy to give you a ride. In fact we will escort you to make sure you don't have any trouble reaching the highway and staying on it, southbound." The major was as good as his word and led them back to the checkpoint, where he jumped out of his vehicle and signaled to Ryan, who was driving, to roll down his window. He called the sentries over and said, "Take a good look at these two. I don't want to see them around here for a while, and if they show up it'll be on your ass, is that clear?"

The two sentries saluted and barked, "Yes sir," then eyed the two WP reporters like vermin.

"We're going, we're going," Angus said as Ryan put the Toyota in gear.

"Why doesn't he just kneecap us and get it over with," Ryan groused.

They both knew the major was technically right. They had broken the pool rules, but after getting away with so much, being ordered out was deflating. They had reported real news from the sharp end, the front line, the story's leading edge. It was almost a compliment to their efforts that they had to be ordered to leave. So with just a flicker of frustration at having to abandon the story, Angus and Ryan headed south back to the restrictions and round-the-clock bickering of the Dhahran Palace Hotel.

At least I have one scoop to celebrate, Angus thought, looking west across the desert painted orange by the setting sun.

Chapter Twenty-Four

THE BOOM of a Patriot missile rattling the Dhahran Palace came as a relief. Angus had returned from the Battle of Khafji to discover that the WP's newly created War Desk in New York was going berserk, peppering the Dhahran bureau with a ceaseless barrage of unhelpful comments, suggestions and questions.

Thea was still on a ship in the Gulf somewhere.

Angus had spent the first morning reading myriad pool reports. He had been uncharacteristically eager to do it, content to hang around the JIB to talk to Colonel Fletcher, Lieutenant Swain or any of the other guys, wanting to be the first to learn any news about Black.

He recognized on one level that Black's disappearance was not his fault. The guy was like the Venus fly trap of producers, ensnaring any news that flitted within his grasp with the same ease that he attracted women. Black likely would have headed for the border whether or not he encountered Angus and Ryan—he'd even crowed about how he'd been hoping to drive north for some time. Still, Angus knew he could have made more of an effort to haul him back.

There had been no news, and after a full day sifting through pool reports about Desert Storm, as the military christened the offensive, Angus had begun to feel queasy. It was bad enough that the press moored in the Dhahran Palace was hoping to make sense of the broad sweep of the war by gluing together copy from scattered points, passing that off as comprehensive war coverage.

The problem was that much of the reporting was crap, either cute features or dull mood pieces describing soldiers sitting around doing nothing. It was as if there was no fighting going on, no dead bodies, no key advances, everything filtered and refiltered down to human interest to the point that Angus felt it would be of no interest to anyone.

He had no idea how he was supposed to spin news of the war from the stuff. Barely one report in four contained something usable.

One profiled a chaplain who left the infantry to work for God. "I went from bombs to bombast," he said.

Another focused on a description of a twenty-two-pound chunk of granite that the 37th Engineers Battalion carted into the field from its home base. "This tradition carries a lot of weight," the story concluded.

Some of the reports were mere diary entries: The bleached blonde columnist he had interviewed briefly on the morning Thea left the hotel focused on her rented Jeep Cherokee getting stuck in the mud. The half-ton army truck that pulled it free started by wrenching the fender right off. "My very own cool little war machine was marred forever," her report pouted.

A British reporter contributed a tone poem: "They came out of the setting sun in a line astern, a platoon of Marine M-60 battle tanks, clanking their way across the desert as they prepared to circle the wagons for the night. As the sun's last rays drowned beneath the horizon, they pierced the dust clouds and the vehicles were momentarily bathed in a rosy glow. But as they throbbed past, the spell broke. Their names stenciled on the sides reminded you of their reason for being here: Grim Reaper. Hell Raiser. Public Enemy."

The air raid sirens mercifully interrupted Angus's attempts to make news from these scraps. Two Patriots went off and he ran for the roof, struggling into the jacket of his chemical suit as he went, thankful that a little action would release him from the task at hand.

Since Saddam had not yet fired a Scud armed with a chemical warhead, the WP bureau decided to keep two staffers on the roof to work the phone. If there were satellite problems, one could retreat indoors to the bureau to file. Angus gave Vandusen the first shot at broadcasting while he did missile lookout.

He glanced around to discover feverish activity. The audience back in the States was lapping up the live broadcasts from the rooftop.

In New York, the tabloids were handicapping various reporters as "anchor material," with Spencer Carr anointed crown prince. The WP's War Desk asked the Dhahran bureau to do a profile of him. Angus ducked that assignment, but he read some of the articles that New York faxed over as fodder: war reporter as pinup.

The *New York Post* anointed Carr the "Scud Stud" and splashed his picture across its front page. All the tabloids included quotes from women gushing about how they never expected war coverage to be so exciting and was that perfect guy Carr married and how they couldn't wait for the next Scud attack so they could see him again.

"Millions of admiring female eyes stay locked on their television sets for hours each night in hopes of even a mere glimpse, or better yet, a Scud attack," wrote another New York media columnist.

A third paper compared him favorably to a movie star: "The Rocky Mountain buck with the unruly blond hair and the bomber jacket plays to the camera with the look of a James Dean bad boy. When he talks to the anchor, he doesn't face the camera, as if addressing his boss, but swivels his head from side to side like a rebellious adolescent yearning to break free," the paper wrote, ignoring the fact that Carr, like everybody else, had been anxiously looking out for incoming missiles.

Out on the roof, Angus discovered that the reporters left unmentioned by the tabloids were rabid to get on the air.

He found the scene at ABC astonishing. Carr was again standing in front of the mirror—tonight testing whether the epaulets on his khaki shirt looked better buttoned or unbuttoned—when an older, taller correspondent named Frank Jergen stepped onto the platform.

"I've been on air far longer than you and certainly working here in Dhahran longer than you, and since you have been doing all the live shots, so if you don't mind, Carr, I'm going to do the broadcast tonight."

"It's like this, Jergen, I do mind," Carr shot back, putting down the mirror and turning to face the guy, planting his two legs slightly apart like a western gunslinger defending his turf. "You saw the messages from New York; they want me. The viewing public will not be denied.

"Get off my platform, buddy," Carr growled, pushing Jergen and making him stumble backward.

Jergen, the far larger man, moved forward and shoved Carr hard in the chest with both hands, knocking him off the platform. "I'll show you whose platform it is, you snot-nosed little shit. Get off and stay off!" he snarled.

Since there had been no Scuds or Patriots after the initial attack that prompted the air raid sirens, the fight hypnotized everyone on the roof.

"You asshole, you can't push me around like that," said Carr, jumping up on the platform and seizing Jergen by the throat, strangling him. Jergen grappled with him and succeeded in reversing their positions, getting Carr around the neck in a hammer lock. The two rocked back and forth on the platform, scattering the chairs and tipping over the potted palm.

A petite producer tried to separate them or at least prevent them from knocking down the flimsy walls. But she retreated after getting bashed a couple times by stray punches. She attempted to referee instead.

"Your faces!" she implored, "Don't hit in the face; black eyes look really bad on camera."

She also appealed to the cameraman, the soundman and various technicians to separate the two, but they shrugged it off, enjoying the spectacle of high-priced talent belting each other. "Let them duke it out, what the hell," Angus heard the cameraman say. "Should I film it for the Christmas video?"

Next to Angus, Vandusen emitted his deep, disparaging laugh. He was on hold to WP radio. "Who knew watching Scud bait was better than professional wrestling?" he said.

After jostling around the ABC platform a few more times, the older correspondent again succeeded in flinging Carr off. This time Carr tripped on a knot of cords and sprawled on his back. Angus heard the ABC satellite technician say, "The bird will be up in thirty seconds; get someone miked on that platform."

Jergen grabbed the microphone, clipped it to his olive green bush jacket and jammed the earpiece into place, then smoothed his brush of gray hair and stood facing the camera. New York evidently didn't like it. Angus heard the producer pleading with him. "You can hear what they are saying, Jergen, you've got to come down. They want Carr; he's boosting the ratings."

"That is bullshit. I've covered more wars than anyone for this network," Jergen said. "I did Vietnam, Beirut, the Falklands; name any war in two decades and I've been there."

"We all know what you've done, Jergen; it's New York's decision, " the producer said, her face softening in a look of pity. "They want Carr because the phones have been ringing off the hook asking about him. There is no question who is going on."

Jergen flushed, ripped off the microphone, flung it to the ground and stomped off the platform. "Fuckin' pretty-faced little pussy. I hope the things are crammed with anthrax tonight," he raged as he retreated back into the hotel.

Carr retrieved the microphone, clipped it on and shook his head back a few times to fix his hair. The cameraman tilted the camera up and down his body, then focused a tight shot on his groin for New York's amusement.

"Hey, I saw that," said Carr, looking at the monitor and grinning. "Knock it off."

Suddenly two Patriots roared aloft, leaving a yellowish plume of fire behind and vibrating the hotel. The reporters now knew the choreography, with each sound seeming to echo because the Patriot batteries fired off two missiles in quick succession for every Scud.

AFTER just two days back in the hotel, Angus found that life developed a loose pattern. Between dodging Scuds at night and reading pool reports all day, he was barely getting any sleep. He would eat the chocolate mint the hotel staff left on his pillow each night and then collapse into bed with his clothes on to save time running up to the roof.

Then Saddam started to lob the occasional Scud during the day, when the number of allied warplanes that patrolled Iraq's airspace seeking the launchers dropped. Angus discovered that daytime Scud attacks proved an excellent time to play tennis since many players failed to claim their reserved courts.

He worked out an arrangement with a junior WBC producer. At the first sign of an attack, if neither drew the assignment to cover it, they would grab their racquets and head for the courts. It felt good to get in a little physical activity outside the hotel, despite the slight risk of metal fragments raining down on his head.

Walking in from one game, he learned that there was plenty of marauding going on during the attacks. Angus found the frowning hotel manager standing by the buffet table in the Dunes, shaking his head. With limited fresh vegetables available after all civilian air traffic stopped due to the war, Brandt had converted the salad bar into meat and potatoes fare. He made everybody laugh by placing a big sign next to it that read, "Scud Spuds." Brandt was reading all the clippings too.

"What is the matter, Mr. Brandt?" Angus asked.

"It is just strange how people react in different ways to this war," he answered, explaining that when the last air raid siren sounded, the almost naked bone in front of him had been a full leg of lamb. "I am afraid I am going to have to assign one waiter to stay upstairs during the air raids, because apparently a whole bunch of reporters are using the occasion to steal free meals. What they say is true, Angus. War really does bring out the best and worst in people."

Angus occasionally descended to the shelter during the attacks: it seemed tempting fate to ignore them entirely. Down there, bored, his thoughts inevitably drifted to Thea. He marveled that the war seemed to be working as prescribed; he had been too busy, too tired and too distracted by the hothouse atmosphere of the hotel to dwell on her absence. She had not been gone that long, but given the rapid pace of unfolding events it proved difficult to figure out where she was, never mind when he might see her again.

Journalism was always like that, eating away great chunks of time no matter what was happening. His attachment to Thea had begun working on him like an avalanche slowly gathering speed, though, upending the established order of his life. Previously he would have worried that any meaningful relationship would undermine his work, distract him from the story, but now he had begun to sense that the opposite was the case, even when he admitted to himself that he didn't have a relationship any more.

The truth was, he missed Thea badly. He constantly imagined their reunion, but given their last encounter, doubted whether it would ever happen. The memory of her parting words had a sobering effect: he should not expect any change. Mixed in with thoughts of Thea was the troubling recollection of his last encounter with Black.

There had been no word from Black and the WBC office had said nothing. Angus had avoided asking too many questions; they might want to know what he had seen or heard about the team up at Khafji.

So he fell back into the old pattern of trying to keep himself distracted by writing stories. Scud attacks were exciting diversions. An even more cavalier attitude toward the risk posed by Saddam's missiles had developed among some reporters, who condemned as wimps anyone who went to the basement or even donned protective chemical equipment during an attack. But it took a spat between Callahan and another WP reporter to reveal the depth of the tension.

Toward the end of a quiet overnight shift, Callahan returned from a short food run in downtown Dhahran to find an air raid warning in progress. He bolted upstairs to get his gas mask, but the door to his room was locked and he could hear the unmistakable grunts and sighs of raucous coupling inside.

Callahan tried to interrupt by tapping on the door, saying repeatedly, "Hey, guys, could I come in for a second? My gas mask is in there." But nobody answered him.

By the time the all clear sounded, Callahan had worked himself up into a righteous outrage: "I could have died during that air raid because Reynolds was humping in my room!" he shrieked. Callahan was infamous for his prima donna outbursts, his eyes rolling around in his head behind his thick glasses. He was making the most of his moral high ground:

"He came back late last night, saying he needed a place to sleep. I gave him the key without even thinking about it. Where does he think he is? Am I supposed to sleep on the same sheets all rank with his sweat and spew? It's disgusting!"

Angus tried not to laugh, since it would set Callahan off again. "Call housekeeping and have the sheets changed," he said, but Callahan wasn't listening. Other WP staffers walked into the bureau and he started narrating the tale all over again.

Then Erik Reynolds sauntered in, looking relaxed and freshly showered, the black hair slicked back on the sides of his otherwise shiny bald head. Reynolds, a fit man in his early forties, had been having an off-and-on relationship with Lydia for months, the two sleeping together whenever they ended up in the hotel but not advertising themselves as a couple.

"You look like a man who just ended a long streak of abstinence," Vandusen joked as Reynolds entered. "News travels fast. It's already been on the wire."

Reynolds chuckled.

Callahan spun around. "What the hell do you think you were doing preventing me from getting my gas mask?" he squawked. "It's one thing if you want to die, but do you have to take me with you?"

"C'mon Callahan, the shelter is for pussies, and so are gas masks. Who wears them anymore?" Ryan said. "What we really want to hear about is Reynolds getting some."

Reynolds looked a little sheepish, drawing himself a cup of coffee and sitting down on the couch with a copy of the *Saudi Chronicle*. "We didn't do it on purpose; it was just that we were both asleep, stark naked, when the first Patriot launch jolted us awake," he said by way of an explanation, opening the paper and hiding himself behind it.

The photographers were not about to let Reynolds get away with that brief description. He was reluctant to go into much detail at first, but gradually they pulled the story out of him.

Lydia awoke first, groggy, and started to cuddle while he argued that the alarm meant they should get dressed and head down to the shelter. Instead she reached for the remote and turned on the television to watch the live reports sent by correspondents standing practically outside their window.

"She refused to leave, saying if we were in any real danger we could find out from the TV."

The two watched Riggs on CBN giving the standard report that Scuds carrying chemical weapons were always a strong possibility. Lydia reluctantly agreed to put on her mask after some arguing but refused to leave the room or get dressed.

"She kept saying, 'Think how romantic it will be if they find us here together, naked, wrapped in each other's arms with only our gas masks on,'" Reynolds said, grinning. "I kept telling her it would look more idiotic than romantic. Well, a little fondling led to more and pretty soon we were all over each other."

"You mean you did the deed with your gas masks on?" Angus asked.

"What was *that* like?" Ryan added.

Callahan interjected, "I could have been poisoned because they refused to follow the rules and go to the shelter and all you guys care about is what the sex was like?"

"Poisoned, my ass, Callahan," Ryan said, shushing him. "Come on Erik, spill, what was it like?"

"Yeah I want to hear this," Vandusen seconded. "Even vicarious sex sounds good to me. It's been so long that plant genitalia are looking good."

"It was kind of anonymous and kind of wild," Reynolds said quietly. "I felt driven in this weird way I've never felt before. I'm not sure it was from not being able to see her or from the thought that we might die at any minute, or a combination of the two."

The suite went completely still. The phone rang but nobody answered.

"We were both sweating inside the masks to the point that it was pouring down our bodies. We were sliding all over each other. But I must say I felt this incredible exhilaration. I mean more than the usual rush. I've never experienced any sex close to that intensity, ever.

"I came like a cork shooting out of a bottle," Reynolds said. He looked up and blushed, realizing he had given a more vivid description than he meant to.

A sly grin spread over his face as he added, "It seemed exactly the right thing to be doing during an air raid—especially since theoretically we could have bought it at any minute. You know, to go out with a bang."

Everyone on the couch groaned at the terrible pun, sacking Reynolds with pillows and then piling on top of him.

When the antics stopped, Angus went over to the CBN bureau to see if he could find out when Thea might reappear. Reynold's story woke him up to the fact that what happened between him and Thea was more important than war reporting. The CBN bureau chief, Kosakowski, wasn't around though, and nobody else in the bureau knew anything about Thea's itinerary.

Angus went back to his office, volunteering to watch the morning military briefing from the Riyadh Hyatt as an excuse to spend time in front of the television so he might catch one of Thea's reports. She would surely want to talk about them whenever she resurfaced.

At least one reporter from WP Dhahran always watched the live broadcast in the unlikely event that something urgent would be announced and they needed to file or follow it up instantly.

In the third floor lounge area in front of two giant television sets, it was all war, all the time. Tomahawk missiles permanently stalked the streets of Baghdad, fighter-bombers never stopped taking off and warships incessantly churned the Gulf. After about fifteen minutes, it always seemed to Angus like the replay button had jammed.

Yet the spilled coffee cups, crumpled potato chip bags and overflowing ashtrays on the glass coffee tables in front of the televisions testified to a permanent reporter encampment.

Angus introduced himself to an Hispanic guy, who turned out to be a senior writer from the Washington bureau of the *Newark Star-Ledger*.

"Working on anything good?" Angus asked him.

"Right now, can't you tell?" the reporter answered, provoking a rueful chuckle from the other characters sprawled on the couches. "I was thinking of commissioning one of the photographers to take a picture of me sitting here, drinking Perrier and watching the daily briefings. The caption would read: 'War Correspondent.' My kid could take it to show and tell."

Angus was bemused by the eccentric cast of war reporting extras more or less stuck in front of the television. They included a fifty-five-year-old former Green Beret, now editor and publisher of the mercenary magazine *Soldier of Fortune*. A tattoo of a sexy cartoon character, Daisy Mae, adorned his still impressive left bicep and he wore green fatigues, a sleeveless black T-shirt, a bulletproof vest and shiny black combat boots. His gray hair was chopped close to his scalp and he sat ramrod straight. He looked menacing even sitting still. His T-shirt read, "A Good Commie Is a Dead Commie."

Near him slouched a lanky, skinny guy with a dishwater blond pony-tail. Angus didn't believe he was really a correspondent for *Audubon* maga-zine until the guy pulled *A Field Guide to Birds of the Middle East* out of his vest. He was wearing jeans and a plaid flannel shirt as well as the vest, which boasted numerous special pockets for various birding paraphernalia.

"Uh, what exactly brought you here?" Angus wanted to know, think-ing to himself that every publication on earth must have dispatched a reporter to Dhahran.

The guy explained the oily cormorant predicament.

In the opening days of the war, Saddam had uncorked the spigots on various coastal oil pumping stations in what many feared was a prelude to igniting the entire Gulf. Instead of burning, the giant oil slick became an environmental disaster. Fouled cormorants washed ashore in such numbers that the reporters in Dhahran were soon grumbling about "more dirty birds" every time they had to file a cormorant update.

"It didn't really sink in with a lot of people in the States just what a bastard Saddam Hussein is until they saw the pictures of the fouled cor-morants," the *Audubon* man said seriously. After he had finished writing his piece, he told Angus, he decided to stay and cover the war rather than pursue his next *Audubon* assignment about the crested grebe.

These journalists had so little hope of getting out to a real unit that they watched the war on television or joined hapless trips put on by the Saudi Ministry of Information in hopes of landing an unexpected story. One day it was to a Saudi factory that made plastic headboards shaped like roses, the next to a poetry slam where a senior Saudi prince insulted the Iraqis in verse.

"They call us the special projects pool," the former Green Beret barked. "But do you know what we call it, Dalziel? The *cesspool!*"

The other reporters hooted.

Angus seemed to have stumbled through a hidden door and discov-ered a parallel world within the hotel. Reporters from large organiza-tions like WP might complain about spending too much time confined inside its walls, but most eventually found an escape route. These guys seemed utterly trapped. It was the first time Angus ever considered he might be lucky.

"Isn't it miserably depressing, knowing you could be stuck here for months like this?" Angus asked.

"It's a lot like covering the White House, except with air raid drills," the Newark reporter said. "You read pool reports, you watch CBN and you write your story. The wardrobe is a little different, but I could see a flak jacket as a useful accessory in the White House press room."

The group laughed, then quieted suddenly as CBN started playing its special Gulf War theme music, the frenetic drumbeats signaling the start of a live report.

Chapter Twenty-five

ANGUS did not learn much sitting in front of the television, but the porn flick incident finally gave him a sense of what Thea was doing.

A WP reporter with Thea in the navy pool befriended a fighter squadron on the aircraft carrier to the degree that they invited him into their ready room while they were suiting up for a bombing run. The tradition of this particular squadron was to screen hardcore porn right before they put on their flight suits, the onscreen action getting their adrenalin pumping before they headed into hostile territory.

The reporter mentioned the movie in something like the sixteenth paragraph of his story in a list of things various pilots did to prepare for combat, including taking a hot shower, reading the Bible, writing home or listening to hard-driving music like the original Stones version of "Satisfaction."

But the admiral in charge of the fleet, who had taken to vetting all copy coming off his ships, demanded that the porn movie be deleted. The WP reporter complied in the interest of getting his story ashore but scrawled "note involuntary change" on the original copy sent via the mail pouch and included a brief note to Dhahran explaining what happened.

Under the pool rules, the news organizations agreed to a degree of censorship, camouflaged as a "security review" in military parlance. But a rumble was swelling in the hotel about officers meddling with copy that had nothing to do with operational details and would in no way jeopardize the security of the units being covered.

Angus suggested a censorship story to WP in New York, dreading the interviews with other reporters but thinking it was a sure route to learning more about Thea's whereabouts, and the War Desk approved.

He figured there would be no better place to start than the ruling rabbi of the press corps, R. Lash Champion, a veteran *Washington Post* reporter of patrician stock who was their Dhahran bureau chief. He was a rabbi in the sense of mentor or godfather—the oldest, wisest member of the press corps, happy to dole out advice to younger reporters. Champion was a legendary figure, as prone to order up a ten-course banquet and describe it in sensual, minute-by-minute detail for the Style section as he was to analyze the administration's foreign policy for the front page.

He hadn't been seen outside his suite in so long that reporters were gossiping among themselves about what he was doing. Then someone spotted him hoisting his substantial frame onto a stool at one of Gabandi's Abu Falafel fast food restaurants in a downtown mall. The joke flashed around the hotel that he was researching a lengthy food piece called "The Glorious Garbanzo: Fashioning a Flawless Falafel."

Despite the jokes, everyone recognized Champion as an old-school reporter who fervently believed serious newspapers should get priority in being assigned to the field. Angus admired the attitude, especially after reading endless pool reports and witnessing some truly idiotic television requests.

Angus had been in the JIB once when the weatherman from the *Today* show piped up. "Can you send me someplace where there is a sandstorm, but not so much sand that it will make it difficult to see me?" he asked in all seriousness. "I'm picturing gentle swirls, with enough wind that the microphones can pick it up as a kind of backbeat, but not so strong that I have to shout over it."

Angus thought the JIB guys would laugh him out of the room. Instead, they treated the request on a par with plans for, say, the Battle of El Alamein, calling dozens of units to collect reports of sand conditions.

On the censorship issue, Angus had no sooner walked into the hotel suite that served as the *Post's* bureau and mentioned the topic when Champion exploded. "Security review! That is utter balderdash! It's not enough that the commanders are fighting a war out here, but now they want to edit copy too," raged Champion, normally a garrulous man slow to anger. "May I remind you of what the guidelines say? Here, I'll read them. They say, 'Material will be examined solely,' I repeat *solely,* 'for its conformance to the attached ground rules, not for its potential to express criticism or cause embarrassment.'"

"Jesus, Champion, I've read the guidelines," said Angus, marveling at the oriental carpets stacked around the room. Everyone had been stuck in the country long enough and was sufficiently bored to buy several rugs, but the *Post* office exhibited a truly imposing collection. He also noted that the usually dingy gray hotel walls had been repainted a quiet shade of white and the bureau had far better lighting than everyone else, although the dusty blue velvet curtains were drawn against Scud attacks as in most rooms. "Save your tirade for the JIB or the Pentagon. What exactly happened?"

"We sent this guy, Max Waldman—young guy, beautiful writer, stories slay you—out with the Stealth bombers. He and the other pool reporter with him got real news—that the planes hit a nuclear facility on their first bombing run—not to mention these incredibly vivid descriptions from the pilots, truly riveting quotes, about flying those bats into combat. You remember Saddam bragged that if the Stealth flew under the radar, the Iraqis would knock them out of the sky with rocks, right? So there was all kinds of fantastic material in this story."

"I'm with you so far," Angus said, trying to write extra fast since misquoting a *Post* bureau chief would be a particularly black mark on his hopes of working there.

Champion continued, "Max wrote an epic story: newsy, interesting, a damn fine read, nothing sensitive in it, but the colonel in charge all of a sudden decides he doesn't like it. It doesn't read like *Top Gun*. I mean, have I ever told them how to fly a plane?"

"So what happened?"

"The colonel started fiddling with the wording. It's unbelievable! Waldman described the pilots coming off missions as 'giddy,' and the guy scratches it out and writes 'proud.' Then the colonel decides that the commanding officer back in Nevada might want a sneak preview since his birds popped their combat cherry on this run. So he transmits the stories to the officers sitting out there in West Butthole, who take their own sweet time changing even more. They called Waldman in the middle of the night telling him what to alter. The guy is young, he wants to get his story out, so of course he says yes."

As his anger mounted in recalling the incident, Champion's face reddened and beads of sweat popped onto his brow. "It took four days, four goddamn days, to get us the story. What do they think we write for, monthly magazines? What would have been a big splash on the front page about the first use of a major new weapon, which bear in mind cost U.S. taxpayers over $100 million apiece, was buried inside as a kind of dated feature. And for what?"

"Well, we all agreed to a security review," Angus noted.

"Yes, we agreed to *one* security review," said the bureau chief, shaking his plump index finger to emphasize the number. "One. We didn't agree to one on every level all the way up the chain of command to God. They may know how to fight a war, and bless them for that, but they don't know the first thing about moving perishable copy. They are doing it on purpose to kill the stuff—it's censorship by delay. That's all I have to say."

Angus told Champion briefly about the porn flick incident and then asked him if he knew of anyone else experiencing similar problems. He gave Angus a few scraps that he had heard, telling him that Thea Makdisi also ran into navy flak using tape from an admiral's briefing and that Reuters got a weather report flagged as information potentially helping the enemy. Angus was about to walk out the door when Champion changed the subject.

"By the way Dalziel, this can probably wait, but I wanted to tell you I had a conversation about you the other day," Champion said, his face still red although his tone was less charged.

Angus, uneasy, stiffened.

"The *Post's* foreign editor asked me who I thought was doing a stellar job reporting around here and I put your name at the top of the list. Don't get your hopes up too high, but he said he was going to take a look at your clips and get back to me. I expect to hear from him any day, so don't disappear before checking with me. He may want to speak to you about a job. Now off you go."

Angus thanked him profusely and left the *Post* suite dancing a foot above the carpeting.

He couldn't quite believe his luck. He now had the prospect of a far better job plus a legitimate excuse to walk into CBN and request to see Thea's work.

"Now why exactly do you want to see this stuff?" Kosakowski, the bureau chief, asked in his slow drawl.

"I told you, Sam, it's for a censorship story."

"I am not exactly sure this here stuff from the USS *Kennedy* would qualify as censorship," Kosakowski said, spitting his nicotine chewing gum into the trash and popping a couple fresh pieces from the pack. "Are you sure you're not trying to get your rocks off?"

Angus looked at the skinny bureau chief sharply, weighing how much he knew about their private life. But it seemed a generic question based on the widely recognized babe factor rather than a specific gibe.

"The public affairs officer on the *Kennedy* doesn't seem to want the press aboard," Kosakowski went on. "In her memo, Thea told us that the material from other carriers is much better because their press officers are pilots. They want to show off what they do, so they drag the reporters into every nook and cranny, let them stand around for hours and watch planes land on deck or whatever they want.

"On the *Kennedy,* Thea said the pool was locked into a ward room when the admiral announced that the war was starting. She apparently told the press officer that he was an incompetent idiot for preventing them from recording an important moment in history, and he answered that he had never met a reporter who was such a bitch," Kosakowski said, chuckling. "He was in the wrong, of course, but I suspect two or three reporters in this bureau might want to shake his hand."

"He really used the word 'bitch'?" Angus asked.

"That's what she told us," said Kosakowski, still chuckling and punching a few buttons.

Thea suddenly materialized on the screen. She was one of four reporters sitting on folding metal chairs while the admiral who ran the Persian Gulf battle force explained the entire deployment, placing little metal ships on a large magnetic map. Thea was wearing her bulky military field parka, with grayish circles etched deep under her eyes from lack of sleep and her hair uncombed. But to Angus she looked stunning, even sensual.

The camera swiveled to show a knot of the admiral's top aides in their crisp white uniforms, nervously chewing their lips in the back of the room while their man talked. Sure enough, he divulged a real stunner.

"And our submarine," the admiral said, placing a little magnetic one on the map, "has performed the first successful launch of a cruise missile from a submarine in wartime."

Angus heard his aides gasp in unison. One hastily interrupted, "Ah sir, excuse me sir, but we are not supposed to mention submarines at all, sir. They are considered highly secret, sir. We are not even to confirm that we have one, sir."

"That so? Well dammit, it's part of my carrier group and I want it recognized," the admiral responded, but then ignored all further questions about it. Still, he said just enough for a fairly exciting lead and the aides knew it. As soon as he exited they demanded that the submarine go unmentioned.

Angus watched Thea put her hands on her hips as she faced the little circle of officers. "Listen guys. He's a big boy. He must know what he's doing, he's the admiral, right? So if the admiral said it was okay to use it, who are we to contradict him?"

The officers grimaced. They couldn't challenge her without making their boss look bad, so they argued that the reporters not mention specifically that the submarine was in the Red Sea. You could see from the expression on Thea's face—the slight grin and the flicker in her eyes—that she knew she was holding all the cards.

Watching her, Angus felt his entire body grow taut. It was the strongest, most thorough sensation of longing he had ever experienced, almost a physical pain. Seeing her onscreen made him vow all over again to get her back.

"Yo," said Kosakowski, snapping his fingers in front of Angus's eyes. "You see a ghost or something? Think that is material you wanna use?"

Angus shook his head, startled. "Well as you pointed out, it's not quite censorship is it? I mean they limited a little bit of what was said."

"Yeah we birded it to Miami last night, so it should be all over the broadcast today, plus I read through the pool reports this morning and saw the print pool used the submarine info too."

"Guess I'll keep looking," Angus said and then added in what he hoped was a casual voice, "Thea and the rest of the pool coming off that carrier anytime soon?"

"She wants to get back here badly because she feels like she's missing the main action. But despite the bickering with the navy she is getting pretty good footage, so I think we will leave her out there until she really screams."

As Angus exited the CBN bureau, he saw Larissa Tyler emerging from the WBC suite next door. She had that hunted look that correspondents get when the boss is in town. The infamously edgy WBC anchorman had arrived the day before and all the network's staffers were scurrying around like mice.

"Hey Larissa," Angus called out softly, jogging a few steps to catch up with her. "You know any censorship anecdotes, or are you too busy leaking exclusives to *People* magazine entitled 'What the Anchorman Ate for Breakfast'?"

"Very funny," Larissa said. "It's not exactly censorship, but we did just get an amazing lesson in the power of the American military. You interested?"

"Sure."

"To make it short, our man had just arrived in Riyadh when Saddam suddenly announced the possibility of a peace deal negotiated by the Russians. There's no equipment in Riyadh for live broadcasts, so New York was desperate to have him anchor the news from Dhahran, but to get here in time he had to fly."

She was whispering and glanced around nervously, tucking a strand of her long auburn hair behind her ear, concerned that the anchor or one of his producers might stroll out of the bureau and catch her spilling network secrets.

"So we requested to charter a jet, even though the air space is closed. We first asked the Washington embassy—I mean Khazzani, that young diplomat here in Dhahran—who thank God reacted fast because it was the anchor. So anyway, he phones the prince in Washington from here and the prince phoned the king, who granted permission.

"But when the request got to Schwartzkopf, who has to sign off on any civilian jet using military air space, he blew a gasket and said no, the airspace is closed to everyone, that WBC would have to drive its anchorman from Riyadh to Dhahran like other mortals."

"Schwartzkopf overruled the *king*?" Angus asked, amazed.

"Yeah, how about that?"

"It must be the first time in history that the military has refused a request from television. I mean it's almost a story! Maybe I can fit it into the censorship theme."

Larissa punched him on the shoulder. "Don't you write a damn thing, cutie pie, and don't spread it around either. Only a few of us know and they will try to trace the source if it gets published. Someone has probably seen me standing here talking to you. I'd better go."

"Any news from Black?" Angus asked quickly, anxious to hear something without drawing attention to himself.

"Nobody's heard a peep," Larissa said, walking away. "I almost feel sorry for the guy."

Angus felt his stomach constrict. He turned and walked toward the WP bureau when a ruckus suddenly erupted in the JIB, someone yelling in a terribly loud voice about the dismal quality of the pool reports.

As he paused to listen, it occurred to him that characterizing the Dhahran Palace Hotel at the height of war as a three ring circus was woefully inadequate. It was too few rings.

"Look at this one!" the voice boomed from within the JIB. "Here we have a report about prisoners of war. Are there numbers? No. Do we know if they are elite Republican Guards or tired fifty-year-old reservists? We do not. The important news in this report is that the American soldiers guarding the prisoners cannot pronounce Iraqi names, so they call them all Elvis. Terribly amusing, I'm sure, but I'm afraid it doesn't rise to the standard required for a newspaper whose readers demand hard facts and actual news."

Angus recognized Champion in full flow.

"What is this dreck? My reporters, all combat veterans, from what you will surely agree is one of the most important papers in the nation, are cooling their heels in this hotel while we are being force-fed what I can politely describe as absolute garbage."

Colonel Fletcher answered in a low voice, so to hear his response

Angus joined a small group of reporters who had edged over toward the pool report mailboxes right outside the JIB, pretending to look busy.

They heard the colonel say, "You surely would not want the military to choose who goes on the pools?"

"The entire system is a travesty," Champion hollered. "Look at these so-called reports. This one quotes soldiers speculating that their piss is setting off chemical weapons alarms because it is so full of the antidotes. This exposé from a fashion magazine reporter reveals that the medical units headed toward the front are carrying neither rape kits nor antidepressant pills. And finally here is a profile of Geronimo, a stuffed bear that a pilot takes on all his missions and has its own uniform and cot. Now I ask you, is this combat coverage?"

"It's not the military's job to vet the reports for quality."

"You and this entire JIB are incompetent; that is the real problem," Champion snapped. "If you dispatched more reporters from the *Post* or the *New York Times* to the field this kind of thing would not be happening. I think you are doing it on purpose to undermine the best papers in the nation and to ensure that the coverage is moronic.

"The most knowledgeable, most accomplished reporters are rotting in this hotel. Even the ones assigned to rapid reaction pools sit idle because their pools go nowhere. My newspaper does not have a single reporter in the field at present and I won't stand for it. Either we get better reporters on these pools or I will personally ruin your career."

"I beg your pardon?" the colonel responded, his voice suddenly flat.

"I will be in Washington next week at the Gridiron Dinner, and I am sure you are aware that the Gridiron Dinner is the most important mingling of politicians and the press all year. And I shall make it a point to tell the secretary of defense, who, by the way, is a very close personal friend of mine, that you have completely lost the confidence of the press corps and should be removed!"

For every decibel that Champion raised his voice, Colonel Fletcher dropped his, so by now no one could hear his icy whisper.

Champion came out rumbling, "We should all just drive north, and to hell with your asinine pool system."

"You are aware that no unilateral reporting will be allowed, and anyone caught risks being expelled from the country, no matter what the paper," said the colonel, standing just inside the velvet rope barrier, raising his voice this time.

The reporters outside the JIB grabbed stacks of the latest pool reports to see what had provoked Champion.

Suddenly Angus felt guilty for wasting time hanging around listening to yet another discussion about the ridiculous reports and not working on his own censorship story. If he wanted to work for Champion or the *Post* one day, he needed to prove himself.

He went back to the WP bureau, retrieved his tape recorder from the top of the television where he had left it to record the Riyadh briefing and rewound the tape to lift any quotes he might need. There was a strange interruption in the middle that he soon figured out was Callahan talking on the telephone. To his chagrin Angus suddenly realized that Callahan was discussing him. Angus rewound the tape to the point where the phone rang and listened to the whole thing.

"Hi Ed, fine thank you. Yes I'm working on it right now." Angus figured out that Callahan was speaking to Devon, the WP foreign editor. After the initial pleasantries, Callahan's tone changes abruptly.

"What do you mean, read you my lead? I am still working on it. What do you think I am, some fucking robot that needs to be guided on how to write a story? I think after all these years I know how to construct a lead and I can't be expected to dictate it over the phone," he said, his harsh tone changing to a whine. "I told you I have good stuff, don't you trust me? Haven't I delivered for you in every damn crisis the world has experienced for the past couple decades?"

Angus knew Callahan was writing a story about how the Gulf War was going to liberalize Saudi Arabia. It repeated a theme of Angus's earliest work, but now he no longer believed it, sensing that the brewing backlash would probably empower the conservatives. The hardcore religious types had awakened and were beginning to howl.

Devon evidently said something about Angus having covered the ground already and that Callahan should avoid repeating it, so Callahan turned to him. "I am extremely aware of what Angus wrote. In fact everybody is aware of what Angus wrote because the Saudis made it quite clear that he and the rest of us might find ourselves with express tickets right out of here because of it."

Angus tensed. Callahan was trying to dodge the flaws in his own story by lying that the Saudis were still seeking to boot him. No Saudi had threatened that for weeks. It was evidently not the first time Callahan had broached the subject with Devon.

"No, I didn't tell you he was a terrible reporter, nor did I call him useless," the tape continued. "You must have misunderstood. I merely said I don't think he is a team player. He kept running off to places like Khafji without talking to anybody about it and that pissed the Saudis off. They said if he or any other WP reporter was found there, they would throw us all out. I think we have enough problems what with the pools and everything without worrying that Dalziel is going to jeopardize the entire WP effort."

There was a pregnant pause while Callahan listened to Devon again. Finally he said, "No, there haven't been any incidents lately that I am aware of, but something more troubling. A reporter from another news organization heard Angus intimating to the Saudis that I don't like Arabs, that all my reporting about them is negative. You know my own visa is due to expire soon and I am concerned that I may not get another one because of what he said. That is obviously a real slap in the face for me, and as far as everybody else in the bureau is concerned, I do think that might smooth things out with the Saudis and give us better leverage to chase harder stories if he was removed. Of course I understand that the final decision rests with you in New York."

Angus turned off the tape recorder, stunned by the audacity of

Callahan accusing him of not being a team player. Callahan always hogged whatever he needed—cars, hotel rooms, translators—without asking a soul.

Angus expected that Devon would be calling to reprimand him, maybe even pull him this time. Anything Callahan said was accepted as gospel. The simple solution would be to get out of the hotel, out to a unit or something, to produce copy like the stuff from the battle of Khafji that would override any thought of removing him.

He brooded about the editors possibly having forgotten Khafji already, although less than a week had passed. Working all day and most of the night had made it seem at least twice that long. But there was a saying in the WP that you are only as good as your last big one.

He heard other WP reporters and photographers coming in through the outer door and vaulted from his chair, deciding it was better to avoid everyone and go write his story in his room. He bumped into Hawxhurst on his way down the corridor.

"I want to get the fuck out of Club Scud, but if I go unilateral not only will I have the army and the Saudis gunning for me, but my own office," Angus said, telling Hawxhurst in sketchy detail why he was concerned.

"Tell me about it," said Hawxhurst, wrinkling his nose. "This place is a stinkin' snake pit. Remember Desirée Shield?"

"One of the most unforgettable women I have ever met," Angus said, thinking back to Thea and the scene that unrolled on New Year's Eve. "Don't tell me she is gunning for your pool position?"

"Not quite. When I went out with my pool I left an envelope of pictures from that party lying around the office. Didn't give it a second thought. When I came in from the field, there was a message from the woman in the office who sent me that doll. She said someone in Dhahran mailed back a few pictures that showed me dancing with Desirée, and whoever received them put them up on the bulletin board in the Washington bureau on a sheet of paper with 'Our Man in the Gulf' written across the top."

"You're kidding! Who would do such a thing?"

"I have my suspicions. But the point is the editors were ready to pull me. The editor who sent me Desirée saved my ass by saying she mailed me the doll as a joke and dared me to take pictures to prove I was in love."

"Like reporting a war in a place like Saudi is not hard enough without this kind of shit," Angus said with rancor.

Chapter Twenty-Six

IT TOOK a week before Black and his crew were confirmed missing.

The WBC bureau grew uneasy after the first twenty-four hours but kept quiet. Black was always scrupulous about checking in. They hoped he would come swaggering back any minute bearing a slam-dunk story.

Then an army recon unit found his team's Jeep Cherokee just over the border in Kuwait, near a tiny crossroads called al-Wafra. The soldiers followed deep vehicle tracks that swerved crazily back and forth across the border in what looked like a chase. The tracks lead eventually to the green Cherokee. The back axle had fallen off and all the doors were open, but there was no sign of violence—no bullet holes, no blood. Expensive camera equipment sat unmolested in the back and a stash of $5,000 in hundred-dollar bills remained safely tucked inside the glove compartment.

The soldiers said it looked like the axle had been torn off by the impact of hitting the ground after the Cherokee launched over a small hummock —the tracks stopped at the hummock. Footprints indicated that the four men walked to another vehicle that had driven north into Kuwait.

Word of the discovery raced through the Dhahran Palace.

Angus stopped by the WP bureau after a late lunch with Lydia to make sure he wasn't needed for anything, finding only Vandusen and Callahan sitting around on the couch discussing the disappearance.

"Fuck, I can't believe all those dark jokes we made about getting an interview with the grim reaper if we set off on our own might suddenly come true," Vandusen said. "I just can't stomach the idea that the military has a real live example to wave in our faces about the consequences."

"Not to mention that all four guys might well be dead," Callahan said.

"Of course," Vandusen added quickly.

Angus didn't want to speculate about it. "Black's a survivor," he said, deciding to adopt Ryan's line and abruptly turning around to escape the conversation. He just wanted to find Thea. Lydia had told him that she was back.

He was turning to leave the bureau when a young WBC producer walked in with a petition demanding that the military deploy all means available to locate the missing team. Colonel Fletcher planned to hold an open meeting that night about the disappearances and the petition would be handed over then. Nobody was looking forward to the meeting, since Fletcher would likely pile on additional restrictions.

Angus quickly scanned the page. "Four of our own have been captured," it started; he was taken aback to find the petition written in the petulant way most television producers speak. "We need to employ all the resources possible to get them. In fact, we demand that they be rescued. If it takes hundreds of troops, so be it. We are not suggesting that we know how to get them, but you do and we the undersigned urge you to apply all possible means toward rescue as quickly and as efficiently as possible."

The producer had already collected hundreds of signatures.

"Is everyone in this hotel delusional?" Angus spat, then considered briefly if it would look bad later if he did not sign. Maybe people would suspect he wanted Black and the rest held captive, and somehow the link with Thea would emerge. Was he actually responsible for all this?

In any case, it was absurd that these guys thought the WBC team could be retrieved from Iraq, risking further lives when the four were either dead or long since hauled off to Baghdad. "Do all these people really believe the army has nothing better to do than send hundreds of men chasing after four journalists?" Angus said.

"Hey, our guys shouldn't have to die just because they were out there telling the army's story," the WBC producer insisted.

"No story is worth dying for, but it happens," Callahan interjected from the couch, pouring scorn on the rescue idea. "Why stop at asking for an entire division? Why not demand that the army go storm Baghdad right now. I mean this really is a crisis. Forget about the oilfields; journalists have been captured!"

"Hey, if it was you, wouldn't you want the U.S. military to save you?" asked the producer, indignant.

"If I flaunted every rule in the military code of conduct, I don't think I would expect the Special Forces to come swooping down like a guardian angel, no," Callahan shot back. For once, the bastard is turning into a rational ally, Angus thought.

"It's the risk we all take," Callahan went on. "Sure it's a game and we have fun with it, but there is a dark side."

"You mean we shouldn't do anything about these guys getting captured, just roll over?" the TV producer said, an angry blush spreading up his neck to his face.

"If you mean this might prevent us from trying to do similar reporting, of course not," Callahan answered. "Black was a fantastic, aggressive reporter. But sometimes, notably during a war, you pay for aggressive reporting."

Angus had heard enough. He walked down the corridor to Thea's room, weighing what he would say. He could hear the soft strains of Fayrouz, the Lebanese diva, through the door. It was her mood music. He knocked softly. There was no answer. He knocked harder.

She came to the door. "Who is it?" she asked.

"It's me," he said. Then realizing they were well past the 'me' stage, he added, "Angus."

"What do you want?" she said, adding hopefully, "Is there news?"

"No, I wanted to make sure you are okay," he said, dismissing the thought as soon as it occurred that maybe he should confess his role in what happened to Black. There was no response. "C'mon, Thea, open up."

She did. She looked utterly drained. Tears had streaked the kohl under her eyes. Her body was wooden when he hugged her, but she held onto him and tapped her forehead against his chest a few times. She didn't look at him.

"So are you okay?" he asked.

She pushed away, sitting on the edge of the bed near the headboard, one leg tucked underneath her. "I don't know, mostly numb really, but look," she said, turning her palms up in her lap. "No slashed wrists." She managed a wan smile and then collapsed. She fell sideways on the bed and smacked a pillow with her fist.

"Oh Angus," she wailed, tears flowing. "I feel cursed. Everything was going so well. I can't understand it. I was finally doing what I always wanted to do and found someone to share it with and now it all seems gone in a flash. Aaron may be dead, and the hotel is crawling with other CBN people who are somewhat less than eager to have me hanging around fighting my way onto the schedule for live shots. Not that I can work anyway."

"I don't know quite what you mean," Angus said, sitting on the edge of the bed and taking one of her hands in both of his.

"I understand I'm not the official widow or anything," Thea sobbed. "But everyone knew about our relationship and it would seem odd, not to say extremely callous, for me to be hanging around the hotel jousting for stories and live shots when the man who was practically my fiancé is missing and probably dead. It would be unseemly. Nor do I want to do it. Yet I feel he would want me to carry on."

She rolled over onto her stomach, her body racked with sobs.

Angus flinched inwardly at the fiancé line. But it was painful to see her so distraught. He wondered how she might react to him trying to hug her again, which he longed to do. Instead, with great restraint, he sat down on the bed next to her and gently rubbed her back. She sniffled repeatedly but after a bit rolled onto one side and hugged him around the waist.

"I am so glad you're here," she said. "You are the only person in this hotel I can face right now, the only one I feel I can trust."

Angus lay down on the bed and pulled her over on top of him, enveloping her in his arms. She lay sprawled across his chest, crying quietly. "Oh Angus, what if he is dead? What am I going to do then?" she moaned.

If he is dead, maybe we can try again, Angus thought, but he knew it was far too soon to voice that idea. She probably wanted reassurance about Black's fate, but Angus decided he wasn't going to lie this time, either.

"I wish I could tell you he will be fine, Thea, but who knows what happened," Angus said, still running his hands slowly up and down her back. "Black was an accomplished, hard-hitting reporter, no question, but it's Iraq, Saddam's Iraq, I don't see them showing any mercy. Remember Bazoft?"

In March, just five months before Saddam invaded Kuwait, a naive British journalist of Iranian origin was caught picking up soil samples, trying to prove that Iraq was producing chemical weapons after vague reports emerged of a massive explosion inside what was thought to be a munitions factory. He was found guilty of spying and hanged.

Thea nodded her head mutely and another wave of keening rolled through her. "And what about that ludicrous petition?" she sobbed suddenly. "Of course the military should not devote those kinds of resources, but it would seem heartless not to sign it and what would people say? And I am so desperate to have him rescued that part of me hopes it would work."

"Hey you shouldn't fret about any of that," he said, hugging her, relieved that she felt the same way he did. "People understand you have had a shock."

"But that's just it! I want to do something," she howled. "I want so desperately to be doing something, to be out there leading the charge, but I can't, I can't do anything publicly. Can't. Can't. Can't. It wouldn't be fair to him, it wouldn't be fair to that wife. WBC would hate me for it. CBN would be horrified. It's funny, but if I was an ordinary colleague it would be different. But I'm the mistress, shunted aside, hidden. Let's face it, I'm not allowed to care, I'm not even allowed to be involved. It leaves me breathless."

With that she collapsed into his chest again and sobbed. Angus wondered how long it would go on before she would exhaust herself, thought maybe he should go root out a shot of whisky to make her feel better.

Eventually the sobbing slowed and Thea lay still for a time before he felt her wriggling. She pulled her tear-stained face up and put both her hands across his chest and rested her chin on them. Her face was inches from his.

"But here I go weeping on and on about me without congratulating you for that fantastic work in Khafji," she said, wiping her tears sideways with the back of each hand. "Of course I always knew you were a true war correspondent. Everyone else hated you naturally, but I was rooting for you, so proud of you."

With that she reached her face up to kiss him. Angus expected a polite peck on the lips but she held it, squeezing him as much as she could since she couldn't get her arms underneath him. Then she rested her face sideways on his chest.

He touched her face to wipe away the new tracks the kohl splotched across her cheek but just smudged it more. She raised her face to him again and he tried to wipe both cheeks. It still wasn't working, but rather than confess that he was making more of a mess, he stopped and looked at her.

The pale gold light of the late afternoon was all but gone from the room. He got up and drew the curtains, plunging the room into darkness, then came back and lay down beside her. He started to speak but she reached up and kissed him once more, then put her right index finger to his lips. "Don't say anything Angus, I don't want to talk about it anymore right this minute. Just hold me please."

He hugged her and kissed the top of her head. They lay still for a time and gradually dozed. Eventually Angus started and looked at his watch.

"Hey," he said shaking her shoulder gently. "Colonel Fletcher called a meeting about the disappearances after dinner. It will probably be starting soon. Do you want to go?"

She rolled over. "I can't imagine anyplace I want to be less. All those reporters turning around and staring at me every time he said anything to see how I was reacting. The British tabloids circling like vultures. That blonde viper from ABC's morning show pretending to be sympathetic. 'Come on the show to tell us who Aaron Black really was,' she'll say again. Then she'll catch herself thinking him dead and say, 'Or is, I mean,' and giggle and try to add something like, 'You knew him so well. Of course we wouldn't mention a thing.'"

"Why don't I go and find out what happens?" he suggested, as much to assuage his own fears as hers.

"No, don't go, stay with me," she pleaded.

Angus suggested he could hover at the back to see if there was any update, any more details from the recon team or possibly a message from Baghdad itself via a sympathetic capital like Moscow. He would return the second it was over. She relented.

As he walked down the corridor, Angus rolled through his head the sequence of events over the past few hours. He couldn't help the slight effervescence that was creeping into his feelings. There had been at least a hint of their old ardor in that first kiss. He just needed to be patient, to help her get over the initial shock.

In the third floor lounge area several hundred reporters sat on folding chairs, facing a podium. A dozen television cameras stretched behind the chairs. Colonel Fletcher walked out of the JIB with a couple news executives from WBC who had flown over from New York.

"The infamous suits, in the flesh," Angus said, sliding into a seat next to Hawxhurst.

Colonel Fletcher announced that Egyptian forces stationed near the border had reported questioning Iraqi defectors who witnessed the four newsmen being detained. The defectors swore that no one was blindfolded or visibly mistreated. The colonel called this a positive development, noting that if eyewitnesses reported them alive, then Baghdad could be held responsible for the men's well-being.

Angus felt a certain relief at the news but had his doubts about the warning to the Iraqis. After the British Iranian journalist was found guilty of espionage, the British government had haughtily announced that it held Saddam Hussein personally responsible for the reporter's safety. Saddam had him hanged that day.

Colonel Fletcher continued, "We are doing everything in our power, but it has been clearly stated by the JIB from the beginning of this conflict that serious consequences can result from unilateral action by reporters. Let me review the rules with you."

"Duck! Here it comes," Angus whispered loudly to Hawxhurst, but before Fletcher could say anything else, the WBC producer who had been circulating the petition stood up and handed it to the colonel.

"This is from the entire press corps. We think it is not only in your power but is your responsibility to get those four newsman back."

Colonel Fletcher, normally an unruffled man, strode out from behind the podium, flushed and angry. He barely glanced at the petition before speaking, delivering each word like he was hitting a hammer on an anvil.

"For those who presume that you can flaunt the rules, flaunt the agreements that you signed, and then turn right around and expect the military to rescue you, let me tell you this: You are living in a fantasy world. From the very beginning you have all approached events here much too casually.

"You treat the entire theater of war like one extended Sand Café. You think you can saunter in and out at your leisure and turn to us or not, as if it's all just one big buffet table. Well, I have a news bulletin. You ought to be able to understand that.

"This is not The Sand Café. This is a war, a real war, ladies and gentlemen, with real consequences, where people may live and people may die and there may be nothing any of us can do about it. There is no U.S. Cavalry at your disposal. The sole means we have to keep you safe hinges on all of you following the rules. Make sure you remember that, all of you, before anyone else winds up in Iraqi hands."

With that he stopped talking and strode off. The reporters sat uncharacteristically quiet, chastened like the schoolchildren they so often resembled, until he disappeared into the JIB, then everyone started babbling at once.

Chapter Twenty-Seven

ANGUS was eating in the Dunes late one afternoon in mid-February when Lydia stumbled in with red-rimmed eyes. She was elegantly attired, as always, wearing a white silk blouse with pearl buttons and tailored black wool pants, but she looked absolutely shattered.

Angus wondered if the worst had been confirmed about Black and his crew.

"What's the matter, Lydia?" he asked after she sat down at a small table and started picking at her salad. "Is there news?"

"How the hell should I know," she snapped.

"Not to intrude," Angus said, "but you look like you've been crying."

"I was watching bitches," Lydia said, swallowing a mouthful of spinach. "And I wish my editor was here so I could strangle him."

"Excuse me? What bitches?" Angus asked.

"Not bitches, *Beaches*," said Lydia, relaxing a little. "The in-house movie channel was showing *Beaches* and I was watching it. If you don't know the story, Bette Midler and Barbara Hershey have this deep friendship and Barbara is dying and everyone is abandoning her except her egomaniac friend who promises to take care of her little daughter. It's this women friendship movie. You know it has that famous song 'You Are the Wind Beneath My Wings.'" She hummed a little bit of it.

"I'm a little confused. You are mad at your editor because the Dhahran Palace was showing some maudlin chick flick?" Angus asked.

"No, silly," Lydia said, and told the rest of the story.

She had worked every day for three months, but with the air war in a monotonous pattern and no sign of action on the ground, she decided to take most of Friday off. She had already written a longish piece for her magazine about how soldiers who saw a woman reporter in the field would come up and share their problems. Friday morning she read through the edits that her desk sent her overnight and the story put her in an emotional mood, so she went to Safeway and bought a lot of junk food and stayed in her room, watching the movie. By the time the closing credits were rolling and that theme song was playing, Lydia was weeping contentedly.

At that point the phone rang and she picked it up without thinking.

Lydia continued, "There was this booming voice on the other end saying, 'Good Morning Lydia Santangelo, this is Bruce so-and-so talking to you live from WSFO, talk radio in the Bay Area!' And I'm thinking I must be dreaming and he bellows, 'Lydia, you are talking *live* right now to our radio audience this morning. Tell us what it is like out there...

"Well Angus, you can imagine. I'm already lying on my bed crying and now suddenly this guy is asking me questions and I'm weeping into the phone and burbling on about God knows what. I can remember saying at one point, 'It's awful, it's terrible, it's war,' or something dreadful like that. In the meantime 'You Are the Wind Beneath My Wings' is playing on and on and on in the background and I'm afraid if I stop talking for an instant all the drivers will hear it, you know."

With that Lydia began to laugh and sing in a smooth voice at the same time, "Did you ever know that you're my hero, You are everything that I wish I could be, I can fly higher than an eagle, You are the wind beneath my wings.

"And I'm sure if Bruce what's-his-name hears the song he will ask me what I am doing and I can't think of anything to lie about that would have that kind of background music. So I keep crying and talking and talking and crying. God! How awful. I was weeping live on all-news radio. I can't wait to get my hands on my editor. If he ever gives my name and phone number to any radio station again I'll castrate him!"

Angus laughed, "Just another grueling day in the life of a war correspondent."

"Oh Angus," Lydia said quietly. "I know I shouldn't get upset about these things, but there is something about this life that warps our emotions. Although I told myself after I heard about Black's note to his wife that at least I am not going through what poor Thea has to put up with."

Angus's heart leaped. Had something happened that he did not know about? Last he had heard Black's wife was in Amman, hoping he would be released from Iraq any day.

"I thought you just said you didn't know anything, that there was no news?" he said, his voice tight with anxiety.

"I don't know anything specific. But there was a report on CBN from Amman just a little while ago that the Red Cross visited the WBC guys and got messages out to their families. Black sent his wife a few lines from Shakespeare about love being eternal.

"It seems captivity has shocked the sentimental old coot back to his former ways, didn't I know it," she went on, shaking her head and frowning. "Poor Thea, I know just what she must be going through, she's probably shattered all over again." With that she finished the last of her spinach salad and pushed her faux bamboo chair back from the table, asking Angus if he wanted anything from the dessert buffet.

"No thanks," Angus answered, standing up, his mind already far away. Leaving the Dunes, he thought it peculiar how the airless, sequestered hotel was such a cloistered environment that you forgot that elsewhere in the world people were doing normal things like driving to work listening to talk radio. He was determined to learn by the end of this war to carve out space for his own life and weighed how long it would take him to figure out if it was going to be with Thea or not.

Angus walked upstairs to Thea's room. He hadn't seen her for a couple days because their schedules had not coincided, but last night she did the overnight shift and he hoped she had woken up by now.

She opened the door wearing a lacy red silk teddy. From her puffy eyes it seemed like she had been crying again. The room was dark, with the curtains pulled, but the bedside and bathroom lights were on and the television was tuned to CBN with the sound off. She turned toward her closet and began pulling out clothes. He decided he would wait a little while for her to bring up the Red Cross message.

"Don't get dressed on my account," he said.

"Do you know what yesterday was?" she asked in a tart voice.

Lydia had mentioned that today was Friday so Angus knew the day before had been Thursday but no other clue sprang to mind. The war rolled on with so little change to punctuate each day that one blended seamlessly with the next like an endless strip of pastry dough.

He looked at the date on his watch. February 15. That would make yesterday February 14. Was it her birthday? Oh shit, he suddenly remembered.

"Of course I do. It was Valentine's Day. Where are those damn roses I ordered?" he lied. "Is that what the luscious underwear is about?"

"I wasn't thinking about Valentine's Day," said Thea, yanking on a pair of ironed jeans. "It was the second anniversary of Ayatollah Khomeini's fatwa sentencing that writer, Salman Rushdie, to death for insulting the Islamic religion."

"And you think we should be marking the date with a story?" Angus asked.

"No, not a story," Thea said, tugging a black turtleneck sweater over her head. "But it got me thinking about life beyond this hotel, how what is happening in the region is so much more important than what we are doing or showing on television. I think I need to get out, get back on the streets, get back to where I belong, back to reporting."

"Hey I was just thinking about life outside the hotel too," Angus said, "I heard the funniest story from Lydia…" He got that far before suddenly grasping that she was talking about leaving the country.

He had grown comfortable around her again. But he recognized that he still had to do something to ensure that Thea and he had a real chance at permanence, not that he had said anything to her about it yet and certainly not while old wounds were still healing. The whole Black thing remained a cloud, a very dark cloud, poised over their heads. Still, he didn't want her to leave.

"What happened to her?" Thea said.

"I'll tell you later, " Angus answered. "What were you saying?"

"I think the reporting on this entire story is askew. Sure the Scud attacks and all the military footage of bombs dropping creates gripping television and it's making me famous.

"But what is the public learning? Those Scud attacks are totally insignificant in military terms. There is no way Saddam can change the course of the war one iota with them. Yet they are shown live night after night because it's the only real action we have access to. The real stuff is happening hundreds of miles away and how much of that have we seen?"

Thea was in her desk chair, twirling a ball cap purchased on one of the aircraft carriers. Angus sat on her bed with his back against the wall and his legs straight out. He'd kicked his black loafers off onto the floor.

"It's an air war; it's not like you can jump on an F-15 and ride along on the mission to take pictures," he said.

"I know that, but it has become completely sanitized. You said it yourself the other day when you were frustrated with the pool reports. What did you call it? Oh yes. 'A fartless bathroom.' Always so vivid, darling, you know how I love you for that," she giggled, and then her face turned serious again.

"I mean what are we up to now? 10,000 air sorties? 20,000? And think how many pictures of dead Iraqis you have seen. Almost none. Suddenly because we have the technology to broadcast live, whatever is live becomes the priority whether it is good journalism or not.

"The old standards were chucked right out the window. I wanted to be Edward R. Murrow describing the London blitz; instead I'm entertainment. Hear sirens wail. See people run. See Scuds explode. Viewers can sit in their living rooms and experience every crash, bang and false alarm in the Dhahran Palace, but is that what the soldiers are doing, is that what they are tasting? No. We may be on twenty-four hours a day, but it is not bringing viewers a real sense of war."

Thea stopped, staring at the silent television.

"But you are, Thea. You are bringing the war to the viewers," Angus said, getting off the bed to massage her neck and shoulders. "Maybe the stuff is repeated to the point where it starts to look like Nintendo, but it's not for nothing that they are calling this CBN's war, just like you said it would be the first day we met."

She dropped her head forward as he rubbed. "On the way back from the aircraft carrier the guy driving us asked where we worked. When I told him he said, 'Oh, CBN, my wife watches CBN back home night and day. She wrote me that she even wakes up in the middle of the night to watch it for a few hours in case she missed any developments.'"

"See, what are you fretting about, everyone is watching," Angus said.

"Yeah, except do you know what he said next? He said, 'My wife's a basket case. I told her to knock it off, no more CBN.'"

Angus laughed but Thea went on: "And you know what? He's right. She is getting upset over nothing. I mean can you imagine the diet of television that woman has been living on? See a Patriot slam into a Scud in midair. Watch the Scud explode. Watch the reporter put on a gas mask and speculate whether the bomb is full of poison gas or not. Maybe so, maybe not, maybe so, maybe not. Watch the video of the pilot using new whiz-bang technology hit his target. And if you miss any of it? If you went to get a sandwich or feed the dog or go to the bathroom? Don't worry; it will be repeated over and over and over again."

"They call it the first draft of history," Angus said. "It's supposed to be a little rough."

"Rough?" Thea shot back. "Can you imagine if they tried to write a history of the Gulf War based on what the press filed? Don't make me laugh.

"The absurd thing is that I have to be in this hotel to get on the air all the time. This sand trap is turning me into a household name, what I always wanted. It's ironic, but if I leave, try to go do something real, I don't get much air time and the viewers might forget me.

"This war could drastically alter the map of the region. God knows what the effect will be on Saudi Arabia. When was the last time anyone turned a camera away from the war and tried to interview one of those religious lunatics like the guy we met in Riyadh together, for example? How are they reacting to all this?

"Instead we are sitting caged in some thrill house for reporters, transfixed by these little firecrackers that fall out of the sky. What we should be doing is chasing real news from the field, what the soldiers are really doing. That is what Black was up to. It was the right thing to do, dammit, no matter what the outcome."

Angus was never quite sure how to respond when she mentioned Black. He managed to keep at bay his conflicting feelings—hoping Black would make it but fearing the consequences of any heroic survival.

"If they have let him live this long I'm sure the Iraqis won't kill him, Thea. Everyone knows he's a survivor. I'm sure they'll all be released when this thing is over. You heard the news today about the message he sent, though, right?"

Even as he asked the question, Angus stiffened, waiting for the reaction. Thea did not talk about Black all that often, but Angus felt he was being silently compared to the missing producer. Sometimes Angus felt confident that she was happy to be with him, but sometimes he was assailed by doubts that he was a lesser draft choice or not her choice at all, just convenient.

She occasionally cried out Black's name in her sleep, and during sex she would tear at Angus's back or chest in a frenzy that felt more like frustration than desire. He had decided not to ask about it, at least not yet. It had to soak out of her like a fever, he figured. He was troubled though, that he was repeating a sin from the past by not broaching the topic.

Sometimes he thought he knew the answer anyway. The spark between them was there but needed oxygen to catch fire, needed to get away from the Dhahran Palace with all its enclosed mildew.

Thea, sitting in the chair, sniffled and wiped her hand over her face. Angus could tell that she was wiping tears away.

"You know, Angus, I think I also told you on the first day, or at least alluded to the fact that having someone to cling to during a war helps keep the fear of death away," she said quietly, still sniffling. "I was wrong about not needing the same reassurance, or at least some reassurance, which is how I ended up sleeping with you both, I expect. Extreme cir-cumstances force odd choices. I don't regret it, but I am sorry if I hurt you. I think I told you that already."

Angus stood behind her stock still with his hands resting on her shoulders, wondering where this was going. She took one of his hands and held it against her cheek as she continued talking.

"Black's message to his wife upset me, sure, but it was hardly a com-plete surprise. Men traumatized by any war often revert to the familiar; it's the fastest way to restore their sense of equilibrium. I am not going to go chasing after him, if you are troubled about that. It's over. I was in love with you once, or at least starting to fall in love with you until I talked myself out of it. I am starting to again, but this whole thing with Black has been too fervent, to intertwined with my work here for me to have any perspective on it. That is another important reason for me to get away."

Angus stepped back and sat down on the bed again, rubbing his fore-head with one hand and then resting his chin in his palms. Everything she had been telling him since he walked into the room seemed a little off-kilter, still wrapped up with Black's disappearance and not strictly about journalism. He couldn't just keep telling her everything was fine. He wished he could summon the right words.

"And another thing about the coverage," she said suddenly, walking over to the full-length mirror by the bathroom door and jamming a brush through her hair with fierce, quick strokes.

"We always mock Quisburt as a war correspondent gone bush, becoming more Marine than the Marines. But have you noticed that the more restrictions they put on our movements, the more everyone tries to make it sound like the press is part of the same team, avoids challenging the Pentagon version of events. Suddenly it's 'Have we targeted Saddam Hussein?' and 'Have we achieved air superiority?' I don't want to be part of this 'we.' I frankly don't want to be a member of this club anymore. I hear the whispering campaign saying they should rename my network PBN, for the Pentagon Broadcast Network, and in many respects it's true.

"We're all becoming Quisburt," she concluded, still raking the brush through her hair.

"Hey, it's still the best story going and you are great at what you do. Just because you're surrounded by clowns doesn't mean you have to surrender," Angus said, answering her, but knowing he had to bring the subject back to them.

"There's no context for what we are doing, Angus," she answered. "It's all about technology, not real information or solid analysis. TV news coverage is a contradiction in terms. It's about making good movies. I know live coverage is nerve-racking and dramatic. Hell, I'm great at it. Viewers can't take their eyes off me. But that doesn't mean it's important."

"What about us, you and me, are we important?" he asked, plunging.

"Of course Angus, I just told you that," she answered, but did not linger on the thought, turning toward him to explain her plans.

"What I am trying to put into words is that all this is feeling overwhelming again. There was a bit of a fight last night over the live shots because there are more reporters who want to do them than there are slots. I got the slot last night, but I am so tired of this mud wrestling that I told the international editor afterward that if he could find a berth for me in any other city in the region, anywhere but this godforsaken hotel, I would jump on it. Miami is due to get back to me with an answer. As a matter of fact I should go to the bureau and see if there are any messages."

Angus wanted a resolution but sensed it was not the time to force one. Journalists could get jumpy when they decided it was time to leave a story, like feral animals willing to chew off a limb when stuck in a trap. He and Thea were comfortable with each other, that was the main thing, but he could not just let time run its course. He had learned that much, so again he plunged forward.

"Do you think we could transfer this whole thing, I mean you and I, someplace else when all this is over?" he asked, hesitating for a beat or two before adding, "I want that more than anything." He felt like he was tumbling, freefalling through the sky as he waited for her to answer.

"Oh Angus, I so want to try," she said in a low voice. "Although who the hell knows what will happen next."

"Hey, that's supposed to be my line," Angus said, making her laugh. She came over and kissed him.

It was not the clear-cut answer Angus wanted, but he would take it for now. He walked with her toward her office, where they parted. He felt both elated and uneasy. He would be damned if he worried about Black's life anymore; it was his own future Angus needed to try to shape.

When he walked into the WP bureau, he was surprised to find Reynolds lying underneath a blanket on the couch with bloodshot eyes. A vague yellow tint hung on his skin.

"You dying or just plain yellow?" Angus joked.

"Very funny," Reynolds shot back. "But it looks like it's gonna be you who gets his ass shot off chasing around the front. I have hepatitis so they flew me back from there. New York absolutely refuses to give up a pool slot with the commander of all the land forces, and since you are the only likely candidate left you have been nominated. New York told me to make it clear you have no choice. We've been looking for you all over the place. You've got about twenty minutes before the press officer will come back. So go get your war stuff together, guy, and then sit here and whimper quietly to yourself until they come and collect you. "

Angus was silent. After weeks of bitching about propping up the hotel end of things, he couldn't refuse an assignment out in the field. He would probably be back in a few weeks, a month at most. Hopefully by then things with Thea would be clearer.

He went to his room and sat down on the bed, knowing that he had no choice: he had to go. But he could depart in two different ways. He could go find Thea and tell her that no matter where she ended up at the end of the war, not matter what assignment she got, he would track her down because he wanted to spend the rest of his life with her.

Or he could just kiss her good-bye and say he would see her soon and hope it was true. That could mean a slow, wasting death and he had taken that awful route often enough before.

Angus glanced at his watch; there was no time to sit there pondering the future. Who was he kidding? He had a deadline to meet, and life would have to be put on pause once again.

He had to tell Thea he loved her before he left, though, so after hastily assembling his backpack, his hand shaking with excitement and his heart beating so that he could feel it in his ears, Angus went and tapped on her door. When he got no answer he rushed to the CBN bureau.

They told him she had been pacing around, railing about the need to get out, and finally a couple of the other women dragged her off to go shopping downtown. They didn't know anything about Miami sending her elsewhere.

Angus groaned, frustrated, but there was no solution. It was an occupational hazard—the other party being absent at a crucial moment. He would find another moment.

Angus scribbled a quick note explaining what was happening to him. His mind was still racing but he knew clearly what he wanted to say. "I hope I'm not leaving you alone and afraid in a world you never made," he wrote. "I will come find you as soon as this thing ends, wherever you are."

Chapter Twenty-Eight

THE GROUND war barely lived up to its name. It was a rout from the moment the U.S.-led coalition rolled forward and the Iraqi forces melted away or surrendered. Saddam yanked the core of his elite Republican Guard back to Baghdad, and the tired, underfed dregs of the regular Iraqi army deployed along the border had no fight left in them.

In previews for over six months, the war shut down after just five days.

Not that anyone covering the thing from Dhahran got any real sense of the action. The communications lines were so badly organized that no stories, film or television video reached the Dhahran Palace from the battlefront. There was one dreadful night when a Scud finally walloped something, a warehouse barracks not far from the hotel, killing twenty-eight reservists. But few reporters managed to get onto the base to cover that either.

Out in the field, Angus watched the system fray. At night, after helicopter forays across the battlefront, he and a *Wall Street Journal* reporter camped with a rear logistics unit made up of army reservists from Kentucky and Tennessee. The unit's officers spent much of their time arguing whether helping the press or burning the outhouse shit was a worse chore.

Filing copy proved a nightmare, although for Angus it should have been easy. The pudgy, bald major in charge balked at the idea of assigning a vehicle to take Angus and the *Journal* guy down the road a couple miles to a little Saudi hotel, where they could use the switchboard to call Dhahran directly.

Pausing briefly from stuffing Fritos into his mouth, the major grumbled in his Kentucky twang, "Might be a road ambush situation," and gave the same stock answer again and again no matter how many times the two reporters argued.

By the time Angus got the commanding general to overrule the timid, dimwitted major and let the reporters drive down the road to file by telephone, it was the last night of the war.

Wanda, who was in the bureau, told him that Thea was gone but she didn't know where. With another guy waiting behind him to file and Wanda juggling dictation from several reporters, Angus couldn't dwell on the subject.

"Any word about Black?" he asked hastily.

"Not that I've heard, and anyway everybody's preoccupied with getting to Kuwait City now that the Kuwaiti resistance, with help from the Special Forces, seems to be in control. New York wants us to focus on that," Wanda told him.

Angus knew there was no point in hanging around a quiet battlefield, so he decided to go back to Dhahran, returning less than a week after he left.

Among the various notes shoved under his door he found a postcard from Thea, a picture of a Bedouin wedding scene, the veiled bride happily milking a goat while the contented husband leaned against the cushions of their low-slung black tent.

"What are you trying to do by disappearing—get my goat?" she wrote. "Next week, month, year (choose one) in wherever, darling, can't wait. Will try to keep the editors at bay and stick around, though. Believe me, you are the best thing that came out of this war. Missyoumissyoumissyoumissyoumissyou!"

Angus smiled but wondered exactly where she was. She was probably in Kuwait, where his own editors would undoubtedly send him.

The Dhahran Palace was eerily empty. The big top had folded. The few reporters in the building were in transit, either heading up to Kuwait in vehicles stuffed with supplies or leaving the area entirely.

No one knew where Thea was, nor did she appear on television. Calls to Kuwait weren't connecting yet. He asked Colonel Fletcher at the JIB if he knew anything, but he said no, the only thing the officer was certain about was that she had not been among the press swarm who joined the unruly convoy that left the hotel.

"What convoy?" Angus asked.

"We organized an official convoy to Kuwait. But we made no announcement and posted no notice. It would have been the whole messy fight over pool slots all over again. In this cathouse trying to keep the news that a special pool was headed to Kuwait was like keeping an elephant hidden under a blanket. When I walked out of the hotel the next morning at 0400, there were like eighty vehicles lined up. I mean the whole hotel emptied in one fell swoop."

"So what did you do?"

"We headed out with all eighty. Boy was that one long convoy."

But the suddenly assertive Saudi border guards wanted nothing to do with the American press convoy. The argument carried on for hours, well past noon. Since nightfall came early in the desert winter and Kuwait City was at least three hours up the road, the officers aborted the trip.

"You should have heard the complaining, bitching and whining; it was unreal," Fletcher said. "By the next day everybody was pretty much gone though."

"So was that the very last trip for the JIB? The last hurrah?" Angus asked.

"Actually no," the colonel said, lifting a sheaf of papers off his desk. "I am organizing something right now. We can squeeze you on if you are interested. It's an overnight up into Iraq."

The colonel explained that on the first night of the war Apache helicopters crossed the lines and picked off Iraqi infantrymen one by one,
shooting them dead with machine guns. They hit others with cannons,
smearing their bodies across the desert. It was war, after all, but word
spread that the attacking forces had launched an unprovoked ambush.

"There is a rumor out that U.S. troops massacred thousands of Iraqis,
which isn't true," Fletcher said.

A few correspondents reported seeing Iraqi bodies sprawled across
the desert, however, suggesting large numbers and an army cover-up.
The JIB was organizing a helicopter ride up there to show that there
weren't thousands of dead, and those killed were being buried properly.

"We are going to show everyone that we are doing the decent thing.
You interested?" Fletcher asked.

Angus wavered, thinking it ironic that with the war more or less over,
the JIB was now offering on a silver platter what he and everybody else
had spent the last months haggling over. He was vaguely worried that it
sounded like a public relations exercise, but he had not seen a single dead
body during the whole war. Few reporters had. Control was so strict that
only one picture of a U.S. soldier in a body bag made it out.

As he was about to say yes, he noticed that a picture of Black was
taped to the milk carton next to Fletcher's coffee mug with the words
"MISSING. Has anyone seen this man?" underneath.

"What the hell's that?" he snapped, the throb of fading guilt returning full force.

The colonel followed his eyes and a bleak smile, more of a grimace
really, flitted across his face. "He's not exactly missing anymore, although
what did happen to him remains unclear. There's a new report floating
around that we bombed the intelligence headquarters in Baghdad where
he and his guys were being held in a basement interrogation center and
they were all killed. Still not confirmed, no body yet, I mean. I'd guess he's
likely done for. Awful way to go, although you know Black was not exactly
loved by the military; everyone thought the guy was out to get us."

Angus was stunned. How could Black possibly be dead, and in an American bombing raid of all things? "Dead," he whispered to himself, his stomach burning and his throat suddenly dry and bitter, the bile rising there burning with the peppery scrambled eggs he had just eaten for breakfast.

Over the past weeks he had convinced himself that he wasn't really responsible for what happened to Black, that the guy would likely have ended up along the border anyway and that he would survive, emerge from jail to write his memoirs. But now his mind raced as he scrolled back through that angry, post-battle morning just outside Khafji, when the bastard took off and the two WP reporters watched his vehicle disappear over the highway.

In recent weeks he had been brooding whether Black, still alive, would cast a permanent shadow between him and Thea. What about dead? Would he end up dragging around Black's memory wherever he went with Thea, like an unwanted suitcase whose contents he could never quite leave behind? That didn't bear contemplating.

He reached his hand out to steady himself against the desk and in the process knocked the coffee mug onto the floor. Both men watched the contents seep into the blue carpet, the muddy liquid merging with the dirt and stains left by so many footprints and fruitless stories.

"Well, do you want to come on this trip or not?" the colonel asked, suddenly impatient. "How hard a decision can that be?"

ARMY bulldozers cut deep trenches in the desert and men with masks over their faces were wrapping the Iraqis in shrouds before placing them in the pits. When one pit was full they would cover the bodies with sand.

Angus walked around watching. The smell was so strong that it occasionally made him gag and stumble. At one point he heard soft crunching underfoot and when the ground seemed about to give way he leapt, thinking it was desert quicksand. The soldiers laughed, telling him that he was walking across one of the first graves they dug. They explained that the graves were shallow, with the bodies close to the surface, so he was probably walking on them.

After that, Angus avoided the graves.

Though the reporters originally planned to fly back in the morning, it was such a brilliantly starlit night that they convinced one helicopter pilot to lift them out.

Since it would take two trips, Angus let the TV guys go first; their material was more perishable. He ate a lasagna dinner with a few of the officers in their mess tent and then went outside to survey the spectacular desert sky.

A lanky army colonel emerging from the tent right behind him told Angus not to stray from the camp because they didn't know where all the minefields were. The colonel was encrusted with layers of dust collected during the four days racing across the desert, a fine powder cracking along the wrinkles next to his eyes as he looked at the heavens.

"Besides, the pilots are not going to want to shut down. They'll just hover and if you aren't around, they'll leave without you," he said.

There was an almost full, gibbous moon right overhead. Jupiter stood closely behind it and Mars appeared off to the west, red but not blazing. Angus slowly took inventory of the constellations: Cancer, Gemini and Leo; Orion the hunter pursuing Taurus the bull, which included the Seven Sisters, off to the southwest; Orion's two hounds, the stars Sirius and Procyon, trailing behind.

This story was over, he knew, and gazing out at the endless sky, he thought of a line from the *Rubiyat* of Omar Khayyam, a long poem he had read repeatedly as a boy with his father. He said it aloud, slowly, to himself: "And that inverted bowl we call the sky, where under crawling cooped, we live and die, lift not thy hands to it for help, for it rolls impotently on as thou or I."

Angus wondered if he would ever again see so many soldiers, or so many reporters, gathered in such a strange place. He hoped not. Sure there had been elements of an adventure, but it proved fleeting and certainly far less momentous than he initially imagined. He recalled various weather-beaten correspondents recounting their past exploits over endless meals in the coffee shop. All those wars—Vietnam, Beirut, Central America—had produced far more dramatic reporting. But once they were over? The sky just kept rolling past.

The freedom to drift that he so prized now seemed like a sure route to eternal sojourns in the Dhahran Palaces of the world. Not much of a life. Sticking to the open water at all costs would lead him no place. Narrowing his horizon, as daunting as that was, would enhance his sense of adventure, not stunt it, give him purpose. He had to go track down Thea.

A tiny, blinking red light in the night sky off to the south intruded on his thoughts, the flashes growing more insistent as the helicopter approached. The clattering machine soon materialized overhead and slowly sank toward him, the poppling sand stinging his face.

It occurred to Angus that this was probably his last night in Saudi Arabia. He would get back to Dhahran, file, and then head up to Kuwait. How long it would take him to find Thea? He hoped they wouldn't end up spending months chasing separate bits of the same story, like two worker bees in the same hive never intersecting. Eventually he would find her again, he was sure of that, but it was all predictably vague.

The sand billowing out from the helicopter enveloped him, blotting out the encampment around him and even the night sky. Angus threw up a forearm to protect his eyes as he ran through the cloud. He clambered aboard, the helicopter lifted, and the night sky reemerged outside the open side door, swelling ever bigger as the desert shrank away. Angus felt he could reach out and sweep his hand through the stars, as if plunging his forearm underneath the surface of a deep, dark lake.

Acknowledgments

Having worked on this book on and off for the better part of a decade, I know that I am bound to overlook some people who helped make it happen. Hence I want to offer a blanket thanks at the outset to everyone who aided my efforts, either directly or inadvertently.

After the Gulf War itself, my initial inspiration for this novel was confirmed by reading through some 1,000 pool reports written in the seven months after Saddam Hussein invaded Kuwait in August 1990. So my first debt goes to all those who participated in the press juggernaut involved in covering the Gulf War and particularly those who filed stories—the good, the bad and the truly abysmal all provided endless fodder.

Where the pool reports failed to conjure up specific events, I turned to some of the officers in the U.S. military's Joint Information Bureau, to my colleagues in the press corps, and to other participants, asking them to dredge their memories. I owe particular thanks in this regard to Gunther Baehr, Bob Dvorchak, George Esper, Major Pat Gibbons, Tom Giusto, Guy Gugliotta, Colonel Larry Icenogle, John Fialka, Peter Ford, Joe Halderman, the late Larry Jolidon, Jim Miller, Don Mell, Carol Morello, Colonel Bill Mulvey, Kim Murphy, Susan Reed, Michael Rosenbaum, Philip Shenon, Captain Mike Sherman and Lieutenant Colonel Pat Sivigny.

In October 1997, some eighteen months after I wrote the first sentence, I was knocked off my bicycle by a runaway bus on Fifth Avenue. It took some three years before I could walk unaided again, and this book would never have happened were it not for the dedicated medical teams who labored so diligently to glue me back together. I am particularly grateful to the Bellevue Hospital Center, New York University Medical Center, the Rusk Institute of Rehabilitation Medicine, and the Hospital for Special Surgery, as well as to my trainer, Joe Garafolo, and my physical therapist, Tamar Amitay, who took what the doctors built and made it work better.

During those years my employer, The New York Times Company, acted with boundless generosity, giving me the peace of mind needed to write by assuring me that the newsroom would wait as long as necessary for me to recuperate and there would be a job waiting whatever the outcome. The many acts of kindness from the company, my colleagues, and friends are too numerous to list. But former Executive Editor Joe Lelyveld and his late wife Carolyn led the effort in making sure that I was supplied with regular supplements of deli food and good reading material, as well as helping my family navigate the city through some of the most difficult moments.

Once I was recuperating, Peter Waldman provided significant encouragement and extensive help in unearthing research materials that I could not readily access. Those of you who were so generous in lending me everything—from broadcast tapes to your dining room tables to a beach house to allow me to work through the various drafts—provided a service that I will find difficult to repay. (The Sellers household was particularly generous, but I will not name everyone in this category individually to avoid your facing a flood of writers expecting similar largesse.)

I am forever indebted to my readers, Frances Dinkelspiel, Nan Richardson, Helen Ward and Kevin Ward. They not only slogged through meandering rough drafts, but supplied much needed enthusiasm when mine lagged. Ethan Canin kindly dispensed periodic dollops of literary wisdom, and there is no institution quite like Yaddo, which gave me a blissful, undisturbed month to work through the final edits.

Last but hardly least, this book could well have ended up being tossed into the Nile River were it not for Tessa Souter leading me to Rebecca Strong, my agent, who believed in the book enough to convince me to rewrite it.

Finally, my deepest gratitude goes to Clive Priddle, my editor, who improved the book immeasurably.